By Clara Bernice Miller

Katie

moody press
chicago

KATIE

All characters in this book
are fictitious. Any resemblance to
real people is coincidental. The
names are incidental although they
are common Amish names.

Moody Paperback Edition, 1974
ISBN: 0-8024-4524-1

Moody Press, a ministry of the Moody Bible Institute, is
designed for education, evangelization and edification.
If we may assist you in knowing more about Christ and
the Christian life, please write us without obligation to:
   Moody Press, c/o MLM, Chicago, Illinois 60610.

To my sisters
Fannie, Lydia, Vesta
Mary Jane, Esther, Anna Mae
this book is
affectionately dedicated.

By Way of Introduction

After reading Bernice Miller's book, I asked myself: Is it not true, no matter what the religious persuasion may be, that at some time or other every thinking individual must settle for himself the question of the validity of the spirit in contrast to the letter?

Katie, the protagonist of the story, is Amish of the Old Order, living in the rich farm country of eastern Iowa. A good-looking girl, as well as a hard and capable worker, she is the sort of person who must think her own thoughts. This is due in no small part to the reading she has been doing. Books are her life and she has been willing to endure ridicule, lickings, anything, so long as she can go on reading; but education for Katie will end at the eighth grade and from then on books will not be easy to obtain. Reading matter, yes--the farm paper, the *Budget,* the Bible, but books that water the roots of imagination and nourish the spirit will be as rare as oases in a desert.

Books for Katie, though a sure delight, have not been an indulgence. The ideas met in them have challenged her to think, to arrive at her own conclusions, to recognize truth and have the courage to rebel against that which is not true. Books have given her ideas which the stilted, perfunctory sermons heard in church did not; ideas that "grabbed at her mind" and led her into conversations through which she "caught a glimpse of a great door opening." Heir to the superstitions and fears which follow in the wake of restrictions and taboos, Katie has gradually been able to find her own inner freedom.

In the midst of her work as one of a large family and later as a hired girl, in the midst of customs that have been practiced for generations, Katie develops the sturdiness of mind to set her own standards, new and high and in keeping with her own time. This is not done easily, but as she had braved ridicule and lickings, she is willing to brave loneliness and the stigma of being an old maid until she finds someone for whom ideas are as meaningful as they are to her. When she does, it is all so right, for tribulation is a word whose meaning has been respectively learned and during the lonely years each one has been made ready for the other.

Bernice Miller is too good a storyteller not to satisfy her readers, but she does not do it soon and she does it out of the stuff that is her world. With steady equanimity, she handles explosive material as new approaches challenge the traditional ways. Out of the things of daily life, she builds and develops character--choring, changing seasons, the weather, the feeling for family, the casual conversations; through a multitude of small details--a woman reaching for the diaper bag, a man unwinding the reins--she creates scenes as the Dutch masters did as they drew on the life at hand. Through these, the reader finds a place in the background; so it is not only Katie whose thoughts seethe and bubble "like a kettle of cooking mush."

This loving attention to detail has characterized the work of George Eliot, of Mary Webb, of many others in the long tradition of English prose, and I find myself wondering where Bernice Miller's developing talent will take her. This is only her second book and she has much more to say. Of one thing I am sure, she will no more conform or be pressed into a mold than would her Katie. She can only grow, and grow she will, for her writer's instinct is sound. I am glad for the roots of faith that go deep within her, for the fact that she has a husband who farms a wide acreage, for the nine children and the strong, warm family life. From all of this there will be material for a long time, with the detail she loves and the problems she delights to solve.

Every book has a keystone; all that has been leads to it, all that will follow leads from it. For me, the keystone of this book is a paragraph almost exactly midway through it. Katie has been tormented by the restrictions that wall her world, by the elders who do things for no other reason than that their forefathers did them. She has come to cherish and to live by the teachings in the Bible and the life of Jesus. In her anguish, she prays; and when her answer comes it is in no dramatic way, but in an inner assurance--

> It was enough. No longer did the demons shriek around her ears. Closing the Bible, she undressed and crawled between the covers. The Bible was to be relied on and the forefathers, good and well-meaning as they had probably been, were only people such as she. Drawing a deep breath of peace, she went to sleep.

From then on, the story moves to an inevitable end as unity is found not in conformity but in the spirit and concord of Christian love.

So, I pose myself another question: Is this what reading can do? The affirmative answer is in Plutarch's line, "The mind is not a vessel to be filled but a fire to be kindled."

Elizabeth Yates

Peterborough, N.H.
Spring 1966

PART 1

1

KATIE stood a good chance of getting a licking for spending a half hour after school at the school library. It wasn't the first time by any means. "If only Mom would quit fussing about reading!" Katie sighed, thinking of the books she had chosen and stored in her desk. She'd not get to start reading them until the first recess tomorrow--and next week school was out! For Katie that meant forever; Amish children in Iowa didn't get to go further than the eighth grade.

Mom had warned her not to bring home any more books after Vernie had tattled on Katie's illicit use of her lunch basket and her secret reading at night. Mom had made her use a paper sack to carry her lunch and told her in no uncertain terms what would happen if she brought the sack home. Katie walked slowly; the evening stretched endlessly before her.

How she wished that Mom liked to read! "If Mom would love to read like Pop," she thought, "the house would be full of books. Pop always reads the daily newspapers, the farm papers, the *Budget*,* and the Bible. When Pop has a free moment, he is always to be found in the living room reading. But what is the use of wishing? Such a thing would be impossible. Mom has no use for books."

Her steps lagged; she blew a wisp of brown hair off her freckled nose and made a face. "I'll get whipped for being late tonight," she thought crossing her blue eyes, turning her pretty face into a hideous caricature of how Mom would look when she grabbed the paddle from the dining room wall and dealt her stinging blows.

"I have it coming to me," Katie thought, her conscience pricking

*Weekly newspaper published in Sugarcreek, Ohio, and catering to the Amish in the United States.

her for making the ugly face. "I've been told often enough to come home on time and not to go to the library. But I'd endure spankings every day if Mom would let me read." She took off her black bonnet and swung it round and round absently on its long black strings, thinking of the books she had chosen. "Maybe, if we weren't Amish, I could read all I want. At least, the children of the high people (non-Amish) read all they want!"

She swung her bonnet round and round. And that black bonnet! She hated the thing. Of all the peculiarities of her dress, it was the thing she hated most and it was the most pounced-on object of ridicule from the boys of the high people. She didn't mind when they teased her about wearing six petticoats under her full sweeping skirts, for she didn't wear that many; she didn't mind when they jerked her pigtails; it hurt her feelings not at all when they made fun of her black stockings. But let some hulking eighth-grade boy snatch off her bonnet put it on his head, and go jumping around the cloakroom, then Katie's spirit was thoroughly aroused.

It did no good to hang it in a dark corner or to hide it behind the cloakroom door; sooner or later one of them found it and invariably put it on, yelling, "Hey, look, kids, I'm an Amish girl," all the while deftly eluding Katie's frantic grasps and entreaties and making everyone howl.

Sometimes, Katie tried to leave home in the morning without it. But, even if Mom wasn't in sight when she let herself softly through the door, by the time she was out on the road Mom's clear voice would call, "Katie Miller, get back in here and get your bonnet on! What do you mean by going without it?" So Katie would resignedly turn back and get it. Maybe, if they weren't the only Amish in town school, it wouldn't be so bad.

She was coming to the last block of houses on the road before it turned into the open country. Ahead of her a little bridge crossed the creek which ran through the west end of town. Would any town boys be under it tonight? Mean old things, who hid under it until the Miller children got halfway across and then came jumping out with demoniac shrieks and showers of gravel and mud clods. How Katie hated them!

"This is what I get for being late," Katie thought. "Because it was library night, I forgot about the bridge boys. I'll really get hit tonight."

Stealthily she crept closer. Perhaps, if she walked softly until she was almost over and then broke into a run, she could get by before they had a chance to jump at her. Hardly daring to breathe, she crept ever so softly until she was almost to the other side. Then she broke into a wild run.

But, for once, no boys came shrieking out at her. Katie slowed down, feeling foolish. She hoped no one was watching from one of the houses on the other side of the creek. She glanced at them furtively, walking backward. Satisfied, she turned and set off more rapidly for home.

Ahead of her stretched the gravel road that ran west and north of town. Up the hill, half a mile out of town, was the Miller homestead, a big square house with the farm buildings around it. She could see Pop out in the south field with the team and Elmer in another field with the tractor. She imagined Mom, paddle in hand, waiting at the dining room door.

It wouldn't be so bad, not being allowed to read much at home, if this weren't the next to the last week of school. Katie sighed a deep sigh of suppressed passion and longing. "If only Amish people went to high school. The children of the high people say, 'When I get into high school next year' and 'When I graduate from high school.' But I'm Katie Miller, one of Lydie Dan's girls, and Lydie Dan is Amish; therefore I, Katie, am Amish, and Amish people do NOT go to high school, and that is that. It does no good to talk about it--at least not to Mom, and Pop won't talk.

"I wish I could tell Pop about it, but he is always so quiet, so absorbed with farm work and his own reading. I can't talk to him. Besides, it is unheard of for an Amish girl or boy to go to high school."

The steady clop-clop of a slow horse and the rasp of buggy wheels on the gravel behind her made her glance around hurriedly and quickly push such radical thoughts back into the farthest recesses of her mind. The horse broke into a little trot.

"Git up," the occupant of the buggy said, drawing up behind her. "Want a ride?"

Katie stopped and looked at the driver. It was Dan Gingerich, a friend who lived way out beyond them. "Thank you," she said, climbing nimbly into the back seat.

Dan clicked to his horse, looked back at her, and grinned. "Kind of late, aren't you?"

"Yes."

"Bet the teacher kept you in," he chuckled.

"Huh-uh," she denied.

"School about out?" he asked, raising his voice above the rasp of the buggy wheels on the gravel.

"Next week," she answered.

She really hadn't been far from home when Dan Gingerich picked her up and already they were even with the south end of the barnyard. He slowed the horse down to a crawling walk. Katie gathered up her skirts and prepared to get out.

"Here you are. Whoa, Fern. Now mind you, get to choring," he said good-naturedly. "Which one of the girls are you?"

"Katie."

"Well, Katie, don't let the teacher keep you in tomorrow."

"I won't," she replied and scampered across the road toward the house. She heard Dan Gingerich chuckle quietly while he tightened the reins and clicked to his horse again.

Katie stole softly across the wide porch and noiselessly opened the screen door. No one was in sight, although from the kitchen came the sound of someone working. She stepped inside the dining room and stopped. The house was as clean as only Mom could make it. Through the big double doors leading into the front room, she could see that every rug was in place across the freshly swept carpet. She caught sight of some freshly baked sugar cookies stacked in rows across the bottom end of the table. She glided over and reached for one.

14

"Katie!"

Katie's arm dropped and she turned quickly around.

"Don't you dare take one of those cookies," Vernie said from the kitchen doorway. "Where have you been? You were supposed to go to Aunt Fannie's place with Mom."

"What does she want there?" Katie asked, relieved. Maybe she wouldn't get spanked!

"She wants to get some raspberry sprouts to plant tomorrow. She took Clarie with her. I bet you went down to the library again. Just wait till I tell on you."

Katie turned toward the stairsteps without replying. "That wouldn't be the first time," she said under her breath, glad she hadn't brought any of the books home. Vernie would seek them out of her best hiding places and show them to Mom.

"How come the house is all straightened up?" Katie asked.

"Pop's cousin from Indiana is coming for supper. So hurry up and get those clothes changed and get to the milking. Pop and Elmer are going to work in the fields tonight as long as they can."

"Who's going to do the milking?"

"You and Emma, of course. Maybe Henry can milk one or two. Hurry up or I'll tell Mom on you."

Katie stuck her tongue out at Vernie, making a terrible face in defiance, then slammed the door shut and sped upstairs two steps at a time.

"Mom spoils her terribly and lets her have her own way in everything," Katie thought. "Just because she had rheumatic fever when she was little and has a bad heart ever since, she thinks she's queen. All she ever does is boss and tattle.

"But at least Mom isn't home now," Katie thought. Exhilarated by this unexpected reprieve from a spanking, she changed into her everyday dress, kicked off her school shoes, and raced downstairs. It was so warm she could go barefooted and Katie loved that. From now on until next fall she would wear shoes only when she dressed up.

She gave only a glance around the clean house on her way out to the barn, hoping to make it outside before Vernie could give her a hard pinch for making a face at her. She opened the screen door and Katie was at the gate before the sharp crack of its slamming reached her ears.

At the barn Katie grabbed up a milk stool and bucket and plopped herself beside the nearest cow. From the back of the cow stable, Emma looked up from behind old Guerns. "About time you showed up," she said severely. "Where have you been anyway?"

"Walking home," Katie mumbled, milking as hard as she could.

"Well, it sure took you a long time to do it. You were supposed to go to Aunt Fannie's with Mom."

"That's what Vernie said."

"Clarie said you were coming way behind them; so Mom took her. She didn't want to wait any longer."

"I could hug you, Clarie," Katie thought. "Even if you disapprove of my disobedience, you never tell on me like Vernie does." Aloud she asked, "Who's this cousin of Pop's who's coming for supper?"

"Ed Bontrager, I think his name is," Emma replied.

"Do they have any children?" Katie wanted to know.

"Not with them. I think they have quite a family though."

Katie turned back to her milking in silence. "I hope they have children," she thought. "I like to hear about other people's children. I like big families, even our own. Although my family never seems big. To be sure, it takes a long table to seat us all at mealtime, but there is only Emma and Vernie and Elmer and Clarie and Henry and Mary Ann and Edna, the baby. And Mom and Pop, of course. Even then there are only eight children in our family," Katie reflected. "Lots of Amish people have ten. And Uncle Abe Millers had thirteen, including two sets of twins. Twins would be nice," Katie thought. "I wish Clarie were my twin. Or, if my twin were a boy, Henry would be nice. But not Vernie!"

Between the two of them, Katie and Emma had the cows milked before Henry was finished feeding the chickens and the hogs. He and Mary Ann were taking turns pumping water into the hog fountain. Katie heard their contented chatter as she started up to the washhouse with the milk. "Mom still isn't back from Aunt Fannie's," Katie noted, hoping she wouldn't return until the cousins from Indiana came.

"I'll do the separating, Katie," Emma said as they brought up the milk. "You and Henry can chase the cows out to pasture."

"All right," Katie replied and started out toward the barn. She liked Emma, too, just about as well as Clarie and Henry. This was the last summer to have Emma at home because she was going to be twenty-one in August and would probably marry in the winter. Katie liked her good-looking boy friend, Mahlon Gingerich.

Henry had let the cows out of the yard and into the narrow lane that led into the back pasture. Katie picked up a stick and joined him.

"Were there any town boys at the bridge tonight?" she asked, swinging the stick around her head.

"Naw," Henry answered, "not when we went over it. Were there any there when you came home? If there were, it served you right for being so poky. Boy, you were lucky that Mom had to go to Aunt Fannie's or you'd have gotten a lickin' for sure." His nine-year-old eyes looked disgustedly into her fourteen-year-old ones.

"I know it," Katie affirmed, spreading her bare feet in delicious enjoyment over the new grass growing in clumps along the lane. "Maybe I will yet. I hope Mom doesn't come home until the company comes. Then she'll forget all about it."

"What makes you go down to the old library and get books anyway?" Henry asked disgustedly. "Always reading! I should think all the lickings you've gotten for reading books would make you quit."

"I can't," Katie said. "I can't live without reading. When I get big I'm going to have a whole roomful of books.

The company and Mom arrived at the front gate simultaneously. Katie, standing behind the washhouse and peeking out through a crack, saw that the man was a tall, bearded Amishman who had a jolly laugh and walked with a swagger of his shoulders. His wife was short and fat with plump, rosy cheeks and blue, twinkling eyes. They stood at the gate for a moment talking with Mom and Amos Yoders, the people who had brought them.

"No, we can't stay for supper," Amos Yoders replied to Mom's hospitable invitation. "We must go home and see to the chores. We've been gone all day and the children are alone." So they drove around the circle of the lane and left after profuse good-byes.

Henry went over to the gate, and Mom sent him and Clarie out to unhitch her own horse and put the buggy in the shed. The raspberry sprouts would be all right until morning. Then, he was to come in and wash up for supper. From the barn, Pop came slowly up toward the group at the gate, a smile breaking across his quiet face.

"Katie," Emma's voice brought Katie sharply around toward the washroom door which connected the washhouse with the kitchen.

"What?" Katie asked.

"Come on in and help us get the food on the table. Don't just stand there."

Katie went inside, still reluctant to meet Mom face to face. Vernie pounced on her as soon as she was inside the door. "Come on in here and help, Katie. You've done little enough tonight."

"Oh, she helped real good with the chores, Vernie," Emma protested mildly, glancing at Katie who was scowling fiercely at Vernie. Emma's quiet words soothed the friction between the two sisters. "Katie, put the silver on the table, pour water into the glasses, and carry the food into the dining room. Mom and Pop want to visit with the cousins."

When the table was loaded for supper, Pop got the cousins out into the dining room and assigned them to their places; Vernie, Emma, and Katie lined up along the wall and watched.

18

"Say, you've got some big girls, Dan," the cousin turned to Pop, a bantering grin breaking out on his face. "Can you keep them at work? Why, say, I believe that one is the best-looking one of the bunch," he said, pointing toward Katie.

She gave an embarrassed snicker; biting her lips, she dropped her eyes in confusion.

"Oh, she is not!" Vernie hissed under her breath, unnoticed in the general titter at the cousin's remark. "Hard-looking old thing!" she hissed again, reaching over and giving Katie a pinch.

Katie retaliated by sticking out her tongue at her while the others had their heads bowed to say grace. Afterward, she stayed as far away from Vernie as possible.

The three girls washed cooking utensils while the others ate. Katie didn't mind because she could snitch chicken while she dried. When at last the others were through eating and had gone to the living room to visit, the girls took clean plates and sat down at the table.

Katie was quiet, only talking when she wanted the others to pass something. It looked as though she weren't going to be spanked. Evidently Mom had forgotten about her being late.

From the living room, the talk drifted out toward them, Katie only half listening, absentmindedly eating.

"Isn't your school out yet?" the cousin's wife was asking.

"Not yet," Mom replied. "It goes out next week though."

"You don't have to send your children to high school here, do you?" the cousin's wife asked.

"High school!" Katie went rigid with attention, the supper completely forgotten.

"No, we don't and I'm glad," Mom replied.

"You should be," the cousin's wife assured her. "It's awful the way they make them go in Indiana. They have to go until they're sixteen, you know."

"That's what I've heard," Mom said. "How many years of high school does that make them take?"

"No more than two, because we don't start them until they are

19

six or seven."

Katie held her breath, then let it out softly. "Was it actually true that there were places where Amish people went to high school--but didn't want to?"

Suddenly Katie wished with all her heart that Iowa could be Indiana. Even as she wished it, she sighed and turned away from the wish. "There is no use thinking about it," she reminded herself. "If the church says you can't go, you can't." For one brief moment a small surge of rebellion against the church shot through her. "Why must it be so everlasting bossy? It told you what to wear, how to comb your hair, how your house must be furnished, what kind of transportation you used, and even what kind of light you could read with. God must be a great, angry being who frowned on everything that was nice and desirable, if He demanded all her church said He did."

KATIE sighed, rubbed her hands together, and wished church were over. Beside her, Dan B's Mary was sitting prim and straight just as though the backless church benches were soft easy chairs. "I can never sit still in church," Katie complained to herself. "In Sunday school, where the benches have backs, you can at least lean back and doze while the lesson is being discussed by the grown-ups, but in church services you have to sit and sit and *sit* on these hard benches for *hours!* There is not even the solace of a cookie," she thought, glancing with envy at the small boys in front of her who were nibbling on cookies and crackers that had been passed around. "At least, that would help pass the time," Katie thought.

But Katie had long ago been too big for cookies. The last time she had taken one was when she was seven, too big to sit with Mom. Dan B's Mary was sitting beside her. When the cookies were being passed that time, she had thoughtlessly taken one. As she had begun to eat in blissful enjoyment, Dan B's Mary had leaned over, pushed her, and whispered, "Aren't you seven years old? You're too big for cookies!" Then she sat back complacently with hands folded primly in her lap, leaving Katie hopelessly embarrassed with a cookie to get rid of. Katie sighed again and shifted around on the bench.

"Hold still," whispered Vernie from the bench in back of her, giving Katie a sharp pinch. Katie sat up straight, a surge of rebellion rushing through her. Glancing back, she stuck out her tongue at Vernie who gave her another pinch. Katie jumped. Susan Gingerich who was sitting beside Vernie snickered; Dan B's Mary turned and frowned. Katie tried to sit up straight and concentrate on the sermon.

"What was the preacher saying, anyway? If he'd make it entertaining, so it was worth listening to, it wouldn't be so hard to sit still in church." She listened intently for a few moments, a frown on her face. "Is he preaching about the end of the world?" she wondered, "because if he is, I'm not listening. I hate to hear of the end of the world."

Ever since she was nine years old, when a great storm and fire in town that could be seen for miles around had followed a sermon on the end of the world, Katie had been afraid of storms, fires, and the end of the world. Someday God was going to come all at once, set the world on fire, and there was no getting away from it. She knew, because Bishop Eli had said so. You couldn't run away. You couldn't hide because you'd have to run through fire.

Once, when she was eleven, she had had a horrible dream of the end of the world. She was in school when it came, and she tried running down the street toward the square, but the fire stopped her. In desperation she turned and ran down an alley, but that was on fire. Then the realization swept over her that

21

there was absolutely no place to go *when the end of the world came!* She shivered.

But John Gingerich wasn't preaching about the end of the world today. Because it was spring and everybody was either plowing or planting, the sermon was on the Parable of the Sower. She listened for a few moments, decided it wasn't interesting enough to bother with, and slumped down in her seat.

Over the backs of the dozing men in front of her, she could see the lovely, spring sunshine streaming across the yard. She thought suddenly that school, for her, was almost over. This week would be the last. No more could she have free access to books and learning. No more would she be able to take an encyclopedia and pore over it. No more could she go to the library and pick out books about lovely heroines and brave, handsome heroes.

No, when school ended this spring, it would be over for her for life.

The minister was closing his sermon. While the other two ministers gave sermon testimonies, Katie watched everybody sit up straight, reach for their songbooks, and breathe a sigh of relief. With the announcement of the closing hymn, anticipation floated over the congregation. Everyone joined heartily in the song.

As wave after wave of unison singing rose up all over the house, squirming children were let down to run as soon as the song was ended. Boys reached furtively under benches to come up with their hats. Beside her, Dan B's Mary moved for the first time, it seemed to Katie, since church had started. The last melodious tone died away, and in front of her, the line of boys got up to file out. Church was ended.

Afterward, when the girls had gone out to stand around on the enclosed porch, Katie found herself alone in a corner. She watched the mothers who, freed from battling bored and weary children, now sat or stood around the kitchen in relieved sociability. Little children scrambled over the benches, playing noisy games of tag and hide-and-seek until stopped momentarily by their mothers who straightened them out while visiting. In the dining room and

22

living room, men cleared the floor of most of the benches and set up the long tables for lunch. Susan Gingerich and one of Dan B's older girls were spreading the tablecloths and setting out the cups and saucers and the tableware.

"Come on, girls," John Henry Sarah was saying. "It's ready now to carry the things in."

The girls started picking up dishes of jam and pickles and red pickled beets that had been dished out by the waitresses during the last half-hour of church. Even Dan B's Mary, who was fourteen and the same age as Katie, picked up a dish of pickled beets and a plate of bread and followed the other older girls.

But Katie stayed in the corner. She felt terribly young and embarrassed. Shy and hesitant, she kept back from others. There were times when she wanted to join in the fun, but this same hesitancy kept her aloof and separated.

"Come on, Katie," John Henry Sarah urged her, seeing her stand alone. "You're a big girl now. You can help, too."

As Katie hesitated, two young mothers who were standing about the kitchen stepped squarely in front of her and began to chat, unconscious of Katie behind them.

Dan B's Mary came out to the kitchen on her second trip, and glancing back into the corner, caught Katie's eye and frowned. "Aren't you going to help?"

Katie bit her lip, blushed and hesitated, too shy to push against the two women in front of her. Dan B's Mary shrugged her shoulders and turned away in disgust.

"Katie, come on and help," Vernie ordered as she came into the kitchen. "Don't be so stuck-up."

Katie sank back into the corner without replying, allowing the two women to hide her from sight. She waited there until all of the food had been carried to the table and the two mothers left to care for their children. Then she followed the other girls upstairs to visit and wait their turn to eat.

She sat quietly on the edge of the circle, content to listen to the gay talk and bits of gossip the others let drop. As usual,

Vernie was the gayest of them all. Katie envied Vernie with her quick wit and ready talk. "If only I could be like that!" she wished. "Why could Vernie charm everyone while she, Katie, sat in corners and bit her tongue with shyness?" Katie sighed.

When Katie had eaten and Pop had hitched up the team, she got her bonnet and light shawl. She found Mom in the washhouse, bundling up Edna and tying Mary Ann's bonnet, talking with Will Yoder Barbrie who was getting her four small children ready to go home. Katie only half listened to what they were saying. Clarie had already gotten her things on and was standing at the gate waiting for Pop. Vernie and Emma were going to stay for supper and the singing, and Elmer had left for the north district to get his girl friend. Katie was glad she was too young to run around. Boys filled her with panicky embarrassment. She'd rather read.

"You'll let me know one of the first days?" Barbrie was asking Mom.

"Yes, I guess so," Mom replied. "Course, I'm pretty sure you can have her, but I want to ask Dan first. Anyway, I hate to promise on a Sunday."

"Oh, I realize that," Barbrie said, carefully tying her tiny Anna Ruth's bonnet. She looked over at Katie and smiled. Katie smiled shyly in return.

Mom caught sight of Pop waiting at the gate. Catching up Edna in one arm and the diaper bag in the other, she started out the door. "I'll let you know for sure before Wednesday," she assured Barbrie in parting.

Katie wondered what they were talking about, but waited to ask until the flurry of seating themselves in the buggy was over. As usual, Henry, Mary Ann, and Clarie all fought to have the coveted place on the front seat with Pop. Katie climbed on the back seat as a matter of course. She could daydream just as well on the back seat as on the front she had found out long ago.

"Mary Ann, you sat on the front seat on the way over," Mom chided her sharply. "Come back and sit between Katie and me."

"Then I can't see," Mary Ann wailed. It was hard to see out over the high back of the front seat.

"Katie can hold you," Mom said. "Katie, take her up."

"Aw, she wiggles so much," Katie protested glumly.

"I don't either," Mary Ann began to cry again. Pop had already clicked to the horses and they were out on the road.

"Shut up, Mary Ann," Mom told her sharply. "Katie, take her on your lap the right way instead of only half holding her. No wonder she wiggles."

"Well, if she wiggles now I'm going to pinch her," Katie mumbled under her breath, taking Mary Ann gingerly and adjusting the lap blanket around them.

"What did you say?" Mom looked at her keenly.

"Nothing," Katie mumbled and subsided into glum silence.

They had gone down the road about a mile, Mom and Pop visiting back and forth by spurts and Henry and Clarie chattering together on the front seat, when Katie thought of Will Barbrie. "What was Will Barbrie talking about?"

Mom gave her a searching look. "Didn't you hear?" she asked. Katie shook her head.

"She wants you to work for her this summer."

"Me!" Katie exclaimed.

Mom nodded.

"How come couldn't one of the other girls?" Katie asked resentfully. "After all, I'm only fourteen."

"Which one of them?" Mom wanted to know. "Emma's going to be home this summer because she comes of age in the fall, and Vernie is not able to go out and work for anybody. You're the only one who can."

"Why do any of us have to work out?" Katie asked. "Why can't we all stay at home?"

"There's not enough work to keep you busy at home, that's why. You're either reading all the time or fighting with Vernie."

"Fighting with Vernie!" Katie was incensed. "I don't fight with her; she's always picking on me!"

"Shut up," Mom ordered. "No back talk. You might just as well make up your mind about it, shouldn't she, Pop?"

Pop, who had been a silent listener, looked around and met Katie's rebellious eyes. "I guess you'll have to go, Katie," he said quietly. "It's just like your mom says, you don't seem to keep busy at home."

"I could help you," Katie urged.

"I have Elmer and Henry to help me," Pop reminded her. "No, Katie, I guess you're the one who'll have to go. Besides, we need the money."

Katie bit her lips in angry silence.

"Don't take it so hard," Mom said, her voice softening as she looked at Katie's set face. "Will Barbrie ought to be nice to work for. I don't think she'll be hard to get along with."

THE Monday following the last day of school, Katie packed her belongings in a battered trunk and suitcase left from Pop's boyhood wanderings and reluctantly went with Will Hershberger to work. It was the first time she was to be gone from home for an entire summer, although she had been at Aunt Fannie's the summer before through strawberry time and at Uncle Henry's for threshing and getting ready for church.

But this was to be all summer! "Chances are that when Emma comes of age in the fall and keeps her earnings, I'll have to work out until--forever! Or grow up and get married," Katie mused. "But that is too far off. Boys embarrass me."

She kept swallowing a lump in her throat all day, although

Will Barbrie was a friendly enough person. And the four small youngsters: David, four; Melvin, three; Pauline, two; and Anna Ruth, barely one; were friendly in a shy way.

"It is no wonder Barbrie wants a hired girl," Katie thought as she plunged into hard work the very first day. The garden needed hoeing badly, and Barbrie wasn't quite finished with housecleaning, although she was going to leave some of it until they had church in the near future. And she was expecting strawberries from an immense patch she'd set out the year before. Katie, seeing the long rows of strawberries stretching out through the orchard, groaned in expectation. "Plenty of backaches here!"

She worked from early morning until late at night, except for the half-hour rest period Barbrie allowed her right after the noon dishes were washed. In the evening, after the chores and supper, they worked in the garden and yard until dark, leaving the supper dishes until lamp-lighting time.

Katie looked forward to Sunday as the one day in the week when there would be some diversion. Never had Mom and Pop looked so beloved and homey as when she saw them in church or Sunday school. Even Vernie began to greet her cordially, and Clarie usually attached herself to Katie the minute church was ended, to follow her around until they left for home.

The first Sunday Katie went home for Sunday dinner with Mom and Pop after Sunday school, she was speechless with gratitude. "Oh, it is good to be home after three weeks' absence!" She went about the house from room to room touching things here, looking at things there, while the others got dinner. Mom, with unusual kindness, said Katie was company and excused her from helping.

"Do you like working at Will's?" Clarie, who was following her around, asked.

"Oh, it's not so bad," Katie said. "We have to work hard though. But Barbrie isn't bossy; so I think I like it. They don't have anything to read though."

"Not a thing? Not even a newspaper?" Clarie, to whom a

27

daily newspaper was as much a part of life as eating, asked incredulously.

Katie shook her head. "Nothing but the *Budget* and some farm papers that don't have anything in them worth reading."

"How do you stand it?" Clarie asked, her eleven-year-old sympathy aroused. "I thought you couldn't live unless you had something to read."

"I don't have time," Katie explained simply. "We're so busy working all day that when night comes I'm too tired to read."

Clarie looked at her in wonder. Katie not finding time to read! Something must be changing in her, that was sure.

"Anyway, Mom bawled me out before I started working at Will's. I haven't dared talk about reading to Barbrie," Katie said. "She said that, if I sat around and read all the time, Barbrie would tell people I was lazy--and you know what everyone thinks of lazy people!"

Clarie nodded. How often had they been warned of that very thing! Being lazy was one of the cardinal sins, along with being fancy and worldly, and on the same low level as being extravagant. It was not to be so much as mentioned among them.

"So I try not to let Barbrie know that I like to read," Katie said simply. Clarie nodded again. She could understand that.

Mom's voice calling for dinner interrupted them. Elmer and Emma and Vernie had gone to the crowd, leaving only the younger children at home for dinner. Katie ate Mom's cooking with homesick gusto. Everything tasted so good. There were potatoes fried only as Mom could fry them and delicious creamed chicken, new lettuce out of the garden, and crisp little radishes. For dessert there were frosted molasses cookies to eat with new strawberries.

"Strawberries already?" Katie asked, dishing a big saucerful.

"Don't you have any at Will's?" Mom asked.

"Not yet, but we're going to," Katie said. "Barbrie's got a great big patch of them."

"Is she going to let people pick on shares?" Mom asked. "Surely she's not going to pick them all herself?"

"I don't know," Katie said. "I never thought of that. She never said anything about picking on shares."

The day was over all too soon. At five o'clock, Wills stopped by on their way home from dinner at John Henry Yoder's and picked Katie up. Katie reluctantly went to get her bonnet. It was so nice to be home when the folks treated you like company that she wished she could stay.

The next week they began to pick strawberries. At first it wasn't so bad, because there were only a few, but by the end of the week, Katie and Barbie were kept busy just picking strawberries and canning them. All the next week they picked and canned and picked and canned, even Will taking time off from his field work to help.

Whereas before she had dropped into a dreamless, restful sleep as soon as she went to bed, she now began to toss and turn fitfully. The days were getting hot, and Katie found her room stuffy and airless in the evening, the curtains at her open window never stirring.

She began to dream of books. She saw shelves and shelves of books! She had never seen this room before. Why hadn't Will and Barbie told her they had books? Why, there were hundreds of them here, some of the very ones she'd been wanting to read and didn't have time before school stopped. Eagerly she ran across the room and reached toward a shelf, almost beside herself with joy.

But as she tried to pull out a book, it dissolved into strong nothingness. Surprised, she reached for the one beside it. That, too, faded before her fingers quite touched it. Desperately she turned to the other shelves across the room, trying to be quicker this time. If she could just get a book in her hands before it vanished into thin air--but no, she didn't quite make it. Katie cried.

She awoke, bitter disappointment making a hard dry sob in her

29

throat. Beside her bed the curtains hung as limp and motionless as they had when she'd come up to bed. Through the window the faint starlight shone softly and the sound of the chirping crickets and chirring June bugs mingled with the sound of a barking dog at the neighbors.

She sat up, swallowing hard, and wiped perspiration from her face. "If only the dream were true! If only for one hour I could go downtown to the library and browse in its musty expanse amid real books! But no, it never could be. I am out of school now," she reminded herself. "Reading is a thing of the past." She lay upon the bed and stared out of the window into the soft summer darkness. "But just the same, I wish the dream were true!"

*　　*　　*

After the flurry of strawberries, Barbrie and Katie took a day off and went to the sewing. Katie liked that. They packed a lunch in the morning and left the two little boys at home with Will who promised to work in the field south of the house where he could keep an eye on them. Taking Pauline and Anna Ruth, they set out for the day's quilting and sewing and a great deal of visiting. In the evening they came back contented and refreshed.

The next week Will and Barbrie and the children took a ten-mile trip to the north district to visit Barbrie's folks. They gave Katie the choice of going along or staying at home and doing as she pleased. It took only minutes for Katie to decide to stay at home. She didn't know Barbrie's folks very well and one whole day to herself seemed the most satisfying thing in the world just then.

"Are you sure you aren't afraid of staying alone?" Will asked good-naturedly as he lifted Pauline and Anna Ruth into the buggy.

"I don't think so," Katie assured him. "I don't know what there is to be afraid of."

"What would you do if a salesman came to the door?" he asked.

"Oh, Will," Barbrie scolded. "There's no need to try to scare the wits out of her."

Will chuckled and climbed into the front seat with Melvin and David, who had been waiting long before Will had hitched up. Unwinding the reins, he clicked to the horses, still grinning. "Well, if anyone comes that you don't know, run into the house and hook the screen door," he called as a parting warning. Katie made a face and waved, watching at the gate until they drove over the hill.

She went back into the house. How quiet everything was with no childish voices from the sandbox just outside the door and no one else in the house. She paused in the middle of the kitchen and listened to the unnatural silence around her. From across the lane came the grunting of the sows with little pigs, while from behind the house came the triumphant crow of a rooster and the contented cackle of the hens.

What should she do now that she had a whole day to herself? It seemed strange not to be picking strawberries or hoeing, washing and ironing, or any one of the dozens of tasks Barbrie usually had her doing. She walked through the house slowly, trying to think of something to fill up the glorious day.

The house was clean and the ironing was finished. There was sewing, but she hardly felt capable of trying it, although Barbrie had been putting her to hemming diapers and tea towels. She turned away from the sewing machine and went back to the kitchen. But a cleaner kitchen was unnecessary, if you weren't having company.

If only she had something to read! How fast the day would go then! But it was only the middle of the month. The farm paper wouldn't arrive for at least two weeks. Today was Wednesday and the *Budget* wouldn't come until Saturday. Once again, Katie marveled how anyone could care so little about reading as Will and Barbrie. Didn't they ever want to read books?

The day, which she had been looking forward to so eagerly, dragged by. Katie found it long and boring--never seeming to end. At last she mowed the yard which didn't need it, and at three o'clock she started choring. She fed the chickens, hunted eggs, and went after the cows. She began to milk, deciding to leave the cow that kicked until last. Perhaps Will and Barbrie would be back by that time.

In the hot cow stable, flies buzzed around even though she had sprayed the cows, whose stringy tails switched and flipped into her face time and again. By the time she had milked five cows and faced the fact that she must milk the kicker, she was ready to cry. Gritting her teeth, she hobbled the cow, keeping as far back as possible. Then gingerly taking the milk bucket and her milk stool, she began to milk.

It didn't turn out to be so bad after all. Only once did the cow make an attempt at kicking. Katie was on her feet in a flash, the milk almost upsetting in her nervous haste to get away. After a moment the cow went back to feeding and Katie to milking.

No sooner had she finished and hung up the milk pail than she heard the familiar clop-clop of horses coming down the road. Will and Barbrie were turning into the lane as she hurriedly let the cows out. Picking up two buckets of milk, she started toward the house.

"Don't tell me that you're finished milking already!" Will greeted her with a grin.

"I am, though," Katie assured him.

"Did you milk that kicker, too?" he asked in surprise, wrapping the lines around the whip socket and jumping down from the buggy to help Barbrie with the two little girls.

"Yes, I did," Katie assured him, feeling rather smug about it.

"Such a hired girl!" Will teased. "Give her a day off to do as she pleases, and she probably did nothing but work all day."

"Did you?" Barbrie asked.

Katie nodded. "There wasn't anything else to do."

She took the milk to the washhouse to separate, then closing the door so the cats couldn't get in, she went back to help Barbrie unload the buggy of babies, diaper bags, and boxes and bags of things sent by Barbrie's folks. After they had everything in the

32

house and Will had gone to unhitch the team, Barbrie dug around in her diaper bag.

"Here," she said to Katie, bringing out a book. "How would you like to have something to read?"

Katie stared at her in wonder. "You mean you brought a book for me to read? How did you know I wanted one?" She was almost too surprised to believe it.

"I supposed you probably did. You've been working so well all summer I thought you deserved to read a little bit." Barbrie laughed.

"How did you know I liked to read?" Katie wanted to know as she took the book, almost trembling with delight.

"Your mother told me before you started working here. She said if I didn't keep after you all the time you'd always have your nose in a book, but I think you've done real well, so far."

"Whose is it? Where did you get it?" Katie asked breathlessly. "Are there more where this came from?"

Barbrie laughed again. "Don't ask so many questions! The book is my sister Mary's. Lavina Miller gave it to her for Christmas last year. And, no, I don't think she has more. You may read it, and if it's very good, tell me, and I'll try to read it, too."

Katie could hardly wait until she had washed the dishes and helped put the sleepy children to bed. Then, taking the book upstairs, she lit her lamp and plopped down on the bed with it.

Although Katie had been reading fiction ever since she was nine, this was the first book of Christian fiction she had ever seen. She plunged at once into the story, heedless of the hot little room.

Long into the night she read. The sounds from downstairs had faded to quietness and only the persistent cry of a whippoorwill from the orchard and the chirping of the crickets rose on the still, night air. It was past midnight when the soft swish of pages being turned one after the other faded. Katie closed her eyes, thinking of the young girl who became "saved"--a new expression to Katie. The author had put the message of the

Gospel in clear and simple terms. Her mind turned it over and over: "All men were sinners," the book said. "When you were sorry for your sins and turned to Christ, He cleansed your heart and came and lived in you by faith."

It was a new idea. She had heard about sin and hell as long as she could remember. Sin was driving a car or wearing fancy clothes or using electricity in your house, if the church said you couldn't. Of course, it wasn't nice to lie and cheat and steal and kill, but, after all, no one was perfect. God didn't expect you to be.

Of course, she had known that Christ died on the cross--didn't they hear the crucifixion story twice a year at communion? But the book's message was so new, Katie couldn't grasp it.

THE whole Miller family plunged into the work of preparing for Emma's Thanksgiving wedding. Katie was almost glad she wasn't going to school. Mom said she could stay home until Christmas and learn to make her own clothes if no one asked to have her work for them. Now she could watch Mahlon and Emma together and lend a hand with cleaning, sewing, baking, and decorating the wedding cake.

"Only Emma would call what you do helping," Vernie said to Katie as she spread icing and arranged decorations.

Emma answered for Katie. "She is too young to wait on tables with a boy at the wedding dinner, but she's really doing a good job on the cake."

Katie and Susan Gingerich, Mahlon's cousin, were to be partners. "We'll have lots of fun," Katie told Emma. Susan was six months older, more sure of herself around boys, and Katie felt safe with her. They were to wait on a basement table for children too old to eat with their parents but too young to be trusted at the big table upstairs.

Katie's romance-loving heart was thrilled with the sight of the bride and groom. Emma had never looked prettier, and handsome Mahlon, who hovered around her, was more exciting than any hero of any book she'd ever read. And when the time came in the evening for the boys and girls to pair off upstairs and come down together to supper and the singing afterward, she watched them, enthralled with their grown-up airs. She could never, never act that way with a boy.

Only the young people of their own district were invited for supper, but the singing was for all of the districts of the Amish. The house was crowded with young people. They had to be seated in every inch of available space. Katie and Susan, with a great deal of giggling, moved from place to place to make room for older girls and boys who had precedence over them. They ended up in the kitchen, wedged between the stove and a table, both loaded with dirty dishes that had been left for tomorrow's washing. There were only two high chairs to sit on; one of them Edna's. Katie just barely squeezed into it. The other was the kitchen step stool. Susan perched on it. They looked and giggled.

In front of them was a short bench where Henry was sitting with Mahlon's youngest brother, and in front of them, on another short bench, were three big boys--well, almost big. Bishop Eli Hershberger's Edward was one of them, and Katie wasn't sure, but she thought that the boy on one side of him was Dave Senior Yoder's Mose. But who was the boy on the other side? She'd never seen him before.

She poked Susan with her elbow. "Who's that homely boy?"

"What boy?" There was so much noise they could talk out loud and not be noticed.

"That odd-looking one beside Bishop Eli's boy."

Susan stretched her neck. "Oh, that's his cousin from away someplace. I forget where. I think his name is Mark Hochstettler. He's here on a visit."

Katie stared at him for a moment. "I've never seen such a homely boy! His nose is too long, his chin sticks out, and his eyes are set too deep. Ugh! What girl would want to sit beside him! Perhaps that is why he doesn't have a partner. But, then, neither do the other two.

"Now Dave Senior's boy is a lot better looking. Any girl would be glad to be his partner! He's not much taller than I," Katie thought. "You can see he is strong. His nose is the right length, he has a dimple in his chin, and his humorous brown eyes don't give the impression of being lost under his brows! When I date, I'll pick the good-looking boys."

After the wedding Emma and Mahlon moved to their first home at the north end of the community; the Miller family settled down to the serious work of the winter. Katie would be fifteen in the spring and she was to learn how to sew her own clothes under Mom's watchful tutoring. Katie was glad to be home, but when she wanted to make her clothes just as fancy as Vernie did--fancier if she could--Mom said she should stay within the church's rules of dress. Home became a battleground. Mom and Vernie against Katie. Vernie liked being called Lydie Dan's fanciest girl and she was determined Katie should be held back. "She's not old enough to go to singings or the crowd. Why should she have such nice clothes?" she complained to Mom.

* * *

That spring, after Katie was allowed to go to one singing, she wanted to go all the time. "Mom, you didn't let me go every time until I was sixteen," Vernie reminded Mom when she almost gave in to Katie's pleas to go every Sunday evening. "Keep her home, too!" she demanded of Mom. So the rest of that spring, Katie, with poorly concealed envy, watched Vernie leave for the singings. Vernie always got the good things in life.

After spring communion Mom told Katie she was now old

36

enough to join church. Katie was glad. If you were old enough to join church, you were old enough to go to the singings all the time and even date boys. To be sure, older people thought joining church was a solemn thing and had to do with whether you could go to heaven or not when you died, but as Katie didn't expect to die for a long time yet, except if the end of the world came, that didn't seem worth worrying about. Now she wanted to have a good time, to be part of the crowd, to go to singings, and have dates.

By fall she was a confirmed singing goer, had dated half a dozen boys, and listened with polite boredom to instructions on how to be a good church member given every other Sunday in the counsel chamber. The ministers found no serious fault with her conduct or in the rest of the class. They were to be baptized the first Sunday in September.

For the ceremonies she got a new black dress in which she felt smug and self-satisfied. Mom had let her make it as fancy as the church allowed, and even Vernie unbended enough to give her a few pointers on its making.

Vernie and Katie became good friends. Perhaps it was because Katie was content to bask in Vernie's caustic wit instead of competing with it, or perhaps the anticipation of being aunts drew them together. Emma was to have her first baby in November. They forgot their differences in the fun of dating and being grown-up together.

*   *   *

Katie was on her knees, facing the congregation. Four other candidates for baptism were lined up beside her: Dan B's Mary and three boys. Katie wished John Gingerich could be baptizing her; he was her favorite preacher, but as John wasn't a bishop, that was out of the question. Besides, John and his family had moved up into Mahlon's district. "Oh, well, I guess it doesn't matter. Once this embarrassing business of baptism is over, I can forget serious things," Katie thought irreverently.

The congregation, which had risen for prayer, sat down. The

bishop came slowly over to the line of candidates, followed by the assisting minister who carried a small bucket of water and a cup. The boys would be baptized first, beginning with the oldest. Then Dan B's Mary--and Katie at the end. She sighed and shifted slightly. Her knees hurt already.

She looked out of the corner of her eyes at the boy at the head of the line. While the assisting minister was pouring water into the bishop's cupped hands, the bishop said, "I baptize you in the name of the Father, Son, and the Holy Ghost."

"One finished," Katie counted to herself. "If I ever get up again, my knees will be too stiff to walk. Two baptized. I'm glad there are only five in this class and not fifteen! How long would it take to baptize fifteen?

"They have finished the boys. Dan B's Mary is next." Katie straightened up and tried to look as prim and solemn as Mary. "In a few seconds all eyes will be on me.

"Mary hasn't moved a muscle since we got on our knees. How does she do it? Maybe she really is serious about this." For a moment, Katie felt ashamed. "After all, it is a serious thing to be baptized--everybody says it is."

They were in front of her. She felt the bishop slip back her prayer head covering, heard, as in a dream, his intoned words above her, and felt the first trickle of water being poured on her head. "Ugh, it is cold--it is running down the side of my head-- oh-hh, it is running down my neck and it is cold!"

5

KATIE, can I speak to you a minute?" Monroe Miller touched her lightly on the arm. Katie turned away from Susan Gingerich and Susan's sister Edna.

"Do you have a way to go home from singing tonight?" he asked softly.

"Not especially," she answered.

"Bishop Eli's Edward wants to take you home," he told her.

Katie considered for a moment. Edward was quiet and friendly-- and as far as she knew, a nice boy. "All right, I'll go with him."

"OK, I'll tell him. He'll come in and take you out. He's not as bashful as some boys."

"Now, Katie," Susan teased as Katie joined the other girls. "Who's going to take you home tonight?"

"Hard telling," Edna said. "She has a different one every Sunday night."

Katie smiled without replying. "That isn't quite true--but there was no use arguing." She wished some of those boys would ask Susan for a date. "She's had only one date since she started to go to the singings--and that's two years ago, " Katie thought. "I've had--I don't know how many dates I've had. Emma used to say when I worked for her last winter that every month a different boy brought me home from the singings. And she was right. I dated each boy about four times and that was enough. Then I'd try another. I'm tired of every boy I know. I've had plenty of chances to go steady but every boy is the same. There's not one who has read a book since quitting school. All they want to do is --ugh.

39

"What is wrong with me anyway?" she wondered as she waited for Edward to come in to the kitchen to escort her out to his buggy. "Boys, dates, parties, and housework--that's all there is to this life. I haven't had a book in my hand since I worked for Will and Barbrie. How I wish I could read! Life surely is more than this."

Maybe it was just because Mom had made her work for Henry Yoders, and it was such a contrast to Mahlon's, Will and Barbrie's, and Dave Yoder Junior's.

Edward came in, cutting short her thoughts.

"Ready?" he asked. She nodded.

"Oh, Katie!" Someone called out as they came through the door. "Out with the boys again, Katie?" and "Why, Katie, Edward tonight!" Whistles and catcalls followed them as they walked on without paying any attention. Such things were common and silly. Boys who had been turned down and couldn't get the girl they wanted stood outside the door to greet all the couples who came out with the same remarks. If an especially surprising couple paired off, these boys would all pile to the home of the girl and do practical jokes.

No one followed them, and Katie and Edward got to Henry Yoder's without any mishap. Katie waited until Edward had tied up his horse, then she led the way into the house. She had learned in her two years of dating that people appreciated your coming in quietly and speaking softly when you kept company with a boy for several hours outside their bedroom door after eleven o'clock at night.

She lit a lamp, set it on the living room table, and deposited her bonnet and covering beside it. Then she looked up and met Edward's gaze.

"Where shall we sit?" he asked, looking around the room.

"Oh, anywhere," Katie said indifferently.

"Let's sit on the couch then," he said, leading her to it.

"Aren't you coming any closer?" he asked, surprised. Reaching over, he tried to draw her to him. She did not move. "You've got the light burning," he said as he moved closer to her and put his arm around her. "Surely you blow it out, don't you?"

"If you want it out, you're the one who has to do it," she replied stiffly.

"What's wrong with you?" he asked ungraciously as he stepped over to the table and blew out the light. "I thought boys told me that you're a good date. You act like a fence post tonight."

His words rankled her. "So the boys discussed her good points among themselves, did they? As if she were a good horse or a new buggy!" she thought. "What if I do?" she retorted, moving to the far end of the couch before he sat down. "Maybe I get tired of being smooched. That's all boys want to do on dates. They have nothing to talk about. I've been dating for two years and never has any boy talked about a book or an idea. All they want to do is kiss, kiss, kiss." To herself she thought, "All they want in a wife is someone to go to bed with and cook their meals and bear their children."

"Well, you must be different from what you used to be. They told me you always make a boy feel at home. Hey, where are you now?" He reached out through the darkness to draw her to him.

Katie was thoroughly incensed. "Oh, they do, do they?" she retorted crisply, slipping off the couch and deftly eluding his waving arms. "Well, I'll give them something else to talk about. If you don't stay at that end of the couch and keep your hands off me, you can go home."

She could hear his surprised gasp. There was a moment of silence. "Say, there is something wrong with you, isn't there? I thought everybody smooched. I never knew you objected to it."

"Maybe I've had my fill of it," Katie answered.

"Well, goodness me, what else do you do on a date?"

"What would be wrong with just sitting and talking?"

"Oh, that's silly," he replied, his voice coming sulkily through the darkness. "What is there to talk about with girls? They don't know anything."

"They don't?" Katie asked, groping her way to the door of the

41

stairway; she hadn't cleaned this room every Saturday for the last six weeks without learning its arrangements by heart. With her hand on the door, she paused. "Here's one girl who knows that she's had enough. You can go home. I'm fed up with you. And I don't care if you tell all the boys I'm tired of kissing and hugging and acting like a silly fool on a date. No boy is worth it anyway." Then she opened the door and sped up the stairway into the darkness.

At the top she paused and listened breathlessly. "I'm safe," she thought. "He wouldn't dare follow me up here. A girl is still safe in her room in our community, even though boys going upstairs to the girl's bedroom is not unheard of in some Amish communities."

She waited a moment, listening. Suddenly she heard his footsteps. Then the front door opened and closed, none too quietly. Quickly she tiptoed to her room and listened at the window. Through the dim starlight she could see him untying his horse and getting into the buggy. As the sound of the buggy faded into the distance, she lit her lamp.

Her face burned; her breath came in gasps; her hair was rumpled; and the bun at the back of her head was loose. She reached up and unfastened it. She might as well go to bed.

"What is wrong with me? If I surprised Edward, I surprised myself just as much!" she reflected. "Edward acted no worse than any of the other boys I've dated. Why did I pick on him?

"Nothing seems to satisfy me anymore. Singings are the same old gossipy affairs Sunday evening after Sunday evening. The girls who are popular are self-assured and disgustingly catty. Those who don't have dates are so jealous it is just as disgusting."

Studying her burning face in the mirror, Katie came to a serious decision. "No more boys for me, if they can't do more than neck. Until I find one who cares enough about the same things I do, who can talk like an intelligent person instead of kissing and hugging, Bishop Eli's Edward is my last date!"

She turned away from the mirror. Her covering and bonnet were still downstairs on the library table; she could get them in the morning. Wearily sitting down on the edge of the bed, she took off her shoes, tears of hopelessness and frustration dropping to the floor. Quickly she wiped them away.

The next morning, when Katie went out to help with the milking, she found Henry already started. With a brief greeting, she picked up a milk bucket and stool and went to the back of the cow stable. She dreaded talking with Henry whose cutting tongue criticized everybody.

"What on earth happened last night?" he began before she was seated. "Did you get into a fight with your date?"

Katie sat down and started milking. "What business is it of yours?" she thought.

"You came home banging doors and you were no more than home when you ran upstairs like a house afire. Whoever heard of acting like that!"

Katie did not reply, her lips set in a straight line.

Henry finished his cow. He set down the milk pail on the shelf beside the door. Picking up an empty bucket, he came over to stand before her. "What was wrong?" he asked in self-righteous indignation. "If it wasn't a decent boy, why did you date him?"

"He was supposed to be decent," Katie answered sullenly.

"Why did you treat him like that, then? They tell me you're as boy crazy as they come; so it must have been that you didn't behave yourself," he said sneeringly.

Katie gave a startled gasp, milking forgotten. "Who says I'm boy crazy?" she lashed out angrily. "A lot you know about it. I don't know as it's any business of yours what went on last night. Nobody got into any trouble."

He gave a short laugh and turned back to another cow. "I can tell you this much, if any of my girls came home and acted like that without a good reason, they'd sure catch it. You run around and do as you please. If you was my girl, I'd make you stay at home and behave instead of letting you work out all the time."

Tears of rage and humiliation blinded her. "Who says I want to work out?" she cried thickly. "Anyway, I find people like you and your wife break your necks to get a hired girl to do your dirty work for you. I didn't ask to come here."

That stung him. "I guess you get paid for doing what you do. I don't know that you've got any cause to complain; you're getting good wages."

She shut her lips in a thin angry line and was silent. The three remaining weeks until August 1 would be cold as winter here-- but she'd endure it.

"They call me boy crazy, do they?" she conversed with herself, as the day went on. "Just because I've had lots of dates the last two years doesn't mean that I'm boy crazy! I don't go asking the boys for dates. Can I help if I'm asked? What are you supposed to do if a boy asks you for a date? Snub him? And as for my behavior on a date--I have yet to see a boy who doesn't try to get at least half a dozen kisses on the first date. Boys who are supposed to be nice boys and well within the rules and regulations of the church.

"I'm sick and tired of such behavior. All the boys think the ultimate in life is dating, kissing and hugging, and then eventually marriage, farming, and a big family! They don't have any books-- and they wouldn't read if they did have them. How I wish I could read! How I wish I had some books! If only I could have gone to high school!"

The Sunday after the episode in the cow stable was church Sunday, and because it was almost harvesttime, the sermon text was Revelation 14:14, 15: "And I looked, and behold a white cloud, and upon the cloud one sat like unto the Son of man, having on his head a golden crown, and in his hand a sharp sickle. And another angel came out of the temple, crying with a loud voice to him that sat on the cloud, Thrust in thy sickle, and reap: for the time is come for thee to reap; for the harvest of the earth is ripe."

Katie found herself listening to the sermon. Today her unhappiness made her seek something outside of herself. Maybe the sermon would help her.

Preacher Joe Yoder painted an eerie picture of the awful end of the world. Katie hadn't thought of that for ages.

"The end of the world is coming one of these days and the harvest of the wicked will be gathered in," he thundered. "The judgment day is coming when everyone will have to stand before the terrible throne of God and give an account of all the things he has done. And if you haven't lived up to the will of God as portrayed in the rules and regulations of the church, what will you do?"

Katie felt terrible. It would be a fearful thing to have the end of the world come before you were ready for it. The thought of meeting God turned her insides into jelly and made her burst out into sticky perspiration. Glancing furtively at those around, she wondered if there was anyone else here today who was afraid of the end of the world. If so, what did they do about it?

That night Katie lay awake in agony of terror, every little noise making her jump, expecting the end of the world. She fell into a troubled sleep at dawn, wondering if the end of the world would come that day.

So as the weeks wore on in the cold atmosphere of Henry Ellie's home, she grew pale and thin, the heat of the July days exaggerating her feelings. Henry and Ellie noticed that she was morose and quiet, and concluded that Henry's lecture at the cow stable had made her too angry to be civil to them.

AS Henry Yoder clattered down the stairs with her trunk, Katie snapped shut her suitcase, and put on her bonnet. She gave one last look around the room to see if she might have forgotten anything. There was nothing. "They say, if you forget something at a place, you'll come back; I certainly don't want to come back to this place," she thought as she started through the door. "Not once in these three months have I felt at home. I hope working for Emery Gingerichs this fall will be better. I'm glad I can be at home for a few weeks."

She found Ellie waiting for her, checkbook in hand. She set the suitcase on the floor.

"How much do we owe you yet?" Ellie asked.

Katie turned to the calendar on the wall underneath the clock shelf. "At five dollars a week, it would be twenty-five dollars for the last five weeks," she said.

"Didn't we advance you some money this month? We usually have to."

"You didn't this time," Katie replied, forcing herself to speak evenly.

"I think that, for the price we paid you, you could have been more dependable," she said as she handed a check to Katie.

Katie stiffened. "What do you mean? I'm sure I tried to do as well here as I did for Mahlons or Will Barbrie or Dave Yoder Juniors."

"Of course, you are young yet," Ellie said condescendingly. "I think your folks should keep you at home for another year or two. But I guess they need the money."

46

For a moment Katie thought of leaving without another word, but on second thought, she made herself stay. After all, nothing spoiled a hired girl's reputation as quickly as falling out with the people she worked for. "Yes, they need the money," she said quietly. With the check in one hand and her suitcase in the other, she started toward the door, wanting to get away as quickly as possible. At the door, she turned briefly. Bare courtesy demanded that she bid good-bye--even if she hadn't liked it here.

"Good-bye now," Ellie said before Katie could speak. "Don't go away mad at what I said. I only said it for your own good."

Katie let the screen door slam behind her before she answered, "Good-bye." Ignoring the rest of the sarcasm, she walked across the porch into the soft summer dusk.

Katie was silent all the way home as Henry tried to make conversation above the rasp of the spring wagon wheels. For the first time since she was thirteen and had begun working out as a hired girl for her aunt, she was sick and tired of it. "It isn't fair for Mom and Pop to make me go," she thought rebelliously. "Mom says, whenever someone asks for a girl for the summer, for a few months, or a few weeks: 'Well, if you think you can get along with Katie, you can have her.' And I have to go.

"Until this summer, I've enjoyed it," Katie mused. "Will and Barbrie were good to me, and Dave Yoder Juniors, and Mahlons treated me like one of the family. But if I work for any more people like Henry Yoders, I'll tell Mom I'm staying at home." Henry turned into the lane. The soft lamplight from the windows of the house reached out toward her troubled soul like a benediction. Before she could alight from the spring wagon, there was a rush of feet and Mary Ann and Edna were greeting her.

"Are you coming home again, Katie?" Edna asked eagerly.

"Yes," Katie answered. "Are you glad?"

"Hello, Katie," Mom, coming from the kitchen, greeted her at the door. "So you're coming home again."

Katie took off her bonnet and placed it on the sewing machine in front of the window, glancing around the room. How peace-

47

ful it looked, with its Saturday evening scrubbed look. Pop came out of the living room with the daily paper in his hand, a faint welcoming smile on his quiet face. "Hello, Katie," he said gently.

She turned and smiled in return. "Where are Vernie and Clarie?" she asked. "I don't see Henry and Elmer either."

"The boys are out in the shop," Mary Ann told her enthusiastically; "they're fixing the lights on Elmer's new buggy."

"The girls are out in the washhouse taking baths," Mom informed her. "They'll be in before too long."

Henry Yoder with much grunting and straining was outside the door with Katie's trunk. "Can you open the door?" he called. "Aren't there any big boys around this place?"

Pop threw the daily toward the table and hurried over to help him place the trunk on the dining room floor. Henry straightened up, red-faced.

"You got quite a girl here," he said importantly, nodding toward Katie.

"So?" said Mom.

"If she tried just a little harder, she'd be a real good hired girl," he said with a snicker. "The wife says that if she were taught a little more, she'd be more dependable."

Pop, who avoided any kind of controversy with anyone, was already backing into the living room, leaving Mom to answer Henry.

"So?" said Mom again, surprise and annoyance making a sharp edge to her reply. "Well, I guess after this, if you want a good hired girl, you'll just have to go somewhere else then."

Henry, who already regretted his remark, snickered again in an attempt to turn it all into a good joke. "Oh, I wouldn't say she didn't do pretty good for her age. She wasn't that bad."

Katie, who had looked at him when he began speaking, turned and ignored him. Mary Ann and Edna looked on in openmouthed wonder. Henry headed for the door. "Well, good night, Katie," he said uneasily.

48

Katie said, "Good night," without turning around.

He let the screen door slam; the sound of his heavy footsteps going down the walk came through the summer darkness.

"What was wrong with him? Didn't he like your work?" Mom asked in puzzled surprise when they heard his wagon going out the lane.

"Oh, Mom, I don't know what was wrong with them," Katie burst out. "I'm sure I tried just as hard at their place as I did anywhere else, and no one else complained about me, did they?"

"Not that I know of," Mom answered doubtfully.

The door between the washhouse and the kitchen burst open and Vernie came in, followed by Clarie.

"Hi," Vernie greeted her gaily.

"Are you home again?" Clarie asked affectionately.

"Yes, Hi," Katie returned, a smile flashing across her face.

"Henrys didn't like Katie," Mary Ann piped up importantly.

"Oh, hush," Mom said quickly. "You don't have to tell everybody."

"What's she talking about?" Vernie wanted to know.

"Oh, Henrys didn't think they got their money's worth out of me," Katie answered with brittle sarcasm.

"Well, now, Katie maybe you didn't work hard enough for them."

"I worked harder this summer than I ever did before, Mom."

"Didn't you get along all summer? You never said anything."

"They never said anything to me either until just the last few weeks." She hated to tell Mom about the episode in the cow stable that Monday morning.

"Oh, well, let's forget it," she said, wanting to change the subject. "I hope I never have to go there again, that's all."

"Why don't we take your things upstairs?" Clarie asked, willing to change the subject.

"Leave the trunk down here," Mom directed. "Katie has to go over her things before she goes to Emery Gingerich's anyway. How soon are they leaving for Colorado, Katie?"

"Not until the middle of August. That's when Emery's hay fever begins. But they want me to come the week after next. I guess she wants me to do some canning and help get ready to go," Katie said as she began to pick up her things to take upstairs. "Oh, here, Mom, I almost forgot to give you the check."

Clarie followed her upstairs, giving a hand with the suitcase. Vernie followed, too. With a sigh, Katie deposited the suitcase on a chair beside one of the double beds. Since Emma's marriage, Clarie had come over to share a room with Vernie, leaving the room she and Katie had occupied to Mary Ann and Edna. Katie looked around the softly lit room, as Vernie and Clarie and she sat on the beds.

"I wish I didn't have to work out," she said longingly, putting her bonnet on the dresser.

"I thought you liked it," Vernie said.

"I always have until this summer," Katie answered.

"Maybe it won't be so bad at Emery Gingerich's," Clarie consoled her. "After they leave for Colorado, you'll have the place to yourself. Wouldn't that be fun?"

"Yes, you can have company every Sunday," Vernie added. "We'll come over and visit you."

"Won't you be afraid to stay alone at night?" Clarie asked.

"I don't know. His folks are just across the road, you know," Katie answered.

"What happened at Henry's?" Vernie asked curiously. "Did you have a fight?"

"Not exactly, although he did tell me that I should stay at home with Mom and Pop instead of working out and doing as I please," Katie answered wryly.

"Of all things!" Vernie exclaimed. "Where would he get a hired girl if everybody did that?"

"That's what I asked him," Katie said. "I wasn't the one who first suggested I work out. I didn't even want to. I went because I had to and ever since then people won't let me stay at home."

"I bet, if anyone hears you're home this week, they'll be here

50

for a hired girl before the week's up," Vernie said.

"I wouldn't be surprised," Katie agreed.

"And here you're hired out until after corn husking," Clarie chimed in. "Or aren't you going to Dave Junior's again this year?"

"I was planning on it," Katie answered.

"Say, that reminds me, Emma asked Mom the other day whether you could work for her next summer. I think she wants you to start around the last of December. She's expecting again," Vernie said.

"Again!" exclaimed Katie. "Goodness me, Johnnie's only going to be a year old in December and Mary Ruth will be two in November."

Vernie shrugged. "I know. I feel sorry for her, but she doesn't seem to care. If she'd have asked two weeks sooner, I would have gone there, but I've already promised to work for Mose Yoders."

"Maybe I could work for Emma," Clarie suggested hopefully. "Then Katie could stay at home next year. She worked for Emma last winter."

"Oh, don't worry about it, Clarie," Katie smiled at her. "If I do work out, I'd just as soon it was at Emma's. I liked working there last year when Johnnie came; Emma's easy to work for. Mahlon's never fussy, either."

"Say, what happened between you and Bishop Eli's Edward?" Vernie asked, changing the subject.

"Who told you?" Katie asked guardedly.

"Oh, Fannie Yoder had some kind of a story. Her brother told her, I think."

"Did Edward tell him?" Katie asked.

"Well, Edward said something about you not being what you're supposed to be, I guess. Didn't he behave himself?"

"You've never dated Edward, have you?" Katie asked.

"No, I've never had that privilege--if you call it that," Vernie answered.

"I guess he wasn't any worse than a lot of others I've dated, as far as that goes," Katie said. Then she burst out abruptly, "Vernie, don't you get tired of hugging and petting? I do."

"So that was the trouble," Vernie said. "Yes, I do get tired of it. That's why I haven't had too many dates in the last year."

"All the boys I've ever dated act as though they weren't enjoying my company unless they neck," Katie said. "None of them seem to consider dating a girl just to talk. I'm tired of being kissed by boys I care nothing about."

"That was all Edward wanted to do, I expect."

"Yes," Katie laughed halfheartedly at the memory of that night. "When I didn't want to let him, he got insulting. What made me really mad was when he said that girls do not know enough to talk to a boy; all they were good for was necking."

"Why, the horrid thing!" Vernie exclaimed. "I'd have told him to go home when he said that."

"That's what I did. I got away from him and ran upstairs. He went home then."

For one surprised moment Vernie stared at her, then she burst into incredulous laughter, with Clarie joining in.

"I never heard of anything so good," Vernie gasped. "Did you really have the nerve to do that? No wonder he's mad at you!"

"I suppose he's going around and saying all sorts of things about me," Katie said ruefully.

"I don't think so," Vernie assured her, turning serious again. "He wouldn't dare tell people you ran away from him."

"Have you had a chance for a date since then?" Clarie asked.

"Last Sunday night. I didn't take it, though."

"Why not?" Vernie asked. "Are you afraid they're all alike?"

"As far as I know, they are," Katie said disgustedly. "I vowed then, and I intend to stick to it, that I'd never date a boy again until I found one who could and would talk with me. I mean, be intelligent enough to talk about something more than his horse and buggy, the singings and crowds, and things like that."

"That will be hard to do," Vernie warned her. "You won't find one like that right away."

"Then I can wait. I've found out that boys aren't the most important thing in the world," Katie said resolutely.

"Oh, you did," Vernie grinned. "I'm glad you know it. It looked for a while as though you didn't."

THE first week at Emery Gingerich's, Katie helped Emery's wife, Sarah, can a couple of bushels of peaches, put sweet corn into the locker, mend, pack, and learned how to do the chores. The idea of staying alone bothered her, but as the busy week came to an end, she heaved a sigh of relief, glad to see the Gingerichs loaded up in a friend's station wagon ready to go.

"Are you sure you won't be afraid to stay alone at night?" Emery Sarah asked at the last moment.

"Oh, I don't think so," Katie said, thinking about storms and fires and the end of the world. "Don't worry about me. I'll be all right."

"She can stay with us," said Emery's father, Dan, who had come over to see them take off. "Go on; we'll see that she takes care of things." He grinned at Katie through his white beard. With good-byes all around, they were off. Katie and Dan stood at the gate watching until they were well down the road.

"Now you're on your own," Dan teased her, as he turned to go home. "If you need any help, don't be afraid to yell."

Katie smiled and assured him she would. Going back to the house, she paused at the steps and looked around her. The yard was beginning to turn brown in places because of the mid-August heat. They could use a good rain although, as yet, nothing was suffering from the lack of moisture. Emery Sarah loved flowers and the garden was ablaze. In the beds around the house plants grew in luxurious foliage. Sarah had picked off slips and put them in jars of water on the back porch to grow roots. Katie was to pot them.

It was an old homestead, this place; one of the oldest of the community. Years of loving care had preserved the buildings. The house gleamed with a coat of fresh paint which Emery had put on this summer. Across the road the grandpa house gave a pleasing sense of completeness to the farm, with its neat yard and garden.

"Everything looks so peaceful and serene. Why am I troubled in such surroundings?

"What causes this unrest in my heart? What makes me so dissatisfied with myself, with life, with very existence itself? I feel old, flat, dull. The strain of working at Henry's and knowing they were dissatisfied with me must have been harder than I realized. Perhaps the fear that I was being gossiped about, because I ran away from Edward, has made me tired. I wish I had some books to read. I wish I could go to the library for books--but Amish people just don't do that.

"Maybe, while living here alone during the next six weeks or longer, the relish for living will come back--"

There really wasn't too much to do. Katie kept the house and yard clean. Until it rained, there was no need of hoeing the garden. There were some tomatoes to be canned. The few chores took only an hour each morning and evening. By the end of the first week, Katie had become so familiar with them that she could do them automatically. Dan came over at least once a day for milk and cream and to see how she was getting along. Usually he lingered long enough for a friendly chat, and Katie began to cherish a real affection for the plump, kindly man.

By the middle of her second week alone, the heat became almost unbearable. The house was shaded by old elm and maple trees. And south of the house stood a grand cottonwood--landmark for miles around. If Katie stayed inside through the day and kept the shades down, the hours passed by in reasonable comfort. But she began to dread the evening chore time. With the heat and the flies, milking became an ordeal.

One evening, when it seemed as though the heat must let up, Katie waited to go out to milk, hoping it might grow cooler.

Wild, dark clouds hovered on the far horizon while she was getting in the cows. Because she had kept the shades down all afternoon, she hadn't noticed them. The grass in the pasture was dry and short under her feet. Little clouds of dust arose from the plodding hooves of the cows and remained motionless in the air.

Katie hurried, keeping a nervous eye on the clouds. Dan came over just as she turned out the last cow to pasture. "Looks like a storm," he commented as he picked up two buckets of milk to carry to the milk house.

"Yes, it does," Katie assented. She took the remaining bucket and followed him through the barn door.

"We need it," Dan grunted, kicking open the little gate beside the barn and holding it open for her.

"Everything's so dry," Katie agreed. "The heat has been awful today. That's why I'm late doing the chores. I thought it might be cooler if I waited a little."

Dan poured the milk into the cans for her and set them in the cooler.

"I'm glad Emery sells milk to the cheese factory. Separating would be quite a job on these hot days," Katie commented.

"Yes," Dan answered. "Need any help to do the other chores?" he asked, pulling out his handkerchief and wiping his face.

"I don't think so. I only have the eggs to gather and the hogs to feed. Thank you, though."

"Well, are you sure you can make it?"

"Oh, yes," she told him, rinsing out the milk buckets and

the strainer and turning them upside down on the bench beside the milk house door. "Don't bother; I can make it."

He left her, trudging across the road toward his house, his eyes on the gathering clouds. Katie watched him a minute, then walked out toward the hog pen to feed the hogs. There wasn't much to do there--just throw a few shovels of corn over the fence and see that supplement was in the feeder. At the hen house door she gazed at the lowering sky toward the southwest.

"This will be a bad storm," she guessed, feeling the cold fear of lightning run down her spine in an icy flash.

She hurriedly gathered the eggs and set them down on the cool basement floor. The eggs she had gathered at noon had cooled enough to be put into the case; so she cleaned and cased them, straining her eyes in the semidarkness.

Closing the basement door, she stood for a moment outside the house, anxious fear mounting as great, lowering clouds rolled and tumbled in the southwest. Flashes of lightning lit the darkened sky.

Katie shivered. For a moment she considered running over to Dan's before the storm broke. "They will think I'm a fraidycat if I go running over because of a summer storm," she thought. Biting her lips, she turned and ran into the house.

She was too fearful to be hungry. By the light of a lamp she washed her hands at the kitchen sink and dried them carefully. A bright flash of lightning swept across the sky. A low rumble of thunder followed. The storm was coming nearer. She dried her hands again. Standing numbly in the middle of the kitchen, she wondered what to do next. Seeing her covering on the table, she walked over, picked it up, and carefully fitted it on her head. Maybe that would keep her from danger.

Lightning flashed so brightly it drowned out the dim glow of her lamp. A loud roll of thunder followed. Desperately she closed her eyes and held her hands over her ears. Another flash of lightning and a louder roll of thunder made her cringe. "Oh, if only Dan had made me come over to his house!"

The wind began a high, whining roar in the treetops. Lightning showed the lilac bushes east of the house lashing about with frantic thrusts as the rain began to fall. It was too late to think of running over to Dan's.

"The open windows upstairs!" Brought to her senses by the pattering rain, she grabbed the lamp and turned quickly toward the stairs. The light flickered. Shielding the chimney with one hand, she crept up the stairs. A bright flash of lightning accompanied by a tremendous crack of thunder nearly made her drop the lamp. It slanted crazily in her hand. For a moment she poised herself on the top step, paralyzed. "What if this were the end of the world?" Knifelike cramps shot through her abdomen.

The sound of the rain coming heavily against the hall window brought her back to the job at hand. "I must get those windows closed!" Fearfully she crept across the hall and opened the door of her room. As she did so, a blast of wind blew out her lamp. Groping her way across the room, she set the lamp on the dresser and turned to close the window behind her bed. Already rain had pelted her bed. Gingerly she pushed down the sash and turned to cross the room to close the other window. An ear-splitting crash of thunder paralyzed her in sheer, melting terror. The blinding flash that accompanied it could mean only the end of the world!

Katie was afraid. Deathly afraid. She felt numb and shaken. How long she stood there, paralyzed, she never knew. Moment after moment brought crack upon crack of thunder, only a shade less terrifying. The wind blew the trees in moaning fury. Rain blasted the windowpanes in its fierceness. It sprayed through the open window in its vehemence, hitting Katie.

Startled to her senses, she dashed across the room frantically reaching for the window. Then she jumped back again into the shadows as a roaring crash deafened her. She stuffed her fingers into her ears. If only she had the lamp! There were matches on her dresser, she remembered. In her raging fear she made her way

57

to the dresser. **There,** fumbling around in the darkness, she finally found them. She lit a match, sighing with relief when its tiny flame flared up. On second thought, she lit her night lamp, too. Setting them at opposite ends of the dresser, she sank wearily down on the edge of the rain-soaked bed.

How long was this storm going to last? It must have been raining hard for half an hour, and it showed no sign of lessening. Wave upon wave struck the windows with renewed vigor. Lightning tore into the room. Katie covered her face.

She sat there wishing over and over again that she were at home with the folks, over at Dan's, or that this awful storm were ended. She *hated* thunderstorms.

When the thunder finally started to abate, she undressed. Leaving a lamp burning, she got into bed, pushing down toward the foot, away from the wet pillows. She was too tired to change the bedding. She was dazed and without appetite. She dozed off into fitful sleep.

AS Katie waded through the morning's mud, with the squashy ooze creeping up between the toes of her bare feet, she was heartily glad for the brightness of the sun. "Perhaps the end of the world isn't as near as I feared," she thought. In the ordinariness of doing chores, the thought of the end of the world seemed farfetched and unlikely. "Maybe it won't happen after all for another hundred years. I hope not," she mused almost aloud. "But even so, I would fear another thunderstorm. I've a notion to hitch up this afternoon, go over home, and get Edna or Mary Ann to stay with me. Emery wouldn't mind. The little girls could keep me company during the day and, if another thunderstorm came along, at least I would have someone to share it with."

"Quite a storm last night!" Dan's voice broke into her thoughts.

Katie glanced around from behind the cow she was milking. "Oh, I didn't know you were here," she said, startled at the unexpected voice. "Yes, it was."

"I wonder if the lightning hit anything last night?" Dan queried of no one in particular. "It sure was close, wasn't it?"

"It sounded like it!" Katie laughed rather shakily.

He paused at the doorway and ran his gray eyes around the farmstead. "Why, I do believe it hit that cottonwood south of the house!"

Katie left the cow and joined him at the doorway, milk bucket in one hand and stool in the other.

"It's been here for years--but look at it now--split in two. No wonder the storm sounded as though it were right above us!"

"It's lucky it didn't fall toward the north; it would have gone full length across the garden," Katie observed.

"I was telling Emery this spring that he ought to cut that tree down. I've told him many times that cottonwoods draw lightning; he just laughs at me. He always said it was a good shade tree for the cows. Well, it's half gone now; maybe he'll come around and cut down the other half," Dan said stoutly.

"You mean all big trees draw lightning?" Katie asked anxiously. This was a new and scary thought, she decided, looking at the tall trees that shaded the house on all sides.

"No, not necessarily. Just cottonwoods," he told her. "Although some of those trees around the house are so old they should be cut down. I expect half of them are partly hollow. But they make such nice shade we hate to cut them down."

Katie went back to milking.

"You should have come over to our place last night," he said from the doorway. "When I got home, Mandy asked me why I hadn't told you to come. She said there was no use your staying over here alone when it stormed. I told her that if you were scared you would come over anyhow."

"Well—" she answered hesitantly, "I thought of that, but I waited too long," hating to tell him how terrified she had been.

"I told Mandy there was no use worrying about you. After all, if you'd be scared to stay alone, you never would have hired out here to begin with," he drawled.

Katie bit her lips, laughed shamefacedly to herself, and wondered what he'd say if he knew what she'd gone through the night before.

After the morning chores she ate a hearty breakfast, hitched up the horse and buggy, loaded the egg case in the back, and got ready to go to town. She needed groceries and decided to go to town first and stop at the folks' after that for dinner. Maybe she could get Mary Ann or Edna to come home with her.

After she had climbed into the buggy and was backing away from the hitching post, she thought of asking Dan and Mandy if they wanted anything from town.

"Naw, I don't think so," Dan said. "I'm going to the sale barn tomorrow anyway; so we can wait until then if we need anything."

"Well, I just thought I'd ask," Katie said. "I thought I'd stop at the folks' for dinner; so I probably won't be home before this afternoon."

"Oh, going home, are you?" Dan asked.

"Yes. I thought I might bring back one of my little sisters to stay with me. You don't suppose Emery and Sarah would care, do you?"

"Naw," he assured her. "It probably gets lonesome for you over there all alone as you are."

"It does," Katie answered. "I've never been alone like this before. Every other place I worked they always had children around."

60

"Why, sure. A little sister around there to keep you company would be just the thing," he assured her.

Katie clucked to the horse and started to drive away.

"Much obliged anyway," he called after her.

It was slow going over the muddy roads. Katie leaned back and closed her eyes, leaving the horse to pick his own pace and path. There was no danger of meeting a car as long as the roads weren't dried off; so she relaxed.

"How bright and glorious life seems this morning after the terror of the night! How could I have felt that life was losing its zest! It is infinitely better than death! No. No. No. Let me live a long time yet!"

She pushed the thought of death and the end of the world to the back of her mind and began to concentrate on the things of life. "Why don't I ask Vernie and Clarie and Elmer and his girl to come over for supper Sunday evening and go to the singing from there? If I see any of the young people in town, I'll invite them too! Next Sunday after church they can come and visit. Maybe I could have an outdoor supper for them." She began to plan the menu.

*　　*　　*

"You want one of the little girls to go home with you?" Mom asked after news had been exchanged as they were sitting at the table after dinner. "I don't know. What do you say, Pop?"

"School starts next week," Pop said quietly. "She could only have her for a week."

"Well, but I could have Edna then, if Mary Ann has to go to school, couldn't I?" Katie asked quickly. Somehow, she couldn't bear the idea of being alone any longer. Especially if another storm came up.

"Edna starts to school, too, Katie," Mom said in surprise.

"Edna! Is she old enough to go to school?" Katie asked, astonished. Edna was still a baby. Only yesterday she had been wearing bibs.

"Why, Katie, of course she is," Mom said. "She'll be six in November."

"Yes, I'm going to kindergarten," Edna turned great, shining eyes toward Katie.

"You're too little to walk that far," Katie teased her.

"Oh, they don't have to walk this year, didn't you know?" Vernie asked. "The school board is sending a bus out this way."

"They'll have it a lot easier than we did," Clarie said. "They won't have to walk a mile each way through all kinds of stormy weather the way we did."

"Oh, it wasn't hard on you," Pop said mildly. "It took a lot of the mischief out of you."

"What's going to take the mischief out of these?" Katie asked laughingly.

"We don't have any," Henry said from the back of the table.

"Oh, you don't," Vernie cried. "I'd like to know what you call it then."

"Aren't you out of school yet, Henry?" Katie asked. "I keep forgetting, because I'm gone so much."

"This is going to be my last year in that jail," Henry assured her loftily. "Then I'll know all there is to know!"

"Do you suppose they can teach you to loosen the checkrein before you water the horse?" Pop asked quietly, a twinkle in his eye. "You forgot to do that to Katie's horse at noon."

"Aw," Henry blustered, reddening. "Aw."

"Aw," said Pop. "I think you have room for quite a lot more learning."

"But what about one of the little girls going home with you?" Mom turned back to Katie. "If you want to bother for just a week, you can take one along."

Katie considered for a moment before replying. "I hardly know what to say," she said at last. "I didn't realize that Edna was that old, I guess. Maybe I'd better just forget about it."

"Oh, I was hoping I could go back with you," Mary Ann said quickly in a disappointed voice.

"Me, too," Edna said.

"You do?" Katie smiled at them sympathetically. "Even if you can stay only the rest of this week?"

"Yes, I do!" Mary Ann affirmed stoutly.

"I want to go, too," Edna insisted.

"Now they both want to go," Mom said in exasperation. "Which one do you want, Katie?"

Katie looked from Mary Ann's pixie brown eyes to Edna's pink and gold prettiness. She'd been away from home so much, she hardly felt acquainted with them. "I'll take them both with me," she decided. "That is, if I may. May I, Mom?"

"If you want to bother with them, all right," Mom said.

"Goody, goody!" Edna clapped her hands.

"Shall we go get ready now?" asked Mary Ann, willing to leave at once.

"Not before we put our hands down," Mom said sternly. "Come on, everybody, we're finished eating. We might just as well put our hands down, then they can go get ready."

They all put their hands down under the table while Pop said a half-audible thanks for the blessings of their food, Mary Ann and Edna poised to jump up the minute it was over.

They buzzed with excitement while Mom got their clothes together. Katie helped Vernie and Clarie with the dishes, talking all the while.

"Come on over and see me Sunday after church, girls," Katie invited. "I thought I'd ask some others Sunday at church, too."

"Just girls or some boys, too?" Vernie asked.

"Oh, I don't know. I'll have to invite some boys so we'll have a way to go to the singing."

"Elmer would probably come, if you asked him," Clarie told her.

"Oh, yes, I forgot," Katie assented. "Where is he working, anyway?"

"In town. His carpenter gang is putting up a new house

63

north of town," Vernie said.

"He's going to get married this fall," Clarie said in a loud whisper. "Don't tell the little girls or they'll blab."

"I'm not surprised," Katie laughed. "I should think he's gone with Lavina Yoder long enough to know her quite well by now."

"Four years," Vernie nodded. "But she's only twenty, even so."

"He's past twenty-two," Clarie said. "He says he's tired of running around; so he wants to settle down."

"Well, anyway, ask him if he and Lavina have planned anything for Sunday evening. If they haven't, tell them to come over."

They went into the living room to sit down a few minutes. Mary Ann and Edna emerged from the bedroom, faces shining with expectation, hair neatly braided, each with a paper sack of belongings. Edna clutched a doll wrapped in one of Mom's discarded baby blankets.

"We're all ready to go," Mary Ann cried.

"Oh, now wait a while," Mom cautioned. "Katie's just finished helping with the dishes. We want to sit down and visit a little before she leaves."

She sank into the rocker beside the library table. "How long are Emerys staying in Colorado?"

"Until frost," Katie said. "Didn't you know? I thought I told you."

"Well, you said frost, but haven't they set a date? You're supposed to go to Dave Junior's through corn husking, you know."

Katie nodded. "They won't be wanting me before the middle of October though, Mom."

"You're going to Emma's by the first of December. You knew it, didn't you?" Mom asked.

Katie nodded.

"She wants you until the fall of next year; so don't count on anything else," Mom went on.

"I know."

64

They were silent, each lost in thought. Clarie and Vernie had settled down with separate sections of the daily paper that had been discarded by Pop and Henry, who had gone back out to work.

"When are we going to go?" Edna broke in impatiently, shifting her doll. "I thought Katie was going back to Emery's place."

"Don't be so in a hurry," Mom said soothingly. "You'll get there soon enough."

"What time is it?" Katie asked.

"Two-thirty." Clarie looked up from her paper and answered.

"Go tell Henry to hitch up," Mom told Mary Ann. "He can tie up at the hitching rack, then Katie can leave when she's ready."

Clutching their burdens importantly, Mary Ann and Edna left to hunt up Henry.

Another hour passed before Katie left. Vernie and Clarie got out material for fall dresses for all three of them. Katie cut off a length for herself and hunted up their dress patterns. Because Vernie and she used the same pattern, they cut an extra one out of a piece of newspaper so that she could take it along and work on her new dress at Emery's.

Mary Ann and Edna seated themselves in the buggy as soon as Henry drove up and tied it at the hitching rack. To pass the time they sang all the songs they knew. Twice they came in impatiently to ask if Katie wasn't ready yet. The third time they appeared, Katie tumbled material, dress pattern, and thread into a paper sack and, grabbing up some cookies Mom had given her went out to the buggy. The others followed.

"Now behave," Mom cautioned the little girls.

"We will," they chorused.

"Be sure and come over Sunday night for supper," Katie told Vernie and Clarie as she clucked to the horse and started out the lane. "And be sure to tell Elmer, too," she called, looking back at them through the open back curtain.

"We will," Clarie and Vernie answered.

Mary Ann and Edna leaned out and waved as long as they could see the others standing at the gate, then settled down in contented anticipation.

As Katie jogged home through the familiar countryside, which looked refreshed and shining after last night's rain, she thought wistfully that it would be nice to stay at home for a change. "But I'll have the little girls with me for the rest of the week," she thought. "I can get acquainted with them for that long." Then, as another thought popped into her mind, she sighed in relief. "The end of the world won't come for the next few days," she thought fleetingly. "Not until I take the little girls home again!"

ALL Katie heard that fall was the end of the world. When she went to a quilting, the ladies talked about the end of the world. If she helped anyone butcher, the men talked about the end of the world. In Sunday school the congregation was studying the twenty-fourth and twenty-fifth chapters of Matthew. How Katie hated those terrifying Scriptures!

"For as the lightning cometh out of the east, and shineth even unto the west; so shall also the coming of the Son of man be."

Just as she had always feared. It would be so quick, there would be no time to get ready.

"Immediately after the tribulation of those days shall the sun be darkened, and the moon shall not give her light, and the stars shall fall from heaven, and the powers of the heavens shall be shaken."

"But of that day and hour knoweth no man, no, not the angels of heaven, but my Father only."

No one would know; so how could you be ready?

"For then shall be great tribulation, such as was not since the beginning of the world to this time, no, nor ever shall be."

Alone in the Gingerich house, she awakened night after night from troubled nightmarish sleep. Through the day she pushed the thoughts back into her mind by sheer willpower only to have them break through her consciousness with such knifelike keenness as to take away her breath and make her tremble with dread. Once, when she was lifting a forkful of food to her mouth, the thought of the end of the world shot through her like a bullet, and she dropped her fork in terror, appetite gone. "I'm glad there is no one here to see how jittery I've become," she thought.

In the middle of October after Emerys came back from Colorado, Katie went to Dave Junior's to work through corn husking as she had the year previously. Dave's little girl, Ruby, was seven; her brother, Floyd Lee, two. Ruby seemed like a little sister to Katie. Dave Mary helped Dave husk corn; Katie took care of things in the house.

Katie was glad to have Mary out in the field through the day. It was hard to act natural when you were feeling distressed. She didn't want Dave and Mary to know how afraid she was of the end of the world.

She didn't fool Dave and Mary though. "What's wrong with you, Katie?" Dave teased once. "Did you turn down some boy that you wish you hadn't?"

Katie smiled and answered halfheartedly. How could she tell them what was wrong, when it was so terrifying she didn't even want to think about it, let alone speak of it?

The weather was cool and clear, and many times when Katie emptied out the supper dishwater she stood in the yard in absentminded silence, her mind on these questioning thoughts.

One Saturday evening when the air was cold and clear, it

was later than usual because Dave had to grind feed for the stock before Sunday and hadn't come in for supper until after eight. She and Mary gave the children supper and baths and put them to bed; then they waited until Dave came in to eat theirs. Now it was almost nine o'clock.

For a moment she stood there, slowly wiping out the dishpan and wringing out the dishrag. "Everything seems so peaceful and enduring, it is hard to realize that someday the end of the world will wipe it out," Katie thought.

"But, what is that?" A long, reddish finger of light slipped up out of the eastern horizon, faltered for a hesitant second, then leaped up high––higher until it reached the zenith in the heavens. Another finger of queer reddish light flew up, up, and touched the zenith, followed by another and another.

Katie turned and searched the heavens. The queer, reddish fingers were shooting all over the sky. One reached up, up, from the east and was met by another one from the north, to hang for a long eerie moment in the reddish radiance that made even the white dishpan shine with a pinkish glow.

"What does it mean? Is it the end of the world?" Terror crept over her as she watched. Sick and nauseated, her stomach cramping sharply, she turned and went back into the house. Forcing herself to look natural, she hung up the dishpan behind the pantry door and the dishrag on the rack behind the kitchen range. "You ought to go outside and look," she said.

Dave looked up from his newspaper. "Why?" he asked curiously, sensing at once that something was wrong.

"Just go out and look," Katie answered, avoiding his eyes. "It's something you ought to see."

Dave slowly laid down his paper and got up from his chair. "Is it a fire?" he asked, as he went across the living room.

"No," Katie answered, wishing heartily that that was all it was. "It's something not made by man."

Mary gave Katie a queer look, then she, too, went outside. Katie waited impatiently.

A few minutes later they came in. "It does look peculiar," Dave acknowledged, giving Katie another keen glance. "I wonder if it isn't just northern lights. Haven't you ever seen them before?"

Katie looked at him sharply. "Northern lights!" she exclaimed. "Is that the way northern lights act? I thought those were just in the north. These are all over the sky."

"I know," he answered reluctantly. "I've never before seen them act this way. Maybe it is something more."

"Maybe it's a sign of the end of the world," Mary said, uncertainly.

"That's what I was wondering," Katie answered, a little break creeping into her voice.

"Oh, I don't know," Dave was matter-of-fact, "I still think it's the northern lights. I'm going to take a bath and go to bed. I'm too tired and sleepy to be scared."

Long after Dave and Mary had gone to bed, Katie sat by the window in her nightgown with a blanket wrapped around her and watched the reddish streaks of light play in the sky. When at last she went to bed, her sleep was troubled. Toward morning she got up to look again; miraculously the sky looked normal. Twinkling stars shone clearly. Katie sighed in deep, thankful relief that the end of the world had not come and went back to bed to sleep soundly for the first time that night.

* * *

"Hi. Here you are," Emma greeted her cordially. "Get back, Mary Ruth, and let Aunt Katie come in."

Mary Ruth backed up slowly until she bumped against Emma, then wrapping herself in Emma's apron she watched with big eyes while Katie came into the kitchen and set down her suitcase. "Cold outside," she volunteered to Emma. "Even with my overshoes and your big heavy bearskin, my feet got cold."

"Come on into the living room where it's warmer," Emma invited, . leading the way, with Mary Ruth at her heels. "I never stay out in the kitchen any longer than I have to."

Katie followed her to the living room, slowly taking off her bonnet and scarf as she went. Placing them on the library table, she began taking off her shawl, her eyes going over the living room and what was visible of the dining room.

"Did you get anything new since I was here the last time?" she asked. "Here, Mary Ruth, come and let me hold you."

Emma drew up a rocking chair to the stove. "Sit down, Katie, and warm up. No, I don't know that I have, except some books." She opened up the door to the heater, took the poker, raked the coals apart, and reached for a piece of wood.

"Books!" Katie exclaimed. "Here, Emma, let me put in the wood. It's too heavy for you."

"All right, I won't argue," Emma said good-naturedly. "The doctor did say I wasn't to do any heavy lifting. Mahlon hates to chop wood; so most of that wood weighs a ton."

Katie filled the heater, then went out to the porch for an armful for the woodbox. "What kind of books?" she asked as she dumped the wood. "And where did you get them?"

"Christian fiction. I got them down at the bookstore," Emma replied, walking over to the bookcase that stood in the farthest corner of the living room. Picking up Mary Ruth, Katie followed her across the room.

"You've got quite a lot of them," she exclaimed. "How does it happen that you buy books? I didn't know that you liked to read that well."

Emma smiled wryly. "I guess I never carried it to excess the way you did. At least I never read so much that I neglected my work and had to be spanked for it."

"Don't rub it in," Katie grinned. "The spankings were bad enough without being reminded of them. Can I read them?"

"Of course! What do you take me for? You can read all you want to so long as you get the work done."

Katie chose a book at random and, going back to the rocking chair beside the stove, sat down with Mary Ruth on her lap.

"What does Mahlon say about this?" she asked while paging through the book.

"Oh, he doesn't care. I buy them with the egg money and there is quite a lot of that this winter. Eggs are more than thirty-five cents a dozen and we have four hundred hens. I'm supposed to have the egg money to buy groceries and whatever's left over is mine to use as I want." Emma explained.

There was a shout from the porch; Mahlon was there with Katie's trunk.

"I'll open up," Katie told Emma, dumping Mary Ruth unceremoniously onto the floor. "Stay sitting."

She flew to the door, book in hand, and opened it wide enough for him to come in. Grunting, he carried the trunk into the house. "What have you in here, Katie? Money?" he asked good-naturedly. "I see you've already found Emma's books."

Katie laughed, "Well, she showed them to me as soon as I was inside the door."

"You asked if I'd gotten anything new," Emma said defensively. "That was the only new thing I have."

"I expect you two will sit here of an evening and have your noses in books," Mahlon said dryly. "If I get a grunt out of you, I'll be doing well."

Katie and Emma exchanged grins at the accurate description of the evenings to come.

"Oh, well, you sleep as soon as supper's over anyhow," Emma reminded him, assuaging her conscience with the thought. "As long as we don't disturb your rest and keep the fire going so you'll be warm, you shouldn't care."

"No, I guess not. Where do you want this trunk, Katie?"

"Upstairs," they both chorused.

"Well, grab hold, Katie. Let's see if we can get it up there. I suppose you brought along everything you ever owned, seeing you'll stay almost a year," he teased.

"Not quite," Katie said solemnly. "I left my dolls at home."

*   *   *

Mahlon had accurately portrayed their winter evenings. As soon as the supper dishes were washed and Mary Ruth and

71

Johnnie were ready for bed, both Katie and Emma picked up books. By that time Mahlon was already dozing over his daily paper in his chair by the fire. The house was quiet. Before they had been reading a minute, they were wholly lost in the stories. They seldom talked, although they constantly chattered in the daytime as they went about their work.

"These books are like the one Will Barbrie brought me," Katie told Emma.

"How is that?" Emma asked.

"Well——" Katie tried to find the right words. "They are romances——but they also tell you how to be saved."

"Yes," Emma said. "They helped me understand that Christ Jesus came into the world to save sinners——and I am one of them."

In the following months, Katie thought and thought. The idea of herself as a sinner needing to be saved was something to think about. It was nothing new to hear that Christ had died on the cross for sinners. She had been hearing that preached in a general way for as long as she could remember. But to own up that she, Katie Miller, was a sinner was——well——disconcerting!

Something in her heart admitted the truth of the matter. The books said that God creates each person in His own image, but that man lets doubt creep into his heart——then disobedience. God, however, loves mankind. He desires their fellowship. When we put our trust in what Christ has done for us, turn from our sin, and ask Christ to live in our hearts, we escape the penalty for sin and live eternally with God.

Each book had the same message. By the time Katie was in the fourth book, the message of the Gospel caught and held her. She accepted it. One evening toward spring, when it had become warm enough to go upstairs with her reading, Katie knelt beside her bed and asked God to save her. Except for Emma, few of her people would have thought it anything special.

PART 2

1

KATIE brushed her hand over her brow, trying to keep a troublesome wisp of hair from hanging into her eyes. Mechanically she dipped diapers into the rinse water and stuck them into the wringer. This was the second load of diapers, besides the load of tiny baby things that were already fluttering on the line in the mild March sunshine. Since the baby's coming two weeks before, Katie had washed baby clothes and diapers by the barrel as Mahlon had said last Friday when Emma had coaxed him into hanging things out for Katie. Today he was busy getting ready for baby turkeys and Katie was washing alone.

She didn't mind. It gave her uninterrupted time to think over all that had happened in the last few weeks. As she sloshed baby things around in the rinse water and automatically hung up diapers, Johnnie's tiny shirts, and Mary Ruth's little dresses, she recalled the message of the Christian fiction she had read last winter. It grabbed at her mind and kept her thinking and thinking until there were times when she grew physically weary.

"So, I, Katie Miller, am a sinner and need to be saved! Well, it's true," she acknowledged. "The books said, 'Everyone is a sinner,' and am I not part of everyone? The books said, 'The only way to be saved is to come to Christ by faith and repent,' and have I not repented? The books said, 'After one has become saved, one must study the Bible and pray.' I have begun to read the New Testament. As for praying, I can't be kneeling down in prayer all the time, but I have begun to kneel in prayer in the evening before going to bed.

"There is so much that is hard to understand in this new life--

so many things--that for the first time in my almost nineteen years I have begun to listen to the Sunday sermons! Never before have I enjoyed--yes, enjoyed--the Sunday-school discussion.

"Was it only last fall when I dreaded going to Sunday school because of the teachings in the end-of-the-world Scriptures? What happened during the Sunday school's winter recess and this spring? I am glad we started studying the Gospel of Mark and so far there has been no mention of the end of the world. But to find Sunday school interesting--she who had before this either daydreamed or sat in fear and trembling, wishing it were over! Well--some change has taken place in me, that is sure."

Katie lifted up the wash basket in strong arms and carried it to the clothesline. The diapers flapped merrily in the wind, almost whipping out of her fingers as she pinned them on the line. With a smile she surveyed the full line stretched across the yard. Would there be ninety diapers again today as there had been last week? "Emma does have her hands full with as good as three babies to take care of; it is no wonder she wants a hired girl all summer.

"I'm glad I can work for Emma if I have to work out all the time anyway. Ever since I've been small, I've liked Emma, with her calm, practical attitudes toward life and her sense of humor."

The basket was empty. Katie picked it up and started back to the washhouse for another batch. "If I hustle, I might get done before dinner," she mused. Taking off the lid of the machine, she began once more to poke clothes into the wringer.

* * *

"May I take Mary Ruth to church with me?" Katie asked Emma, clearing off the table and carrying the dishes to the work counter.

"Oh, I don't care," Emma paused in the act of getting the baby's bath water ready. "Are you sure you want to bother with her all day? It's counsel meeting, and she might be quite a pest before the day's over."

"I'll risk it," Katie assured her. "She'll surely sleep this afternoon, won't she? If I take her along, you won't have quite so many on your hands."

"Well, if you want to risk it," Emma shrugged. "If she gets too bad, you can send her in to Mahlon."

"Is he staying all day?"

"I suppose so." Emma picked up the baby's bathtub and started for the living room. "He usually does," she said over her shoulder.

After the dishes were washed and the house swept, Katie began getting herself ready, hurrying a little so that she would be done in the washroom before Mahlon wanted to shave. As yet, he was still finishing chores, although the milking and separating had been done before breakfast. "He should be in any minute," thought Katie, fitting her side combs into her hair, before she began on her long brown braids.

By the time she had her hair braided and pinned up, with her hair net tucked over the braids, Mahlon was on the back porch kicking off his overshoes. With one more look into the mirror, Katie rinsed and wiped off her hands and left the washroom. Through the window she could see the horse and buggy already tied up at the hitching rack. The kitchen clock showed nine o'clock. It was time they left.

"Need any help with Mary Ruth?" she asked Emma.

"No, thanks," Emma assured her. "Go get yourself ready. All I have to do is bathe her and get her clothes changed. I'll have that done by the time you're ready."

Upstairs, Katie opened her closet door and surveyed the row of dresses hanging there. Which one should she wear? Not the black one, because in two weeks, if they had communion, she would have to wear black. Black brought back the memory of her baptism--and she wore it no more than was positively necessary. She finally decided on her winter blue; she loved that dress and in a few weeks the weather would be too warm for it. Slipping hurriedly into it, she pinned it shut and, reaching into her dresser drawer, drew out her white shoulder cape. It was too early to start wearing her white apron; so she pinned on her blue apron to match her dress. She reached down behind the row of

77

dresses for her good shoes.

Should she wear heavy black cotton or thin rayon stockings? It was too warm for cotton, but black rayon had better not be risked at counsel meeting; so she settled on a pair of black lisle. There was sure to be some old woman who mentioned rayon hose in the counsel.

The hose and shoes on, she opened up her covering drawer and took out her black covering, taking deep pleasure in its trim fit. "I'm glad Mom finally let me make it of organdy," she thought; "organdy is so much more chic! The only people who still make their girls wear black silk coverings are old-fashioned."

Grabbing up her shawl and bonnet and taking out a bunch of hankies from her drawer and a pink chiffon head scarf, she went downstairs. There was no Sunday school today; so she didn't need her Testament. She found Emma in the living room putting the last touches on Mary Ruth, who stood smiling widely over her new pink dress and white organdy apron. Katie smiled too. Mary Ruth did look sweet.

"My, all ready to go!" Katie laughed. "Isn't that a pretty dress?"

Mary Ruth smiled in womanly fashion at all her finery.

"She's got it already," Katie chuckled.

"Don't I know it!" Emma said wryly. "Don't brag about her or you'll make her worse. Are you ready?"

"All but tying my shoulder cape. Can you do that?" Katie turned and presented her back to Emma.

"Sure. I'll be glad to." Emma took the ends of the shoulder cape. "How does it happen you don't tie it before you put it on? I thought most girls did."

"I never can make a decent bow," Katie said impatiently. "Besides, it's too much bother when you can get someone else to do it."

"There it is," Emma gave one last pat to the perky white organdy bow that adorned the center back of Katie's waistline.

78

"Mahlon's getting dressed; so you'd better get your shawl and bonnet on. He'll be out here any minute."

While Emma put on Mary Ruth's coat, scarf, covering, and bonnet, Katie flung her own shawl around her shoulders and fastened a sparkling pin in front. Then, slipping back her covering, she fitted the small pink square of chiffon over her head and tied it securely under her chin. That done, she pulled up her covering carefully over her scarf and then lowered her bonnet over the covering. In a few weeks it would be warm enough to go without a scarf, but right now the air was still a little too chilly in a buggy.

"Daddy, go by-by," Mary Ruth chuckled. Katie turned to see Mahlon coming out of the bedroom. His dark blue frock-style coat fitted him perfectly, and with his smooth shaven cheeks and handsome Roman nose, he looked every inch a man. No wonder Emma considered him good-looking!

"Are you going along, too?" he asked Mary Ruth in mock surprise. "With your pretty new dress?"

Mary Ruth gave a pleased look at herself. Even though Emma had covered up the new dress with her coat, she knew it was there.

"Think you can get on alone?" Mahlon asked Emma.

"Yes, yes, don't worry about me," Emma assured him. "I don't suppose anyone will come anyway, since it's counsel meeting Sunday."

"Someone from another district, or Poplar Hill Church, might come," he suggested, giving his hat a final brush and throwing the brush down on the library table.

"No, I don't think so," she assured him. "Other districts are either having counsel meeting, too, or else fast day; so I'm not looking for visitors. Go on or you'll be late. Should anyone come, I'll entertain them," Emma said positively.

*   *   *

The voice of the presiding preacher droned on and on, and around Katie many had succumbed to the lullaby of the droning voice and were dozing discreetly behind the backs of others. Katie, seeing those around her, was strongly wakeful. The sermon was the familiar story of the fall of man and the call of the patriarchs, known to her as the old-father Scriptures.

Preacher John Gingerich's voice rose and fell in a regular singsong chant that made even the most strong-willed sleepy, but Katie listened as though for the first time. As the morning advanced, Mary Ruth grew restless, wanting her purse and the playthings in it. Katie was relieved when the cookie plate was passed around, for Mary Ruth decorously ate her cookie and became quiet again.

Later there was a stir behind her. Looking around, Katie saw two girls go out to help get the lunch ready. In a few minutes she heard the soft chatter of their voices in the basement, for services continued right over the noon hour.

About her, groups of three and four quietly went outside to go down to the basement to eat the lunch of coffee, bread, butter, jam, jelly, or a mixture of peanut butter and corn syrup, a favorite of the children. This, with beet and cucumber pickles, was the accepted fare.

Seeing so many around her leave for lunch, Mary Ruth wanted to go too; so at last Katie, with Susan Gingerich and Katie Hershberger, went downstairs. The group in the basement was rapidly thinning. The older men and women filed sedately out. Only a few younger girls remained at the ladies' table, although many of the boys were still at the men's table, cleaning up whatever the waitresses put on it. If they waited long enough, the main session would be over and, not being members of the church, they would be excused anyway; so why go back in?

Katie met Mahlon as he was leaving, toothpick in his mouth. "Is she getting to be too much for you?" he asked, nodding toward Mary Ruth. "If she is, I can take her."

"Oh, she's just fine so far," Katie assured him. "Besides, she hasn't eaten yet."

"Well, if you get tired of her, send her in to me," he told her, turning to go back into the services.

Katie smiled into Mary Ruth's questioning eyes and led her toward the table. "You'll stay with Aunt Katie, won't you?" she asked quietly, mindful of the people upstairs, who could hear the softest voice. Mary Ruth nodded, her eyes already on the plate of pickles.

By the time they had finished eating and returned upstairs, the main service was almost ended. Preacher John Gingerich asked for testimonies of the sermon's truthfulness; the next meeting place was announced; and all those who were not members of the church were asked to leave. Only members could stay for the counsel session that began after the closing hymn. The restless boys grabbed caps or hats and quickly filed outside. With a stir and rustle children and young mothers moved from the kitchen into the bedroom, closing the doors so that the children would have a warm place during the next hours of the counsel session.

The remaining people grew quiet. Every eye turned to Eli Hershberger, the bishop, who before this had been sitting composedly on the bench just inside the living room door. For the first time that day Bishop Eli rose to address the congregation. He did it slowly, dramatically, knowing that the main business of the day was now to begin. Before the evening all of those within the sound of his voice would be resentful and dissatisfied, wholeheartedly approving, or blandly indifferent to the afternoon's session.

He cleared his throat quietly as he rose to his feet. "Brethren and sisters, we are gathered here together in the name of God," he began his lengthy preamble to the hushed congregation. Gone were all signs of drowsiness. The only sounds were the muted chatter of small children and the jabber of some baby.

"It is alarming when we see how many of our people are leaving the true church. Not just young married people, who are always the first to show their dissatisfaction, but older families, too, are leaving for more progressive churches. Some with married children comfortably established in the church are going, leaving the children to follow or stay. People just don't want to practice self-denial anymore and obey the true precepts of God and the church. Therefore, it behooves one to speak sharply to those here this afternoon so that you will be sound in the faith."

After this foreword, he gradually led up to the main business of the meeting. Telephones, electricity, and automobiles were named first as being worldly and therefore strictly forbidden. Everyone breathed normally because none of them had those things, therefore none felt guilty.

Then he began condemning rubber-tired implements and rubber-tired tractors. By this time, several young married farmers started to fidget and gloomily looked at their hands. "What could you do when steel wheels were so hard to get and more expensive than rubber?" more than one asked himself resentfully.

Katie quietly held the sleeping Mary Ruth, making no mental comments. She was still untouched. The unmarried women were usually the last to be admonished.

Warming up to his subject, Bishop Eli commented on the young unmarried men. Shingled haircuts, parting the hair on the side, flashy rings and buckles on the buggies, zipper jackets, narrow-brimmed hats, hats with creases in the crown--all these were worldly and fancy. Some of the boys shifted uneasily and rubbed their hands together.

"And the young unmarried women. Where should one begin--with their short dresses and hair nets and rayon stockings!"

Katie tensed at once. "Rayon stockings? Who had been tattling now? Usually only silk stockings were mentioned at counsel meetings!"

Bishop Eli stormed on, "How could they expect to serve God with their flashy shawl pins and hair clasps and dresses in all kinds of fancy colors of yellow and peach and pink? What of their fancy hairdos, with coverings so small they sat on the back of the head, not covering it the way they were supposed to do? And bobby pins in their hair with all kinds of waves there to make a vain show instead of looking meek and humble? Where was their love for God and the church if they aped the worldly fashions and went after the ways of the flesh?"

Katie shifted uneasily in her seat. She hadn't thought of it until now, but Mary Ruth was getting heavy.

"Christ died on the cross for each one of you," Bishop Eli reminded them. "If that means anything to you, you would love His blood; if you love His blood, you would love the church; if you love the church, you would love the rules of the church. If there is rebellion in your hearts at what I am saying, you would do well to examine yourselves and see what manner of worldliness is in you."

"Do I really want to serve Christ?" Katie asked herself. "Haven't I gotten down on my knees and told Christ I am a sinner and want to be saved? Don't you want to do the things now that Christ wants you to do?" she asked herself. "I don't want to serve the world, that is sure," she reassured herself.

"Where is self-denial," Bishop Eli asked, "if you have all these things? Didn't Christ say that whoever wouldn't deny himself couldn't be His disciple? Hadn't He said that they were to take up their cross and follow Him? How could you follow Him, if you don't obey the rules and regulations of the church?" Bishop Eli stopped for breath.

"If this is self-denial and following Christ, then my evil things will have to be put away. The rayon stockings. The bobby pins. The fancy shawl pin. The hair net. Before another Sunday, all my dresses will be longer," Katie decided.

All at once tears came into her eyes. "I do want to serve Christ and be saved and escape the wrath of hell. If this is the way to do it, away with all these silly, vain things! If eternity is at stake, what are silly ornaments, rayon stockings, and short dresses? I am going to deny my flesh and serve God and the church!"

"MAY I use the sewing machine after supper?" Katie asked Emma the next night.

"Why, of course you may!" Emma answered. "Go ahead and use it all you want. You don't have to ask. What are you going to sew?"

"Oh, I--well, I thought I'd let down the hems of my dresses," Katie stammered, not meeting Emma's eyes. "They're all so short."

Emma took the baby's bottle out of the teakettle where she had been warming it and squirted a drop expertly on her wrist to test its warmth. "Did someone say something to you about them?" she asked.

"No, but--well, I thought it wouldn't be practicing self-denial if I had them too short," Katie said.

Emma looked at Katie. What was happening to her? "Help yourself," she said, turning toward the bedroom where the baby's wails were growing louder. "Use it all you want to."

After doing dishes, Katie opened the sewing machine. Then going upstairs, she brought down her Sunday dresses and aprons. All that evening she ripped out hems and put in new ones, making her dresses an inch or two longer. None of them had been too short--Mom had seen to that, but now Bishop Eli couldn't complain that she was following the fashions of the world.

There was one new dress that Katie had been looking forward to wearing, but as it was definitely a summer dress, she now left it hanging in the closet. Of soft, thin pink cotton, it had been the occasion of a long verbal battle between Mom and herself, Mom declaring pink was too fancy. It was only after Susan and Edna Gingerich, the two daughters of Preacher John Gingerich, had told Katie that they had made dresses of similar color that Mom had given in and let Katie have one, too. Now, with a pang of sadness, it seemed to Katie that Mom was right. The color was too fresh and bright. "I will not be practicing self-denial if I wear that dress." Katie pushed it way back in her closet, not knowing what else to do with it.

All that week she worked on her dresses. By Friday night she had let out the last hem, and the dresses and aprons were pressed and ready to wear again. While religious zeal was still gripping her, she slipped off her fancy shawl pin and hid it in her bottom dresser drawer. From now on she would use the unworldliest and ugliest of fasteners, a diaper pin. She didn't want to be gratifying her vain nature.

Katie reread all Emma's books. The hens laid as well as ever, but the price of eggs had dropped so that there was no extra money to buy more books. Katie decided it didn't matter too much. "With the beginning of outside work and a new baby to care for," she said to Emma, "I'm too tired to read much in the evenings. After I help Mahlon with the baby turkeys and milk three more cows, I fall asleep when I try to read at night."

As the spring days wore on, Katie found a strange melancholia creeping over her soul. A heavy, burdening sense of dread that seemed unexplainable. As she worked outside, raking the yard, planting the garden, cleaning out the raspberry patch, even the atmosphere seemed full of despondency. The soft soughing of the wind in the trees, the chirp and chatter of the birds seemed in a minor key. She felt sad. "What is wrong with me now?" Katie wondered.

She turned for help to the books she had been reading. They pointed to a more certain source of help, the Bible. When Katie sent her paycheck to Mom and Pop, she decided to ask for money to buy her own Bible.

Eagerly she awaited their reply. The day the money came,

Emma went to town to take the baby to the doctor. "Just buy me an inexpensive Bible," Katie told Emma hesitantly. "One with a center reference column, if you can." Then she worked all day in an agony of suspense until Emma came home in the late afternoon with a shiny Bible.

Not only did the Bible have a center reference column but, what was much better, pages of Bible helps in the back. There were texts on how to be saved, how to believe, how to know you are saved, and how to grow in being a Christian. If she could stay awake in the evenings, she would begin to study.

She knew so little! Of course, many of the stories were familiar. But what did they mean? Why were the Jews so important in the Old Testament? What relation did all of those old rites and ceremonies and sacrifices of the Jewish people have to do with Christ and His death on the cross? She felt that there must be some connection, but for the life of her, she couldn't have told what.

Communion services followed two weeks after the counsel meeting although Bishop Eli had to stretch the point a little to have a unanimous vote. Some of the young married men were noticeably dissatisfied, but most of them had given their assent for communion services when the vote was taken. Even Mahlon, good-natured as he usually was, was dissatisfied with some of the things Bishop Eli said and muttered of inconsistencies and narrow-mindedness to Emma.

The Sunday morning of communion services dawned in a low mist of gauzelike vapor over the vivid green of an April morning. There was a promise of beauty ahead in the faint azure tints of the mist. Katie stood outside the door of the milk house, pails in hand, and drew in deep breaths of the fresh morning air. Was there anything that could surpass the scent of spring? How peaceful this morning seemed in contrast to the many mornings recently! Far across the fields she heard the faint insistent crowing of a rooster suggesting life from beyond the depths of the mist. "If I have to see the end of the world, I hope it will be in the fresh **promise of a morning like this,"** she thought.

"But there isn't time to stand here and moon over the beauty of the morning." Emma had decided to attend communion, too. "When you have three children to get ready, that means some hustling to finish in time. Besides, if we are away all day, Mahlon will take extra care of the young turkeys this morning, and chances are I will have to milk alone." Katie opened the gate of the barnyard and, kicking it shut behind her, went to let the cows into the stable. She milked all but two of the seven cows before Mahlon came in.

"About done?" he asked, grabbing up a milk stool. "I'm sorry I took so long at the brooder house, but those crazy turkeys take so much care."

Katie grinned. "Only one thing dumber than a turkey," she teased.

"Yeah, I know, the man that raises them," he grunted wryly. "But it takes a smart man to outwit the stupid things. Here, let me milk Spot; she's such a hard milker. What would you rather do--go start the separator or finish the other cow?"

"Oh, I'll finish the other cow," Katie said, taking up another empty pail. "I don't mind milking."

They finished milking in silence, each busy with his own thoughts. Katie was thinking of the coming communion services. Now that she wanted to do what was right before God and the church, there was a fear in her heart of not doing the right thing. "Is my black dress really long enough and am I really committed to the rules and regulations of the church?" she asked herself. "Am I above reproach? If there is still anything fancy in my dress, I want to put it away before I take part in communion."

The thought of that pink dress still in the depths of the closet made her uneasy. "What else can I do with it? I can imagine Mom's reaction if I should go to her now and say I want to get rid of it! No, the only thing to do is to let it hang. I'll push it out of sight--so I won't be tempted to wear it."

"I wonder who will help Eli with communion services," Mahlon broke into her thoughts, showing that he, too, had been thinking of the coming meeting. "I hope one of the bishops of the other districts comes over today."

"Why, what's wrong with Eli?" Katie asked. She squirted the last final drop into the pail and got up.

"Oh, I don't know." Mahlon said hesitantly. "Seems to me he is getting too strict."

"Maybe that's what we need," Katie said. "We don't want to practice self-denial anymore."

Mahlon got up from his milk stool. "Well, I know, but what can a man do? Especially about these steel tractor wheels. He forbids us the ownership of a rubber-tired tractor, but he turns right around and gets his neighbor with a rubber-tired tractor to do his plowing!"

"How do you know?" Katie asked, astonished at his outburst.

"I saw it. I went past there the other day and he had a great big, rubber-tired outfit in his south field doing his spring plowing."

"Well, if he hired somebody to do it, what's so wrong in that?" Katie asked. "We hire people with cars to take us on long trips and things like that."

"Yes, I know," Mahlon grunted in a dissatisfied voice. "I'm beginning to wonder how much sense such ideas really make."

"Why, Mahlon!" Katie protested. "Surely you aren't saying that you think it's right to have a car?"

"I didn't say that. I just said I'm wondering why it's any bigger sin to own a car or a rubber-tired machine than it is to hire one." He hung up his pail of milk and let out the last of the cows while Katie stood flattened against the wall to let them past, a bucket of milk in each hand. As the last cow disappeared through the door, Katie turned and slowly followed.

"Oh, well, don't take it so hard," Mahlon grumbled good-naturedly, following her with two overflowing buckets. "I just had to blow off some steam, I guess. I'll settle down and be satisfied, I hope," he grinned as he held the gate open for her with his foot.

She deposited the milk on the milk house floor in silence and turned to leave to feed the hens. "Does Emma know how you feel about this?" she asked in a strained voice.

"She didn't until last night," he answered without looking at her, as he poured milk into the separator tank.

"What did she say about it?"

"Oh, not too much. She thinks about it the same as you do."

"Well, see!" Katie said triumphantly. "How can you be practicing self-denial if you have the latest, most modern machinery? Besides, aren't we to be obedient to the church?"

"Yeah, I know. That's what stops me when I get to thinking such thoughts. I told you not to take it so hard. I have no intention of disobeying the church." He grabbed the crank of the separator and began to work up speed.

The whine of the separator made further conversation hard and besides, if they didn't hurry, they'd be late for church. Katie left the milk house and went across the lane to feed the hens. The mist was beginning to fade, and, through wisps of it, she could see across the wide expanse of fields around the neighborhood. By the time she had finished feeding the hens, the pungent smell around the hen house had lifted with the rolling mist. Mahlon was through separating and had left to feed the hogs.

Katie went back to the milk house to wash the separator and milk pails. She hoped Emma had breakfast ready to fill her famished stomach. Stacking the last milk pail on the shelf, she covered the separator with a white cloth before she took the broom and washed out the milk house. She gave one last look to see that all was clean and in place, then, closing the door firmly, she hurried to the house for breakfast.

THE delicious smell of bacon greeted Katie. Taking off her coat and milk apron and hanging them in the cellarway, she turned to the wash sink. Breakfast was on the table and Emma was bathing baby Paul. Mary Ruth and Johnnie were already at the table on their high chairs, each with a cup of cereal.

"Katie, is it you?" Emma called.

"Yes."

"I was going to fry eggs for breakfast; then we'll eat when Mahlon comes in."

"I'll do it," Katie assured her. "Here he comes now."

There was no mention at the breakfast table of the conversation in the cow stable. Mahlon left for another look at the turkeys and to hitch the horses to the new buggy. Since the increase in his family, he had bought a double buggy from one of the families who had left the church for Poplar Hill.

In a flurry of activity Katie and Emma washed the dishes and tidied the house. By the time Mahlon came in again, Katie had already gone upstairs to dress for church. She glanced into the mirror. "Surely I'm not gratifying the desires of the flesh," she thought as she surveyed herself. "My hair is drawn back tighter than I've ever had it before and is devoid of all vain folly, such as hair net, bobby pins, and hair clasp. My legs are encased in thick black cotton stockings and covered by a dress a good two inches longer than before." She tried to feel solemn and pious as befitted one who wanted to deny the flesh. As she took up her shawl and bonnet to go downstairs, she gave one last look at her reflection. She felt quite proud of her ability to mortify the body and practice self-denial.

Through the green countryside, fragrant with the odor of spring, the team trotted briskly. By the time they pulled up at John Gingerich's, buggies were coming from every direction.

"We arrived at just the right time," Emma noted with satisfaction. "If we come too early, the little ones get restless before church starts, and I do hate to be late."

"There's Bishop Dan Miller from the southwest district," Mahlon observed. "I hope he preaches of the crucifixion."

"There's Preacher Abe Miller of the middle district, too," Emma answered. "I'll bet Bishop Eli won't preach today."

Mahlon muttered something under his breath which might have been, "Good thing." They had drawn up to the gate to take their turn to unload. His remark went unheeded. Emma and Katie lifted the children down and walked to the house. Mahlon turned the team out toward the field behind the house where others were unhitching.

Bishop Dan Miller did preach the crucifixion sermon. He was a gifted speaker and, as the congregation was not used to hearing him, few slept that day. The noon lunch was over before he began and as he unfolded the story of Christ's ministry and His waning popularity, gradually working up to the events of His capture and trial and the crucifixion, Katie found herself listening with tears.

When the assisting ministers had brought in the loaves of bread wrapped in a white cloth, the bottle of wine and a mug, with a knife to cut the bread, she stood with the rest of the congregation for prayer before partaking of the elements.

A hush hung over the congregation as Bishop Eli slowly went from person to person, handing them a bit of bread which he had broken from the thick slice in his hand. Little boys, who had been sent out of the counsel session two weeks before but now were kept in to watch communion services, followed his slowly moving figure intently.

The men and boys were served first, Bishop Eli slowly working his way into the bedroom where the older women and the unmarried girls were standing. As Katie saw him approaching, her heart beat faster. "Am I really fit to partake of this bread which represents Christ?" she wondered. "Oh, I want to be!"

He was in front of her now and handing the piece of bread to her. With trembling fingers she took it, made the little reverential curtsy, and slipping the bread into her mouth, sat down. Bishop Eli was already breaking off another piece of bread for Susan Gingerich beside her.

"Oh, I want to do right," Katie was thinking to herself. "I want to die to the world, and the flesh, and the devil." All the long minutes that followed while Bishop Eli passed out the bread to the young mothers, Katie sat with bowed head and clenched fists. "Oh, I want to die to the world, God! I don't want to follow my own fleshly lusts!"

After distributing the bread, he motioned with his hand and said distinctly. "Let us all stand up for prayer." The congregation arose. Bishop Eli gave thanks for the bread and asked the blessing on the forthcoming cup.

"Oh, I want to be fit to drink of the cup," Katie thought. "I want to mortify the flesh; Christ died for me on the cross and I must do something for Him!"

This time Bishop Dan took the cup and passed it to the remaining ministers, each one taking a sip and handing it back to him. Then he passed it to the congregation, John Gingerich following with the jug so that the cup could be refilled as it was emptied.

"Take the cup. Sip. Hand it back to Bishop Dan. Sit down." Katie's thoughts made a rhythmical pattern as Bishop Dan worked his way around the men in the living room.

He came toward the bedroom now, and once again, Katie was one of the first to partake. Holding the cup reverently, she took a quick sip and handed it back to him, making a quick little knee bend as she sat down on the bench. Bishop Dan passed on to Susan.

As soon as all had partaken of the cup and the last hymn

had been announced, John Gingerich and the other assistant ministers went out to the kitchen to bring in buckets of warm water and towels for the foot-washing ceremony. Placing these at strategic points among the congregation, they seated themselves. Foot washing was ready to begin. Katie looked at Susan in wordless questioning and Susan gave a slight nod. They would wash together.

"This is what Jesus did for His disciples," she thought, as she bent to wash Susan's slim, white feet. "He stooped so low as to wash others' feet--are we any better than He? O Jesus, help me to wash others' feet as you did," she thought earnestly. "Help me to be as humble as you are!" Taking up the towel, she wiped Susan's feet slowly, trying to imagine she was doing it to Jesus. " 'Inasmuch' as ye have done it unto one of the least of these my brethren, ye have done it unto me,' " she thought suddenly. "O Jesus, make me like Thou art!"

She felt drained emotionally, as she sat down to let Susan wash her feet. She sang along softly with the rise and fall of the cadence of the chanted hymn. All over the house people were washing one another's feet.

At last it was over. The hymn was brought to a close. As the girls got up to file out, Katie felt a surge of elation. "I am a Christian and have overcome the desires of the flesh. Never again will vain, worldly fancies have a hold on me!"

Outside, the warm afternoon sun flooded the countryside with a sunny glow. The Gingerichs' garden back of the house was showing rows of new plants coming through the ground.

"Will you stay for supper tonight?" Susan asked Katie as they stood together beside the house.

"Oh, I guess I could," Katie answered slowly. "Are you having the singing tonight? I thought you weren't having it this time. Didn't Millie Joes want it?"

"They said they did to begin with," Susan said in an exasperated voice. "Then just last Monday Millie saw Pop in town and said we could have it after all."

"Why?" Katie asked, absently, brushing some lint off her sleeve.

"She said she had some relatives coming from Indiana and it wouldn't suit them. Edna and I wanted to have a whole bunch of young folks for supper when we had the singing, but we didn't get the chance to invite very many," Susan said.

"Oh, well, you might get a lot of them anyway," Katie comforted her. "There are always some who come for supper because they don't have any other place to go."

"Yes," Susan said gloomily. "Oh, well," she said and went on more calmly, "I did get to invite Vernie and--"

"Vernie?" Katie looked at her. "Where did you see her?"

"She was here to help get ready for church."

"Oh, yes," Katie replied. "I forgot she works for your aunt."

"Well, anyway, I invited her," Susan went on. "And Edna wrote a card to Clarie and told her to come, if she could."

"They'll probably come before too long, then. It's getting late."

"I expect I'd better get in and start cleaning up."

"Looks as if most of the people are leaving," Katie said. "They won't stand around and visit after communion."

Men made short work of hitching up. It had been later than four-thirty when church had been dismissed, and already buggies were turned homeward. Katie caught sight of Mahlon driving up toward the gate and was mildly surprised that he hadn't been ready sooner because of all the small turkeys to look after.

"There's Mahlon," she told Susan. "I'd better go and ask Emma whether I may stay."

"I'm going inside," Susan told her. "Come on in, too, after you've talked with her."

Katie went to the washhouse where the women had left their wraps, arriving in time to put Mary Ruth's coat and bonnet on and to carry her to the buggy where Mahlon had already seated Johnnie. She put Mary Ruth on the back seat and held the baby while Emma got in. "Have a good time," Emma said, waving good-bye as Katie went back to the house to hunt Susan.

She found her in the living room shoving the benches together and getting ready to sweep. Edna was picking up the wet towels to take outside and hang on the wash line.

"Give me a broom," Katie told Susan. "I can sweep."

"Here it is," Susan grinned at her. "I'll carry out these buckets of water. It'll be unhandy to sweep, though. All these benches will have to be left in here."

Katie swept up the dust and dirt of the dozens of men and boys who had been sitting in the living room that day. The Gingerichs had taken out their carpets, as did most people when they had church in the spring, for bare wood floors were easy to sweep of loose dirt sure to be brought in. Katie shoved the benches backward and forward until she had reached every little nook and corner.

She went toward the bedroom. By now everyone had left except the family and a few boys. Katie met John Gingerich at the door of the bedroom. "I'd like to get my clothes out of the closet," he smiled at her genially. "Then I'll go upstairs to change and let you clean up in here."

Katie drew back bashfully.

"I'll come in later on and pile up the benches," he told her.

"Thanks," Katie said.

After he had left, she shoved benches back and forth and swept the bedroom. From the dining room and kitchen she could hear Susan and Edna talking with their mother, discussing the food for the coming supper. She listened absently, her mind on the events of the day.

By the time Katie had finished the bedroom, Susan stuck her head around the doorframe. "Come upstairs with us, Katie. We're going to change our clothes before we start supper. Just put the broom there by the door."

As they were going upstairs, Katie said, "I hope my sisters come; I haven't seen them for two weeks. I wasn't at the singing for the last two Sundays."

"I noticed that," Susan opened the door of their room and

95

stood aside to let the others enter. "Didn't you have a way to go or didn't you want to go?"

"Both," Katie sank down on the edge of a bed. "We had a lot of company, and I was so tired I didn't care to go. I hated to let Emma entertain all of those people alone; so I went home after Sunday school last Sunday. Two weeks ago I went home to help with the chores so Mahlon wouldn't have to do them alone."

"I'm glad you stayed here tonight," Susan's voice was already coming from the depths of the closet, while Edna was taking off her shoulder cape and apron in front of the dresser where she could observe herself in the mirror.

"I wish Pop would let us use bobby pins," Edna said, half resentfully. "My hair has been coming out and hanging in my face all day. If we could use bobby pins, we could keep it back."

"You didn't pull your hair back tight enough," Katie said trying to sound teasing, but feeling good within herself because of being able to do what Edna hadn't--put the bobby pins away without a pang.

"Oh, who wants to pull their hair back tight like an old woman?" Edna demanded. "You sound like Pop!"

"You know what he said about preachers' children," Susan warned her humorously, as she emerged from the closet.

"I don't suppose I'll forget it right away," Edna sighed. "Sometimes I wish Pop wasn't a preacher. Somebody's always coming to him and telling him his girls are setting a bad example for the young people."

"Well, you try hard enough," Susan laughed. "Did you put your hair net away?"

"You know I did," Edna was reproachful. "Even if I wanted to keep it, Pop was so nice about it, I couldn't use it anymore. But I still can't see why a hair net and bobby pins are sinful."

"Well--they're actually just vanity," Katie began hesitantly. "They don't make us warmer or colder."

"Well, but they make us neater," Edna retorted laughingly. "I felt like an old witch today with my hair hanging in my face

96

all the time. I'll have to put up my hair again after supper," she backed into the vacant closet.

"Which will be about midnight if we don't hurry," Susan cut in dryly. "Hurry up, Edna, get your clothes changed. One of us will have to help milk, you know."

"I will," Edna's voice was muffled as she pulled off her dress inside the closet. "I'd rather milk than help get supper."

Susan opened up a dresser drawer and took out a starched apron, which she tied around her slender figure. "I'm ready to go, Katie. Do you want to go with me or stay here and be corrupted by Edna?"

"I don't corrupt anybody," Edna muttered, emerging from the closet. "My head is just as devoid of vain folly as Katie's!"

"Yes, but your thoughts aren't," Susan commented dryly.

"My thoughts are my own," Edna said loftily.

They all laughed and Katie got up. "I'll go with you, Susan. Do you have an extra apron for me?"

"Sure, put on this one," Susan said, pulling another apron from the drawer. "It's really Edna's, but if she milks, she won't wear it anyway."

"Yes, but watch out that you're not corrupted by it," Edna warned Katie solemnly. "It's got a *pocket* on it!"

They all laughed gaily and turned to go downstairs, Katie tying on the apron on the way. Just as they got to the bottom of the stairs, the door opened.

"Here you are!" Vernie's voice came gaily toward them.

"Why, Vernie!" Katie cried.

"So you really did come!" Susan exclaimed.

"Did Clarie come, too?" Edna asked excitedly.

"Here I am!" Clarie peered around Vernie's shoulder. "Vernie, get out of the way, so they can get down."

"How did you come?" Katie asked.

"We got cousin Lewis to bring us over," Vernie explained.

"Is he here, too?" asked Edna quickly. She thought Lewis Miller was just about the best-looking boy she had ever seen, although so far, he had been too bashful to date. Edna secretly hoped she could get him over that.

"Oh, sure!" Vernie laughed. "It didn't take long for him to decide that this was the only place he could eat supper when we asked him to bring us."

"I think maybe tonight is the night," Clarie assured Edna.

"Oh, go on!" Edna exclaimed. "You aren't funny."

"Girls, just make yourselves at home," Susan extracted herself from the rest. "I'll have to go and help Mom get supper. Take your things upstairs and do as you please; come down and visit or stay upstairs until supper's ready."

"We'll come down again," Vernie assured her. "I don't know why we'd come here if we couldn't visit with you."

"I'm going out and help Edna milk," Clarie put in, seeing Edna tie on a chore apron. "Edna, do you have another dress for me?"

"Come upstairs and I'll give you one," Edna invited, leading the way.

"How is everyone at Mahlon's?" Vernie asked Katie.

"Oh, just fine. Emma was in church today. The baby grows like a weed and he's real good."

"Does Johnnie walk yet?"

"Oh, he runs around all over," Katie said. "Yesterday we let him go out to play, and he was halfway out the lane before we caught him." They were all proud and fond of Emma's children.

"What have you been doing to yourself?"

"Why?"

"Well, you look so different. Did you lengthen your dress?"

Katie looked down over her dress, following Vernie's gaze.

"I did lengthen it, yes," she replied slowly.

"Goodness me, you sure did!" Vernie exclaimed bluntly. "You look like an old woman! Whatever made you do it?"

"I thought it was too short," Katie mumbled. How could she tell Vernie why she had really done it? How could she explain to self-assured Vernie that she had died completely to the world and the flesh? Would Vernie understand if she told her that never more would the vain things of the world appeal to her and that from now on she would take the cross upon herself and follow Christ through obedience to the rules and regulations of the church? Vernie would stare at her incredulously and break into unbelieving laughter. Abruptly, she changed the subject.

ALL the next week Katie alternated between an honest desire to do the will of God and smug, self-assured feelings of triumph. She had scored a major victory over the world and the flesh. How pleased God must be with her! Many of the other girls giddily took pleasure in daring to keep on the edge of the church's rules. She was glad those days were over for her forever. God could count on her to obey the teachings of the church.

But why, if she had pledged her lifelong devotion to the denial of the flesh, should she at times be despondent and pessimistic? In the morning she would feel most confident of life, of hope, of her own standing with God. But gradually as the day progressed and she meditated on what was taking place in her heart, and on the teaching of the church, despondency would descend on her until in the dusk of the evening nameless despair surrounded her. There was no good in life.

Mahlon was getting dissatisfied with the church. "What will happen to him?" Katie wondered. "If he could only see that life was too short and serious for any deviation from the will of God! If he began to question the teachings of the church, he would soon follow the ways of the flesh. Young people and older, not willing to live the life of self-denial, were getting rubber-tired tractors, rubber-tired machinery, and much worse, leaving the church completely for a more progressive one where they were allowed cars!" Katie reiterated the bishop's warnings.

Saturday morning a post card from Susan told her that they were having the crowd after Sunday school and that she had written Vernie and Clarie to invite them. She wanted Katie to be sure to plan to stay. Pleased, Katie put the card on the buffet. She liked being with the Gingerich girls.

While washing the dishes after breakfast Sunday, Katie thought of the pink dress. The scene from the kitchen window delighted her. This morning was even fresher and lovelier than the Sunday before. Only the faintest suggestion of mist touched the air, just enough to give every leaf, bush, and blade of grass a tiny little dewdrop of silver. If ever a day was made for wearing a new, pink, summer dress, this was it.

Weakly, Katie tried to battle the growing thought. Maybe she shouldn't wear it, but really--Her arguments got weaker and weaker as she finished the dishes and swept the kitchen. By the time she was ready to change clothes, every trace of resistance had vanished. Straight to her closet she went and, reaching behind her other dresses, pulled out that wonderful, lovely, worldly, pink dress.

All her defenses crumbled. Shutting out thoughts of worldliness and self-denial, she laid it carefully on the bed. Oh, it was pretty! Quickly she took off her old dress, slipped the pink dress over her head, and surveyed herself in the mirror for a long moment while she fastened the dress up the front. Never had her eyes seemed so blue and her cheeks so pink, matching exactly the color of the dress, and she herself so lovely.

All but her hair. She pulled her hair looser around her face. As she took her hand away, a troublesome strand fell across her forehead. Impatiently she brushed it back.

"Oh, what was the difference? She couldn't be expected to pull her hair back so tightly that it remained that way all day!"

She fumbled in her dresser drawer and pulled out some bobby pins, combed her hair back, and deliberately stuck the pins above her ears. That ought to keep her hair back--even if it lay loosely around her face.

Her shoulder cape pinned and her apron settled into place, she got her shoes from the closet, then opened her handkerchief drawer for hose. She pulled out a rolled-up pair of black cotton ones.

"Oh, who wanted to wear those horrid, old, thick, cotton hose with a new pink dress?" Disgusted, she threw them back, fished around for a pair of lisle hose, and regarded those. Even they didn't seem to suit a pink dress. The occasion demanded something special.

Slowly she reached back into her drawer and touched her black rayon hose. Did she dare wear them? Almost she drew back-- and might have succeeded had not the pink dress sleeve on her slender arm shone so softly.

It was her undoing--that glimpse of pink. Resolutely she took the forbidden rayon hose, slammed the drawer shut, and, picking up her shoes, sat down on the edge of the bed to put them on.

"You couldn't always be denying the flesh," she thought resentfully. "You had to be young and well-dressed sometimes."

"You're wearing your pink dress!" Emma said pleasantly, as Katie came downstairs. "You look nice."

"Umm," Katie murmured, feeling detached and noncommittal at her own daring. She lifted Mary Ruth to a chair and tied her tiny bonnet over her braided hair.

"Pretty!" Mary Ruth smiled, stroking Katie's dress. "Pretty new dress!"

"Oh, you little thing!" Katie said indulgently. "You're only two years old and already interested in clothes!"

"No wonder, with her mom and all the aunts that way," Mahlon chuckled. "I see you've got on a new dress. My, it glistens and gleams and shines and swishes! What will the preachers say?" He grinned at her.

"Oh, it doesn't either!" Katie said rather shortly, ignoring his question. Mahlon's words unwittingly cut deep. She thought of changing.

"We'd better hurry," Emma said coming to the dining room with Johnnie. "Here, Mahlon, take your boy while I get the baby."

It was too late to change. The clock pointed to 9:30; Sunday school began at 9:45.

"Come here, *nix-nutz,*" Mahlon clapped hands at Johnnie, who, smiling obediently, toddled across the room. Mahlon grabbed him, threw him high into the air, then caught him expertly while Johnnie howled, half in fright and half in glee. Katie watched them unsmilingly, Mahlon's teasing words still rankling.

Silently she picked up her Testament and handkerchief from the buffet, avoiding the large mirror behind the buffet. Very seldom did Katie pass it without looking at herself, but this morning she could not bear to glimpse her own weakness.

By making the team trot all the way, Mahlon managed to get his family to Sunday school before the first hymn was announced. Katie took Mary Ruth and slipped through the benches to the place where most of the girls were already seated. The opening song was announced as she put Mary Ruth on the bench beside her.

"Oh, you've got on your new pink dress!" Susan Gingerich whispered from behind the hymnbook she offered to share with Katie. "You look real snazzy!" She gave Katie a light pinch.

"Mom wouldn't let us wear ours because we're having the crowd. We'd ruin them," Susan whispered. Katie nodded in reply.

*   *   *

"Oh, you've got a new dress, Katie! My, it's pretty! Where did you get the material?" All the girls commented to her after Sunday school as they filed out into the warm sunshine.

"Let me see it," someone else echoed, touching the corner of the apron. "Oh, it's the prettiest stuff!"

Katie began to be vexed at herself and at those who fussed over the dress. "You would think you'd never seen pink material," she said, her conscience bothering her more and more about her broken vows and resolutions. She was glad when the boys drove up and the girls piled into the buggies to drive to Gingerich's for the crowd.

Vernie and Clarie arrived with Henry as driver. He was considered old enough to take the girls to the crowds but not old enough to go to the singings, much to his disgust. They came gaily up the walk toward the porch where the girls were still standing.

"Oh, you've got on your pink dress!" Vernie squealed by way of greeting. "You look good enough to eat!" Her eyes traveled all over Katie, taking in the rayon hose and the length of the dress in one quick glance.

Katie suddenly remembered that, because she had resolved not to wear it, it had been the only one to escape lengthening. Now she felt it must be indecently short--even to Vernie. Vernie's eyes rested on that hem--a superior smile playing around her lips. When she raised her gaze and met Katie's eyes, Katie changed the subject, asking quickly how her mother was. Vernie laughed a short, knowing laugh. And Katie felt suddenly sick at heart, wishing she'd never seen a pink dress.

* * *

Tiredly Katie pulled her chair to a better position to catch the light from her dresser lamp. She sank gratefully down, glad to be at the end of another busy Monday. There had been ninety-three diapers; she'd counted them to keep her mind from rehashing yesterday's fiasco.

But while working in the yard tonight, her failure grew in proportion to the number of weeds she pulled. Her life was full of weeds. God could not count on her to be obedient to the church. She had failed. Utterly, miserably failed.

"Was I ever saved if all I can produce is weeds? Yesterday

103

morning I felt sure I was saved; now I feel like a thistle. If only I tried harder. If only I'd said a loud resounding *no* when I first thought of wearing that accursed dress!"

She didn't want to live for the flesh and go to hell when she died! She knew the tares would be burned. How could she escape hell if she didn't produce wheat as the Bible said?

Wearily she picked up her Bible, leafing through the pages in a desultory way. Perhaps there was something in Psalms that would help her. Hardly daring to hope that God would hear her, she let her Bible open near the middle. There at Psalm 103 she began reading the first few verses halfheartedly. They spoke only dimly to her until she came to the ninth one, "He will not always chide: neither will he keep his anger for ever." Slowly tears filled her eyes.

"He hath not dealt with us after our sins; nor rewarded us according to our iniquities."

"Did it mean that God would forgive her? That was too good to be true!"

"For as the heaven is high above the earth, so great is his mercy toward them that fear him," the psalmist assured her. "As far as the east is from the west, so far hath he removed our transgressions from us."

Katie gave a strangled heartbroken sob. "If God is like that, I needn't be afraid of Him! Maybe He isn't big and awful and terrifying after all!"

"Like as a father pitieth his children, so the Lord pitieth them that fear him," the thirteenth verse told her lovingly. Katie didn't doubt it.

"For he knoweth our frame; he remembereth that we are dust."

Katie sobbed and sobbed. "God understands that I want to be saved. The Lord has mercy to forgive me. I can try again." Katie felt forgiven. "O God, help me to be saved!" she prayed. "Help me to do what's right!"

5

Spring flew on to summer in a quick succession of work-laden days.

"Do you have to go on picking berries?" Mahlon demanded one morning after Emma and Katie had worked until midnight canning strawberries.

"Well, you know how you like canned strawberries," Emma reminded him rather shortly. "If they are so plentiful that people come and ask you to pick, I hate to turn them down."

"You've picked our own and on shares for two other people. Has anybody else asked you to pick?" he questioned.

"Aunt Fannie asked me Sunday to pick her patch tomorrow. I said I would, but unless you go, I don't see how we can. Johnnie seems to have a cold and yesterday, when we picked at Ed Miller's, he and baby fussed so much that Katie had to do most of the picking."

"Oh, that was all right," Katie assured her.

"No, it wasn't. That patch seemed a quarter of a mile long, and I thought we'd never get finished--especially when I was running into the house every ten minutes to quiet the children."

"Well, I'm not going to put up hay until tomorrow afternoon," Mahlon volunteered. "I can go with Katie tomorrow and pick your Aunt Fannie's patch, if we can get back before one."

"Oh, would you?" Emma exclaimed gratefully. "Maybe I can get the ironing caught up. We haven't touched it this week, and today we must can peas."

"OK, I'll help tomorrow," Mahlon said cheerfully, pushing away from the table and starting for his hat. "Can we be gone by six in the morning?"

"Six o'clock!" Katie echoed. "That means getting up at four-thirty and hustling through the chores, leaving Emma alone to wash the dishes and the separator."

At six, when they set out with a half-dozen dishpans, Katie's chore apron, and some large bowls, the dew was thick on the grass. "Might just as well be picking berries; we couldn't put up hay," Mahlon observed, the reins held firmly in his hands. Lady felt frisky and Mahlon let her run. After all, even though Lady trotted most of the way, it would take them almost an hour to drive the eight miles.

"There would be a lot quicker way to get around than with a horse and buggy," Mahlon said moodily.

"What do you mean?" Katie asked, instantly panicking. "You're not saying that you're dissatisfied with a horse and buggy?"

"I'm beginning to be," he acknowledged shortly. "If God asked it of us, it would be different, but I'm beginning to think we're doing nothing but following traditions of men."

"Why, Mahlon!" Katie exclaimed, shocked. "How can you say that? You know that God wants us to deny the flesh. How can you think that God doesn't ask us to live as we do?"

"Just what did Christ mean when He said we are to deny the flesh?" Mahlon countered her question with one of his own.

"Why--why--by not following the world in having cars and--and all the modern things of the world," Katie stammered in reply.

"Is that really what He meant?" Mahlon asked. "What does it mean then in Galatians where Paul speaks of the works of the flesh as being adultery, idolatry, variance, murders, drunkenness, envyings, and so on?"

"Oh, sure, yes," Katie said, nervously biting her lips. "We're not supposed to do those things either, of course."

"Of course!" Mahlon exclaimed. "What do you mean--of course? Those are the things God is concerned about. Those are the main issues of the matter."

"You mean that, if we didn't do those things, that would be

all that was needed?" Katie asked heatedly. "Do you really mean that driving a car and having all the modern conveniences isn't displeasing to God at all?"

"Can you read in the Bible that it's wrong to drive a car?" Mahlon asked quietly.

"Well, no, of course not. They didn't have cars then," Katie answered. "But what else does it mean when it says that what is highly esteemed among men is an abomination in the sight of the Lord and what is more highly esteemed in the world than cars?"

"Money and the love of it, for one thing," Mahlon put in. "And we can't point our finger at the world about that, because our people like money just as well as the world does."

Katie was silent. That was true; so what could she say? Many of their own people had the reputation of pinching pennies until "Lincoln hollered," as the saying went.

"Then another thing, if what our people are teaching is so nearly the truth, why is there so much sin and wickedness going on among the young people in some localities? Drinking and carousing around and--Do you think God is going to overlook those things just because we don't have cars and modern conveniences, but dress the way we do?" Mahlon asked.

"Well--" Katie stammered, helpless.

"Well," echoed Mahlon decisively. "That's what I say."

They were both silent, Lady trotting briskly. In the brush along the roads, birds were flitting. Spider webs covered by dew sparkled and glistened. At farmsteads along the way men were busily choring, intent on getting out into the fields. A few enterprising ones were already cultivating the young corn or raking up hay. Mahlon commented from time to time to which Katie replied halfheartedly, her mind painfully trying to digest Mahlon's forceful words.

"Can it be true that we are following the traditions of men instead of the Word of God? It seemed unlikely! We believe what we are taught, don't we?" She was glad when they turned into

107

Aunt Fannie's drive. Aunt Fannie greeted them heartily, her merry laugh supplanting Katie's questioning thoughts.

"My, you must not have gone to bed last night," she teased, helping Katie set the dishpans on the loading block. "Maybe you just stood in the corner to sleep, so you wouldn't have to get up."

"Oh, I was in bed," Mahlon grinned. "Not very long though."

Down the walk came Sam, Aunt Fannie's husband, leisurely chewing a toothpick, followed by Katie's cousins.

"Looks like you're just picking out your teeth from supper," Mahlon grinned.

"Yeah, we ate supper and breakfast all in one." Sam drawled slowly. "Saves trouble that way."

"Now, Sam, you know it wasn't that bad," Aunt Fannie denied, chuckling. "We ate late last night and early this morning, but there were a few minutes between."

"Forty winks," drawled Sam, flicking away the toothpick.

Katie smiled silently. Aunt Fannie was always like this, ready to burst into good-natured ribbing.

The children gathered around Katie, grinning silently.

"Coxey's Army," Mahlon commented humorously. "Bet the work really gets done when these fellows get at it."

"Coxey's Army, when it comes to feeding them!" Aunt Fannie chuckled. "As for getting the work done, if the straw boss keeps after them, they get it done."

"Much obliged, Mom," Sam drawled. "She has to keep after me, too."

"I guess I do!" Aunt Fannie gave back as good as she got. "Are you going to help Mahlon and Katie pick strawberries?"

"That's what you tell me," Sam said.

"Oh, you don't have to help," Mahlon protested. "That's not in the deal. We'll pick them alone."

"I guess you will not!" Aunt Fannie said indignantly. "That would be some way to treat my own niece! I don't get up there to help Emma and this is one way to help her out. With all those little ones she has, she needs help."

"Yeah, I'll help you," Sam said. "That way I can visit with Mahlon. The boys can cultivate without me. Lewis, you can go out and start and, Chrissie, you go hitch up the rake and start raking that hay."

"You got hay down, too?" Mahlon asked. "I have to get back in time to put up hay this afternoon."

"Oh, but you'll stay for dinner, won't you?" Aunt Fannie paused, halfway up the walk to the house.

"I don't think so," Mahlon said. "If we would, you'd go to a lot of extra bother for us."

"Now, Mahlon, just for that I'll not make a thing extra, not even strawberry shortcake. You can eat sausage and potatoes like we do," Aunt Fannie cried, with another ripple of chuckles.

"Well, if it's not too late when we finish, we might stay, but sausage and potatoes are good enough for me," Mahlon picked up a nest of dishpans and stood waiting to go to work. "Where is your patch? We'd better get to work."

"Sam will go with you," Aunt Fannie said. "I'll be out to help just as soon as I get the girls to washing dishes. Come on, girls, don't just stand around."

Katie followed the men around the corner of the house and through the early garden into the well-strawed paths of the strawberry patch. The rows stretched out, going to an end at the far side of the garden. The dew would be gone long before all the berries!

Katie put down her dishpans. Picking up her chore apron, she tied it absently in place. Mahlon had already started picking. He and Sam began at once to talk of crops, weather, and farm work-- their tongues as busy as their hands. Mahlon said nothing about leaving the church.

Katie was setting aside a full pan of strawberries, brilliant red against the white enamel, when Aunt Fannie came out and began picking.

"You've already got a panful!" Aunt Fannie exclaimed. "I was afraid you wouldn't find many today. They're beginning to slow down from what they were."

"They're real nice though," Katie observed.

"They're not bad, but you should have seen them at first. They were monstrous big. But they aren't bad, even now. Does Emma have a lot of them canned yet?"

Katie gave the sum, and Aunt Fannie told how many she had canned and how many jars of preserves she had made and still wanted to make. "For church, when we have it," she explained. Aunt Fannie chatted on about already canning thirty quarts of peas with more coming tomorrow and her early beans were going to be ready to eat by the end of the week. The garden needed hoeing again.

Katie glanced around her at the clean, well-kept garden rows and smiled to herself. How like Mom Aunt Fannie was! Never satisfied unless she had a half-dozen jobs needing attention at once.

"Your garden looks fine to me," she told Aunt Fannie with a smile. "I can't even see a weed."

"You don't look right," Aunt Fannie chuckled. "If you took the hoe out there, you'd find plenty of weeds."

"Hey, you," Aunt Fannie called to the men now halfway down the length of the patch. "How does it happen that you're so far?"

"Oh, we pick fast," Mahlon called back.

"Ha, ha, you don't get them all," Aunt Fannie chuckled, leaning over and inspecting their row. A quick twist of her hand revealed a large ripe berry and she pounced on it at once.

"Just look here, Mahlon Gingerich!" she cried, holding it aloft by the stem. "How many others like that did you leave in the patch? You're as bad as the children." She went off into a perfect spasm of chuckles at his abashed look.

"That was the only one," he called back. "Anyway, I think that was in Sam's half."

"Now, Mahlon, own it up," she cried, still chuckling. "I've

got Sam trained better than that."

Katie laughed. If anyone could make you laugh, even when you didn't feel like it, it was Aunt Fannie. The look on Mahlon's face was amusing. He didn't like being called a careless picker. After that the men slowed down.

Aunt Fannie picked for half an hour, then, loaded with two huge dishpans, she went back into the house. There were still two rows to be picked. Katie stood up for a moment and rubbed her tired back. Without Aunt Fannie's cheerful talk, Katie thought the rows seemed twice as long. The sun began to be hot. Katie took off her bonnet and brushed back her hair to catch a cooling breeze that came over the garden.

When Aunt Fannie's two little girls came out with a cold drink, Katie was more than glad for the interruption. They wanted more strawberries.

"Mom's stemming them for you," they told Katie importantly.

"Oh, now, she shouldn't," Katie prostested quickly. "She's got enough work of her own to do."

"Oh, we're helping her," Lydie, the oldest, said.

"That's nice of you," Katie said, her nose crinkling in amusement. "With big girls like you to help, she probably gets lots of work done."

For a moment Lydie regarded her questioningly, not sure whether Katie was poking fun or giving an honest compliment. She decided on the latter when Katie added, "I always felt I did lots of work when I was your age."

"Oh, we don't work all the time though," Mary, the youngest, cut in before Lydie could answer. "Mom lets us play sometimes."

Soon after eleven, when they were at last within ten feet of the end of the last row, Aunt Fannie sent the girls out again to say that dinner was ready.

"Mom said to tell you it's nothing but sausage and potatoes but you can stay anyway," Lydie said.

"You tell your mother that nothing would taste as good as that," Mahlon replied. "It's been a long time since breakfast."

111

Big platters of canned sausage and great dishes of creamy mashed potatoes, with garden lettuce, new peas and dumplings, and strawberries, were welcome fare. Katie, taking a second thick piece of homemade bread, didn't care that there was no shortcake. With bread like this, spread with fresh butter, who wanted shortcake?

After the meal Aunt Fannie insisted that they ignore dishes and start for home. She had stemmed two big dishpans of strawberries for them and apologized for not doing more. She sent along a loaf of homemade bread and some cookies.

"Thanks for everything," Mahlon said loading the buggy. "You shouldn't have given us so much."

"I'd like to know why not," Aunt Fannie gave a parting chuckle. "I guess I can give away anything I want to."

"I thought you acted like that," Sam said wryly. "You'd better not try to give me or the children away."

"You know that I didn't mean it that way," Aunt Fannie protested. "Anyway, good-bye and come again," she called to Mahlon and Katie, who had already started away from the loading block.

They were both too drowsy to talk. Mahlon kept a tight hand on the reins, though, with Lady doing a slow trot. Katie leaned back against the side of the buggy in dreamy abstraction.

By one o'clock they were home. Emma came out to the gate to help carry in the strawberries. "My, you got a lot of them! I thought Aunt Fannie said there wouldn't be many."

"I think she gave us more than our share," Mahlon told her.

"Yes, she did," Katie added. "I wanted her to keep more, but she said she had more than she wanted already."

"Well, we'll be busy the rest of the day. Did you eat yet?"

"She made us stay for dinner," Katie explained.

"I thought she probably would; so the children and I ate a long time ago."

"What time is it?" Mahlon asked.

"Fifteen after one."

"Anybody come yet to put up hay?" Mahlon inquired.

"Not yet," Emma replied. "Say, are we going to have to feed them supper?"

"I expect you will," he called above the crack of the screen door's slamming.

"And all these strawberries to can!"

"Give them bread and milk and strawberries," Katie suggested absently, taking off her bonnet and adjusting her covering.

"I've got a lot of jars ready; so we have that much less to do. Who stemmed these berries?" she asked in surprise, her eyes falling on the strawberries Mahlon had brought in.

"Aunt Fannie and her girls."

"Oh, she shouldn't have," Emma protested. "She gave us more than our share and then stemmed a lot! Isn't that just like her!"

"I know. I told her not to, but she said she didn't get a chance to help you very often," Katie explained. "Shall I pour these berries onto the table to stem?"

"Yes. I wonder if I have any more empty dishpans around here. Wait, I'll pull out the wing, then we'll have more room." Emma reached down and pulled out the other wing of the table.

They stemmed in silence. The chidren were taking their naps, and except for the sound of hens cackling out in the hen house, the place was quiet. The neighbors were already out in the field helping Mahlon load up hay.

Katie wanted to talk to Emma. "Does Emma realize what heretical thoughts Mahlon is harboring?" she wondered. "If she does, she never lets on."

Finally she blurted out, "Is Mahlon thinking of leaving the church?"

Emma looked up, startled and wary. "Did he say something about it?" she asked quietly.

"He didn't come right out and say that he was thinking of leaving, but the way he talked sounded as though he wanted to."

"I know," Emma said. "He gets more dissatisfied every week."

"What's wrong with him? Can't he see that if he left the church he would be gratifying the flesh?" Katie cried.

"Do you really think he would be?" Emma asked.

"Doesn't the Bible say we aren't to be conformed to the world? And wouldn't he be conforming to the world if he got a car?"

"I'm beginning to wonder whether that Scripture really means what we were always taught," Emma said guardedly.

Katie was appalled. Was Emma getting heretical ideas, too? "How can you say so?" she cried. "What else would it mean?"

"Does it stop with 'be not conformed to this world'? Doesn't it go on and say how we're not to be conformed?"

"Well--" Katie faltered. Emma had her there. She really didn't know what the rest of the verse said. Or where it was found, for that matter.

"No, I really think it means more than we were taught. It says we are not to be conformed to the world, but to be transformed by the renewing of the mind. That sounds as though more were involved than just not having cars and such things."

"Yes, but doesn't the world have its mind full of cars and such stuff?"

"I don't think the world has its mind as full of cars as we think," Emma replied gravely. "After all, most people have had them so long they take them for granted. Don't you suppose there are other things that take up their thoughts?"

"I don't know--" Katie found herself faltering again.

"What about pleasure? Or money? Or indifference to God? I think those are some of the things meant by the Scripture."

For a moment Katie was silent. If what Emma was saying were true, all her standards were in danger of crumbling. With a desperate attempt to find some foundation to stand on, she tried again. "If what you are saying is true, were all our forefathers deceived? Didn't they have the truth at all?"

"Oh, Katie, I don't know. I can't judge what they did. I only know what's happening to me--to us. God has taken care of our forefathers, whether for good or bad. I don't believe that He took

114

them all to heaven because they were Amish, though!"

"Well, no, of course not," Katie faltered again. "But if they tried to please Him by keeping the traditions of the church, He surely did."

"Katie, are we saved by what we do? Aren't we saved by our faith in what Christ has done for us on the cross? Doesn't the Bible say: 'By grace are ye saved through faith . . . not of works, lest any man should boast'?" Emma asked searchingly.

Katie paused, motionless, her stained hands poised above the heap of berries on the table.

"I guess you're right, Emma," she said huskily, and felt at once as though she had caught a glimpse of a great door opening.

By three o'clock the sweetish odor of cooking berries was lying like a fog around the house, but Katie was too busy trying to absorb this strange idea of being right with God by faith in Christ's work on the cross to give it a thought. But for years afterward, whenever she smelled strawberries cooking, the scene in the kitchen that afternoon flashed to her mind: Emma dipping strawberries from kettle to the jars with quick deft movements and her own inner confusion as she stemmed berries.

"What on earth will we have for those men for supper, besides strawberries and bread and milk?" Emma asked.

"Oh, I don't know," Katie answered. "Lettuce sandwiches and radishes. Same thing we always have."

"I expect that's what they'd have at home," Emma assented. "But I hate to give only that when they're haying. I expect you and I will have to do the chores alone, too."

"It will take us more than an hour to finish here," Katie sighed.

Emma went to the table for clean jars and glanced automatically out of the window. "Oh, here comes a buggy!" she exclaimed. "And a woman is driving! Who in the world is coming in here to catch us in our mess?"

Katie half rose from her seat and looked intently out the

window. "It's Bishop Eli Mattie, I think. I wonder what she wants."

"I'm sure I don't know," Emma said. "I won't be ashamed of our mess. With the family she's got, she knows what it's like."

"I'd think so," Katie agreed.

The buggy was in front of the gate by now, and they saw Bishop Eli's wife climb out and tie up the horse at the hitching rack. Then she made her way up the walk to the house, glancing here and there across the yard as she did so.

"Come right in," Emma called as Bishop Eli's wife knocked. "If you can get in through our mess." A pleasant-faced woman with a sweet, low laugh opened the screen door.

"My, it looks like somebody's got strawberries," she said.

"Doesn't it though? But not of our own," Emma replied, reaching for a chair. "Here, sit down."

"Just go on with your work," Eli Mattie told her. "Did you pick somebody's patch on shares?"

"Aunt Fannie's," Emma answered.

"Oh, Sam Fannie's! Yes, I guess she has a big patch. Has she been getting a lot?"

"More than she wants," Emma told her, busy once again ladling berries into jars. "She didn't seem to want very many of those she picked today; she sent most of them home to us."

Eli Mattie turned to Katie hesitantly. "You're busy and I don't want to keep you up; so I'll tell what I came for, then go," she began. "Are you hired out all fall, Katie?"

Katie looked at her quickly. "Just until the first of November."

"November," Eli Mattie echoed. "Are you working here? With Emma?"

"No, I'm only staying here until the first of August, then I'll begin at Dave Junior's."

"Oh, I see. Are they going away or something, or how does it happen they need a girl?" Eli Mattie asked.

"They plan to remodel their house this fall," Katie explained.

116

"Oh, yes," Mattie nodded. She was silent for a moment, then began hesitantly. "You could take other work, then, after the first of November?"

"As far as I know, yes," Katie said, reaching for another strawberry. The last dishpanful had been poured onto the table.

"Could you work for us?" Mattie asked. "I was hoping I could get you by the first of October, but November will be better than nothing."

"I can so far as I know. But I'm not of age yet, you know. You'd have to ask Mom, too," Katie said.

"Oh, yes, of course. I just wanted to know if there would be a chance before I asked her," Mattie hastened to explain. "I wonder, could you help me next summer, too?"

"I don't know of anyone else who wants me. I don't know whether anyone has asked Mom, either. You'd have to ask Mom about that, too."

"Then I'll do that." Mattie rose from her chair. "I'll either write or go down and see her."

"Well, it looks as if you've got yourself some more work," Emma remarked after Mattie had taken her leave. "You'll have your hands full at that place. Ten boys to take care of!"

" 'IF ye then be risen with Christ, seek those things which are above,' " Katie thought, reaching back into Dave Junior Mary's cupboard for another box of spices. " 'If ye then be risen with Christ. If ye then be risen with Christ, seek those things which are above.' " Last night she had been reading Colossians 3; today the first verse repeated itself over and over in her mind. " 'If ye then be risen with Christ; if ye then be risen with Christ.' "

Suddenly there was a cheery whistle outside the door. "Open up," someone shouted.

Katie scrambled down the step stool and hurried to open the door, catching a glimpse of Mose Yoder, Dave's brother, through the window.

"Hi," he grinned, his arms full of lumber.

Katie pushed open the screen door and stepped well back out of the way. "That's quite a load!" she commented.

"Got that cupboard cleaned out yet?" he asked, raising laughing eyes after he had dumped the lumber with a bang.

"Mose, watch out for that lumber," Dave Junior Mary called to her brother-in-law. "Don't break it all up to splinters before you start."

"Don't worry, Mary. This is just frame lumber. When I bring in your birch, I'll carry it with gloves."

He exchanged an amused glance with Katie as she closed the screen door and came back inside. He stood with feet wide apart, head slightly thrown back, hands on hips. The merry look in his brown eyes made little crinkles at the corners, and one eyebrow was slightly higher than the other. No doubt about it, Mose Yoder was a good-looking boy.

Katie stepped lightly across the kitchen and climbed the step stool, acutely aware of Mose's laughing eyes on her. Katie thought, "Of all the boys among the young people, he has never asked me for a date."

He watched her for a moment. Her quick fingers flew in and out of the cupboard, getting out spices and putting them in the box on the counter. "I don't suppose you could use any help," he drawled.

She met his laughing eyes. "Not just anyone could do this right," she answered solemnly.

"Tom Sawyer!" he challenged chuckling. "I don't have any rabbit's foot or broken marble to swap you for the chance to help; so I guess I'll just have to watch until you're finished."

"Have you brought in your tools to take out the old cupboards?" Mary's voice came again through the dining room door.

"They're outside the door," he assured her. "Just as soon as your hired girl has everything out of the cupboard and gets down from the step stool, I'll bring them in."

"There you are," Katie told him. "Now get the crowbar and make pieces."

"Just watch me," he chuckled in return and made for the door to get his tools.

Katie picked up the box of spices and carried it into the dining room. Mary looked up from the sewing machine where she was making a school dress for Ruby.

"Here's the last of the stuff," Katie told her, placing it in the corner on top of a box of little-used dishes.

"That Mose," Mary said in amused exasperation. "He always has an answer for you."

"He kept one jump ahead of you, didn't he?" Katie replied, smiling at the recollection.

"Yes, but she keeps me jumping fast," Mose called from the kitchen. "I've had to learn how all these years since Mary's been in the family."

"Mose! You weren't supposed to hear that," Mary sputtered. "You go on with your work. Where's Dave?"

"He went over to the neighbor's to phone the hog market. Think of all the hogs that'll have to be sold to pay for this remodeling. Could have bought a new tractor for the same money!"

"Now, just wait a minute," Mary said indignantly. "Who needs a new tractor? This house needs working on worse than anybody around here needs a new tractor."

He came to the door and leaned against the doorjamb. "I'm sorry I made you mad," he apologized, laughing humor in his eyes. "It wouldn't do to make the women mad."

"Oh, go on with you!" Mary sputtered again. "The trouble with you is you're always teasing. Sometime you will get me mad."

He broke into a grin at that, and held Katie's eyes with a laughing, flashing look that seemed to include her in the joke. As he turned to go back to the kitchen, Katie caught her breath.

*　　*　　*

" 'If ye then be risen with Christ; if ye then be risen--' " Katie picked up her Bible from the dresser and, seating herself on the edge of the bed, opened to Colossians. "That bit of Scripture again! It keeps ringing through my mind. Maybe if I read it again I can get a little meaning out of it.

"Here it was. 'If ye then be risen with Christ, seek those things which are above, where Christ sitteth on the right hand of God.' " She read it twice, still not able to comprehend it. "Maybe if I reread the chapter before, I can grasp what it is talking about."

She turned back and began reading the second chapter, quick eyes taking in the words. As she came to the eighteenth verse, her mind lightly tossed it aside as not for her: " 'Worshipping of angels'--I don't worship angels." She raced on to the next verse--and the next.

"Wherefore if ye be dead with Christ from the rudiments of the world, why, as though living in the world, are ye subject to ordinances, (touch not; taste not; handle not; which all are to perish with the using;) after the commandments and doctrines of men?" The words leaped out and she felt dazed.

"Why, that is talking to me, to my people, to the Amish church. No, no, it might be all right to say that one was saved by faith in what Christ had done for you on the cross, but to come out and believe that no traditions, no standards of church rule were necessary--why, that was going too far! You had to have traditions and ordinances or you couldn't have a church!

"Maybe I've gotten the wrong thought out of it." Hastily, she ran down the page again, trying to make herself believe that it meant something--someone else.

It leaped out again; it caught her eyes; it would not be denied.

"Why, as though living in the world, are ye subject to ordinances, (touch not; taste not; handle not; which all are to perish with the using;) after the commandments and doctrines of men?" The question mark at the end of the twenty-second verse looked as big as a pencil. "Why? Oh, yes, but--why, you had to have rules and regulations; you wouldn't have church order if you didn't."

She closed the Book with a loud slapping noise and put it back on the dresser, turmoil raging in her heart. "If this were true, why hadn't someone seen it long ago? Why didn't the preachers and bishops quit teaching the ordinances and traditions? Furthermore, if you didn't need traditions, rules and ordinances to keep you from being worldly, what would you need?

" 'If ye then be risen with Christ, seek those things which are above.' That verse again! What did that have to do with it?" She rubbed her chin. "This is something too serious to think out alone; I need a preacher to help me. But of course! In a few weeks I'll be working for Bishop Eli. What better help could I get!"

*   *   *

The last hymn was finished. Over on the men's side of the Sunday-school house, boys reached under benches for hats, scuffed big feet, jammed elbows into each other, and dived or filed out into the late afternoon sunshine. Because of fall communion next Sunday and fasting day that morning, Sunday school had been in the afternoon.

Over on the girls' side, Susan Gingerich looked at Katie for a moment, gave a short nod when the last boy had disappeared through the door, then rose to file out through the women's door.

"Nice day," Susan remarked absently, when they were standing outside in the late September sunshine.

"Um-hum." Katie assented, stretching herself.

"Where's Edna?" she asked after a moment.

"She's working down at Emery Gingerich's while they're in Colorado. Didn't you know?"

"Oh, yes, I forgot." Katie nodded. "Won't this be your last fall at home?"

"Yes, I'll be of age in January, you know."

"What's Dan B's Mary doing over here? Is she working in this district?" Katie asked, catching sight of her.

"Somebody said she's working at Bishop Eli's," Susan said. "I didn't know it either until today. When will you be going there?"

"First of November."

"She's probably there until you start," Susan surmised. "I bet she hightails it around there with all those boys looking on."

"Don't be so catty," Katie chuckled. They grinned at each other and subsided into silence again.

"Where are you going for supper?" Susan asked as she and Katie watched the men drive up to the loading platform for their womenfolk, in a hurry to go home and chore before night came on.

"I don't know. Mary said I didn't have to come home to chore. Where is the singing, anyway?"

122

"Down at **Ira Hochstettler's** in the southeast district. Are you going?"

"I expect," Katie said indifferently. "I don't know how I'll get home, though. Are you going?"

"I guess so. Edna wrote me a postcard and said she told Lewis to bring me along when he picks her up. That gets me there, but I don't know how I'm coming home either."

"Too bad you don't do what Vernie says you should."

"What was that?"

"Get yourself a boy friend."

"Hum," Susan said wryly. "Why don't you? Anyway, can't you get Mose to take you home?"

"I hate to ask him. I don't know what he's planned."

Buggies were waiting in line three deep in front of them. Women came out of the Sunday-school house, clutching babies and diaper bags and, sometimes, chubby hands of reluctant children.

"What's Clarie and Vernie doing tonight?" Susan asked.

"I don't know. I haven't been home for a month, and last Sunday night I didn't go to the singing; so I don't know what they're doing."

"Is Vernie going to work in town all winter?"

"She says so. She likes it, I guess. The people pay pretty well, too."

By now only a few buggies were left and those belonged to the young unmarried men, who, like Susan and Katie, had made no definite plans for the evening. Katie could see them standing around the horse barn, talking. She saw that Mose was still there. Evidently he, too, had made no plans for the evening.

Of the other girls, only Dan B's Mary and Fannie Yoder were left. They crossed over now to Susan and Katie.

"Are you going to the singing?" Dan B's Mary asked.

"We were thinking of it," Susan admitted guardedly.

"Edward said I could go with him," Mary said importantly. "I see he's still out there with the rest of the boys."

123

"They're coming up here," Katie observed, catching sight of the boys moving toward the Sunday-school house. The girls drifted over to the loading platform and seated themselves to await the boys.

"Nobody seems in a hurry to leave," Mose grinned by way of greeting.

"I should have gone home with Dave and Mary," Katie yawned. "I'm sleepy."

"Where's the singing?" Lewis asked, dropping down on the platform.

"At Ira Hochstettler's. Anybody invited down that way for supper?" Edward asked, trying to avoid looking at Katie. Ever since that memorable night, they spoke as little to each other as possible.

"I'm thinking of going down there for supper," Fannie's brother, Sammy, said.

"Why don't you all go home with me for supper?" Susan asked suddenly. "We didn't especially plan to have company, but we'll get you something to eat."

"I might do that," Mose said. He picked a blade of grass from the sod at his feet and began to fit it between the palms of his hands, thumbs touching. "Are you going, Katie?"

"I could, I guess. I don't have anything else in mind. Can I drive along with you to the singing?"

"Oh, sure. You can go home with me afterward, too," he answered. He bent his head to blow on the grass between his thumbs. There was a piercing shriek.

"Mose Yoder! Quit that!" Dan B's Mary exclaimed. "That makes the shivers go up my back."

The boys grinned; Susan and Katie exchanged amused glances. Mose laughingly threw the offending blade of grass to his feet.

"I think I'll go down to Ira Hochstettler's for supper," Edward ventured. "They probably expect some to come anyway."

The sound of a buggy coming around the building surprised

124

them. "Any of you girls got any bonnets in the building yet?" asked Henry Beachy, an older man who did the janitor work.

"Where'd you come from?" Mose asked as the girls scrambled up to get their bonnets, light shawls, and Testaments.

"Oh, I went up the road to visit Ben Miller a while. I figured I could come back and lock up after everyone was gone." He climbed out of the buggy, leaving his wife to hold the reins, and shuffled toward the men's side to lock the door. As if his appearance had been a signal they were all waiting for, the boys left to untie their rigs.

Edward drew up first, followed by Samuel. Dan B's Mary stepped primly off the platform into the buggy and settled the duster around her. Fannie Yoder settled herself beside her brother and turned to flip a hand in good-bye to Susan and Katie. After they were out on the road, Lewis and Mose drove up.

"You're coming home with me for supper then, aren't you?" Susan asked Mose as she stepped into Lewis's buggy.

"Yes, go home and get the fatted calf ready," Mose told her, his laughing eyes seeking Katie's.

"Fatted chicken, more likely," Katie said lightly, settling down beside Mose and taking her end of his proffered duster.

"Whatever you have," Mose called to Susan. "Nice day," he commented conversationally to Katie as they started up the road.

"Um-hum," Katie murmured, wondering why she was so acutely aware of this slender, wiry, good-looking boy at her side.

"The sky is the same color as your eyes," Mose said suddenly.

She lifted startled eyes and found his own merry, brown ones regarding her intently. "I didn't suppose you had ever noticed," Katie bantered with a smile.

"You gave me a good chance to see right now," he chuckled. "I've had lots of chances to see them the last few weeks."

"Quit looking at me, then."

"I like blue eyes," he said. "But I've been wondering what's behind those eyes. I think there's more there than I gave you credit for."

"Mose!" she protested indignantly. "You talk as though you thought I were a nitwit."

"You aren't though. I think that daydreamy look you have makes people think you're only half aware of what's going on."

"Daydreamy look! I'm sure I'm just as much aware of what's going on as most people. Maybe more so, if I do say so myself."

"I know you are. At least, you're the first girl I ever talked with who knew what was in the newspapers except who had a baby or who married or who died."

"Thank you," she said with a twinkling smile.

"Now listen, I'm not making fun of you," he hastened to assure her. "I'm glad to find someone who reads a little more than the *Budget* and the Bible."

"I read the Bible and the *Budget*, too!"

"Oh, I know. You know what I mean," he protested.

Katie broke into a rippling chuckle, almost like Aunt Fannie's.

"Well, anyway, you're smart," he broke into her chuckle.

"My, my!" Katie chuckled again.

They were silent after that. The horse trotted smoothly along without any promptings, the buggy wheels rumbling quietly over the dirt road. Crickets chirped loudly, a continuous sound, which was as much a part of fall as picking corn or cleaning off the garden. The ditches were overgrown with long grasses accented here and there by a clump of brilliant red sumac. A trailing bittersweet vine filled up one fence corner, its orange berries waiting for a nip of frost to break them open to the darker orange inside.

"We'll get frost one of these nights," Katie thought, pulling her light shawl over her hands. "I wonder whether my light shawl will keep me warm tonight if I go home with Mose in his open buggy."

Ahead of them the Gingerich homestead gleamed white in

126

the late afternoon sun, the red barn a bright accent in the shade of huge maple trees that were dropping golden yellow leaves on its roof. The garden was a patchwork of color: green feathery carrots, grayish black of ground already raked, a crimson velvet band of coxcomb around two sides, bold-colored dahlias along the road, and a blazing trail of marigolds.

As they followed Lewis and Susan into the lane, they caught sight of John Gingerich already in his chore clothes at the gate, milk buckets strung over his arms. As the two rigs stopped and the girls alighted, he paused to greet them. "Oh, so we're having company," he smiled at them. "Susan didn't say anything about it."

"I didn't know about it myself, but I knew you wouldn't care; so I invited them," Susan said.

"That's right," he said. "Just drive over there and unhitch, boys. Andy's out there somewhere. He'll show you where to tie your horses and where to get oats to feed them." He turned to the girls. "I don't think I can shake hands with you, Katie. My hands seem to be full."

"That's all right," Katie smiled bashfully.

His blue eyes twinkled pleasantly above his straggly gray beard. His strong nose and jagged-toothed smile made him one of the homeliest men Katie knew, but his gentle spirit and quiet goodwill made her forget he was homely.

"Mom will take care of you," he assured them. "Just go on in and make yourself at home."

Susan was already going toward the house. Katie slowly closed the gate, the latch clicking loudly, and followed her. With a rattle of milk pails that grew softer and softer, John proceeded toward the barn.

John Sarah met them at the door. "Hello," she greeted them with a genial smile. "So we're having company for supper?"

"Oh, not really company," Katie protested.

"She didn't have anything else planned; so I told her to come home with me," Susan said, unpinning her shawl and taking it off with a flip of her shoulders. "Here, let me take yours," she said to Katie.

"Why, that was just fine," Sarah assured them. "You are welcome to come here anytime you wish. You might not get much for supper, but you'll get something."

"Don't go to any bother for us. Popcorn and sandwiches would be fine," Katie said.

"That might be all you'll get, too," Susan warned her. "I'm going up to change my dress, Mom; then I'll be right down to help you."

Katie followed her up the carpeted stairs, down a narrow hall, and into the large, airy girls' room.

"Did you get anything new since I was here last?" Katie asked.

"Oh, you Lydie Dan girls! That's the first thing you always ask. Every one of you. The only new thing we got was material to make some new, navy blue dresses."

"You did!" Katie exclaimed delightedly. "What kind of material? Where did you get it?"

Susan was taking out the pins from her shoulder cape and apron quickly, folding the cape, and putting it into a drawer.

"It's downstairs in the cupboard. I'll show it to you when we go down. It's crepe, and we got it in the city."

Katie settled down on the edge of the bed to wait for Susan. Her eyes rested contentedly on the room: the white half-curtains at the windows, the polished oak floor with its handmade rag rugs, and the pink bedspread. How she had grown to love it! She liked coming to the Gingerich's. You were always sure of a welcome.

Susan had dived into the closet to take off her dress. "That's all we got new that I can think of," her voice was muffled. "Oh, I forgot, we did get something else," Susan was out of the closet again, reaching for pins to fasten her dress.

"What?"

"Pop sent for some little booklets. Maybe you'd like to have one. He said we could pass them out."

She was reaching into the drawer again, feeling around among her capes. She handed Katie a small pamphlet.

"What's it about?" Katie asked.

"Courtship," Susan said wryly. "Pop thinks we young folks need higher standards than we've got."

"He's right, I think," Katie said slowly. She turned the booklet around and began to leaf through its pages. "Where did he get it?"

"From some man he knows in the East. He sent for about a dozen." Susan had her dress fastened, a clean apron pinned around her waist, and was reaching for her everyday covering. "I'm ready to go downstairs. Do you want to go down with me or would you rather stay here?"

"I'd rather go down with you," Katie answered, rising. She kept the little booklet in her hand, though, and followed Susan.

While Susan and her mother planned the evening meal, Katie wandered into the living room and began to read. Only vaguely aware of the sounds from the kitchen, she completed the booklet before laying it down. "It certainly does come out in plain words," she thought. "Though our community looks upon bundling as a sin worthy of public confession just as the booklet does, we need the last part about not necking. I can agree with letting a lamp burn. That seems like common sense although I've never done that except for that time when I ran away from Edward Hershberger. But wearing the covering is something I'd never heard of before. In fact," she mused, "on a date our people seem to consider it a disgrace to wear the covering--or even the apron for all I know," she thought with a flash of humor.

"This is definitely a new idea: to wear the covering on a date. But why not? If it isn't considered proper to go without a covering in public in the daytime, why lay it aside at night when one is keeping company with a boy? It seems to me," she mused, "that if ever it was needed, it was then!"

"Would Christ be honored if I wore it?" she questioned. "If only there were more definite statements in the Bible! How could you know which way to take if you were young and inexperienced and had so many crosscurrents running in your heart?

"Like this question in Colossians. How could you know which was the Holy Spirit talking to you and which was your own desire? If only I could go to someone older, more experienced, and get an explanation. A preacher maybe." Once again she thought of Bishop Eli and when she'd work there. "He knows so much Scripture by heart and is such an eloquent speaker, surely he will be able to give me answers to these issues--

"But as for wearing my covering on a date, I have a notion to try it," she decided. "If I ever have a date again," she thought wryly, thinking suddenly of Mose Yoder's slender wiry figure. With a soft sigh she arose and went to the kitchen.

*   *   *

Katie was standing between Vernie and Clarie ready to leave the singing. Clarie had told her all about things at home and Vernie had finished telling her that she liked working in town and boarding at home. Susan had already left with someone who was going past her place. One by one the girls in the kitchen had been leaving, the steady couples first, with each boy coming in and escorting his girl out to his buggy. Even Lewis and Edna, who had been going steady for only two months, had made their way past the unattached boys with their whistling and catcalls. Katie wondered if Mose was ready to go. All at once the door opened and his merry eyes searched the girls grouped around the kitchen.

"Bus leaving for up Dave Junior way. Have I got a passenger?" he sang out.

"One," Katie couldn't help laughing at his jesting as she stepped out of the waiting group of girls. "Did you have anybody else you wanted to take along?"

"Not that I know. Anybody else want to go along?"

"Somebody else might want to if you were going some other way," Vernie called.

"Not tonight," he waved that off. "Well, Katie, I guess if no one else wants to go along, we'll just go alone."

They made their way through the jam of boys on the porch. "Oh, Mose!" someone gave a shout that trailed melodiously at the end. "This could get serious!"

"Think so?" Mose answered jauntily. "I'll have to see what she says about it." They were at the gate and he snapped on his flashlight. "Over here, Katie," he directed, waving his flashlight so that its beam shot up into the air and ahead of them as she followed him. He lighted the buggy step while she climbed in, then, snapping out the light, he went up to the horse's head to untie. In a moment he was back and leaping lightly into the buggy. "All set?" he asked, unwinding the reins from around the whip socket.

"Um-hum."

He backed away from the fence where the horse had been tied and turned toward the road. Katie drew her shawl more tightly about her and settled back against the buggy seat.

"Are you warm enough?" he leaned forward and looked at her. "It's going to be pretty cold riding in this open buggy. I'll have to get the top put on before bad weather comes."

"I'm all right," she said. "I like an open buggy sometimes."

"They're fine if it's not too hot or too cold or rainy."

"I know. On a day like today, they're nice," Katie said.

"Pop gave it to me the other week, and I just haven't gotten around to taking it to have the top put on."

"Even though it is getting cooler, the night is lovely," Katie said. A small sickle moon was setting in the west, its silvery ends turned down.

"Moon's turned down; means it's going to rain," Mose observed.

"I thought that meant it had emptied itself out and we'd

have nice weather," Katie laughed mischievously.

"Hum. Now you might have something there," he said.

The horse was trotting steadily through the clear autumn night. Here and there clumps of trees marked silent homesteads wrapped in sleep. Everyone was in bed except the young folks. The stars winked at the thin moon.

"It seems a shame to think that all of this loveliness will disappear when the end of the world comes," Katie thought. "Even if I know I am ready to meet God when it happens, the end of the world will end all that is known and familiar." She pushed away the thought as they turned the corner to the road that would take them to Dave Junior's farm. Only a half mile further lived Mose's folks, Dave Seniors. Mose slowed the horse to a walk.

"You know, what that fellow said back at the singing wouldn't be such a bad idea," he said suddenly, turning toward Katie.

"What did he say? Which one? So many of them were shouting," Katie said.

"The one that said this might get serious," he replied.

Katie held her breath. So--Mose was beginning to be as aware of her as she was of him. "Oh," she said, a small rising inflection at the end.

"How about it? Would you care to have me come in tonight?"

She was silent a moment. "It would be embarrassing tomorrow."

"I can take it if you can," he assured her. "But nobody need know about it."

"Could you wait until I finish working at Dave's?"

"When will that be?"

"The last of October. That's only a few weeks from now," she said quietly..

"I'll wait if you want it that way," he said. "But as far as working together at Dave's, I won't be over there all the time from now on. Pop needs me at home. So that wouldn't be too bad."

"Oh, I know but--" she broke off lamely.

"But what?"

"People would **talk**. It **wouldn't** look nice," she finished.

He laughed, an amused, indulgent chuckle. "You're funny, Katie. But I like it. If I wait until you finish working at Dave's, **will** you go steady with me then?"

"We'll see."

DAVID Junior took Katie to her home the Saturday night before she was to begin working at Bishop Eli's the last day of October.

She and Vernie and Clarie sat on their beds wrapped in robes and quilts, talking far into the night.

"Did you know Mahlons became members at Poplar Hill last Sunday?" Vernie asked.

"*Really?*" Katie exclaimed quickly, regret flashing through her. "Who told you?"

"I met one of the Poplar Hill girls in town this week. She **said** they admitted three families last Sunday."

"Mom thinks it's terrible," Clarie put in. "She's always thought that to leave the church was the unpardonable sin. I guess she never realized any of her own family would go."

"Now she's afraid we're all thinking of leaving," Vernie added dryly. "She thinks my working in town is a sign of it."

Katie smiled sadly. "I wish Mahlons hadn't gone."

"He was bound to go. He's good to Emma, but after he had made up his mind, I don't suppose anything she said could have kept him back."

"I don't think she said much against it," Katie said slowly.

133

"You mean she wanted to go?" Clarie asked in a shocked voice.

Katie nodded.

"What does Pop say about it?" Katie asked after a moment.

"He doesn't say anything," Vernie shrugged under her cocoon of quilts. "It's hard to find out how he feels about anything. I don't know if even Mom knows how he feels. But then, she says enough for two."

They heard someone moving around downstairs, then the stair door was opened. "Girls, go to bed," Mom's voice came up. "Don't you know that it's almost eleven-thirty? Tomorrow you won't be able to get up." With guilty giggles, the three burst out of their separate quilts.

"Are you going to sleep with me?" Clarie asked Katie, as they flung their quilts across the bed again.

"I suppose so," Katie answered. "Don't you and Vernie sleep together when you're alone?"

"She kicks," Vernie said disgustedly. "I like to sleep alone."

When she was almost asleep, Katie roused up to ask, "Where's the singing tomorrow night?"

"Same place as our church is--Chris Yoder's," Clarie mumbled.

Katie settled down under the covers. Was Mose going to take her home tomorrow?

* * *

The three Miller girls, with Susan and Edna, had gone laughing and chattering outside to get a breath of air after the singing. Katie tried to act as unconcerned as possible, but she wondered. "Had Mose meant what he had said?" She had purposely stayed away from the singings since that night, fearing she would have no way to Dave's except with Mose.

But she was finished working at Dave's now. "Will Mose still be counting on dating me tonight? He knows I start at Bishop Eli's in the morning. People will probably laugh good-naturedly and say that we must have fallen for each other when we both

134

worked at Dave's, but there should be no raised eyebrows and insinuating remarks."

By the dim light of the lantern hanging at the gate, she caught sight of a group of boys across the yard. "Was that--? Yes, it was Mose, talking with Lewis and Bishop Eli's Edward and a few others." Katie tried not to be aware of him. She joined in the gay chattering of the girls.

Eventually they broke up. "It's cold out here," Edna said. "I'm going inside."

"Me, too," Vernie said. "It's time to go anyway. If we can find a way. I wish Henry were old enough to run around."

"That might not help you much. He'd probably get a girl friend right away," Susan pointed out.

"One who lives twelve miles out the other way. I know," Vernie assented gloomily. "Katie, couldn't you or Clarie do something about it? Where is Katie?" she asked curiously.

"I don't know. I thought she was coming," Clarie said puzzled.

"Oh, well, she's old enough to take care of herself," Susan said.

Katie hardly knew how she had gotten separated from the others. One minute she was with them and Mose was across the yard, and the next minute he was at her elbow, guiding her around the corner of the house.

"Remember what you promised me?" he asked in a low voice.

"Yes," Katie answered huskily.

"I'm counting on that tonight," he told her, flashing on his flashlight long enough to look into her eyes.

"Are you? I didn't know if you still wanted to," she answered laughing softly and a little bit self-consciously.

"I do though. Don't you?" he demanded seriously.

She nodded.

"I'll be coming in to get you then," he told her.

"I'll be ready," she said lightly.

Inside, she met Vernie and Clarie at the worktable where they had put their wraps.

"Do you girls have a way to get home?" she asked in a low guarded voice.

"We found a way for two of us with Melvin Miller, but we need a way for one more," Vernie told her, looking sharply at Katie's brilliant eyes and pink cheeks.

"Then don't worry. I've got a way," Katie said softly.

"Who?" Vernie asked suspiciously.

"Oh, you'll find out; keep your eyes open."

Vernie looked at her with raised eyebrows, opened her mouth to speak, then closed it. That Katie! If she wasn't a sly one! Who on earth was good enough for her?

The steady couples left in a rush, but before the last ones had gone, Mose came into the kitchen, searching the room for Katie. Without a word, she crossed the room and waited while he opened the door. Vernie and Clarie looked at each other.

"What in the world!" Vernie exclaimed. "So that's how she's going home! I wonder how long this has been going on?"

The unattached boys outside were saying the same thing. They were too surprised to do more than look at Mose and Katie until they had gone through the mob unmolested. Then the wonder broke. By the time Katie was in the buggy, a small pack of howling boys was upon them all yelling at once. "Why, Mose, not really?" and "Katie, how did you do it?" and "How long has this been going on?" and "No wonder they wanted to work at the same place."

Mose untied the horse, jumped into the buggy, backed the horse clear, and started toward the road before the boys realized it.

"I hope that bunch of cutups doesn't follow us," Katie laughed nervously.

"I hope so, too," Mose said fervently. "I don't think they know for sure where we're going, and we got out of there in a hurry. That should confuse them."

They got home a half hour before Vernie and Clarie. Katie

went into the house ahead of Mose, lighting the lamp above the worktable so that he could see to come in. She took matches and went to the living room. Softly pulling the bedroom door shut, she felt her way across the room to the library table where the Aladdin lamp stood. Katie hesitated a moment. Burning a lamp while she courted, yes, but one that bright? She decided to light it and turn it down.

When she heard the door open it told her Mose was coming in. Taking off her shawl and bonnet, she put them on the library table. Then she turned toward Mose, who had found his way through the kitchen to the living room.

"Nice and warm in here," he said conversationally in a low voice, aware that Katie's mom and pop were behind the closed bedroom door.

"They must have built a fire before they went to bed," Katie answered softly. "Here, give me your hat."

He held out his hat, and she laid it beside her bonnet while he took off his light topcoat. His eyes took in the room. Katie suppressed a desire to giggle, remembering the last boy she had dated.

They drifted toward the davenport, exchanging light talk. "Aren't you going to take off your covering?" Mose asked in a puzzled sort of way.

Katie took a deep breath. She might just as well make things plain at the beginning. If Mose didn't agree with her, it was best to know it at once. Faltering, she explained everything: How she had decided to wear her covering on a date. How she thought it best to burn a light. And--hardest of all to say--How she didn't think it was good to neck. Her fingers were tightly knit in her lap. She did not dare to look at Mose. She hated to offend him, yet knew she would hate herself far more for being a coward.

"Did you think this would make me mad?" he asked her, his eyes burning holes through hers. "No, no, Katie, I don't care if you burn a lamp and wear your covering. About--about necking, I agree with you. At least until we have gone steady longer. There's something more important on the first date."

"What?" she asked breathlessly, looking into his eyes.

"Talking, getting to know each other."

"That wasn't what Bishop Eli's Edward thought," Katie said involuntarily, then wished she hadn't.

Mose chuckled. "Edward's a fool. So that's what your fight was about."

"Didn't he tell you?" Katie demanded.

"He didn't dare. We would have rubbed it in too much. No, it was his attitude toward you after that. We all knew something had happened, but we didn't know what."

Katie gave a sigh of relief. Then he hadn't told the boys!

"From then on I began to look at you," Mose said suddenly. "Then, when we both worked at Dave's, I saw that there was a side to you I hadn't noticed before. I hate to say this but--but I used to think you were boy crazy."

Katie's cheeks burned. "I don't blame you," she said simply, avoiding his eyes. "I was silly."

"Then, when you turned down one boy after another, I changed my mind about that, but I was afraid to ask you for a date for fear you'd turn me down, too."

"I probably would have," she broke in mischievously.

"When we worked at Dave's, I thought it looked as though you might accept me after all."

"Oh, here come the other girls!" Katie exclaimed. "Why don't we mix up a pan of fudge or taffy for all of us?"

138

AT Bishop Eli's there were so many boys to tell apart! All the way from Edward, who was eighteen, to small Daniel, who could barely walk alone. An older boy, Jerry, was already doing his I-W service.* Then there was Marvin, who was just sixteen. The others were all lumped together and called the little boys by both their mother and Bishop Eli. With all these boys, the household was always lively. "No wonder Dan B's Mary liked to work here," Katie thought.

Daniel and three-year-old Paul were at home. The day was quiet after the others had left for school in the morning until they burst into the kitchen at four-thirty. Katie laughed to see how doors slammed, coats flew, and lunch buckets were thrown about carelessly each evening, as the boys came in eager to raid the pantry. By the end of the week she knew them apart.

Mattie wanted to get the fall work done in time to have church near Christmas. There was plenty to do--yard raking, cleaning off the garden, wrapping up fruit trees, and digging up carrots. Just the cooking and dishwashing alone kept Mattie busy.

Katie was shy and reserved around Bishop Eli. He had such a commanding personality and his authority was so unquestioned, it seemed impossible to be on easy speaking terms with him.

"His office sets him apart," Katie summed it up. "I dare not ask him for answers to my questions. Perhaps I will find them in his sermons." She listened closely to them, longing to be assured that she was doing the right thing.

She came away more troubled than before. "Is it just my

*Two years' service, as an alternative to going into the armed forces, usually spent for the public good.

139

imagination or does he preach that salvation is impossible outside our church? If he did preach that, did he mean that no one else was going to be saved? Oh, surely not! If he meant that you had to be a member of their church to be saved, how did he explain 'whosoever shall call upon the name of the Lord shall be saved,' or the verse in Revelation which spoke of a great multitude of all nations and kindreds and people? I must have misunderstood him," Katie thought.

Two weeks later John Gingerich's quiet talk comforted Katie, but Bishop Eli's main sermon set her off on a wave of dismay again.

"Are we to believe what some people try to tell us that traditions don't make any difference?" he thundered. "Are we to believe those who have left their first love and broken their vows made on bended knees to God and the church? We can just see how the devil works in their hearts. First, he makes them believe that ordinances don't make any difference; next, they begin to lust after things of the world and the worldly churches; then, they break their vows and leave the church! People, let's be on the watch that we aren't moved from what we took upon ourselves!"

He paused, turned to another portion of the audience, and began again. "Oh, yes, they tell us the worldly churches do so much good. They tell us they have God's worship oftener than we have; they tell us they study the Bible more; they even tell us they have prayer meetings. People, what are prayer meetings but aping the worldly churches? What are they but something new started by those who aren't satisfied with the way our forefathers set things up?"

Katie sat numb with confusion.

"And then there's another thing they try to tell us," he continued. "They tell us we can know that we're going to heaven before the judgment day. People, don't believe such heretical talk! If we could know in this life, what would be the use of having the judgment day? No, people, we can only hope in this life. 'Hope

140

that is seen is not hope: for what a man seeth, why doth he yet hope for?' Let's not give place to such an erroneous belief.''

Katie was stunned. "Doesn't Bishop Eli believe that you can know you are saved? Do all my people really think it is erroneous to believe you can know you are saved? The Bible plainly says, 'If thou shalt confess with thy mouth the Lord Jesus, and shalt believe in thine heart that God hath raised him from the dead, thou shalt be saved.'' Of course, you can know you are saved, right here and now!"

Katie hardly spoke after church. Even Susan couldn't draw her out.

*　　*　　*

"Those boys! If you let them alone, they'll throw the house out the window," Bishop Eli complained Monday evening. Katie turned slightly from her job of washing dishes and smiled. She hadn't known he was in the kitchen, but he had settled himself complacently on a chair at the kitchen table and had begun to unfold the daily paper. She hoped he had not followed her into the kitchen to make friendly conversation. She was in no mood to talk to the gray-bearded man whose sermons distressed her.

The noise from the living room rose to a crescendo of thumps and shouts. "Dad, come straighten up these boys," Mattie called from the dining room.

With a few giant strides, he was in the living room. The thumps and shouts died out abruptly. In a minute he was back in the kitchen, having settled the boys right and left. David followed him, grinning shamefacedly.

"Now wipe the dishes," Bishop Eli ordered. "Don't monkey around at it, either."

There was silence for a few minutes, broken only by the sound of dishes on dishes. Mattie glided back and forth from the dining room noiselessly, bringing out piles of dishes and going back for more.

"Oh, these newspaper stories," Eli's exasperated voice cut

across the silence. "Sometimes I wonder why I bother to subscribe for the paper. Nothing in it but silly stuff or stories of sin. Murder, fights, robberies! I am tired of reading it. How glad we can be that we're removed from the world's lust!"

"The world is in a sorry state," Katie admitted, looking around to see whether Bishop Eli expected an answer. She caught him looking at her. "But are our own people always good enough to be bragged about?"

"What do you mean?" he asked.

"Well, we hear stories of other communities where our people do things they shouldn't do," she answered bravely.

"Oh, I wouldn't believe too many of those stories," he said. "They are put out by people who aren't satisfied with the ordinances of the church; so they try to justify themselves by things like that."

"You mean they aren't true?"

"Oh, I wouldn't say that some things might not have happened that weren't for the best," he admitted with an uneasy laugh. "We aren't perfect, you know. We're all just sinners saved by grace. If we live up to the rules and regulations of the church and live faithfully by what we took upon ourselves on bended knees, God will forgive us our imperfections."

"I thought the Bible says, 'Not by works of righteousness which we have done, but according to his mercy he saved us,' " Katie said, wiping off the stove and noticing that Mattie was nowhere in sight.

Bishop Eli drew himself up with a jerk. Was this young girl presuming to contradict him? Didn't she know that the young were to listen to their elders?

"Oh, yes, it says so." His voice was loaded with ponderous authority. "But you can't just pick out one verse of Scripture and build on that. Jesus said, 'He that hath my commandments, and keepeth them, he it is that loveth me.' "

"What are His commandments?" Katie asked in a tight voice.

"Why, communion, feet washing, giving alms, and being

142

faithful to the rules of the church," Bishop Eli almost thundered at her.

"John said, 'This is his commandment, That we should believe on the name of his Son Jesus Christ, and love one another.' Christ didn't set up the rules as we have them," Katie heard herself saying. "He didn't dress like we do or things like that."

"Oh, now, yes, that might be true, but who are we to question what our godly forefathers thought was best? Are we better than they? What was good enough for our forefathers is good enough for us," he told her in a tone that assured her the final verdict had been given.

"Yes, but our forefathers might not have had as much light as we do," Katie persisted. "They didn't always have the Bible and not everybody could read. Besides, they were just people, too, and made mistakes."

"Now, Katie, I think you're going just a bit too far," he warned in an ominous voice. "I think you'd better listen to your elders when it comes to serious things. I'll make allowances for your youth and inexperience, but if I were you, I'd be a little more careful about believing just anything. People have gone far astray from the church by doing that."

Katie was silent. She had finished the dishes and David had disappeared. Mattie was still nowhere in sight. She investigated the dining room to see whether the table had been completely cleared. It proved to be; so she wiped the oilcloth, outwardly calm, but inwardly seething.

Bishop Eli was disappearing through the outside door when she returned to the kitchen. Rinsing the dishrag, she hung it behind the stove and wiped her hands on the roller towel. Giving one last glance around the kitchen, she reached for a handful of matches from the matchbox above the stove and went upstairs.

Warfare raged in her heart. Bishop Eli thought she was too young to know much about serious things. "Even the young can think!'' she said almost aloud as she lit her lamp. His bland assurance that, because the forefathers had done thus and so, the younger generation must do likewise was more than she could take.

Opening her Bible, she leafed aimlessly around, hearing only a thousand demons shrieking around her head: "You're wrong. You're wrong. You're wrong!"

The pages stuck on the fifteenth chapter of Matthew. She began to read, hoping the raging would cease. The ninth verse caught in the confusion of her mind. "In vain they do worship me, teaching for doctrines the commandments of men." Katie noticed Colossians 2:20 listed in the center reference column. "That is the very passage that's been troubling me," she said aloud. "Wherefore if ye be dead with Christ from the rudiments of the world, why, as though living in the world, are ye subject to ordinances, (touch not; taste not; handle not; which all are to perish with the using;) after the commandments and doctrines of men?"

She sat motionless, unaware of the cold about her. "If this means what I am beginning to believe it means, why is my church teaching traditions and ordinances?"

"And why don't rules and traditions work?" she questioned. "Our forefathers must have believed they were a vital part of life, yet the Scriptures warn against traditions of men! What makes traditions wrong? As soon as one puzzling question is explained, another one pops up."

*   *   *

Someone else wanted to have church at Christmas; so Mattie decided to wait. She let Katie have three days off. Christmas came on Thursday, second Christmas the following day, and the Saturday after wasn't enough to bother with; so Katie didn't have to go back until Sunday evening after the singing.

There were church services on Christmas in Bishop Eli's district, with the singing at the same home. Susan invited Vernie, Clarie, Henry, and Katie to her house overnight. Henry

144

was allowed to take the girls, much to their delight. Lewis and Edna were there, too, and they, with Katie and Mose, sat up.

Edna had decided to wear her covering, too, and burn a lamp. The two couples had a delightful time talking, although once they got too loud and John Gingerich rapped on the closed bedroom door.

Friday, they all went to the crowd where everybody exchanged details of the night before, and the girls tried not to look too sleepy. Some of the boys went coasting in the morning. After the big carry-in dinner, they gathered in the house and played I, Yes, No; In the Barrel; and Dollar, Dollar, Thou Must Wonder; and Telegraph. Some of the more musically inclined spent the afternoon singing from songbooks they couldn't use at the singings. Katie was aware of Mose throughout the day, although it was not until evening that they were alone.

*   *   *

Katie leaned back against the buggy and yawned. Mose had his new top on and they were snug and warm in its boxlike interior.

"Tired?" Mose turned to her, his eyes caressing her tenderly.

"Sleepy," Katie corrected him.

"I am, too. I'm glad there aren't three days of Christmas!"

"A bunch was going over to Dan B's tonight for a party," Katie volunteered. "I wonder what kind of a party it will be."

"I wouldn't know. Nobody said anything to me."

"They didn't to me either. I guess it's just for special people. I heard a couple girls talking about it. Fannie Yoder and Sammy were going; so I can imagine what kind of party it will be."

"Card party," Mose guessed.

"Um-hum."

"Let them have it."

It was not yet dark. Before them, the last traces of a gold and crimson sunset were vanishing. By its frail, pinkish light, Katie watched Mose. How good-looking he was! His slightly Roman nose was counterbalanced by his firm jaw. Even though his

145

mouth was a little bit too wide, the thinness of his lips kept it from dominating his face. But his main charm lay in his eyes. Dark brown, with darkly fringed lashes and slender well-defined eyebrows, his eyes could say things without his mouth uttering a word. They could look at you intently when you were saying something, telling you that no one else would have dreamed of such a special statement. Or they could poke fun at you gently, daring you to be serious. Or as now, they could caress you without lifting his hand to touch you. Katie had fallen hard.

"I've got something for you," he said as his eyes met hers. "I didn't have a chance to give it to you before, with so many people around us."

"Oh, Mose, I've got something for you, too. It is in my box under the seat."

"Mine's down there, too. I wonder if I can get it without getting out."

He slowed the horse to a walk and, reaching under the seat, fished around. "Here's something," he came up with a package. "Mine to you. Merry Christmas, Katie."

"Oh, Mose, thanks. Can you get my box?"

"I have it. Here you are."

Quickly she opened it and took out a small package. "And here's mine to you. Merry Christmas, Mose," she echoed.

"Well, now, maybe I'd better stop the horse while we unwrap them." He pulled on the reins with a firm hand and cried, "Whoa."

Katie unwrapped hers and found a lovely purse. At the same time Mose drew out a handsome leather billfold.

"Now doesn't that beat all!" he grinned. "We must have had the same idea."

"Oh, this is pretty!" Katie exclaimed. "Thank you."

"You're more than welcome. Thank you. How did you know I needed a billfold?"

"I didn't. I just took a chance."

"You couldn't have suited me better," he assured her, clucking

146

to the horse to start up again. His eyes met and held hers again, laughing at her and caressing her. Katie gave a little choking laugh and looked down at the purse.

* * *

It was after New Year's Day before Bishop Elis finally had church at their place. The cleaning they had done in the fall had to be redone. The last week was filled with feverish activities. On Tuesday the first of the help came. Someone came every day after that. On Friday, Henry Ellie, who was Mattie's niece, came with Dan B's Mary, who was working for her. Mattie put Mary and Katie to cleaning the downstairs bedroom while Ellie ironed, and Mattie and Harvey Miller Annie baked cookies.

There was little conversation between the two girls. "She thinks the sun comes up ten miles east of her home and sets five miles west," Katie thought caustically, hating herself for her nasty thoughts about Dan B's prim Mary. "She is pretty in a colorless way," Katie mused. "She combs her pale brown hair smoothly enough to suit the strictest people; no bobby pins and hair nets for her!" And yet, Katie saw her constantly peeking into Mattie's small mirror and adjusting her covering or tucking in an imaginary wisp of hair. She was slow and disorganized, and Katie worked circles around her, secretly exulting in it.

Katie was down on her hands and knees in the closet washing the floor while Mary dusted the woodwork when she heard Henry Ellie's loud voice. "Say, did you hear that some of the girls are getting so good they want to wear their coverings when they have a date?" Henry Ellie called into the kitchen to the other two women. Katie froze, the closet floor forgotten. The replies of the two in the kitchen were muffled.

"That's what they say," Ellie said loudly. "There was a bunch of them at Dan B's Christmas night and if they didn't have a time with them!"

"Dan B's!" Katie thought.

"They said some of those young girls got hold of a tract somewhere that said you should wear coverings."

147

"What girls?" came Mattie's voice.

"Oh, some of those snooty young things that don't know a thing about it. Mary told me."

"Where did they get the tracts?" Harvey Annie asked.

"I forgot who she said passed them out. But, anyway, if that isn't a way to act! I can just imagine how my covering would have looked if I had worn it on a date! Tee hee hee."

The two women's replies were muffled again.

"And the same bunch thinks you have to burn a light, too," Ellie tittered again. "They think they're so good!"

Anger surged over Katie. If those girls wanted to wear coverings, what business was it of Henry Ellie? If it was right to wear a covering all hours of the day, why should it be wrong to wear it when daylight faded? And it was Mary who had told Ellie!

Fresh anger broke out over Katie. "Simpering, vain thing! She and Ellie were cut out of the same cloth," Katie thought with a rush of contempt. In her vehemence she scrubbed the closet floor cleaner that it had ever been before. Sitting back on her heels, she dipped the rag into the water and wrung it out methodically, too angry to get up and speak to Mary and the other women.

The water was too dirty to use, though, and whether she wanted to or not, she had to go out to the kitchen to get clean water. Reluctantly she arose. Mary was nowhere in sight.

Katie opened the kitchen door and walked out into the cold air. She threw the dirty water from the pail across the lane. For a moment, she stood there, oblivious to the cold. "Should I tell Ellie that I, too, wear my covering when I have a date?" she wondered. "If I do, Ellie will include me in her ridicule. Yet, if I say nothing, I will hate myself for being a coward."

Shaking the pail to get out the last drops, she turned and walked slowly into the house. She filled the pail with clean hot water, shook in some detergent, and got a clean rag from the drawer in the wash sink without saying a word. Only when she was on her way back to the bedroom did she pause at the dining room door for a moment.

"I'm one of those girls who wears her covering when she dates," she told Ellie in a level voice. "I burn a light, too. I didn't think anyone would object to that. What would be wrong about it?"

Abruptly she turned toward the bedroom, leaving Ellie standing in openmouthed astonishment.

SUSAN had heard about the Christmas episode, too, and filled Katie in on the details the next Sunday night. "Edna had given a courtship pamphlet to one of the younger girls, who had immediately taken it to heart and passed it on to her good friends," Susan explained. "These girls had been at Dan B's place visiting Mary's younger sisters. Mary had dated Sammy, and Fannie, Bishop Eli's Edward. None of the younger girls had had dates.

"One of the younger girls told Edna that they'd gone upstairs to talk. After a while they decided to go down for something to eat and had been horrified to find the couples stretched out on the open davenport in the darkness. Then one of the younger girls had been courageous enough to bring out the pamphlet and read it to the group."

"That must have been quite a scene!" Katie interrupted.

"Yes, Bishop Eli's Edward got mad. Sammy Yoder told the

girls that the only thing wrong with them was that they had never known what it was to have a date and that he'd be glad to show them!"

None of the covering bunch (as they were beginning to be called) were prepared for the storm of abuse that followed. Many of the married people spoke against them. Some of the ministers treated it lightly and predicted it would pass when these young girls began to date.

If Bishop Eli and Mattie had anything against it, they never told Katie. After that evening when the bishop and Katie had disagreed, they had kept their conversations strictly casual.

Between Katie and Edward there was a sort of truce. If he ever thought of that evening when she had run away from him, he never mentioned it.

Katie grew more and more disatisfied with Bishop Eli's sermons. Sometimes she wondered whether he would ever go further than preaching against the wicked people who had broken their vows and left the church. At other times when she would honestly try to receive his words with an open heart, she came away doubting whether she was a child of God.

She felt better when John Gingerich preached. It was true he had to be prompted at times before he could finish quoting a verse, but he made its meaning clear. Katie sensed that he dared not preach too plainly for fear of disagreeing openly with the bishop.

One Sunday, in late winter, a visiting minister preached the main sermon. Katie had never heard of him before, but he wasn't preaching five minutes before she was listening breathlessly. He couldn't use a text because the church frowned on that, but he could develop a theme, which he did without vague wanderings and repeatings so common to Bishop Eli.

"We all want our own way more than we want to follow God," he told the congregation. "This is the essence of sin. Unless you repent sincerely of this self-centeredness and ask Christ Jesus to come into your heart, you are utterly without hope for eternity.

"Some of you might ask, 'How do I repent? Is it by being baptized and joining the church? Is it by being faithful to the traditions and ordinances of the church?' No, people, that's not repentance. You can all do that and still be utterly lost. True repentance is when you see that there's nothing you can do to make you right with God except turning to the cross of Golgotha.

"The sins to be repented of are not things like being unfaithful to the traditions of the church. No, in Galatians 3 we're told what God wants us to repent of: adultery, fornication, uncleanness, lasciviousness, idolatry, witchcraft, variance, emulations, wrath, strife, and all of those things. You might say that you're not guilty of the first two or three, but what about wrath? Or variance? Or emulations? Or covetousness? God says that if we fail in one point, we're guilty of all of them.

"No, people, don't think that anything you can do can erase the guilt of these sins. The Apostle Paul told Titus, 'Not by works of righteousness which we have done, but according to his mercy he saved us, by the washing of regeneration, and renewing of the Holy Ghost.'

"Some persons believe we can't know whether we're right with God in this life, but must wait for the judgment. The Bible says in John 5: 'He that heareth my word, and believeth on him that sent me, hath everlasting life, and shall not come into condemnation; but is passed from death unto life.'

"Do you see, people? If we repent and believe that Christ came to take away our sins and trust Him, we pass from death into life. Furthermore, the Bible says in I John 5, verse 13: 'These things have I written unto you that believe on the name of the Son of God; that ye may know that ye have eternal life.' We can know that we are right with God in this world."

Bishop Eli looked like a thundercloud on Monday. There were services for the visiting preacher in one of the other districts that afternoon, but he disdained to go, saying he

151

didn't have time. It was just an excuse, Katie knew, because two weeks before he had taken off three days to visit and attend church services for a visiting preacher who agreed with him.

Katie felt rested and peaceful. There were other people who believed as she did! She wished she could talk to someone about it. Mose seemed rather indifferent to discussing it; so Katie decided the matter would have to wait.

Because Bishop Eli was going to butcher the next day, Mattie put Katie to cleaning out the washhouse and washing the butcher tools. Bishop Eli and Edward brought in two big barrels and set them in the middle of the washhouse, then lowered the tabletop carefully onto them. While Katie was washing it with hot, soapy water, Eli brought the sausage grinder and the lard press down from the attic and set them beside the table. He sent Edward out to begin the choring.

"Is that visiting preacher going to stay long?" Katie asked.

"I don't know," he replied grumpily.

There was a moment of silence. "If he doesn't want to talk, why doesn't he go outside," Katie thought. "He isn't really helping. He's just moving things aimlessly about." Aloud she said, "Has he been a preacher very long?"

"Not long enough to know what he's talking about," Eli exploded. "A young man should listen to his elders when it comes to interpreting the Scriptures."

Surprised at his vehemence, Katie asked, "Didn't he quote Scripture?"

"He did that," Eli conceded reluctantly. "But such a way to interpret it, picking out a verse here and there and trying to justify himself with it!"

"I thought he quoted a lot of verses," Katie said quietly. "Do you believe that the Bible teaches that we can know we are saved right now?"

"No," he said flatly. "What would be the use of the judgment if we could know now? The Bible says we can only hope. Hope

152

that is seen is not hope. If we could know it now, where would hope come in?"

"Christ is our hope," Katie thought. Aloud she asked, "What do you think about being saved?"

"Oh, that's something the liberal churches dragged in, in the last twenty-five years. I wouldn't pay a bit of attention to it. They're always wanting something new."

"But doesn't the Bible say something about 'unto us, which are saved'? That sounds as though there were something to it?" Katie persisted.

Bishop Eli drew himself to his most commanding height, his eyes regarding her coldly. "I'm afraid you're beginning to lose your love for the church," he warned in his sternest voice. "I'm willing to make allowances for your youth and inexperience, but, if I were you, I'd take care what I believed. What happened to the children of Israel when they went after strange gods? What this preacher taught yesterday is not what the church says. If our forefathers saw fit to give us the teachings they did, who are we to contradict them?"

Katie found herself weak and trembling, ready to cry. And yet, she could not keep back the next words. "Yes, but if our forefathers say one way and the Bible another, shouldn't we believe the Bible first? Our forefathers were just people such as we are."

There was a thumping across the porch, the door burst open, and the excited school children trooped in. "Oh, boy, we're going to butcher," David shouted. "Can I stay home and help?"

In the hubbub that followed, Katie left quietly to empty her pail of water behind the woodshed. For a long moment she stood there, trying to calm herself. How could she face Eli's cold gaze. "Help me, God; oh, help me," she prayed silently.

When she went back into the washhouse, it was empty. She caught sight of Bishop Eli's square figure going toward the barn. From the sounds coming from the kitchen, the school children were begging Mattie for their usual after-school lunch. Katie was glad to work in solitude.

Her thoughts seethed and bubbled like a kettle of cooking mush. If the Bible and the traditions of the fathers differed, were you to ignore the Bible and believe the church? If the Bible was to be quoted and believed when it spoke of living by hope, why wasn't it to be trusted when it spoke of knowing you were saved? Once again a thousand demons seemed to be shrieking into her ears. "You're wrong; you're wrong," they screamed. "You've been misled; you're way off!"

Throughout the evening Bishop Eli made only a few inconsequential remarks. Katie was glad when she had finished the dishes, straightened up the kitchen, and was free to go upstairs.

Wrapping herself in a quilt against the chill of the room, she picked up her Bible, turned quickly to the back of it, where past experience had taught her to look for specific subjects, and found the heading: "Assurance of Salvation--How I may know I am right with God."

I John 5: 13. The very verse the preacher had quoted Sunday. Turning to it she read for herself: "These things have I written unto you that believe on the name of the Son of God; that ye may know that ye have eternal life."

Flipping back to the helps she found John 1:12. "But as many as received him, to them gave he power to become the sons of God, even to them that believe on his name."

John 5: 24. "Verily, verily, I say unto you, He that heareth my word, and believeth on him that sent me, hath everlasting life, and shall not come into condemnation; but is passed from death unto life." The preacher had quoted that, too.

John 6:47. "Verily, verily, I say unto you, He that believeth on me hath everlasting life."

"Help me, Jesus; oh, help me," she prayed silently. "I know you died for me. I know I'm not worthy of your forgiveness, but I want to be a true child of yours. Give me something to cling to!"

John 6:37. "All that the Father giveth me shall come to me; and him that cometh to me I will in no wise cast out."

It was enough. No longer did the demons shriek around her ears. Closing the Bible, she undressed and crawled between the covers. The Bible was to be relied on and the forefathers, good and well-meaning as they had probably been, were only people such as she. Drawing a deep breath of peace, she went to sleep.

By the time the sun was up, all of Bishop Eli's household had finished eating breakfast. Despite their pleas, the children were not allowed to miss school because of the butchering. Disgusted, they hung around and watched as long as they dared. At eight o'clock, Henry and Ellie arrived. Ben and Sarah Hochstettler, neighbors who exchanged help with Bishop Eli on butchering day, came soon after.

Katie baked pies for dinner. Then the sausage casings were ready to clean. Until dinner she worked alone at this detested job, glad only that it gave her a chance to think in solitude.

From the kitchen came the sounds of the women as they prepared the early dinner. Their hard work would begin when the hogs had been cut up. Ellie studiously avoided Katie.

By the time the men had scalded, gutted, and split the hogs in two and hung them on beams under the foreshoot of the barn, Mattie went out to call for dinner. Katie gave the last bit of casing its final cleaning and surveyed her work with satisfaction. The casings lay clean and pinkish white in salt water, ready for stuffing.

After dinner Mattie sent her out to the washhouse to help the men cut up the meat. As soon as sausage meat was cut, her quick fingers diced it for grinding. Occasionally one of the women came for more meat to clean. Otherwise Katie was alone with the men. They talked of everyday happenings, bits of news about the neighborhood, or exchanged views on farming.

The talk drifted to honesty. Henry told of a man who gypped a neighbor in a horse trade--not so much by what he said as by what he didn't say. "The horse never balked for its owner. Of course, it didn't. He had never hitched it to a buggy," Henry laughed. "He knew the horse was a balker; that's why he had

155

got it cheap. He had thought he could break him, but he was afraid to try."

"Well, now, we do things like that sometimes," Bishop Eli drawled slowly. "We're all just sinners and we make mistakes. That reminds me of a happening I had once."

"What was that?" Ben asked.

"Oh, one time I had six heifers--the nicest Guernsey heifers you ever did see. I was planning on keeping them for cows, but one day a buyer came in here and saw them, and don't you know, he wanted me to price them. Now I wasn't anxious to sell them at all, but I finally priced them. Put the price so high I never thought he'd take them, but he took me up right away. Said he'd come back the next day and pick them up. That night, when I told the wife what I'd done, she said, 'Don't sell that one heifer! It's the only stock we have that comes from the cow I got from home.' So I got to thinking about it, and I decided that man didn't need that heifer. I didn't think he'd even seen her because she was behind the barn, and he probably thought there were only five of them.

"So the next morning I penned that heifer in a box stall and let the five others out in the yard. But wouldn't you know, when the buyer came, the first thing he said was, 'I thought there were six heifers.' 'No,' I says, 'just five.' He loaded them up and gave me my check, and we kept the other heifer.

"But you know, she never did amount to much as a cow. Her first calf almost killed her, and she gave bloody milk, I finally had to sell her on the market. Taught me that I didn't gain a thing after all."

Katie listened. The more he progressed with the story, the bigger her contempt for him grew. She wished she dared to ask him whether he had already been ordained bishop when it happened.

"Did you ever make things right with the man?" Ben asked, too casually.

"Naw, by that time the man had forgotten it and there was

no use raking things up he'd forgotten. It just taught me a good lesson," Bishop Eli drawled smoothly.

Katie met Ben's eye. "Why, he feels the same way I do about it," she thought with a shock. "He thinks it was mean and despicable, too."

Six months afterward, when Ben and Sarah joined Poplar Hill, Bishop Eli couldn't understand what had made them turn against the church.

SUSAN asked Katie to go home with her Sunday after church. Leaving word with Mattie to tell Mose to meet her at the singing, she gladly went with Andy and Susan. She loved going home with Susan, for she always received a welcome from the whole family. After a short visit with them, she felt refreshed and contented, as though life had a purpose.

The elder Gingerichs stopped to visit an invalid after church. Katie and Susan went upstairs to take off their bonnets. Katie spied one of the little covering pamphlets lying on the dresser.

"So you still have one of these!" she exclaimed, motioning toward it with her hand.

"What? Oh, that. Yes, I guess we gave away enough!" Susan answered.

"Judging from the sounds we hear," Katie said with a short laugh. "You'd think we'd committed an awful sin by wearing the covering when we date."

"I know. I wonder how they'd talk if we really did do something bad?" Susan asked.

"Why are they so opposed to it?" Katie cried earnestly.

"Oh, our mothers didn't do it; our grandmothers didn't do it; and if our mothers and grandmothers didn't, why should we?" Susan asked with mock severity.

"Yes, and if they admitted they should have worn their coverings, they'd be owning up to some more things! Things like lying together on the couch and doing all that heavy petting," Katie said.

"I know, and you won't catch very many doing that."

Susan changed into her everyday dress and hung her Sunday dress carefully in the closet. Katie stared with unseeing eyes through the window at the late winter landscape.

"Susan, are you saved?" she asked abruptly.

"Yes," Susan answered simply.

"Are you really?" Katie cried delightedly. "Oh, I'm so glad."

"What makes you ask?" Susan wanted to know.

"Oh, I just wanted to know. I felt that we agreed on so many things and--I just wondered. How long have you been--saved?"

"I don't know how long. Ever since I was twelve or thirteen, at least," Susan said quietly. "I can't even say when it did happen. All I know is that from then on I asked the Lord to guide me and show me His will."

"I've only done that in the last year or two," Katie confessed.

"I've noticed that you've changed," Susan said. "You used to act as though nothing were more important than dates and fun."

"I was awfully silly," Katie admitted. "I'm surprised God cared enough to call me."

They could hear steady clop-clop coming down the road. The horse and buggy turned into the lane.

"Mom and Pop," Susan commented.

"Susan, what do you think about the church? Are you satisfied that it always teaches the right thing?" Katie asked.

"That depends on who's teaching," Susan answered. "If it's someone like Pop or that preacher the other Sunday, I'd say yes."

158

"Bishop Eli didn't agree with him at all," Katie said.

Susan gave an unladylike snort. "That doesn't surprise me. Pop said Eli disagreed so much he wasn't polite to him afterward."

"He really exploded the next day," Katie said.

"Bishop Eli gets worse and worse," Susan acknowledged.

"How does your pop get along with him?"

"Pop gives in a lot. He doesn't want to cause a fuss. He says it's a serious thing to challenge a bishop; keeps reminding us what happened to Korah when he challenged Moses. In the Bible, you know."

Katie nodded. "I thought it was awful when Mahlon and Emma left the church. I still couldn't bring myself to leave, but I don't know--"

"Andy says he's not going to join the church," Susan said. "He is old enough to take instruction this summer and be baptized in the fall, but he told Pop he wouldn't do it."

"What's he going to do then?"

"I guess he'll join Poplar Hill," Susan shrugged.

"What does your pop say?"

"He doesn't like it. He told Andy it would look bad if a preacher couldn't keep his own family in the church, but Andy hates the idea of joining so much he'd rather quit going to any church than join ours. Pop said, if he felt that way, he'd better join Poplar Hill."

They heard the elder Gingerichs move around downstairs. There was the sound of the stairway door being opened.

"Susan, are you up there?" Sarah asked.

"Yes."

"Are you alone?"

"No, Katie's with me," Susan answered. "We'll be down soon to help make supper."

That evening Katie, Susan, and Andy arrived at the singing early enough to get to the singing table. They slipped quietly in, took places, and opened their songbooks to the number being sung. Edna wasn't there yet; neither were Vernie and Clarie. The few boys at the opposite side of the table were doing their best to carry their end of the singing, but as yet the girls outnumbered them. With a stir half a dozen more boys came in, Mose among them.

There was still room for them on the boys' side of the table. By the time they were seated, Mose was exactly opposite Katie. For one long moment their eyes met. "There's no one else like you," his eyes said. "You're the prettiest girl here tonight." He smiled faintly and Katie dropped her eyes in confusion, almost losing her place in the melody. Susan gave her a playful jab with her elbow. "Save that for tonight," she whispered softly to Katie.

The room was rapidly filling. With the increase of singers, the singing picked up in volume. Katie caught a glimpse of Vernie and Clarie, with Edna, taking places in the back row.

It seemed to Katie that every time she looked up, she met Mose's eyes. She was glad when the singing ended and she could go outside for a moment before finding her sisters.

Mose came in for Katie before she had finished catching up on the news from home with Vernie and Clarie. When she caught sight of him, standing by the door in his hat and coat, flashlight in hand, obviously waiting for her, she hurriedly dug around among the wraps on the worktable for her shawl and bonnet. Mose had never before come in before she was ready. With a few murmured good-byes to her sisters and the Gingerich girls, she joined Mose. He opened the door for her and snapped on his flashlight so that she could see. Closing the door, he put a firm hand to her elbow to guide her to his buggy.

There was an urgency about him, new to her. Usually they took their time to get to the buggy, he matching his stride to her shorter steps; but tonight she had to run to keep up. Fortunately he had tied the horse at the hitching rack right outside the gate. Mose got into the buggy, snapped on the headlights, and wove his way through the tangle of buggies

160

and boys around the yard. By the bright gleam of the lights, Katie stole a glance at him. While he was busy getting them out to the road, she studied his profile. A current of determination showed in the set of his jaw and the thin line of his lips. Katie didn't quite know what to make of him.

Out on the road Mose could have snapped off his headlights, leaving on only the red warning lights. Instead, he turned to look at Katie. He gave a low, humorous chuckle. "I wonder if you realize how pretty you are tonight."

"Pretty?" Katie echoed inanely.

"I've thought so before, but tonight you were prettier than I've ever seen you. What makes your cheeks so pink?"

"I don't know. The lamplight maybe, or perhaps the heat in that room." Katie was only half conscious of what she was saying, her heart beating wildly.

He snapped off the headlights. Then taking a firm grip on the reins with one hand, he put his free arm around her and gathered her in a close embrace. "You have a good mind, you're the prettiest girl I've ever seen," he said fervently. "No wonder the boys kept you rushed with dates! What made them quit asking you?"

"I turned them down. I got tired of them."

"And took me! I'm the lucky fellow." Reaching up with the reins in his hand, he snapped on the overhead light. By its dim glow he searched her face. Then he bent down and kissed her.

*   *   *

Katie lit the lamp and set it on the table in Bishop Eli's living room. She laid aside her shawl and bonnet, settling her covering carefully on her head. Mose was taking off his topcoat and hat with quick, lithe movements. After laying them over a chair, he turned to her. His glance rested on her covering. "Why don't you take if off?" he asked abruptly.

For a moment Katie stared at him blankly. "Why, Mose, what do you mean?"

"Your **covering. You don't have to wear it,** do you?"

"I thought—why, Mose—didn't I tell you I was going to wear it when we had our first date? I thought you felt I should wear it," Katie stammered.

"Oh, that was then. We didn't know each other so well. Besides, people didn't--" he broke off, not wanting to say the rest.

Katie took a step away from him. "People didn't what? Talk?" she asked in a strained voice, **not wanting to hear** what she was hearing.

"Forget it," he evaded.

She dropped down on the couch, dazed and bewildered. "Why don't you want me to wear my covering?"

"I can't put my arm around you without mussing it," he said laughingly.

"Maybe that's why I wear it," she said. "I told you in the beginning how I felt about petting."

"Yes, but that was with just any Tom, Dick, and Harry. We've been going steady for four months," he pointed out. He had dropped down on the other end of the couch; now he sat moodily rubbing his chin.

Katie looked at him, but for once he avoided her eyes. "Mose, I didn't realize it at the time, but I know now that if I quit wearing my covering and blow out the light when we date, I'm only asking for trouble. Susan and I were talking about it today. You say people talk. I know they do. One reason is because they're ashamed to admit what went on when they did blow out the light and the girls didn't wear their coverings."

He didn't answer for a moment. Then he mused, "It's something new. Our forefathers didn't do it that way."

"Forefathers!" Katie exploded. "You're as bad as Bishop Eli. That's his standard answer to anything different."

"Well, you have to admit it is something new. We can't ignore the way our forefathers taught us," he argued.

"If what our forefathers taught us was good and according

to the Bible, we can't. But they were just people like we are and made mistakes," Katie answered.

"You can't read in the Bible that you have to wear a covering when you have dates," he persisted. "Besides, the church doesn't ask it of us. If the church had a rule like that it would be different."

"I don't know why the church would make a rule like that, if it doesn't want to believe a lot of other things the Bible does say," Katie said caustically.

"I didn't come to argue with you," Mose said abruptly. "I came to see you because you're my girl. Wear your covering then, if it makes you feel better. And burn a light. I can see you better when you do." He gave her his old humorous smile from across the couch.

Katie sighed in resignation.

11

OUTWARDLY things were patched up between Mose and Katie. Mose protested no more about the covering, carefully avoiding any reference to church rules. Because Katie liked him more than she cared to admit, she tried to forget their disagreement.

In the last weeks of winter, ominous undercurrents of dissatisfaction were apparent all over the community, reaching even the young people. They seemed to be splitting into two factions. "It is all because of the covering bunch," Henry Ellie said. "The young people were getting along just fine until those girls came along." She quoted Dan B's Mary to prove her statement. "The covering bunch thought they were so good! To think that a preacher's girls were their ringleaders! John Gingerich should be ashamed of himself for letting them go. But then, you can see what kind of a leader he is if he lets his own son join Poplar Hill. Who is going to buy a car for Andy? John? Andy is only sixteen and everybody knows he has no money to pay for one."

Katie, hearing Henry Ellie's words from Mom whenever she dropped in at home, became frustrated and resentful. Except for Susan, there was no one who knew how she felt. Vernie thought she was silly and Clarie seemed puzzled. And Mose refused to discuss it. Because her heart was hurt at the unjust talk, she longed for the assurance of knowing she was doing God's will.

"I'll begin to read the New Testament at its beginning," she determined. "Surely, God will speak to me. Surely, He will show me how to think about the traditions."

The Gospel of Matthew seemed wonderfully new. When she reached the fifteenth chapter, she almost gasped at the similarity between the Pharisees and some members of her church. She became convinced that, when traditions said one thing and the Scriptures another, it was best to follow the Bible.

She was at this stage when spring counsel meeting was held. A minister from another district came to help. As he preached, Katie realized he saw eye to eye with Bishop Eli. His words were sharp against the heretical teachings creeping into the church. "There were some," he said, "who dared be so presumptuous as to say they knew they were right with God! The same people were saying that traditions made no difference! He was scandalized. Were they better than their forefathers who had set up the traditions? No, the forefathers were right and good. What they had set down was the way of the cross."

Katie could have wept. "Hasn't he read the New Testament?" she wondered.

The day passed slowly. At last the children were dismissed and the real business began. Bishop Eli had a long prologue: "To condition the congregation for what comes next," Katie

164

thought, a bit unkindly.

There were the usual things first: cars, telephones, electricity, life insurance. Then he pounced on people who had rubber tires on their farm machinery. He told them in no uncertain tones that, unless the rubber was put away, the guilty would not be allowed to partake of communion.

Next he tackled the question of dress. His voice went on and on. As he mentioned the things that were forbidden, laying down the rules of what should be, Katie grew sick at heart. "How could that which was put on the outside cleanse the heart? Jesus said: 'In vain they do worship me, teaching for doctrines the commandments of men.' It is out of the heart that life issues.

"Could anyone or anything but Christ make the issues of the inward life right? Oh, dear God," she prayed, "help me look at it in the right way. Help me, oh, help me!"

At last it was time to take the vote of the church for communion. "What should I say?" Katie wondered. "Shall I say I agree with the rules and traditions? No, no, better openly disagree than lie," she thought. "But do I dare say how I feel? I am only a young girl. It is a serious thing to challenge the teachings of the church."

John Gingerich was coming toward the women. Katie gave a sigh of relief. If she had to disagree, it would be easier to tell John. She relaxed a little. "Shall I tell him that we should study Matthew 15 and 23 and the last verses of Colossians?" she wondered. Then to her dismay John took the vote of only the first row of women in the bedroom and passed out into the kitchen to the young mothers. Would she have to give her vote to the visiting preacher?

Ah, it was hard to disagree! She could imagine how her dissenting vote would be twisted when told to the congregation. Almost she was tempted to say she agreed with everything.

"Coward," her conscience whispered. "If it means so much to you, speak up! You're brave and bold in your thoughts, but afraid to let the church know how you feel!" She shifted position uneasily.

John was going to be busy for a while--with the kitchen so full of women--but perhaps he would get to her before the visiting preacher. Others were giving dissenting votes, judging by the murmurs of voices from the men in the living room. "The guest minister will be a long time coming," Katie thought, dreading the long minutes of suspense. When he finally reached the boys on the back bench, and began to move a little faster, Katie found her hands growing clammy. If he took her vote, would she dare speak out? She could imagine his cold stare when he heard how she felt. "Oh, please, God," she prayed, "Let John take my vote!"

There was a stir in the bedroom door; John came back from the kitchen. She gave a sigh of relief. She could give her vote to him after all. But relief gave way to consternation. John was taking the end bench and working toward the back of the room away from her. The other preacher was crossing over to the bedroom to help John take the vote of the women. "O God, will I have to give him my vote after all?" she prayed, panic-stricken at the thought.

"Coward," whispered her conscience fiercely.

The visiting preacher was taking the vote of the girl at the end of the bench--was listening intently--had taken it and was before her. There was no getting out of it. She must give her vote to him whether she wanted to or not. In a trembling voice she began murmuring her vote. All at once she knew she couldn't give lip service to something she disagreed with. Let the preacher twist it as he would, let the congregation hear it; she must tell how she felt. Surprised at her courage, she said, "I disagree with the rules of the church; I feel it would be well to study Matthew 15 and 23. I believe the message of the Bible could be put in these words of Paul: 'By grace are ye saved through faith . . . not of works, lest any man should boast'; and I would like to keep communion."

166

It was over! The preacher's lips were compressed into a thin, incredulous line as he turned to the next girl.

* * *

Mose was gay and talkative that evening, trying to bring out Katie's usual warm response, but she listened with only half an ear, still hearing Bishop Eli's thunderous warning to the dissenters of the church. "It is because of you," he had said, "that there can be no communion services for the present. Until all displays of worldliness, such as rubber tires, are put aside, no one may keep communion.

"And what is to be done with the dangerous manifestations of heresy that are being heard among the congregation? Heresy that says you can know you are right with God in this life. You can only hope!"

"We're having church in two weeks at our home," Mose broke into her reverie. "Communion services. Would it suit you to come? You could keep communion in our district instead of Bishop Eli's."

"I don't know how that would work," she roused herself. "I didn't get any encouragement to keep communion this afternoon."

"Why not?"

"I gave a dissenting vote at counsel meeting," she said.

"About what?" he asked in surprise.

"About the whole system of rules and regulations."

He stared at her, too stunned for words.

"Oh, Mose," she burst out of her reserve at last. "Why fuss about things being done just as our forefathers did them? Our forefathers didn't die on the cross for us. Keeping a certain set of rules doesn't make us right with God."

"Well, but the church has set things for us to follow. Who are we to try to change them?" he retorted. "Are we just to do as we please and not live by any rules? What kind of a church would that be?"

"I'm not saying we should do as we please. I said keeping

a certain set of rules doesn't make us right with God," she told him passionately.

"What does make us right with God?" he asked.

"Confessing we have a sinful nature and turning to Christ in faith."

"You mean--just believing in Christ will make us right with God?" he asked incredulously. "Where would the works come in?"

"If we could perfect ourselves by our works, why would Christ have had to die for us?" she asked in return.

" 'Faith without works is dead,' " he reminded her. "You can't be right with God without works."

"Oh, Mose, what I'm trying to say is that if you put your whole trust in what Christ has done for you on the cross, you will have works."

"Exactly," he assented. "You'll be faithful to the rules of the church and you won't go after worldly things like cars."

"Oh, Mose!" she almost wept. "Is there anything in the Bible like that? Doesn't the Apostle Paul tell the Galatians to walk in the Spirit and not commit the sins of the flesh? Those seventeen sins do not mention material things we can touch. They're all things that have to do with our hearts."

He was silent for a moment, his chin in his hands as he stared moodily at the floor. Katie picked up a cushion from the couch and began to worry the fringe along its edge.

"There's nothing wrong in living as we do," she began after a moment in a quieter voice. "We can have our rules and regulations, so long as we don't feel that keeping them is our salvation! But the danger lies in doing just that. The Apostle Paul told the Ephesians (2:8, 9), 'By grace are ye saved through faith; and that not of yourselves: it is the gift of God: not of works, lest any man should boast.' "

He made no reply, still staring at the floor.

"Don't you see?" she pleaded softly. "If our way of rules and regulations were the way to get in right standing with

God, everyone who got to heaven would have to do as we do. Jesus said that He was the way, and no one came to the Father but by Him. You don't believe that everyone else will be lost but our people, do you?"

"I wasn't talking about them," he replied. "I don't know anything about the other churches. I promised on my bended knees to be faithful to God and our church, and that's what I intend to do. I wish you'd get these ideas out of your head. Don't you suppose I can see where you're heading?"

"Where am I heading?" she asked thinly.

"Out to some other church. Poplar Hill, I expect."

"I didn't say anything about joining Poplar Hill," she protested.

"Oh, I know you didn't, but that's where this heresy will lead you. Katie, can't you reconsider? I hate to get into an argument with you, but--but--I love you. What kind of a future is there for us if you keep on like this? Doesn't my love for you mean anything?"

"Oh, Mose," she buried her face in her hands. "Don't you suppose I was thinking of that, too?"

*   *   *

"Get over," Mose slapped his horse lightly and by the light of the lantern stepped in with the harness. After fastening the bellyband, he slung the tugs across the horse's back. There was a noise behind him and he turned to see Bishop Eli's Edward regarding him.

"Getting ready to take the girl friend home?" Edward teased.

"Um-hum," Mose's answer was noncommittal as he took the bridle from the hook inside the stall.

"How can you two get along?" Edward asked suddenly.

"What do you mean?" Mose paused in the act of unfastening the halter.

"All the crazy ideas she has! She's always trying to set Dad right on the Scriptures, just as if she knew more than he. She's

169

one of the covering bunch, too, isn't she?"

"Yeah," Mose replied and began to pry the bit into his horse's resisting mouth.

"I wouldn't stand for it," Edward declared emphatically. "I'd tell her to act like everybody else, or this was the last she'd see of me."

Mose was silent until he had the bridle in place and fastened securely. Taking the hitching strap in his hand, he backed his horse out of the stall. "If I knew I'd get her in the end, I'd quit her for a while," he said moodily. "Maybe it would teach her a lesson."

KATIE and Mose tried to ignore their differences. When she wasn't with him, Katie felt a small wedge of doubt being driven into her heart. How could she and Mose go on if he refused to discuss the very thing that was growing to mean life itself? Wasn't there something in the Bible about "Can two walk together, except they be agreed?"

At other times she tried to tell herself that they weren't very far apart. Mose believed in God; so did she. Mose believed that Christ had been crucified; so did she. Mose believed in living a peculiar life; so did she. Oh, but her heart told her that this was where the difference lay. Mose believed you must be peculiar in outward things because the church said so. She was coming to see the peculiarity as an inward condition of the heart, possible only after you had put your trust completely in Christ.

170

Yet, she could not bring herself to sever their relationship. Mose was the only boy she had ever cared for. How could she quit him? His way of caressing her with his eyes, his rapt attention to her small talk, and, above all, his way of making her seem special had captured her fancy until life seemed impossible without him.

It was almost the last week in May before Bishop Eli felt the congregation was united enough to have communion. Some of the most dissatisfied had left for Poplar Hill; a few put away the offending things reluctantly and kept communion.

While he didn't threaten to withhold communion from the heretics who believed they were right with God, he solemnly exhorted them to repent and turn back to the truth. "It would be funny," Katie thought, "if it weren't so tragic, asking those who trusted what the Bible said to put it aside for what the church said!"

After communion Katie carefully avoided a discussion with Bishop Eli. She was going to be there only through harvest until the first of August.

One evening Bishop Eli came home in high good humor from helping a neighbor who had hired a boy from town to work for the summer.

"That town boy's quite a worker," he told Katie.

"Oh," she answered absently.

"I told him he did so well he could come over and work for me."

"Um-hum," she replied, wondering what he was leading up to.

"What do you suppose he said then?" he asked. Not waiting for an answer, he continued, "He said he would if he could sleep with the hired girl!" Bishop Eli guffawed loudly.

Katie gave him a long incredulous look of withering contempt. "You, a bishop of the church, can find that funny? You make a fuss about not having cars, yet laugh at a suggestive joke!" she thought.

171

The guffaw faded hollowly. Abruptly he picked up the day's mail and went into the living room.

* * *

Later Bishop Eli began talking while Katie did dishes. "Old Dan Gingerich's making a nuisance of himself--passing out tracts. He's even gone to the state prison! Spent a day there giving out tracts and counseling anybody he could talk to. He's been doing this for some time, and people didn't know it!"

Katie felt a warm rush of admiration for Dan. Had he been interested in such things when she worked for Emery two years ago? Could he have helped her?

Bishop Eli muttered darkly of public confessions or cutting him out of the vote. "Dan is trying to interest more people in this work. He's gathering them together to pray for it. The church is taking steps. Such behavior may not be tolerated."

"Why?" Katie asked him. "What's wrong with giving out tracts?"

"Tracts?" he asked in the same tone he would have said, "Cars!" "What are tracts but things people have written? If we want to read something, why not read the Bible? Besides, it's not our business to go out and judge the world. God will do that!"

"I didn't know Dan was judging the world. I thought he was giving the good news of Christ to people who were lost," Katie said. Katie had begun to iron. She was trying to finish it so that Mattie wouldn't have it on her hands next week. Quietly she thought, "Tomorrow is my last day--and I'm glad, glad, glad."

"We don't have any business carrying that out to the world," Bishop Eli assured her.

Katie gasped. "You mean God's people aren't supposed to tell the world about Christ?"

"No. God will take care of the world. We have all we can do to take care of ourselves. What business do we have going out trying to clean up other people? If we keep ourselves clean,

172

that's all we'll get done!"

For a moment Katie was silent. Then she asked, "What about Matthew 28? Jesus told the disciples to 'go . . . into all the world, and preach the gospel.' Isn't that command for us, too?"

"That was meant for the apostles," he said quickly. "The apostles have already preached the Gospel. We don't have to anymore."

"But Jesus said also, 'Lo, I am with you . . . even unto the end of the world.' That sounds as though it were meant for more than the apostles!"

Bishop Eli drew himself up and regarded Katie with cold enraged eyes. "Katie, you have lost all love for the church. To think that a fine young girl like you should be so bold and forward! That's just what happens when you take the teachings of the church under your feet. I shudder to think what will happen to you now. I certainly wouldn't want to be in your shoes!"

* * *

"I'm going down to Lydie Dan's tomorrow," Bishop Eli told Mattie. "I'm going down in the forenoon and you can take Katie home in the afternoon."

"Why? Can't you wait and take Katie with you?"

"No. I want to talk with them alone. It's time they found out what kind of a daughter they have."

* * *

Sunday evening after the singing, Susan told Katie that her father had told her that Bishop Eli had convinced Dan Gingerich's bishop and ministers to put him out of the vote of the church if he didn't make public confession.

"Susan told me they are going to put Dan Gingerich out of the vote," she burst out to Mose on their way home. There was no need to explain why; Mose lived in the same district as Dan.

"They should," he answered contemptuously. "He thinks

173

he's so good he can go around and tell other people what to do."

"Mose!" she cried. "That's not what he's doing. What is wrong with our church? Can't it tolerate a man who is only doing what Christ wants him to do?"

"I'd like to know what else it is. Who told him to go out and hand out tracts? The church didn't."

"It would be a good thing if it would," Katie answered. "But you wouldn't catch it doing that. It's too busy trying to preserve the traditions of the forefathers."

"What more is asked of us?" he demanded. "If we do our duty in the church and clean up ourselves, that's all we'll get done. We don't have any business going out and trying to clean up the world."

"Are you sure? How shall we explain Jesus' promise to be with those who go into all the world with the Gospel?"

"I wish you'd quit trying to interpret the Scriptures and listen to the church," Mose pleaded. "How do you know what they mean? You're not even of age and you think you know more than the preachers!" His voice was sullen.

"If it doesn't mean what I think, what does it mean? Bishop Eli couldn't tell me. He just got mad and told me I was wrong." Katie laughed bitterly.

Mose took a firmer grip on the reins, cleared his throat, and turned to her. "Katie, how can we keep on together, if you don't get these ideas out of your head?"

Katie took a deep breath. "I don't think we can. I've been afraid of this for a while."

"What do you mean?"

"I think we'd better quit."

"Oh, Katie!" his voice was full of genuine anguish. "Can't you reconsider? Doesn't my love for you mean anything? Why must you let all these ideas come between us?"

"Why ask me to give up all the way?" she demanded. "Couldn't you try to see my side?"

174

"I don't want to. I'm satisfied with what I believe."

"That's what I thought. Oh, Mose, we can't get along. We might just as well stop seeing each other."

Ahead of them the farm buildings of Katie's home were a dark blot. In silence Mose drove the remaining distance and turned into the lane.

"If that's the case, I'd better not come in," he said dully, as the horse slowly walked to the gate and stopped.

"I think so, too," she assented, throwing back the duster.

As she stepped down from the buggy, hymnbook in hand, he burst out, "Katie, please! If I let you believe as you wanted to, couldn't we keep on?"

She stopped at the gate. "Mose, it just wouldn't work. It means so much to me I'd like to talk with you about it all the time, and you don't want to hear it. I don't see how we can go on."

By the pink glow of the taillight, he stared at her. He couldn't see her plainly, but he knew her blue eyes would be clouded with emotion, her cheeks pink and smooth, her lips rosy and tender. Giving a sigh he slapped the reins across his horse's back and turned toward the road.

She was too depressed to think clearly. Snatches of conversation with Susan and with Mose chased each other around her head. Automatically Katie climbed the stairs, lit a lamp, undressed, and crawled into bed.

It was no use. She heard Vernie and Clarie come in. The low mumble of their voices changed to excited whispers as they discovered the empty living room. They ran upstairs.

Vernie came in first. "Katie, what does this mean?"

"I'm trying to sleep," Katie said laconically.

"Yes, but where is Mose?" Vernie persisted.

"He went home. We quit."

"What on earth! You didn't either. Why?"

"Because," said Katie, rolling over.

*   *   *

175

PART 3

1

KATIE was helping Mom fold the wash Monday afternoon. "What's this I hear about you thinking you know better than the preacher?" Mom began.

Katie's hands froze. "Who said anything like that?"

"Oh, don't bother about that! I've been suspecting it for a while anyway. I told Pop that you were getting heretical ideas way last spring, but he wouldn't believe me. What's the matter with you anyway? Since when does a young girl like you know more about the Scriptures than the preachers do?"

"I never told anybody that I knew more than the preachers. Someone has been telling you things that aren't true," protested Katie.

"Don't try to deny it," warned Mom. "I know too much about it. Ever since you worked for Mahlons you've been losing your love for the church. I blame Emma and Mahlon as much as anybody. He wasn't satisfied to leave by himself; he had to try to drag you with him."

The accusation was so absurd Katie had to suppress a hysterical giggle. She had been horrified when Mahlon talked of going.

"Why did you give heed to his talk?" Mom went on. "Don't you realize it is serious to break vows made on bended knees?"

"What vows?"

"Why, the promise you made to be faithful to God and the church when you were baptized."

"I haven't broken any vows!" Katie exclaimed with some heat. "Besides, where in the Bible does it say that making vows to the

179

church is going to save us? **The Apostle Paul** says, 'By grace are ye saved through faith; . . . not of works, lest any man should boast.' "

"Are you trying to tell me that all you have to do is believe? Where would the works come in?' 'Faith without works is dead.' Don't you know that?"

"This is the work of God, that ye believe on him whom he hath sent," Katie heard herself quoting.

"There you go! I can well believe that you're bold enough to try to set the preacher straight! Where do you get those ideas?"

"From the Bible," Katie answered, her voice trembling.

"You can just watch yourself! You'll go crazy—studying the Bible so much! It's one thing to read a little in it, but an entirely different thing to study it so much."

"Why, Mom," Katie burst out. "How can you study the Bible too much?"

"If you study it just to try to justify yourself the way you've been doing, you can get too much in a hurry," Mom said positively. "Besides, you read all those misleading books that Emma's been wasting money on, and, if anything would give you a wrong interpretation of the Bible, they would! Why should we listen to such trash? They lead away from the church."

Katie, remembering her terror of meeting God before she had read those books and the change in her life since then, felt that her most precious things were being threatened. What were the teachings of the church compared with the release from that awful, insides-melting fear? "O Lord, help me!" her heart prayed.

"Give up these misleading beliefs! Think of what you took upon yourself when you were baptized! Give them up before they pull you away from the church entirely!"

Katie blindly folded the forgotten towel.

"Oh, Mom! Don't ask me! I would sooner give up life itself!"

"That's just what Emma said when I talked with her last week," Mom said disgustedly. "You're just as bad as she is."

Katie folded towels methodically in the silence that followed. Her mind churning and twisting, she tried to face this new opposition. Couldn't Mom see that what she believed wasn't something she had dreamed up to justify herself, but the very Word of God? No one had spoken to her about her soul until after she had committed herself to Christ. Now that she finally knew that salvation came only by repenting and putting her trust in Christ, why must they try to pry her loose from the promise of the Scriptures?

"What does that young man you're going with say about this?" Mom asked. "Does he agree with you?"

"He thinks like you do," Katie said, with an effort to speak evenly. "We quit last night because of that."

"What?" Mom cried in consternation. "You mean to tell me that he's not good enough for you? What is wrong with you?"

"I didn't say that he wasn't good enough for me. I said we couldn't agree about this thing you're talking about; so we decided we might as well quit."

"You beat everything I ever heard of," Mom cried in bitter exasperation. "I don't know where you'd find a better chance than Dave Senior's Mose. I never thought one of my girls would think herself too good for that boy."

"Oh, what is the use of trying to explain?" Katie thought. For a moment, remembering Mose's handsome face and protective care, a piercing regret knifed through her. "No, no," her heart cried out. "He's not worth it. Not if he asks you to give up your commitment to Christ. Life wouldn't be bearable if you did that!"

Mom folded clothes angrily, thumping the tea towels as she put them on a pile. What possessed this strange girl beside her to throw aside one of the best catches among the young people just because of some silly, heretical ideas? She had prided herself on Katie being Mose's choice. Vernie was a sore spot—refusing every boy until it looked as though she were going to be an old maid for sure. How Mom hated the stigma of an old maid in the house! Now Katie had thrown away the best chance she'd ever get! It was just too much.

As time passed, Katie hated to be alone with Mom, for every time they were, Mom would renew the attack. Once it was about the assurance of knowing you were right with God, with Mom quoting the now familiar verse about hope.

"Yes, but, Mom, what does Paul mean when he says to the Roman Christians: 'Therefore being justified by faith, we have peace with God through our Lord Jesus Christ'?" Katie asked. "Doesn't that sound as though we were right with God as soon as we put our trust in Christ?"

"There you go again! Picking out a verse here and there to justify yourself," Mom said bitterly.

"Well, what does it mean?" Katie persisted.

"I don't profess to know all about the Bible. After all, we must be willing to let those who are set up to be our leaders explain those things," Mom answered shortly.

"Oh, Mom! Those leaders are just people such as we are and just as apt to make mistakes." Katie's voice was sharper than she realized.

"Are you suggesting that these men who have been put in as leaders by the lot aren't ordained of God?" Mom asked in a shocked voice. "If God ordained them, they are His mouthpieces. If you resist them, you are resisting God!"

"Then why do you criticize John Gingerich?"

"Criticize John Gingerich! Who wouldn't criticize a man who teaches misleading things like he does? He split the young people in two with those covering tracts!" Mom retorted sharply.

"Yes, but he was ordained by God," Katie said doggedly. Mom was back in a corner and she knew it. For a moment she was at a loss to answer. "You needn't twist my words so you can justify your actions," she replied. "Besides, anyone who gets as violent in his arguments as you do is wrong for sure."

Katie stared at her. This was Mom, her own mother, saying

hard, cutting things to her--things that wrenched and burned and left her crying! Her lips quivering with silent sobs, she turned blindly away.

* * *

Vernie frankly told her she was crazy. "You mope around like a sick hen," she told Katie disgustedly. "You used to be a lot of fun, but now you're the wettest wet blanket I ever saw! You sit around with a face a mile long and act as if it were a sin to crack a smile. I'm getting tired of it. Why don't you act decent for a change?"

Katie wished she could talk to Pop about it. Did he, like Mom, think she was being misled? He was always so quiet, intent, so reluctant to take part in any controversial conversation. But deep down in his heart, he surely must have convictions that meant something to him. Was he convinced that the church was always right? Did he ever question its teachings?

* * *

From the woodshed Katie got out a basket, hoe, and garden rake. Already the chill of another autumn was in the air, with a faint haze shimmering across the ripe cornfields and green meadows. A killing frost had browned the zinnias and dahlias and marigolds whose panorama of color had brightened the garden. Yesterday Katie had dug sweet potatoes. Today Mom had told her to dig the dahlia roots and put away the gladiolus bulbs after she cleaned the pantry and finished ironing.

It was unusually quiet around the house. Pop and Henry were busy in the neighborhood silo ring frantically filling silos. Today Mom had gone along to help cook the noon meal at their closest neighbor's. Mary Ann and Edna were in school; Vernie was working in town; Clarie had begun to work at Dave Junior's. Katie was alone. Not that she minded. It was so unusual to be alone, she was glad for the chance.

She had forgotten the shovel. Dropping the rake and hoe and basket in the path, she turned back to get the shovel. "I might

183

as well get the butcher knife to cut the tops off the dahlias and gladiolus," she mused. Going through the washhouse, she let herself into the clean sunny kitchen. She hoped Mom would be satisfied with the way she had cleaned the pantry. Mom's standards were high; no halfway measures with her. Katie remembered how they had grumbled among themselves when they were younger because Mom made them do a job over if it didn't come up to her expectations. Getting ready for company was an ordeal they had all dreaded; the house was turned upside down in her zeal to clean every corner lest someone say Dan Lydie was a careless housekeeper. Once Vernie had said that, if the president of the United States came, Mom couldn't go to any more pains than she did for the next-door neighbor. "It is funny now, but it hadn't been then," Katie thought, remembering with a faint smile.

Butcher knife in hand she left the house and went out to the shop to get the shovel. In the murky interior of the shop, she looked around for it, finally discovering it on a nail in the farthest corner. In a moment she was back outside the shop with the door closed behind her.

Oh, it was a lovely day! Was the sky ever as blue as in early October? Only a few white clouds drifted across the horizon, looking twice as white against the blue of the sky. A jet moved soundlessly far to the north, leaving a thin pencil of white behind it. To the south the town lay vague and shadowy, wrapped in haze. It was all so lovely it brought a faint pain to Katie's heart. Oh, if only things were as peaceful around her as the landscape!

With a start she aroused herself from her reverie and turned back to the garden. She would never get those flower roots dug if she stood around thinking. Perhaps, if she did a good job, Mom would be a little more understanding. Her strong young limbs handled the shovel easily. Automatically she pushed the shovel into the ground with one foot, her mind going back to her inner pain. "If only Mom could see that faith in Christ is more essential than obeying traditions."

"'A man's foes shall be they of his own household.' Oh, it is true, it is true," she thought in agony. All at once she was sobbing so much that there was no strength left to push the shovel. Her body shaking, she bowed her head against the handle, sobbing out all of the misery of the last two months at home: Mom's sharp censure, Vernie's blunt frankness, Pop's indifference, the whole church's displeasure.

Suddenly a presence was beside her. A strange peace swept across her pain-filled heart, making her lift her wet face in wonder. It was almost as though she could reach out and put her hand in the hands of Christ. For the first time since she had committed her life to Him by faith, she knew what it was to feel His love for her, healing the pain and giving her strength.

"Christ, O Christ!" she prayed silently. "You know what it's like, don't you? They called you a heretic and said you were crazy. Some of your own family didn't believe in you. Dear, blessed Saviour. Dear, precious Lord Christ!"

Tears of joy ran down her face. She reached into her pocket and took out her handkerchief. Halfway up to her face, her hand paused. So this was how He might have felt. The warm autumn sunshine and the soft, fragrant wind dried the tears from her face while she stood, lost in the glory of sharing in Christ's suffering.

DAN Gingerich was given until spring to repent of his missionary endeavor. If he made a public confession, he would be left in peace; if he refused to do that, he would be excommunicated. There were many who felt the church was going too far. Because Bishop Eli was known to be one of Dan's strongest opponents, there were complaints against a bishop who meddled into the affairs of another district. More than one family left the church because their convictions told them Dan was in the right. If everyone had taken the bishop's attitude down through the ages, they reasoned, who would have told their own forefathers about Christ?

It led to more dissensions for Katie. She came to recognize with dread Mom's statements that inevitably led up to another disagreement. "Dan Gingerich is just doing this to make himself a great name," or "Why can't he work among his own church, if he thinks he's got something?" or "He thinks he's so good, he can go and tell other people how to act."

"Oh, dear Christ," Katie would pray frantically, "keep me from saying too much or from losing my temper! O Father, help me!"

She would struggle desperately to be silent and let Mom's unkind remarks go in one ear and out the other. For a while she would seem to have success. Then all at once some especially sharp remark would loosen her tongue. Words would pour forth, tumbling over each other in her effort to convince Mom, to make her see, that Dan and others like him were only doing what the Word of God told them to.

186

Each such episode **would break** her heart. The humiliation she suffered because of **losing her temper** when she **wanted to** be calm and quiet before Mom, brought her crying to **her** knees before Christ. Then He seemed dearer than ever. "**How** often He forgives my weakness!" she would exclaim. Often **she** wanted to reach out and touch Him.

Fall passed on into winter. Clarie stayed at Dave **Junior's** until Christmas, taking care of a new baby. At home, **Katie** found herself getting really acquainted with Mary Ann and Edna. Mary Ann was now twelve and Edna, eight, both with an intense love of dolls and doll dresses. Katie wondered that neither of them seemed as interested in books as she had been.

Because they struggled so hard with their diminutive sewing, Katie helped them cut out and sew countless dresses for their family. In a spurt of endeavor she even designed little coverings **and bonnets** for their dolls as Christmas presents, working on them while the girls were in school and whisking them away in the evenings as soon as she saw the bus coming up the road. Mom caught the spirit of it and let her have some of her finest organdy for the coverings.

For once no one had asked for a girl through the Christmas holidays. They would all be at home, Mom decided. For a few weeks the girls could catch up on winter sewing, braid the carpet rags, and perhaps even quilt a quilt. Vernie still had her town job. Coming home overnight, she could help quilt in the evening, seeing this quilt was to be hers.

Christmas came and lingered two days, waned, and **was** gone. Katie had no dates; would have refused anyone **who** would have asked. Clarie **had one**, though; the two **girls,** with Vernie, invited guests Christmas night. Dan B's Mary was not among them. That night Dave Senior's Mose dated Mary for the first time.

The day after Christmas the young folks had a crowd, **where** the usual jokes were cracked, the usual games played.

Because they had lost so much sleep through entertaining

house guests and going to the crowd, Mom let the girls take a nap the next afternoon. Katie was deep in sleep when someone shook her shoulder. For a moment she thought she was dreaming.

"Katie, wake up. Katie, do you hear me?" Mom was saying, giving Katie's shoulder another urgent shake.

"What do you want?" Katie mumbled, her voice thick with sleep.

"Henry Yoder is here and he wants a hired girl." Katie half raised herself on her elbow.

"He what?"

"He wants a hired girl. Ellie and the children have flu. Get up and get your things together."

"Mom!" Katie was outraged and thoroughly awake. "You said we didn't have to go out over the holidays."

"I know, but when someone is sick it's different. Come on and get up."

"Do I have to go there?" she asked indignantly. "Don't you remember what he said the last time I worked there? Let him go somewhere else and get a good hired girl."

"Get up and get your things ready, I said," Mom's voice stung like a whiplash. "You're always talking big about missionary work. This is as good a chance as any. If you really mean what you profess, you'll go and work there without another word."

With set lips Katie got up and began to toss her things haphazardly into a suitcase.

She found the Yoders really sick. Katie had her hands full, for Ellie and Anna Mae, the oldest girl, were burning with fever. The two younger children, already convalescing, whined and fretted. Even Henry was sicker than he cared to admit, dragging himself out twice a day to help Katie chore.

By the next week, the younger children returned to school; Ellie, able to be up and around, helped Katie patch socks. Anna Mae spent her time embroidering.

188

Katie, who had always disliked fancywork, was tempted to suggest that Anna Mae, too, might help mend. But her experiences at Henry's had taught her that you didn't make suggestions to Ellie. You kept your opinions to yourself and it was best even to refrain from asking the children to do something for you.

Their conversation was stilted and strained. Some of Bishop Eli's strongest supporters, even though they weren't in his district, Henry and Ellie scorned John Gingerich with his fancy girls and heretical ideas. It broke out in their conversation more than once.

By Friday, Henry was well enough to go to the sale barn for the day. In the evening he came home with the news that Dan Gingerich's wife had suffered a stroke.

"Maybe that will open up his eyes," he commented at the supper table. "You can just see that God is punishing him for the way he's been carrying on. If he doesn't watch out, God will take away his wife."

Katie ate for a moment in silence. Should she speak up what was truth and be called bold and argumentative or keep her mouth shut and despise herself afterward? How often she had had to make one of these hard decisions the last year or two! "Dear Christ, help me," her heart prayed silently. "Don't let me say anything that would disgrace Thy precious name. Give me the right words to say."

"Maybe he won't have time now to go around trying to be so good," Ellie observed. "He'll have his hands too full to fuss about other people."

Katie took a deep breath and laid down her fork. "Here we go," she thought. "I can't keep still and swallow this." Quietly she said, "I thought Dan was fulfilling Christ's last commandment."

The eyes of everyone at the table were instantly riveted on her.

"What commandment?" Henry asked coldly.

"Why, the one in Matthew 28, where Christ says, 'Go ye therefore, and teach all nations, baptizing them. . . .'"

"That was meant for the apostles," Henry said. "Those times are past for us. That doesn't have anything to do with us."

"If that were true, why would Christ say, 'Lo, I am with you alway, even unto the end of the world'?" Katie persisted, fighting the old familiar rush of indignation that she felt sweeping over her.

For a moment Henry was at a loss to reply. He wiped bread crumbs from his beard with a calloused hand, avoiding her eyes. "Even if it says that, that man has no business taking things in his own hands," he burst out. "Why doesn't he let the church take the initiative? Let the church have the say so."

"Why doesn't it take it then?" Katie asked, trying to keep her voice calm. "Maybe that's why Dan went ahead and did it. Maybe he saw the church wasn't going to."

"All that's wrong with him is that he'd like to be a preacher and God never saw fit to let him be put in by the lot; so he thinks he can do it this way," Ellie broke in. "He's always thought he was so good."

"That's just it." Henry supported her triumphantly. "He's as thick as nettles with John Gingerich. There's another man who's always giving out tracts. Two of a kind, if you ask me."

"Just look at the damage to the young folks John Gingerich did with those covering tracts!" Ellie pointed out.

"Damage to the young folks!" Katie gasped. "How on earth did those covering tracts damage the young folks?"

"It split the young people wide open, that's what it did!" Ellie said. "Dan B's Mary told me the young people were getting along just fine until John's fancy girls started giving those tracts out. Ever since then the young people have been divided. I think it's a shame!"

"John ought to make a public confession just as well as Dan," Henry declared solemnly.

Katie's heart was beating so loudly she felt sure the others could hear it. With an effort she pulled herself together. "I can't see that Dan Gingerich was out of place in being concerned about the lost people of the world," she said thinly. "I think he's only doing what God wants all of us to do. I'm glad he has the nerve to stick up for his convictions."

"Dan Gingerich is crazy!" Henry burst out pounding the table. "Crazy I tell you. He's out of his head!" Henry's face was livid with anger. The veins on his forehead protruded with the intensity of his anger; his eyes were burning holes of hate.

Katie recoiled in surprised horror. She felt weak and trembly. Her appetite had disappeared. The others were quiet, too. Henry shoveled in his dessert without looking up.

Katie cleared the table and escaped to the kitchen. She had been washing dishes alone all week, but tonight Ellie, in an effort to smooth over Henry's outburst, sent Anna Mae out to wipe the dishes. In her intense preoccupation with the scene just past, Katie was only half aware of her. Katie scraped plates and got out the dishpan. She tried to bring a measure of calm to her spirit, but the picture of Henry, livid with rage, would rise up before her again. In all her life, she had never seen anyone so violently angry.

"When I get big, I'm not going to be one of the covering bunch," Anna Mae burst out unexpectedly into Katie's reverie.

"You're what?" Katie turned to her in surprise. She had almost forgotten Anna Mae was there.

"I'm not going to be one of the covering bunch like you are," Anna Mae repeated. "Mom says the covering bunch is just awful."

A grim smile played across Katie's lips. "Oh?" she asked, rising inflection on the word. "I'd be sure I knew what it was all about before I talked so big if I were you."

"Covering bunch girls think they're so good. I'm never

going to be like that! I'm going to be the way my mom was!" Anna Mae gave the tea towel a careless fling across the drying rack and went back to the living room and her latest fancywork.

Katie continued on in the kitchen, methodically emptying the dishwater and wiping out the pan. Rinsing out the dishrag, she put it carefully on one side of the rack and hung Anna Mae's tea towel neatly beside it.

A slow burning anger began to replace her first surprised shock at Henry's outburst. "Who did he think he was fooling with his pious talk about letting the church go ahead with missionary work? The church would never do it, because there were too many in it like Henry. It is nothing but an excuse, this pretended indignation at Dan for running ahead of the church. They want it like it's always been," Katie thought with sudden clarity. "It's easier for them to stay in the comfortable rut of the traditions of the forefathers than it would be to own up that they had a responsibility to carry the Gospel to a lost world. They don't want to admit that, because none of them care who goes to hell, just so they escape it themselves," her thoughts tumbled over each other.

Katie stood smoothing the tea towel on the rack. "That is it. My own people are desperately trying to save themselves, caring only for themselves and their traditions. Their eyes have never looked upon the people of the world as lost and needing the Gospel. Many of them admit openly that they want nothing more from anyone outside of their group than to be left alone. In return, they, too, would let the world go its way. No battles to fight and no principles to stand for," Katie thought. "It's a far cry from our Anabaptist ancestors who gave their lives for the sake of spreading the Gospel. Or from the apostles who went everywhere preaching the Word and called it an honor to suffer for Christ."

Not trusting herself to speak, she walked angrily through the dining room on her way upstairs without so much as bidding Henry and Ellie good night, glad that tomorrow was her last day with them.

AFTER her weeks at Henry Ellie's Katie stayed at home all winter, helping to butcher and quilt, and giving a hand to neighbors who were having church. In the spring the Millers had church--and, of course, the singing.

The three girls and Henry invited all their best friends for supper. There were so many that Katie and Susan were still washing dishes when it was time to begin singing. Katie quickly emptied the dishpan as Susan whisked the last dish out of sight. Clarie emptied the dustpan, and Vernie shoved the broom into the closet. Pop began setting up benches in the kitchen as the girls dashed upstairs to change their clothes.

There they found their room crowded with a gay, chattering bunch of girls, including, of all persons, Dan B's Mary and her friend, Fannie Yoder. As they had not been invited for supper, the others could only conclude that they had come early, un-noticed, and, hearing the noisy girls upstairs, had gone up to join them.

Girls were everywhere: on the beds, on the window seat, on the floor, but most of all, in front of the dresser mirror. Katie wormed her way between them to the closet and bumped against Dan B's Mary.

"Excuse me!"

"Oh, of course," Mary assured her with saccharine sweet-ness. "It was so clumsy of me to get in your way."

Katie bit her lip. She wondered if she would ever get to the

193

place where Mary would have no power to irk her.

"It's too crowded in here, girls," Vernie sang out with gay bluntness. "If the rest of you are done combing hair and putting on perfume, why don't you go down and sing?"

"Vernie!" Katie protested. "You're being impolite."

"Maybe I am, but I need room to get ready," Vernie replied nonchalantly, unpinning her hair. "I can't even run a comb through my hair without bumping someone."

"I'll go down," Dan B's Mary cut in. "They're singing downstairs anyway." A thin, reedy strain of song came up through the floor. "I only came up for a few minutes to see your room. I didn't think you'd mind."

"Sure, that's all right." Vernie said with false cheerfulness. "Look all you want to."

There was a flurry as girls got off the beds and up from the floor. Their noise completely drowned out the sound of the singing. In a few minutes they had gathered songbooks, shawls, and bonnets and gone chattering downstairs. As the last one vanished, Vernie gave a sigh of relief and closed the door with a tiny slam. "Thank goodness, now we can dress in peace."

"You've still got me," Susan said wryly.

"Oh, you're like one of the family," Katie assured her. She had changed and, going to the dresser, was beginning to take down her hair.

"That Dan B's Mary!" Clarie broke out.

"What's wrong with her?" Katie asked with assumed indifference.

"She makes me sick," Vernie said.

"Me, too," echoed Clarie.

"I can't say I'm head over heels about her," Susan added.

"Who is?" sniffed Vernie.

"Fannie Yoder," Katie replied.

"Mose Yoder must like her," Clarie put in. "He's still going steady with her."

Katie avoided their eyes. She knew that each of the others

was secretly wondering whether she cared. She didn't want to talk about that.

"She looks like a milk soup, but she's got a barbed tongue," Susan said in her customary dry voice. "You should have heard her last Sunday evening at Henry Yoder's before the singing. On second thought, it's a good thing you didn't!"

"What did she say?" Vernie asked mischievously. "Did she talk about us?"

"And how!" Susan rejoined. "She laid you girls wide open."

"I'll bet it would have been fun to hear it," Clarie grinned. "I suppose Lydie Dan's girls are the fanciest, worldliest girls among the young folks."

"Yes, you are. She didn't know for sure which was the worst. Vernie, here, is as green as grass. Katie is positively wicked, and Clarie does nothing but giggle and cut up through the singing."

"Wow!" Vernie exclaimed. "What else?"

"Your dresses are too short and you pick the fanciest colors!"

"Huh, who'd want the colors she chooses?" Vernie said spitefully. "Old mustard green and odd blues and rusty browns that make her look more like a milk soup than ever."

"What did you say?" Clarie asked.

"It took me by surprise when she started. She knows we're good friends; so she must have realized I'd tell you about it."

"She probably wanted you to," Vernie cut in.

"I expect. Anyway, I told her I liked the colors you choose. She shut up after that."

"Good for you," Katie told her.

"I think it's time we went down," Vernie observed, taking her hymnbook from the dresser and giving her covering a final pat. "By the sound of it, everybody is down there but us."

"I'm ready," Clarie was at the door, waiting for the others.

"I am too," Katie said. "Oh, I forgot. Susan, before we go down, I'll get you that embroidery pattern you asked for."

"We're going down." Vernie said, her hand on the door with Clarie's. "You come when you're ready."

Katie reached up to the closet shelf, pulling down the box of patterns.

"I'm going to work for Dan Gingerichs this summer," Susan said when Katie had come back with the box.

"You are!" Katie paused. "How does that happen?"

"Dan asked me. He really does need help. He can't take care of Mandy alone, and Emery Altie must stay off her feet. She'd been helping Dan."

"What if he gets put in the ban?"

"As far as I'm concerned, the ban won't make any difference. You know Dan isn't doing anything worthy of punishment," Susan said staunchly.

"I know."

"I'm not going to pay any attention to it."

The two went downstairs. Every little nook and cranny was filled with singers; the only places Susan and Katie could find were in the kitchen with Mom and Pop and the little girls.

As she leafed through the pages of the hymnbook, trying to find the song, Katie's mind was on Dan B's Mary. Her lips curled into a sarcastic smile. "So Mary openly told people Lydie Dan's girls were worldly. And fancy. And Katie was wicked. Yet, Mary had pretended to be so friendly tonight! Two-faced little snake in the grass!" she thought unkindly. Hot anger surged through her. "Mary, Henry Ellie, Henry--the whole church--pretend piety and self-denial. They fuss about loving the rules and traditions of the church, professing to obey God, but they don't believe what the Bible says! And when they do have a member such as Dan Gingerich who honestly wants to obey Christ's teachings, they belittle and ridicule him! What is far worse, they reject his Scripture-based counsel and threaten to put him out of the church." Katie was angry. "Were I of age and my own boss, I'd leave the church before next Sunday," she thought determinedly.

*   *   *

When Dan Gingerich was put out of the church at spring counsel meeting, Katie thought she couldn't bear its self-righteous intolerance until she was twenty-one.

All the old differences between herself and Mom were stirred up. Mom, strongly on the side of those who had worked for Dan's excommunication, maintained that only by ousting the heretics could the church resist the forces of change. For change it would be, were the church to adopt Dan's views!

Condemned in her own home and regarded with suspicion by the church, Katie was unhappy. But even more distressing was the feeling that a veil had dropped between herself and Christ. No longer did He seem near enough to touch.

Every time she opened her Bible or picked up a bit of Christian literature, she read something about loving one's enemies. "Love my enemies! Love those who reject the very things that mean life itself," she thought. "No, I can't love those who flatly reject the teaching of Scripture rather than give up their own traditions! How could anyone do that?"

Katie passed her twenty-first birthday and became officially of age. She went to Will Yoder's for the rest of the summer and early fall. Katie liked to work for Will and Barbrie. Even though they were content to stay with the church, they took a firm stand for the authority of the Scriptures over the traditions of the church. When Katie mentioned leaving as a way out, Will shook his head decidedly.

"If everyone who feels as we do would leave, who would be left to tell them?" he said.

It was a new thought to Katie. Perhaps she had been too hasty in thinking of leaving. At least she hadn't made the actual break. For the time being she put it off.

One Sunday evening in early fall Barbrie said, "You're too young to stay at home all the time, Katie. You haven't been to a singing more than twice since you came to our place. Will will take you to Yoder's and, if you do not get a way home, you may stay at Will's folks overnight. Will can pick you up in the morning. It is only two miles."

Katie, glad for a chance to be with the young people, consented to Barbrie's plans.

"Hi!" Katie cried delightedly to Susan after the singing. "I was afraid you wouldn't be here tonight."

"I was thinking the same about you," Susan said. "If I wouldn't have seen you tonight, I would have written you a letter. Let's go outside so we can talk. What have you been doing with yourself?"

"Working," Katie answered vaguely. "How are you doing at Dan's?"

"I'm doing fine, but I'm not going to be there much longer. That was one reason I wanted to see you. Do you suppose you could work for Dan this winter?"

"I suppose I could," Katie answered slowly. "But what are you going to do?"

"I just knew you'd ask," Susan laughed. "I was going to tell you, but don't you dare tell it further. Edna and Lewis are getting married on Thanksgiving and Mom wants me to come home a week or so before to help get ready for the wedding. Then afterward, Lewis and Edna and the folks are going to Florida for the winter. They want me to stay home to help Andy take care of things."

"I'm not surprised. About Lewis and Edna, I mean," Katie said. "I've been expecting they'd get married; Lewis will be twenty-two in February. It's unusual for a fellow to wait that long! Won't he be eligible to take his two years of service?"

"Yes. If he does, Edna's going with him."

"But about working at Dan's, I don't know," Katie said slowly.

"You haven't promised anyone else, have you?" Susan asked quickly.

"No. I'm staying with Wills until the first of November. I had an offer or two, but I haven't promised anyone yet."

"Then, why don't you go to Dan's?"

"I could, I guess. The only thing is, I don't know how good

a nurse I'd make," Katie said.

"Oh, don't let that bother you. Dan helps a lot, and his wife is not hard to take care of--I mean not grumpy or complaining. I'm sure you'd like it," Susan assured her. "You'd have spare time after the fall work. You might have to help Emery Altie one day a week, but she's easy to work for, too."

"Do you like it there?" Katie asked.

"I love it," Susan said slowly. "If it weren't that the folks want me at home, I'd stay. Dan is such a kind, jolly person, you'd have to be an awful grouch not to get along with him. And, then, I found out that I loved the nursing," Susan spoke more slowly. "In fact, I love it so much I've been thinking of taking some kind of nurse's training and make my living that way."

"Nurse's training!" Katie exclaimed. "How could you take nurse's training? You didn't go to high school!"

"Just for practical nursing. I discovered a correspondence course," Susan said. "That's enough for me. I could get plenty of work around here, if I were a practical nurse."

"Taking care of baby cases," Katie laughed. "You'd be nurse and hired girl both."

"I wouldn't have to take those cases. There are plenty of others. But I like babies; so I wouldn't mind caring for them."

Katie looked at her friend with new respect. "You're brave," she said.

"I've already written to a correspondence school and asked for literature. I should hear this week," Susan said.

"What about having Dan in the ban? Doesn't that make things unhandy?" Katie changed the subject abruptly.

"I don't pay any attention to it." Susan said stoutly. "That man didn't do anything worthy of the ban and you know it."

"I agree," Katie assured her. "I just wondered if you ate separately and things like that."

"Oh, well, as far as that goes, we don't eat together, but that's because he feeds Mandy three times a day."

Katie nodded.

"All right, you can tell Dans I'll work for them--just as soon as they want me."

"I guess that's it," Emery Gingerich said matter-of-factly, setting the last suitcase on the ground beside the loading block. "Two big suitcases, one little one, a shopping bag--"

"And a box or two, my chore coat, and my overshoes," Katie finished with a grin. "You can be glad I travel light."

"Travel light!" Emery echoed. "What do you call traveling heavy? You're as bad as Altie is when we go to Colorado. What happened to that big trunk you used to have?"

"It was handed down to Clarie," Katie grinned again. "It was Pop's old one. I'm on my own now; so I had to buy my own baggage."

"Hello. So you got here!" came the voice of Dan from the porch. They both turned toward him.

"Yes, I'm here." Katie smiled at him. "Emery was just looking forward to bringing in my suitcases."

"I guess I was," Emery said dryly. "I'll have to tie up my rig first."

While he tied the horse to the hitching rack beside the gate, Katie picked up the shopping bag, her coat, and a box, and started for the house. Dan came down the walk to greet her and took the small suitcase and her overshoes.

"Just take them on into the kitchen," he told Katie. Seeing her hesitate at the door, he said, "Wait, I'll show you where to put your things."

She stood aside to let him pass into the kitchen. Following after him, she put her bundles down on a chair beside the table.

"Well, well, so it gives a wedding!" Dan began genially.

"Yes, it does. I was expecting it all fall," Katie answered.

"I suppose you've already got a seat for it," Dan said.

"Not officially yet. Last night Edna did tease me about being sure to choose the right present for her. I expect Lewis will be here today or tomorrow."

"I told Susan she'll have to dance on the hog trough now-- what with her younger sister marrying first!" Dan chuckled.

"You aren't the only one." Katie laughed. "Poor Susan. Everyone was teasing her about that last night. It's a good thing she doesn't get mad easily."

"Yes, Susan's a pretty steady girl. We might just as well take your things upstairs. Here comes Emery with your suitcases."

Katie went swiftly to open the door for Emery. They followed Dan upstairs to a bright little room at the head of the stairs. "Here you are," Dan threw open the door. "Just make yourself at home. I think I'd better see how Mom is getting along."

"All right, I'll be down in a minute, too," Katie assured him.

After the two men had gone downstairs, Katie took off her bonnet, put it on the dresser, and threw her shawl across the bed. Susan had left everything in perfect order; the curtains freshly laundered, the bedding clean.

Opening one of her suitcases, Katie took out an everyday apron and a handkerchief. After she had unpinned the apron she was wearing, she tied the other around her slim waist and peeked into the mirror to be sure her covering was adjusted properly. Then, tucking the handkerchief into her pocket, she went downstairs to begin her work.

She heard Dan and Emery in the bedroom with Mandy. Going softly to the bedroom door, Katie stood quietly awaiting recognition.

"Here she is, Mom," Dan turned toward her.

201

Hesitantly Katie went to the bed. Mandy muttered something and slowly held out a shaky left hand. Katie gently took it in her own limber hands.

"How are you?" Katie smiled.

Again there was the unintelligible mutter. Katie raised quick eyes to Dan in an unspoken question.

"She's a little better," he said cheerfully. "You can talk now, can't you, Mom? You couldn't talk that much two months ago."

A faint glimmer of a smile lit up Mandy's drawn face. It was easy to see that she was completely paralyzed on her right side. Katie's heart contracted with pity. That one so active as Mandy had been should now be so completely helpless seemed hard to understand. She gave the gnarled hand, still cradled in her own soft ones, a gentle squeeze, and laid it on the bed.

"I'll try to take care of you the best I know how," she assured Mandy. "I'll see if I can do as well as Susan did."

"Oh, we're not afraid of her, are we, Mom?" Dan assured Katie.

"Naw, you needn't be," Emery, who had been a silent bystander, spoke up. "If Katie does as well here as she did when she worked for us, you won't have anything to worry about."

Katie gave him a surprised, grateful look.

"I'd better go on home," Emery went on. "Altie's having dinner ready early so I can get out and shuck corn again this afternoon. Take care of yourself, Mom," he turned to his mother. "And make Katie behave."

"I always do," Katie laughed.

"Speaking of dinner, reminds me," Katie turned to Dan. "Do you tell me what you want or shall I do the planning?"

"I'll take you out to the kitchen and you may make yourself at home," Dan said. "That's what Susan did. I'm sure you can find plenty of things to make. If you want something we don't have, we'll go to town for it."

She followed him out to the kitchen, her quick eyes taking in the cheery living room. The windows sparkled and the white

202

half-curtains hung in starched folds. Susan had mentioned finishing fall work, but Katie saw nothing that needed finishing --at least not in the house.

Before the week was up she felt as though she had been there a long time. Dan was a cheerful, jolly employer, and, as Susan said, you would have had to be critical indeed, not to get along with him. Mandy, even though she could barely make her wants known, had a twinkle in her eye.

Mandy's painful cooperation at bath time wrung Katie's heart. The first time Katie bathed her alone, Katie's fingers were all thumbs and she almost spilled the basin of water. Once Mandy tried to say something, and Katie, not wishing to admit she couldn't understand her, said humbly, "I'm being terribly clumsy and stupid, aren't I?"

Mandy muttered something unintelligible and slowly reached out a trembling hand to Katie's strong, steady one. Katie smiled and gave it a light squeeze. By the time she had tucked in the last corner of the bedding, given the pillow a final pat, and buttoned Mandy's nightgown, Katie felt as though she had finished her greatest achievement.

Picking up the soiled sheets from the floor and gathering up the basin, wet washrag, and bath towel, Katie turned to leave the bedroom. At the door she almost ran into Dan.

"Are you done already?" he asked in surprise. "I ran out on you, didn't I?"

"Oh, I got it done," Katie assured him.

"I really intended only to mail the letter, but when I got out to the mailbox, John Gingerich came along and I got to talking--"

As Katie had predicted, Lewis stopped in to invite her to the wedding, and before she knew it, the wedding day was upon them. Katie finished her work early, even preparing food for Dan to heat for dinner and supper. A cousin, Earnest Miller, stopped in for Katie. It was a big wedding and a gala day. At noon Lewis's older brother, Perry, and Susan had little hog troughs beside their plates. No one seemed to know how they had gotten there, but everyone thought it a huge joke. Susan filled them with salted peanuts and mints and passed them to the bridal party.

That evening Katie was chosen by Lester Gingerich, a cousin of Edna's, to be his supper companion. As he was barely sixteen and terribly shy, Katie knew he had been asked to do so by Edna, partly to spare him the humiliation of picking out a girl for himself and partly because she wanted Katie in the wedding party. Since she had quit Mose, Katie had not been dated. "Boys have been the least of my worries," she thought, amazed at her discovery. "If God wants me to have a husband, I guess I'll get one. If He doesn't, I am better off as I am."

*   *   *

"But won't they get after Mandy for taking something from your hands?" Katie asked lightly during her first month of work. Seeing the look in Dan's eyes, she bit her lip in shame. She was filling the dinner tray, and Dan had ambled out to the kitchen to talk until it was ready to take into the bedroom.

"I don't know," Dan said simply. "I can't let the opinions of the church stand in the way of serving someone who needs it."

"It's not fair!" Katie burst out hotly. "They put you in the ban because you serve God and then turn around and overlook their own sins of disobedience and self-righteousness."

"There are a lot of things that aren't fair in this world, Katie. I don't suppose it was fair when Christ was made sin for us."

"I know."

"And besides, as long as I am doing what the Word of God tells me to, the ban really doesn't hurt me. I'm not banned from God."

"How can you stand it, though? Why don't you leave the church?" Katie cried.

Dan walked to the window and looked out across the fall landscape with unseeing eyes. Katie watched him for a moment and then went back to dishing gravy and mashed potatoes, half afraid she had said too much.

"It's hard for a younger person to understand, I guess," Dan answered at last. "If I were young, I'd probably consider leaving the church. But as far as material things are concerned, I'm satisfied. I don't mind driving a horse and buggy and doing without electricity and a telephone. And I don't farm; so I don't need rubber-tired machinery. I realize those things tempt a younger person more. And my family is grown and they've made their choice whether to go or stay; so I don't feel any responsibility to them," he stopped.

Katie was silent.

"And as far as dress is concerned, I don't mind the rules of the church. I'm too old to change that anyway."

"Younger people don't think like that, though," Katie said.

"That's true. But, when they get to be my age, they'll see that clothes aren't the main issue."

"I think I see that already."

"I've noticed that. That's one reason why I'd hate to see you leave the church."

"Me? Who said I was leaving? Besides, to hear some people talk, the church would be better off without me," Katie said with a touch of bitterness. It was hard to forget what Dan B's Mary and Henry Ellie were saying.

"Don't think things like that. I know it hurts when people say unkind things about us, but really, the church doesn't realize what a blessing it has in young people like you and Susan."

Katie felt ashamed and humbled. While she was ready to retaliate, Dan was kind and forgiving to the very ones who had hurt him most.

"If you think the church has a blessing in people like me who get mad and bitter when they're called heretics, what do you suppose it has in people like you who truly forgive your enemies?"

"Oh, well --"

"How can you do it?" she burst out. "How can you love those who say you're a heretic? I haven't been able to do it."

"Ah, Katie, I thought you were having that trouble--"

"I expect I show it in everything I say about them," Katie cut in. The tray was ready to take in, but she was loath to stop talking.

"No, no. It's not that bad. But you asked how I do it. I don't alone."

"I know, Christ gives us grace to do it," her voice was a shade impatient.

"He does, but that's not what I was going to say right now. I couldn't forgive them if I didn't love them."

"How do you get to love them?" Katie asked.

"I haven't been learning that just in the last eighteen months, Katie. That is something I've been growing into the last thirty years."

"You mean it's a gradual process?"

"It was for me. It may not be that way for everybody."

"You're not talking about the new birth or being saved?" she asked uncertainly.

"No, no. Don't get me wrong. I realize there comes a definite time when you enter into the spiritual life, but what I'm talking about is something else. Let's call it growing in the Lord, or growing in the Christian life. When I was younger I felt like you say you do. When someone crossed me, I had a hard time forgiving him. The Holy Spirit showed me that I wasn't going to grow in the Lord, if I let it get the best of me."

"How did He show you?"

"Well, every time I read the Bible, I'd read something about forgiving one's enemies, or if I read a Christian book or paper, invariably it would be on the same thing."

"That's the way it is with me right now," Katie confessed. "What did you do then?"

"I didn't have peace until I went to the people I felt bitter toward and confessed it. After that I found I had a compassion and love for them that would have been impossible before."

Katie was silent. How hard such a path would be! Could she bring herself to go to Dan B's Mary and Henry Ellie and Henry and Mom and Bishop Eli and confess the bitterness she felt toward them? Every fiber of her being shrank from it.

"That's why I can love the church now," Dan went on. "I had to empty my heart of bitterness all these years so Christ could put His love in it for just this situation. The church really isn't hurting me. It's hurting itself--and God pities it. I forgive it, but, oh, how it needs the very thing it's rejecting. His voice cracked.

Katie aimlessly fumbled with the tray, close to tears. Her own hurts already seemed of less importance.

"Here, let me take that tray. Why didn't you tell me things were ready? I wouldn't have gone on talking." Dan came back to prosaic facts abruptly.

"I wanted to know," Katie said. "I expect everything's cold again. Let me warm it."

"No, I'll take it this way. At least, I'll not be burning Mom's tongue today."

OH, it was hard for Katie to follow Dan's sound wisdom! More than once that winter she was ready to go to those toward whom she felt bitterness, but each time she was on the verge of going, she drew back. In the rare times she went to the singing, Katie's heart would prod her all evening to tell Dan B's Mary she was sorry she felt bitter toward her, but at the last moment her mind won. "It doesn't suit," she would decide. Or she couldn't get Mary alone, or Mary wasn't there. And each time she put it off, she hated herself more and more for her cowardice.

And, if the thought of going to Mary who was her equal was hard, the thought of going to Mom and Henry and Ellie and Bishop Eli was ten times harder. Especially Bishop Eli. Each time she thought of speaking to him, she seemed to shrink and shrink until she was barely a foot high and Eli loomed bigger and bigger, his look of outraged self-righteousness staring her down.

"No, it was asking too much. Besides," she would argue with her persistent heart, "it wasn't as if she had begun it. Why should she go to these who had wronged her and said spiteful things about her? They were the ones who were in the wrong."

"Oh," but her heart persisted, "they may be in the wrong, but the thing you need to get rid of is your hot anger toward them and bitterness that keeps you from seeing them as people for whom Christ died."

"Let them go to ruin," she thought darkly. "You can't tell them anything. Let them come before the judgment with nothing but their traditions and rules. Let them try to achieve perfection by doing without cars and modern conveniences and see if I care. If they won't believe it if someone tells them that works of righteousness won't save them, they have no one to blame but themselves."

She had looked forward to reading Dan's books, but as the weeks went by, she picked the books up less and less. "All they talk about is loving your enemies and not being bitter toward them," she thought petulantly. "I'd just like to put someone like Moody or Torrey or Isobel Kuhn in my place and see if they could love my people!"

At other times she thought of Christ and dissolved into hot tears. "My people think I have an erroneous faith and all I want to do is live for Christ. It isn't fair."

Whenever Christ was nearest, her one desire was to please Him. When someone like Dan B's Mary or Mom or Henry Ellie claimed her thoughts, she felt mean and guilty.

One Sunday after Sunday school reorganized for the summer, Katie brought Susan along to Dan's. The two church districts were merged into one for the use of the Sunday-school house; consequently on alternate Sundays the two girls saw each other.

Susan helped Katie make dinner and wash the dishes.

"How long are you staying on?" Susan asked, after they were comfortably settled upstairs.

"I don't know. As long as they need me."

"How is Mandy?"

"I think she's getting a little better. At least we can get her out on a chair in the morning when we change her bedding."

"Do you like nursing?"

"Oh--" Katie answered slowly. "I like the satisfaction I get from knowing I'm helping someone who needs it, but--"

"But you aren't crazy about nursing?" Susan finished for her.

"Not nursing for the sake of nursing."

"Well, I am," Susan said. "I love it. Just nursing for its own sake. But to you it's a means of doing something for others, is that it?"

"Something like that," Katie admitted. "I don't suppose I'd care for it, if it weren't that I know Mandy needs it. Then, too-- well, how can I say it? I feel that I can serve Christ that way," she finished hesitantly.

"You make me ashamed," Susan broke the silence. "I never gave that a thought--I mean serving Christ that way. I like nursing so well I was just thinking of my own pleasure in it."

"You're the better nurse, though," Katie assured her loyally. "You can keep your wits about you and nothing flusters you. Girls like that probably make the best nurses."

"I hope so. But why don't you take the same course I'm taking? Maybe you'd find it just as interesting as I do. You'd

209

have plenty of time to study here at Dan's."

"Oh, I could, I guess. I never thought of it. Is it very hard?"

"Not that hard! You could pass it just as easily as I do," Susan assured her.

"Give me the address, then, and I'll write for information," Katie said. "But I won't promise I'll go all the way with it."

"Well, I am," Susan vowed. "I'm going as far as I can."

"What do you mean?" Katie asked.

"I've been thinking lately that I might try to get a job in one of the hospitals in the city."

"Oh, Susan! Not really!" Katie gasped at such daring. "What would the church say?"

"I expect some people would say plenty. But why couldn't I work in a hospital? Our people like hospitals as well as anybody else when they get sick. I can't see anything wrong in working there. A lot of girls from Poplar Hill work there," Susan pointed out.

"That's different. They're on the wrong track anyway; working in a hospital can't make it any worse!" Katie laughed.

"Sez you," Susan retorted. "Well, anyway, I'm going to apply for a job, I think. I've got a job in town with an old lady, but as soon as I'm not needed there, I'm going to try to get into the hospital."

"I wish you luck," Katie told her. "I hope the church doesn't kick up too much."

"Let it kick. There are more churches."

"Don't tell me you're getting thoughts of changing churches?" Katie asked in surprise.

"I don't know what I'll do. If it gets too bad, I might do just that. Lewis and Edna are going to."

"No, not really!"

Susan nodded.

"What in the world will Aunt Fannie say? The first of her children to leave the church!"

"I don't suppose she'll like it, but there's nothing she can do

210

about it. Didn't you know Lewis was dissatisfied?"

"No. Oh, I knew he had everything the church allowed but--" Katie's voice trailed off into silence, her mind's ear hearing Aunt Fannie's jolly, chuckling laugh. It would probably have a touch of heartache in it now, if one of her children left the church.

"He's been talking of going for a year at least. In fact, he would have joined Poplar Hill before their marriage, but Edna wanted an Amish wedding. She told him if he'd wait, she'd leave the church without a fuss after they got married."

Katie was silent, digesting this. "All around me people are leaving--and I still hang on," she thought. "Why? Why, when I am so dissatisfied it seems unbearable to think of staying? Last year I vowed to leave as soon as I was of age, but as yet I've made no move to go!"

She asked herself the same question all that spring. Spring counsel meeting came again, and once more left her heartsick and disgruntled. Nine members of her church were accepted as members at Poplar Hill. Bishop Eli thundered louder than ever against the lust of the flesh. Other bishops and ministers shook their heads and wondered when people would accept exhortation and turn from their erring ways.

In the two weeks between counsel meeting and communion services, Katie daily battled with herself. One minute she would be seething with anger and bitterness; the next she was ashamed and contrite. Above all, she loathed herself for her cowardice in not going to those toward whom she felt most bitter and humbly confessing her fault. Several times she was on the verge of taking a day off and going to see Henry and Ellie and Dan B's Mary and Bishop Eli, but each time she weakly put it off. Before she knew it, communion services were upon them.

To her surprise, Dan announced his intention of going.

"You!" Katie exclaimed. "After all the church has said and done to you! You wouldn't be allowed to partake anyway."

"I know," Dan's voice held a touch of pathos. "I'm going anyway. If I stay at home, everyone will think I'm sulking. It

211

might be that someone will turn to God, if they see me there as usual."

"You make me ashamed," Katie said humbly. "If the people of the church did to me what they did to you, I'd have a hard time showing up in the services just once, let alone being there as often as you can. Especially communion services."

"Oh, well—" Dan avoided her eyes. "Christ gives me the grace to do it."

Katie sighed. "I'm afraid I'd have to have a lot more grace from Him than I've had so far before I could do as you do."

They drove to church that morning in silence. Two weeks before, on counsel meeting day, Emery Altie had stayed with her mother-in-law. Today she wanted to go to communion; so Will and his wife, members at Poplar Hill, had volunteered to be there. Katie and Dan would stay until after the services in the late afternoon.

The bishop of that district, Dave Miller, was one of Bishop Eli's staunchest followers, and it was no surprise to see Bishop Eli in church. Katie, seeing him stalk majestically toward the house as they drove up to the gate, felt her heart sink. So they were in for one of his thunderous sermons again.

"If you want to talk with him, here's your chance," her conscience told her as she got down from the buggy. Only half admitting its whisper, she made herself think of other things. She couldn't—couldn't face Bishop Eli!

By evening she felt emotionally sick. There had been so little in the sermon to give her any spiritual help and so much she disagreed with, she almost decided at noon to abstain from partaking of the bread and cup. And yet, by the time the congregation was ready for the passing of the emblems at three that afternoon, she took the morsel of bread and the common cup with the rest of them. Maybe the next time things would be different.

Seeing Dan's gray head among the others out in the living room, Katie felt small and mean and humble. How could he go

212

on loving those who treated him as the church did? Very few people had talked with him in the morning before services, but Dan was invariably kind and gracious to those who gave him only a cold stare and limp handshake. He refrained from going to the kitchen for lunch, since the church was forbidden to eat with him. And yet, he refused to leave them.

"Only God can give a love like that," Katie thought. "If the situation were turned around, and the very people who shun and condemn him were in his place, I wonder how many would take it the way he does?" Suddenly she wanted desperately what he had. If he could have grace from God to love his enemies, she wanted it too. If he could love the church, she wanted to too. If he could be patient and kind to those who stared at him coldly and whispered about him behind his back, she wanted to be, too.

Oh, but it would be a hard thing to follow Dan's counsel on how to attain such love! And yet, it would be worth it. All at once she decided to follow it. For the first time, love like that loomed larger than the shame and humiliation to be gone through to get it. Before another Sunday she was going to every one of those people she felt especially bitter toward and ask their pardon.

*   *   *

Her voice was quiet and subdued the next morning when she asked to take the rig and see some people.

"Why, sure," Dan said heartily. "Anytime you want the rig, just say so."

"I'll plan an early dinner, then I'll leave after that," Katie said diffidently, avoiding his eyes. "I don't think I'll be back until suppertime."

"Something is bothering her," Dan thought. "She has been too quiet all last night and this morning. I wish she would tell me what is wrong. We all have our troubles," he mused. "Young or old, we all have trials we can't understand."

After she put the last touches to the kitchen and checked that there was nothing more Mandy needed, Katie went resolutely upstairs to get ready for the afternoon. Now that she had definitely decided her course, a detached calmness possessed her. There was no more shrinking away; she had done all that before.

As she jogged slowly through the fertile countryside glistening with spring sunshine, she planned her route for the afternoon. She would go to Bishop Eli's first. "I might as well meet the giant when I'm freshest," she thought shakily. "Then I'll cut across and stop at Henry Yoder's. From there I'll go down to Andy Miller's where Dan B's Mary is working. Then home," she thought slowly.

She sighed. Next to Bishop Eli, it would be hardest to face Mom. Bishop Eli might loom large with all the authority of a church leader, but Mom loomed almost as large with all the years behind her when she had been Katie's sole authority.

As Katie drove up to Bishop Eli's hitching rack, the screen door flew open divulging half a dozen children. In spite of the seriousness of her errand, Katie grinned when she saw boys of all ages come tumbling and wrestling down the lawn toward her.

"What's going on, boys?" she called. Abashed and grinning, they gathered around her, tucking in shirttails and making wild swipes at disheveled hair.

"Hi, Katie," David was the first to speak.

"I see you fight just as much as you did when I worked here," she said with pretended severity.

"Aw, we weren't fighting," David protested.

"Yeah, we were just playing," Paul, the youngest, piped up.

"It looked like fighting to me," Katie laughed. "Is your dad here?"

"No, he and Mom went to Indiana," David informed her.

"To a funeral," Daniel added.

"They left this morning. They found out about it last night," David said.

Katie nodded. "How long are they staying?"

"Dad said over a week," Paul said importantly.

"Yeah, he said if communion is over out here, they might stay until the next church Sunday," Jerry added.

214

"So he will be gone almost two weeks. What shall I do now?" Katie wondered. Aloud she asked, "Are you boys alone?"

"Naw, we've got the hired girl," David answered.

"Oh, I forgot. Fannie Yoder is working for you, isn't she?"

"Yeah, and I don't like her," small Paul said. "She's not as good a hired girl as you were."

"Oh, is that right?" Katie laughed. "Why not?"

"She's bossy," Paul explained.

"I should think that's what you'd need," Katie laughed again. "The way you were acting when I drove up."

"Yeah, and she wants Edward for a boy friend," Daniel put in.

"Oh, she does?" Katie raised her eyebrows. "How do you know?"

"Shut up," David gave him a shove with his elbow. "Mom said you weren't supposed to tell."

"David Hershberger, you quit that," Daniel flared up, flying at David with clenched fists.

"Boys, stop your fighting. Daniel, quit that!" Katie's voice had a needed ring of authority. Daniel subsided with only a glare at David.

"If your dad's not here, I'll go on," Katie said in a quieter voice.

"You'll have to come back later on," Paul said. "Come and work for us again sometime."

"If I do, I'll be bossy, too," Katie warned as she turned back to the hitching rack to untie her horse. "You'll think I'm worse than Fannie."

"Huh-uh," Paul shook his head. "You weren't the other time."

She untied her horse and backed away from the hitching rack. Getting into the buggy, she gathered up the reins and clucked to her horse.

"Shall we tell Dad you were here?" David asked as the horse began his slow plod toward the road.

"Oh--I don't care," Katie leaned forward to look past the

buggy curtains. "Maybe I'll just write him a letter."

"Good-bye," the little boys shouted and waved when she was out on the road. "Good-bye. Come work for us again."

She gave the horse a brisk slap with the reins and settled back against the cushions, a smile hovering about her lips. "So the boys think I am a better hired girl than Fannie Yoder! Yet, Fannie is one of Eli's staunchest supporters. Only Dan B's Mary is as loyal," Katie reflected.

"But at least God has spared me the trial of talking with Eli," she thought with relief. "It will not be cowardly now to write what I wanted to say. I came with the intention of talking with him; it is hardly my fault if he wasn't there!" Feeling happier, she cut across the section toward Henry Yoder's.

That would be another hard trial. It was too much to expect them to be gone. "They'll probably be hateful enough to make up for missing Bishop Eli," she thought, drawing her shawl around her with a slight chill. "Eli might be terrifying with his arrogant authority, but Henry and Ellie are downright hateful." She visualized Henry's little eyes burning at her savagely.

By the time she had reached their place, she was sick with nervous apprehension. "O God," she prayed as she tied up her horse, "give me the grace to meet them. I'm a coward, dear Lord, and, oh, I dread this."

Making her way slowly to the door, she knocked with more force than she felt. For a long moment there was no sign she had been heard. With wild hope she knocked again. Maybe they, too, were gone. Her hopes were dashed at once. There was a slight stir at the door curtain, then Ellie herself opened the door.

"Oh, it's you," she said without cordiality. "I wondered who would be coming now."

"Yes, it's just me," Katie murmured, feeling ill at ease. How on earth could she say the words in her heart if at the very beginning Ellie showed animosity?

"Come in," Ellie invited her ungraciously. "It's too cold for me to stand out here and talk."

Katie followed her into the house. Her heart seemed to be beating loud enough to be heard by Ellie. Nervously she wrapped her hands in her shawl to dry their clamminess. Around the corner of the dining room door she caught sight of Anna Mae looking at her curiously. Henry was nowhere in sight.

"Take a chair," Ellie shoved one toward her and sank into another one. Folding her hands across her stomach, Ellie sat back in silence. Evidently she was determined to show Katie as little goodwill as possible.

After clearing her throat, Katie began at once. "I came over to make a confession and apology," she began with a rush.

"Oh?" Ellie's voice rose in polite surprise. "For what?"

"For--for feeling bitter toward you," Katie stammered. This was even worse than her worst expectations.

"So? I'm afraid I don't know why you should have felt bitter toward us."

"You know that we disagreed on--on--some things when I worked here the last time," Katie floundered.

"I knew you disagreed with some very important things, yes," Ellie's voice dripped sarcasm. "If you've come over to apologize for some of your erroneous beliefs, I can only say I'm glad you see it at last."

Katie bit her lips. "I didn't come to apologize for any erroneous beliefs--I don't think I have any."

"What did you come for then?"

"I came because I let bitterness come into my heart toward you because we disagreed so much. I know now it was wrong to do that," Katie said evenly.

"Humph!" Ellie spat out. "If that's all you came for, I'd say you're pretty far off yet. As long as you don't make a clean break with your erroneous belief about knowing you're saved and think you know so much more than your elders, your halfway apology for feeling bitter toward us doesn't amount to anything."

Katie stared, her blue eyes dark pools in her white face, the bridge of freckles dark across her nose. "Then you won't accept

217

my apology and forgive me for feeling bitter toward you?"

"You're not ready to be forgiven yet," Ellie said in self-righteous superiority. "When you come and own up you're wrong in your erroneous belief, then you can be forgiven. But not before that."

Katie rose from the chair and started toward the door. "Then I'm afraid you'll never forgive me. I honestly came to confess my bitterness to you because we disagreed, but to come and apologize because I have put my trust in Christ and because I know I'm saved—never. I'd rather die than do that."

"Well—" Ellie shrugged. "You're doing it for yourself."

"I don't think so. Christ has done it for me," Katie's voice was calm and steady. She opened the door and left.

All at once her calmness left her and she began to tremble. How could Ellie have been so utterly unforgiving and self-righteous? Wasn't there ever any doubt in her mind about following the traditions and regulations of the church? Yet, remembering how she, too, had believed unquestioning in traditions only a few years before, a keen stab of pity for Ellie touched her. Perhaps she had been too hard on her. How much would she, herself, agree with Ellie, had not the Holy Spirit led her to study the Bible?

She slapped the reins briskly across the horse's back, trying to get a little more speed. He was fat and old and rather lazy and not used to impatience. Dan always let him pick his own gait, loving the slow drives for quiet meditation. But Katie's meditations were anything but quiet. If she met with antagonism from Mary, it would be hard to go on home and talk with Mom. Besides, at the rate the horse was going, it would be dark before she got back to Dan's.

With nervous dread she approached Andy Miller's homestead. "I must not keep Mary from her work for long," she thought. "Perhaps I can get her to step outside the door for a few minutes, then Andy's wife would be none the wiser."

Turning into the lane, she guided her horse toward the

hitching rack beside the gate. She glanced around the yard and buildings, hoping to see Mary. But there was no one in sight, and she went slowly up the walk toward the house.

"Hello," Mary greeted her in surprise. "What brings you here?"

"I wanted to see you for a few minutes," Katie answered, twisting the fringe of her shawl. "Could you come out so I could talk to you alone?"

"I'm alone in the house," Mary said. "Andy Lydie went to town. Besides, it's too chilly out here. Just come on in."

She held open the door for Katie to pass through, then, closing it, she motioned Katie toward a chair. Katie sat down and hesitantly unloosened her shawl, letting it slip down over the back of her chair. "I came over-- I wanted to see you--" she floundered nervously. "I felt I should come over and apologize to you."

"Oh?" Mary's eyebrows rose in surprise. "I'm afraid I don't know just what you mean."

"I've been feeling for some time that I should talk with you," Katie explained slowly, trying to keep her voice even. "You must know that we don't agree on--on some things. I just wanted to confess that, because of that, I've allowed bitterness to come into my heart against you. I know now that--that God doesn't want that, and so I came over to apologize."

"Oh, I forgive you," Mary assured her in a condescending voice. "I know that we who are strong ought to bear the infirmities of those who are weaker than ourselves. I've often felt sorry for you."

"Sorry for me!" Katie echoed stupidly.

"Yes. You do have such a time denying your self-will. I've often thought that I wasn't thankful enough that I'm not tempted that way."

Katie stared at her, too astonished to find words to reply.

"And then, when Mose and I began going steady, I noticed that you seemed to hate me. But I realized it must have been a blow to have him quit you and go with me right away."

"But I never did like you," Katie thought wildly, and for one awful moment she was afraid she had said it aloud. "Besides, I quit Mose, and he didn't start going with you until six months afterward!" With effort she collected her thoughts, battling a sense of frustration. "It would give me great pleasure," she thought resentfully, "to wipe that holier-than-thou smirk off your face."

She felt a sudden sense of shame. After all, she had come to dispel bitterness, not to cause more.

"Then you can forgive me for--for--everything you hold against me?"

"Oh, yes," Mary assured her with the same maddening superiority. "No, I don't want to hold anything against you. I even feel I should ask your forgiveness for--for going with Mose so soon after he quit you," she blushed prettily.

Katie bit her lip in vexation, thinking, "Why must you harp on that? Evidently it feeds your vanity to believe that you can take a boy away from one of Lydie Dan's fancy girls." All at once Katie wanted to laugh. Suppressing her feelings, she got up and fastened her shawl. "I must get out of here or I'll laugh in your face and undo everything I've done in the last few minutes," she thought wildly. "I guess that's all, then," she said aloud evenly.

"Oh, must you go so soon?" Mary asked. "There's no need to rush off."

"I wanted to go over home a bit, too," Katie was at the door.

"Come back again," Mary invited with a show of cordiality. "I hope I didn't say anything to make you feel bad."

Mumbling something, she didn't know what, Katie let herself out of the house, thankful that Mary chose not to follow her outside. "You hope you didn't say anything to make me feel bad," she thought, her mouth twisting sardonically. "You did, though. I knew you were a self-righteous little prig, but I didn't realize you'd be utterly without shame in letting me know you thought so. You're so glad you're not tempted to be fancy the way I am, but you don't realize how bad off you are!"

As she guided the horse out onto the road again, the giggles she had suppressed broke loose in waves. "Oh, it is too funny! Mary thinks I dislike her because Mose started dating her. Nothing could be further from the truth. Right now, I couldn't care less who went with Mose, as long as it isn't me."

Then the other side of the situation struck her. "How could anyone be so shamelessly self-righteous? Why, Mary was acting like the Pharisee who thanked God he was not like the publican! O God," she prayed, "help me have a broken and contrite heart. Mary is only one of many among my people who have the same attitude." Soberly Katie slapped the reins across the horse's back and gazed with unseeing eyes down the road. "If only I could tell them--if only I could say the right words, the right Scriptures, to show them that unless their righteousness is better than that of the Pharisees, who, too, relied on traditions, they will in no case enter into the kingdom of heaven!"

By the time she turned down the hill toward home, she had almost forgotten why she had come. Only when she saw Mom in the garden, did she realize that she still had to make one more apology. "Will Mom be as hard to talk with as Ellie and Mary had been? If I knew Mom would be, I'd not say anything at all. I can't bear the thought of Mom being as smugly self-righteous as Mary or as violently opposed as Ellie. Oh, please God," she prayed silently, "don't let her be like that."

By the time Katie had reached the hitching rack, Mary Ann and Edna were there to greet her.

"Hi," Edna shouted.

"What brings you home?" Mary Ann wanted to know. "Can you stay for supper?"

"Hi, yourself," Katie smiled, getting out of the buggy and tying up her horse. "I came to see Mom a bit and, no, I'm not staying for supper."

"Mom's out in the garden," Edna said.

"I know. I saw her when I was coming down the road. How

come you aren't choring yet?"

"Edna just got home from school," Mary Ann answered.

"When I was your age--"

"Yes, I know. You used to stop at the library after school," Mary Ann broke in. "You got a licking for it, too."

Katie laughed. So Mary Ann remembered that.

"I'm going out to the garden to see Mom. I still think you girls had better go and start choring."

She started around the house toward the garden, hoping the girls would take the hint and leave her alone with Mom. They hesitated a moment, then Mary Ann turned toward the house.

"Come on, Edna, she's right. It's time we started choring."

Reluctantly Edna followed.

As Katie came toward the garden, Mom straightened stiffly. "Hello," she said cordially. "What brings you home?"

"I wanted to see you a few minutes," Katie spoke guardedly. "I see you've got the garden half full already."

"Yes. Pop plowed it last night and it was too late to plant anything then; so I've been working out here all day."

"I haven't made any garden yet. Emery is supposed to plow it and he's not finished sowing oats. He might get at it tomorrow."

"Oh, so you're planting a garden?"

"A small one. Dan and Mandy don't eat much, but I thought I'd like a garden anyway. Susan had one last year."

"If you can wait a few minutes until I've got these radishes sown, I'll go into the house and we can talk."

"I can wait, but I didn't want to stay long. Here, let me help you plant the radishes. I can make the trench for you," Katie reached for the hoe.

"You've got good clothes on," Mom protested.

"Not that good. Here, let me make the trench."

Reluctantly Mom yielded the hoe, and Katie began making the trench along the marking twine which was stretched taut from one side of the garden to the other. She was careful to make it as Mom had taught her--wide and not too deep, with only

222

soft, crumbly earth along its floor. When she had finished digging, she went back to the other end and covered up the tiny seeds behind Mom's careful sowing.

"There," Mom said, looking over the garden with satisfaction. "Now that's done. Come on, let's go into the house."

She began to gather up her seed box, now nearly empty. Katie helped her, tossing empty seed bags into it. Mom hated the sight of them blowing over the garden and yard. "If I want to say something to Mom, now is the time," Katie thought, taking a deep breath. "Mom--Mom, I wanted to talk to you alone."

"Yes?" Mom looked at her questioningly.

"I just wanted to--that is, I felt I should come and apologize," she broke off.

"Apologize?" Mom echoed.

"Yes, Mom, you know we've had so many disagreements in the last few years."

Mom's face was noncommittal.

"And I'm afraid we still disagree, but I want to confess that--that because of those disagreements, I've felt pretty bitter toward you. It's for that I want to apologize," Katie finished in a rush.

Now that she had said it, she waited with dread for Mom's reaction. Would it be like Mary's or Ellie's?

"I forgive you. I could wish you weren't so stubborn, but--"

Katie felt hot tears in her eyes. "Oh, Mom. I don't want to be stubborn. All I want is to do what God wants me to do. But it seems I've got such a battle with myself--"

"Don't we all?" Mom's voice was unexpectedly sympathetic. "But God doesn't ask us to be perfect; all He asks of us is that we really want to be."

"Well, I want to be--" Katie said with feeling.

"I'm glad of that," Mom said. "I wish that we could agree better. You think I'm strict and all that, but you don't realize I want only what's best for you."

"The only trouble is, we can't agree on what is best," Katie gave a sad, little laugh.

"I guess that's it," Mom's voice sounded tired and old. "Come on, let's go in. It's getting cold out here."

"I can't. I should be getting back to Dan's. It will be dark before I get there the way it is."

She couldn't get away, however, before Mom had taken her into the house and given her some sugar cookies, a piece of fresh beef liver from butchering the day before, and a few sprigs of daffodils from the bed in front of the porch. It was almost time for the crisp, spring twilight to begin when Katie started for Dan's.

The slow, old horse must have sensed that his own barn and manger were at the end of this run, for he picked up his feet and ran faster than Katie had dreamed possible. As he trotted briskly past one homestead after the other, Katie's mind went over the events of the afternoon: Ellie's open hostility, Mary's smug self-satisfaction, but above all, Mom's unexpected sympathy. "Mom will probably never realize how much her sympathy helped my discouraged heart," Katie mused. "And, dear Father," she prayed, "help me to live such a life that will make Mom see Thee in me. And, oh, help me to love Ellie and Mary."

IN July Mandy, who had gained enough strength to sit on a chair, was suddenly stricken with another stroke. Katie and Dan doubled their care of her, but by the end of the month she quietly died.

There were those who shook their heads gloomily and said that this was to be expected. Was not God giving Dan one last chance to repent of his error? If this did not bring him to his knees in solemn repentance, what drastic measures would God use next?

Katie, hearing these, wondered whether to laugh or cry. Knowing Dan as she did, it was hard to imagine anyone who lived more of a life of righteousness and true holiness. She was challenged by his quiet, good will, and total absence of bitterness toward those who said such things. Ever since she had made confessions to Mary, Bishop Eli, Henry Ellie, and Mom, Katie had felt no bitterness toward her people. But love them with the same compassionate love that Dan had--that she could not. She gave up all thought of leaving the church and wondered what Susan was going to do.

After Mandy's funeral Susan spent a Saturday night with Katie.

"I'm not going to take any more," Susan said grimly. "I'm sick and tired of being reprehended for working in the hospital."

"From who? Your folks?"

"Oh, Mom and Pop have said they'd be glad if I would quit for their sakes rather than cause trouble, but no, it's not them."

"Bishop Eli?"

"Yes. And Henry Yoder and Ellie are forever running over to Bishop Eli and egging him on. I honestly think he'd give me a breathing spell between spring and fall counsel meeting, but they won't let him."

Katie sighed. "That sounds like them."

The two girls were up in Katie's room at the head of the stairs. The heat of the day still lingered there, although a faint breeze blew the organdy half-curtains, folded up over the rods to let in more air. From her chair by the south window, Susan faced Katie who had thrown herself across the bed on her stomach, her head propped up by one slender, browned arm. They had left the door to Katie's room and the bottom stairway door open to let the breeze have free circulation. From downstairs they heard the faint creak of a rocker as Dan rocked in the living room. They were silent for a moment, listening to the shrill chirp of crickets in the yard below, punctuated by whispering thuds as some night moth beat against the screen.

"What are you going to do now that Mandy isn't--" Susan changed the subject abruptly.

"I don't know for sure," Katie roused herself from the dreamy state of listening to the night sounds.

"Does Dan want you to keep on here?"

"He doesn't think so. Emerys want him to go with them to Colorado next week, but he hasn't quite made up his mind."

"Oh, so they're still going? I thought they might give it up this year."

"They would, but Emery's hay fever is pretty bad. They would have gone before this, but they didn't want to leave as long as Mandy was sick."

"Are you going to do their work while they're gone?"

"Um-hum."

"What will Dan do when they get back from Colorado?"

"Stay here, I guess. But he told me this morning that I wasn't obligated to stay; he doesn't think he needs anyone. He can eat one meal a day at Emery's and get the rest himself. Altie can easily do his cleaning and washing, no more than there is to it."

"So that means you're looking for another job. Well, you can always get one at the hospital."

"Um," Katie smiled at her. "I have something else in mind."

"What? You don't happen to have a boy friend hidden around somewhere, do you?"

"Susan!" Katie protested. "You know I don't."

Susan chuckled.

"It must be on your mind, or you wouldn't have thought of that." Katie sat up and rubbed her elbow.

"Not me. I'll always be an old maid."

"As far as I know I will, too," Katie answered. "If there's a boy friend around, I've yet to meet him."

"Well, what are you going to do? You sounded so secretive I thought that might be it, but if it isn't, what is?"

"You sound like a tongue twister," Katie observed wryly. Their eyes met and they burst into laughter.

"I'll tell you what I'm thinking of, but for everyone's sake, keep it to yourself," Katie began, after their laughter had subsided.

"You know I will," Susan said.

"Well, this is it. Dan found out from someone that there's an old people's home in the Ozarks that would like to have Amish girls work for them."

"What?" Susan asked in surprise. "I never heard the like."

"They do, though. I thought I might go down and try it," Katie said simply.

Susan stared at her. "How in the world did they find out about Amish girls? There aren't any living down there."

"I know. But it seems they found out about us from someone in one of the western churches. Anyway, someone from Kansas mentioned it to Dan in a letter the other week--some friend of his who's been writing to him for years."

"And you're thinking of going down there?"

Katie nodded.

"For how long?"

"Oh, I don't know. A year or two. Maybe longer if I like it and don't get too homesick."

Susan considered her a moment. "What do you suppose the church will say to that? They might not like that any better than they do my hospital job."

"I don't know what will be said. It seems to me that it's no worse than going to Colorado for the summer or south for the winter and working there. I'll be back at least once a year for counsel meeting and communion. If I stay within the rules of the church as much as I do at home, I don't think that anyone could object."

"Aren't you ever tempted to leave the church? You aren't satisfied with it any more than I am."

"Oh, I can't say that I haven't been tempted," Katie said slowly, rubbing a mosquito bite on her forearm absently. "But

I thought that if I went for a year or two, things might be--"

"Different," Susan cut in. "I don't believe it."

"No, I wasn't going to say that. I thought--that is, I might have a different attitude toward our people."

"Different attitude? You don't mean you'd go back to your old way of thinking--that you have to do as our forefathers--and all that?"

"No, no. I don't for a minute mean that. What I meant was that perhaps, if I were away from them for a while, I'd--well, just feel different. I know that doesn't explain it very well. Anyway, I'm going to keep my membership with the church until I get back."

"Well, I'm not," Susan said grimly. "I'm going to apply for membership at Poplar Hill."

"I wish you God's blessing," Katie said shyly. "If you're really sure that's what He has for you."

"That's nice of you," Susan's voice softened. "I wish you the same in the Ozarks."

*   *   *

By the next week Katie was alone. Emery, who had been suffering agonies of hay fever, hustled the others around to get a hurried start for Colorado. Dan had gone somewhat reluctantly. Emery meant well; he seemed to feel that a change of scenery would lessen Dan's silent grief over Mandy's death. Because it pleased Emery, Dan humored him by going along. With a few last-minute instructions to Katie about what to feed the horse and where to forward mail, they were gone.

Except for washing and putting away the things Mandy had needed during her illness, Katie left the house as it was. If Dan chose to close up some of the rooms, he could do that when he got back. Katie passed the silent hours working in the yard and garden and doing the few chores. In anticipation of her stay in the Ozarks she made a few dresses and coverings.

On Sundays Katie hitched up the slow old horse and went to church and Sunday school. Now that Susan was going to

228

Poplar Hill, Katie missed having one good friend to keep her company.

Driving home from services in September, Katie wished pensively for something to do in the afternoon. There was no crowd for the young folks and no one had invited her home with them. She had thought of inviting Clarie and Vernie out Saturday evening, but as this was their church Sunday, Katie had given that up. Mom disapproved of missing church services unless you had to. Neither could Susan stay with her because she was working on the night shift.

For a moment Katie toyed with the idea of going to Mahlon's. They had had another baby, and as yet Katie hadn't seen it. But, if she went to see Mahlons, she preferred going during the week when her chances of being alone with them were greater. Chances were they would have a houseful of company, for they had so many friends at Poplar Hill, young couples their own age who had left the Amish church.

Slapping the reins across the horse's back in an effort to get more speed out of him, Katie decided there was nothing else for the rest of the day. Somehow the thought made her lonely.

"Oh, this horse is slow!" she complained aloud. It did no good to slap him with the reins. She wished Dan carried a whip. And yet the irony of it made her grin. If there was nothing to do at home and nobody to meet her when she did get there, why hurry? With a sigh she settled back and let the horse pick his own speed. She was sure that it was past one o'clock when she finally turned into Dan's drive and drove up to the hitching post. Thinking she would go in and change before she unhitched, she clambered out of the buggy and went to the horse's head to tie him up.

At that moment a car came down the road, slowed down with obvious intention of turning in, and drove toward her. A glance showed her it was Lewis and Edna with Susan.

"What in the world do you want?" she greeted Susan, as she got out of the car and came toward her.

"What are you doing this afternoon?"

"Nothing," Katie said.

"Good. We came to take you over to the folks with us."

"What for? Are you just lonesome for me or is something special going on?" Katie asked, her hands busy unfastening the tie rein from the horse's bridle and fastening it to the hitching rack.

"Both. But really, there is something special going on. Did you ever hear of Mark Hochstettler?"

"Mark Hochstettler! Who's he?" Katie asked.

"He's Bishop Eli's nephew," Susan explained. "He's from one of the western churches, but the last two years he's been in South America as a volunteer with the Mennonite Central Committee,* helping refugees who have settled in Paraguay. He's giving a talk about it at our place."

"Is he Amish?"

"Yes. But not Bishop Eli's kind," Susan said.

Katie laughed. "I just wondered. I couldn't imagine his kind going to South America. I don't suppose Bishop Eli is going out of his way to welcome him, if he's that kind of Amish."

"No, he isn't. But Mark is related to us, too, distantly, and Pop would like to hear about his experiences; so we decided to invite some people in this afternoon to hear him. Can you come with us?"

"Sure. You'll have to wait until I unhitch and put this horse out in the yard. I haven't eaten anything, either."

"You can eat at our house. We've got all kinds of food left from dinner," Susan told her. "Here, let me help you unhitch."

Lewis got out of the car. "Let me do that," he volunteered.

"Thank you," said Katie. "I'll go in and wash."

"Where do you want the old plug?" Lewis asked, his experienced hands making quick work of unhitching.

"Now, Lewis. Don't make fun of that old horse. He may be slow, but he gets you there. Put him in the back barnyard and

*An overseas relief service committee.

230

push the buggy into the shed. And thanks for unhitching for me."

Susan followed Katie into the house. Glancing at the clock on her way to the washroom, Katie exclaimed in surprise. "What in the world! Is it already a quarter past one? That horse is slow!"

"Get a car," Susan advised.

As she came out of the washroom, hands clean and cheeks flushed with excitement, Katie asked, "Did you say you'd already had your dinner? You must have eaten on the run."

"We did hurry," Susan admitted. "But services at Poplar Hill end at a quarter till twelve and we left right away. Edna and I had dinner ready by the time the folks came home from Sunday school with Mark."

"Oh, was he in Sunday school? I didn't see him, but then, I can't see the boys from where I sit."

"He was there, though."

"Did he stay at your place overnight? I'm ready to go now."

"Yes," Susan answered, as she led the way out to the car.

"Didn't he go to visit Bishop Eli?"

"Oh, yes, he went there the very first day, but evidently he sensed he wasn't welcome; so he came over to our place. His mother and mine are cousins of some sort, black cousins, I think. Pop has been taking him around visiting."

At the car they met Lewis coming back from the shed.

"Hi." Edna greeted Katie as Lewis held the door for Susan and Katie. "I was too lazy to get out of the car. How are you?"

"Fine. I haven't seen you for a long time."

"You know where we live," Lewis told her, backing the car out on the road and turning toward John Gingerich's.

"Oh, I know. But you never invite me," Katie laughed.

"Good friends don't need invites," Edna told her. "Clarie and Vernie were there last Sunday night for supper. Henry brought them and then left; so we drove them over to the singing."

"I haven't seen them for ages," Katie sighed. "I haven't been to a singing since before Mandy got sick the last time."

"You're not missing much," Susan snorted. "Say, I forgot to

tell you that this **Mark Hochstettler** was here when Mahlon and Emma got married. Don't you remember asking me that night who that strange boy was?"

"Oh, you mean he's the one who's here now?" Katie exclaimed.

"That's the one."

"Is he still as odd?" Katie grinned.

"In a nice way. No, really, when you get to know him, you forget about his looks."

"He's such a nice person," Edna put in.

"He's as common as an old shoe," Lewis added.

As they drove into the Gingerich yard, they saw several buggies tied up, with cars also making their appearance. A few men were talking on the front porch. Susan and Edna hustled Katie through the back door and into the pantry.

"I feel as if I were a little kid sneaking," Katie laughed, a chicken leg in one hand and a pickle in the other.

"Sneak all you want," Susan told her. "Here's some pie and a plate and fork. Take all the time and food you want. I'm going to go help Mom get more chairs from upstairs."

By the time Katie had finished eating, Susan and her mother had brought out all the chairs they could find, with Lewis and John and Andy carrying in two benches kept in the unused summer kitchen. Katie made her way slowly toward the dining room where Susan and her mother were having a consultation about where to get more chairs if they were needed. As yet, she had not seen Mark Hochstettler, but a group of men stood in a circle on the porch listening to someone, and Katie surmised that Mark was in the center.

From her chair in the corner of the dining room, Katie noticed a stir on the porch. The circle of men broke up as they began to come into the house to find seats. Katie watched them, automatically noting their identity as they made their way into the living room. Lewis, Susan's brother Andy, Will Yoder (yes, he would be there), even Mahlon.

And then--a strange young man, with deep-set eyes, thin

232

face, Roman nose, high forehead, whom she knew at once to be Mark Hochstettler. Except for an older look about him and more flesh on his thin body, he was the same boy she had seen almost eight years before. "Let's see," she thought, "if he had been eighteen then, he'd be about twenty-six now. I'm twenty-two," she bit her lips in annoyance at her thoughts.

He was directed to a seat by John, who then arose and asked that a song be sung. The congregation joined in the singing; then John arose to read Luke 10:30-37. After finishing the Parable of the Good Samaritan, John asked them to kneel in prayer. When the congregation was seated again, John briefly introduced Mark Hochstettler, then sat down. Mark Hochstettler got up and began speaking.

After that she never looked away. At first, his homely face fascinated her, but gradually she forgot his face and only listened to what he was saying. He described his work for the past three years among refugees from Europe who were struggling for existence in the jungle of South America. Katie felt as if she were an onlooker of that struggle. She suffered with them from the heat, feared with them because of the terrors of the jungle, felt the same hopeless frustration they felt when crops refused to grow. Their hard work brought in only meager returns.

He brought his talk to a close with a plea for more concern for those in need, more compassion for a world who needed Christ, and more devotion to Christ. He had spoken for an hour, but to Katie it seemed only a few minutes. How little she had done for God!

*   *   *

"What did you think of him?" Susan asked after the meeting.

"I never heard anyone like him," Katie said slowly.

Susan looked at her sharply. Katie was downright beautiful. Funny she'd never noticed it before. Then a sudden idea came to her. "Why don't you stay for supper and see more of him?" Susan asked.

"I've got to get home and chore."

"Oh, chore!" **Susan** waved that aside. "It won't take you fifteen minutes to do that. Don't worry about choring."

"How am I getting home anyway?" Katie asked suddenly. "Are Lewis and Edna taking me home?"

"Oh, someone will," Susan was purposely vague. Perhaps she could work things so that Mark could take Katie home, or at least go along. "You stay for supper, and we'll work things out then."

After the crowd had thinned out to only the Gingerichs, with Lewis and Edna and Mark Hochstettler and Katie, they found themselves gathered on the front porch. Mark was talking with Lewis on the steps. Katie, sitting on the porch swing with Edna, was trying hard not to watch them. Susan and her mother had brought out one of the benches which Andy was to carry away, and they both sat down to rest a minute. John was coming back from the summer kitchen with Andy, where they had already taken one bench.

"What are your plans for tonight, Mark?" John asked, breaking into his conversation with Lewis.

"I was thinking of going to the singing," Mark looked up. "There are some boys I'd like to see who will probably be there."

"Where is the singing?" Susan asked. "Does anybody know?"

"I asked around this afternoon," Mark turned toward her. "They told me it was at John Yoder Senior's. Whoever that is."

"Oh, yes, they do have church today," Katie remembered. "They live down in my home district."

"Were you going?" he asked Katie. His deep-set eyes were on her at once.

"I don't have a way to go," she blurted out unthinkingly, and could have bitten her tongue at once. "He will think I'm shamelessly hinting he take me!" she thought, turning pink.

"I'd be glad to take you," he said courteously. "I'll have to have someone go with me, or I'll get lost on these strange roads."

"I couldn't--that is--I have chores to do at home," Katie floundered. She sensed Susan was grinning at her confusion. "I

234

wish I could pinch her," Katie thought.

"Where is your home? I could pick you up there," he offered unembarrassedly.

"I work for Dan Gingerich, about two miles from here," Katie made her voice even and dignified.

"Dan who?"

"Dan Gingerich," John answered for her.

"Not the Dan Gingerich who's been in the ban because of his missionary work?"

"That's the one," John said, while Katie nodded.

He gave her a piercing look of respect. This was no ordinary girl, if she dared to work for Dan Gingerich. Besides, he had never seen a prettier one.

"I haven't introduced you to each other yet," Susan said. "Mark, this is my good friend, Katie Miller; Katie, you know who Mark is."

"Glad to meet you," Mark smiled, his eyes lighting up. He came forward to shake hands, not mentioning that he had already asked Lewis who she was and had been waiting for a chance to talk with her.

"I'm glad to meet you, too," Katie said, getting up from the porch swing. "But how do you know about Dan Gingerich?"

"Those things get around. Even if they live in another locality, people who are interested in mission work find out. Our people, I mean."

"I enjoyed your talk about mission work," Katie said shyly.

"Oh? Well--I'm glad you did, although I don't feel I did much missionary work. Most of the people I worked with have a strong faith in Jesus Christ."

"Are you the only boy of the Amish church who was down there?" Susan asked, joining the conversation.

"No, there was one from the East, too. I stopped to visit him on my way home last spring."

"Do you know any young people here?" Katie asked.

"I remember a few from my visit here eight years ago. Mose

235

Yoder, I believe, was the name of one."

"Dave Senior's Mose!" Lewis said. It was on the tip of his tongue to tease Katie, but a warning look from Edna stopped him.

"Yes, that's the one. Is he married?"

"Not yet," Susan said. "He's going with one of Dan B. Miller's girls, though."

"He'll probably marry this winter," Edna predicted.

"Then there are Bishop Eli's boys. How many are with the young people?"

"Edward and Marvin. And David's just beginning," Katie spoke.

"Edna, it's time we went home," Lewis got up from the porch steps.

"I know. I've been wondering why you didn't say something sooner. Katie, are you going with us?"

"No, she's not," Susan said, determined to keep Katie there with Mark. "She's staying for supper."

"I should go," Katie said, opening the screen door. "I've got those chores to do."

"But Mark should have somebody to go with him to the singing," Susan protested. "I have to work tonight, and no one else is going."

"How are you going to the singing, Mark?" Lewis asked.

"I told him he could have our rig," John answered him. "He can use Andy's old buggy. It's got lights."

Katie came back outside with her bonnet. "I'm ready to go if you are," she told Edna, avoiding Mark's eyes.

"Katie! You don't have to leave so early to do those chores," Susan said. "There's no reason why you can't stay for supper first."

"Yes, there is," Katie, who was already halfway to the gate, called back. "I have to chore and, if you're going to work tonight, you'll have to get some sleep."

Lewis and Edna exchanged knowing looks as they followed her

to their car. **Behind them on the porch Susan gave an exasperated snort, while Mark watched Katie's retreating figure with a questioning look.**

"Are her chores at home really so pressing?" he thought as he waved with the others on the porch as the three left. He stood on the steps for a moment, watching the car disappear in a cloud of dust. Behind him John went into the house to change his clothes, and his wife, with a word about supper to Susan, followed him. Andy had already gone upstairs.

"Where does Dan Gingerich live?" Mark asked Susan.

"You go west half a mile, then north a mile. Then, another half mile west [Susan waved her arm in the general direction] there are two houses, one across the road from the other. Dan lives in the new, little one on the north side."

"Is Dan at home? I'd like to talk to him."

"No, he's not," Susan said regretfully. "He went to Colorado with his son for the fall. That's why Katie has chores to do."

"Is Katie taking care of his wife, too? I thought somebody said she was an invalid."

"She was. She died the other week, though. That's why Dan's son took him to Colorado--to help him over the first shock, I guess. His son has hay fever and goes every fall."

"Is Katie going to keep on working for Dan after he gets back?"

"No," Susan answered slowly, remembering Katie's request that she keep silent concerning her future plans. "I guess Katie has something else in mind."

He gave her a searching look. Such secretiveness could mean only one thing--Katie was planning to marry in the near future. But hadn't she said she had no way to go to the singing? That didn't sound as though--and yet, it could mean her friend was gone even as he had been.

"Who's her friend?" he asked, wondering if it were someone he knew.

"Whose? Katie's?" Susan looked at him in surprise.

He nodded.

"She doesn't have any. What made you ask?" Susan's eyes twinkled.

"I thought--well, you sounded so secretive when you said she had something else in mind--"

"You thought she was going to marry," Susan laughed, finishing his sentence.

"No, Katie has a plan in mind, but it's not getting married. She asked me not to tell anybody. But I'm sure it's a job you'd approve of. Katie wants to work for the Lord the same as you did."

* * *

Mark didn't ask for directions to reach the singing when he set out that evening. If John Gingerich thought it strange, he kept it to himself. Susan might have had suspicions, but, as she had gone upstairs to sleep before she left for the hospital, no one was there to voice any wonder that Mark calmly set out toward the west as though he were well acquainted with the locality.

KATIE washed her hands slowly. The long, empty evening stretched ahead. The cow had been milked, the hogs fed, the hens watered, the eggs gathered, and the cold ones cased, and still the clock showed only a quarter after six. What could she do tonight to make the time go faster? She had been staying at home from the singings most of the summer, but then there had been Mandy to take care of, or Dan to talk to, besides welcoming company who dropped in to visit the sick woman.

She wished she hadn't been so hasty in refusing Susan's supper invitation. Andy would have brought her home on his way to evening services at Poplar Hill had she stayed. It wouldn't be the first time he had been pressed into service for Susan or one of Susan's friends.

What had made her rush off? Her pride? Just because Mark Hoch-- She wiped her hands on the towel and went into the kitchen. She didn't want to think about him. Drawing herself up to dignified five feet five, she stood in the middle of the kitchen and looked about her. At least she could get herself something to eat. She opened the refrigerator door and looked inside, trying to push all thoughts of Mark Hochstettler out of her mind.

But even that didn't help. As she glanced into the well-stocked interior, his story of the refugees flashed through her thoughts. "Hungry, facing famine because of crop failure-- And I have so much," she thought, eyes suddenly wet with tears. "There's so much in this thing that I can't decide what to eat." Suddenly she wanted no food. Pushing the door shut, she leaned against it.

"O God," she prayed, "I've never suffered anything like that. I thought it was hard to take the condemnation of my people for heresy, but I've never really gone hungry and thirsty; I have a place to sleep and plenty of clothes to wear. I've never been driven out of my home in the middle of the night by soldiers. Dear Lord, help me to share with those who have less than I have. And, oh, dear Lord, help me to do something worthwhile for Thee! Something like Mark Hochstettler did."

She wandered aimlessly about the house, coming to rest at last before the bookcase. Her eyes roamed over the titles, trying to decide which book would be interesting enough second reading to make her forget her loneliness. Deciding on a book by Isobel Kuhn, she settled herself in the chair by the library table with its overhead lamp and was soon engrossed enough to lose all sense of time. Every now and then there was the sound of quick hoofbeats and buggy wheels from the road. "Someone going to the singing," Katie thought absently, intent on her book.

She must have been reading an hour, for twlight had already given way to darkness, when she heard another rig come down the road and slow down almost to a stop. She lifted her head at once. Was it turning in? It was. Who on earth was coming to see her? Perhaps the folks had decided to drive the six miles out here. It had been a long time since she'd seen them.

Laying down the book, she crept stealthily to the dining room window and peered out, being careful to stay in the shadow of the living room door so that she couldn't be seen by whoever was outside. A quick glance showed her it wasn't Mom and Pop, or at least if it were, they didn't have the double buggy. Besides, the buggy had lights, and Mom and Pop had nothing but a buggy lantern for their old, single buggy.

The rig made a circuit of the yard and came to a stop at the hitching rack. A young man jumped out.

What on earth! Well! She didn't want to be caught peeking out the window. Slipping through the shadows of .the dining room, she made her way into the kitchen, to the bathroom, through the empty bedroom, and into the living room again, giggling nervously at the picture she made. Then her heart gave a great lurch. Suppose it was Mark Hochstettler. She gasped and clapped her hand to her mouth.

By this time steps were coming up the walk, followed by a knock at the door. Panic overcame her. She couldn't walk calmly out to the door and let him in. The first sight of him would make her do some silly thing like falling over the rug on the porch or holding the lamp so crookedly the chimney would fall off.

A louder knock brought her to her senses. She went through the dining room and out to the kitchen. She could find her way around well enough without a lamp, but she stopped and lit a lamp, carrying it with her to the porch.

240

Shielding the lamp with her hand, she opened the door. "Come in," she said, pushing open the screen door, after she had recognized Mark Hochstettler.

"Did you get your chores done?" he asked.

Katie smiled. "Yes, I did. It didn't take long, but they had to be done."

He nodded. "Did you have something planned for the evening?"

"No!" she replied.

"I thought you might want to go to the singing, too. You said you had no way of going."

So he thought she'd been hinting for a way to go! Humiliation made her hands tremble and the lamp flickered.

"Really, I wasn't expecting to go," she said stiffly, determined to make him realize that she had not been hinting.

For a moment he was quiet, his eyes roaming over the porch. Then they came back to her. "I was hoping you'd care to go," he said simply. "I don't know how to get there, and--"

That put things in a different light. Not stopping to wonder why he hadn't got directions from John, and how he had found his way to her, she said quickly, "Well, of course, if you really want me to."

"I wouldn't have come over if I didn't," he pointed out. "Besides, I wanted to visit with you."

"I will have to get ready."

"Oh, yes. I expected that. I tried to leave earlier, but John and I got to talking--"

She smiled understandingly. He and John would have a lot to talk about.

"Come on in, then," she said, leading the way into the house. Setting the lamp on the kitchen table, she led the way through the shadowy dining room into the living room. Motioning him toward a chair, she turned to go upstairs. "I won't be long," she assured him. "The book I was reading is on the table. Make yourself at home," she invited.

"All right. Where there are books, I feel at home."

"You like to read, too?" she asked.

"Yes. Do you?"

"I love it." Katie's eyes shone.

He nodded. Turning once more to the stairway, Katie opened the door. Their glances met again--hers shy; his the peculiar look she had noticed before. All at once he broke into a smile which lit up his deep-set eyes with an inner glow. "Take all the time you need," he assured her.

She closed the door and sped up the stairs in the darkness, her steps muffled by the rag runner. Up in her room she lit the lamp on her dresser and looked at her face in the mirror. It was flushed with the unexpected happening of the evening. She closed her eyes and rubbed her hands across her burning cheeks. Then, remembering that Mark was waiting, she opened the closet door to get a dress.

In a few minutes she had changed into a good dress, combed back her hair, and put on her good, white covering. Grabbing her light shawl and good bonnet from the closet shelf, she put them on. A deft fling settled the shawl in place. Her hands smoothed down her covering before she put on her bonnet. Picking up her hymnal from the dresser, she blew out the lamp and went downstairs.

Mark was sitting in the chair she had been using, reading the book she had been reading. He glanced up quickly and smiled. "It didn't take you very long. I was just getting to realize how good this book you were reading is."

"It's one of my favorites."

"Have you read any others by her?"

"No. I've wished I could."

"I read a few. They were good, too. What I like about this one is that her problems were much the same as mine—or of any Christian for that matter. Being on a mission field brought them to light quicker, that was all. I expect we'd better go, don't you?"

She nodded, reaching up to pull down the lamp and turn it

242

out. By the light from the lamp in the kitchen they made their way out to the porch. She stopped a minute to turn it down so that she could later find her way in.

He stepped outside ahead of her and shone a small flashlight across the steps so that she could see.

"Problems on the mission field aren't so very different from those at home," Mark said, picking up the conversation as they walked across the lawn. "The only thing is, they're intensified."

"That's what Mrs. Kuhn says," Katie answered. "I never realized it before, though. I thought missionaries never had any troubles with their old natures."

He chuckled. "Many missionaries could tell us that wasn't true."

"Where we are doesn't make any difference; we'll always have a fight with our old nature."

"I've found that out, too." He was untying the horse, while Katie got into the buggy. "When I was in South America, I had the same problems of hate and jealousy and envy and bitterness that plague me here in the States. But then, I've also got the same Lord to help me overcome them."

He got into the buggy and unwrapped the reins from around the whip socket. Clucking softly to the horse, he backed the rig away from the hitching rack and turned toward the road.

"That's the main thing," Katie observed quietly, in answer to his statement. "Jesus said, 'Lo, I am with you alway.'"

"I know. That's what makes life worthwhile. Where do we go from here?"

"East to the north-and-south road, then straight south about five miles, then about half a mile west again."

"Well, we'll get the horse on the track and let him go his way while we talk. He's not a fast horse; so we'll have plenty of time."

"Dan's horse is like that, too."

"How does Dan stand in the church?"

"Just the same."

"You mean he's still in the ban?"

"Yes."

"All because he was missionary-minded?"

"Oh--mostly. I really think that was just an excuse, though. A lot of people didn't like him before that."

"Why? Was he overbearing and self-righteous?"

"No!" Katie was indignant. "Nothing could be further from the truth. It would be hard to find someone who lives a godlier life than he does. Oh, he's got his faults; we all do."

"That was it. He told me he's had the assurance that he was saved for years. Well, just saying something like that to our people is enough to turn them against you."

"I know. We're supposed to keep the traditions of the fathers and do the best we can and hope that God will save us at the judgment."

"Exactly! And yet the Apostle Paul says that we're saved by grace and not by works. In Ephesians."

"Was Dan telling people that through the years?"

"He tried to. Especially to the leaders of the church. The bishop in this district is indifferent more than antagonistic, but Bishop Eli comes over and stirs him up. I hate to say this about your uncle, but it's true."

He chuckled again. "I don't know why being my uncle would make him either better or worse. You talk as though you had had some dealings with him."

"I did. I worked there a year."

He glanced at her, seeing only her dim outline by the rosy reflection of the taillights. "Was he pretty bad?"

"Bad enough. Oh, I'm not saying that I always said the right thing. Looking back, I can see I had more zeal than tact. You might have been able to talk to him, but I couldn't. Even if I quoted Scripture after Scripture."

"I can't tell him either," his voice had a touch of sadness.

"Oh, you tried it, too?"

"I've been trying to for the last eight years--"

"You mean you were already--oh--saved then?"

244

"Yes. When I was twelve years old, I asked Christ to come into my heart and use me as He wanted to," he said simply.

"I only did it a little over three years ago," Katie confessed. "And it's been only since I'm around Dan and his good books that I've never had any doubts about being right with God. For a year or so after I first asked Christ to forgive me for being a sinner, I still thought that the way to please Him was to keep the traditions of the fathers."

"What showed you it wasn't?"

"Well--" she hesitated. "This sounds awful, but working for your Uncle Eli cleared that up quicker than anything else. He kept all of the letter of the law perfectly and--"

"Abused the spirit of it," he finished.

"That's it. He preached the doctrine of humility with the arrogant assurance that he knew all there was to know about interpreting the Scriptures."

"That's a good way of putting it," he chuckled.

"It's true, though. For all his condemnation of high-mindedness he is the proudest person I ever met."

"Ah--you know those things are so tragic!" his voice was deep with compassion. "I know what Jeremiah meant when he said: 'Oh that my head were waters, and mine eyes a fountain of tears, that I might weep day and night for . . . my people'!"

"That's what Dan says."

The horse settled into a slow trot, his hoofbeats muffled by the dust of the dirt road. They had left the gravel and, now that the rasp of the buggy wheels no longer made so much noise, the soft, night noises were a background for their talk.

"How does it happen Dan stays on? Hasn't he ever thought of leaving?"

"He says if he were younger he might consider leaving, but since he is older it is different. He's really content to be Amish. He says he's too old to start driving a car anyway!"

"Maybe the leaders were hoping he would leave."

"I don't know whether they hoped he would, but I think they

245

expected it. That's one of the first things they say when you tell them that keeping the traditions of the fathers won't save them."

"All you want is a car and telephone, and you're trying to justify yourself by the Scriptures," he quoted.

"Yes. You've probably heard a lot of that, too."

"Too much."

"What's going to happen to our people? How can you show them that they have the same sinful nature everyone else does and that getting right with God means trusting Christ instead of keeping the traditions of the fathers?"

"I don't know. I keep thinking of that, too."

Again they were silent. They passed a field of corn, the breeze bearing the rustling of a thousand leaves. There was a harsh grating of the buggy wheels as they crossed a cement culvert. Faint faraway lights twinkled from the homes around the country.

"I've often wondered," Katie began again, "if they put Dan in the ban for doing something the Scriptures tell us to do, what would they do with someone who really got into sin?"

"That would depend on who it was. If it were one of the covering bunch--"

"Who told you about them?" she cried in astonishment.

"Uncle Eli was the first to mention it. He said just enough and put them in a bad enough light to make me believe the opposite of what he was saying. I asked John about it, and he told me."

"Did John tell you he got the tracts that started it?"

"Yes. He said his girls gave them to some more girls, and it went on from there."

"I suppose Bishop Eli told you it was the fault of the covering bunch that the young folks don't get along."

"Something like that," he admitted. "He said that the covering bunch think they're so good that it antagonizes the others. He said that it would be better if those covering tracts had never been passed around. The young folks were using the same method of courtship their forefathers used and why drag in a new way?"

246

Katie gave a despairing little laugh. "You wouldn't think an intelligent person could be so blind, would you? Here's the corner where we turn west."

He guided the horse around the corner and up the hill. There were other rigs ahead of them, and the horse slowed into a walk behind them. Once more they were on a graveled road; the rasp of the wheels made them raise their voices.

"Didn't Bishop Eli ask you to stay there?" she wondered.

"He didn't invite me, although Mattie said I could come and make their home my headquarters."

"She's nice. I feel sorry for her."

"I do, too. But John's wife is related to me, too, and I decided to go there. We'd have more in common."

"When are you leaving?"

"Around the middle of the week."

"So soon," she thought. "Why, I've hardly begun to know you." And then bit her lip, glad Mark couldn't read her thoughts.

There was no more conversation until they turned into the lane. The lights of the house shone out across the lawn, making dense shadows where the trees and picket fence cut it off. He threaded the rig through the yard to the gate and turned the horse so that she could get out of the buggy easier.

"I've only begun to talk," he said. "I'll save the rest for the way home."

"All right. I talked more than you did, though."

"I liked it. Can you find your way into the house?"

"Oh, yes. I've been here before."

A wave of singing enveloped her as she slipped through the back door into the kitchen which was crowded with boys debating where to sit. She put her shawl and bonnet on the table with other wraps. The only other girl in the kitchen waited until Katie was ready to go in and join the singers.

The house was already crowded. They found a vacant place in the dining room. Glancing around, Katie caught sight of Vernie at the singing table in the living room with Clarie on a bench behind her. My, it was good to see them again! Vernie looked up, saw her, raised an eyebrow, and smiled, all the while singing without a break. Katie smiled in return and, as the song was familiar, joined in the singing, too.

There was no sign of Mark. Either he hadn't come in yet, or he had been directed to the bedroom for a seat. Two benches in front of her, Mose Yoder was sitting beside Bishop Eli's Edward and Samuel Yoder, carrying on a conversation--the hum of their voices a discordant note.

She let her eyes linger on Mose for a moment. Edna had predicted he'd marry this coming winter, and Katie expected it, too. He still had the trick of raising an eyebrow and smiling his crooked little smile while he listened, as if what he was hearing was of the greatest interest. His shoulders had filled out the last year, giving his slender body the appearance of strength and bigness. "And yet, there is a dissolute twist to his mouth," Katie thought. "He's taken to smoking and, some whispered, he likes the beer that finds its way to the singings. I'm heartily thankful I broke with him! Especially now that I've met Mark Hochstettler.

"No, no, this will never do!" Katie chided herself. "Just because he invited me to this singing is no sign anything more serious will come of it--even though we found so much to talk about." Determinedly she put him from her thoughts.

*　　　*　　　*

"Did you get to visit with Dave Senior's Mose and Bishop Eli's Edward?" Katie asked lightly as Mark and she were on their way back to Dan's.

"A little bit. It wasn't very satisfactory, though. Most of the time they gave me the impression they were making fun of me."

"I'm not surprised. They probably were."

He considered this a moment in silence. "Eight years ago they both seemed pretty decent boys. But then, they were young and--"

248

"The covering bunch came along and offended them, and they turned wild to get even."

"Is that what people are saying?"

"Some of them. That's what Mose's girl friend says."

"Isn't it funny how some people will blame almost anything but themselves?" he mused. "It's easier than facing the truth. I suppose Mose keeps all the required traditions."

"On the surface, yes. But he's got plenty of things behind people's backs. Things like an accordion and a record player and playing cards. Edward is just as bad."

The moon threw a big elm before them into sharp relief; the light and shadow marbling the horse's back as they approached and passed under. Somebody's late cutting of alfalfa was ripe and pungent with dew, waiting to be put up in the morning.

Katie looked shyly at her companion. The pale moonlight showed only the rugged outlines of his face--the strong forehead and the crooked nose, balanced by the firm jaw line, made his eyes seem more deep-set than ever. No one could call him handsome, but neither could anyone be around him for any length of time and not be impressed by his personality.

"You said you were leaving by the middle of the week," she broke the silence. "Are you going to South America again?"

"No. I might go back later on, depending on where the Lord leads me. But the next thing for me is college."

"College!" she echoed in amazement. "Not really going to college!"

"Why not?" he sounded amused.

"Well, but--I mean, I never--"

"Heard of an Amishman going to college?" he finished for her.

"Well, yes."

"I don't know that I have either, but I'm going anyway."

"What made you decide to go to college?" she asked.

"Oh, seeing so many people who had never heard the

Gospel made me decide to be a missionary, and the mission board I'd go under wants you to have a college education before they send you out. So I decided I'd go to college," he explained simply.

She looked at him with new respect. Except for Dan, no one she had ever before met was a missionary (even an embryonic one). She put missionaries on a higher spiritual plane than ordinary people. Even Isobel Kuhn's book hadn't dispelled the idea that they were more consecrated with less faults than those who stayed at home.

With the new respect for him came also something else--awe, restraint, and a withdrawing. People who were missionaries had given themselves to the Lord. Surely they were better people than she! Mark probably never got impatient with those who disagreed with him the way she did. Did he ever have to go to somebody and ask pardon for bitterness as she had had to? Surely he had conquered that a long time ago, even as Dan, while she still felt impatient with her people whenever a new accusation was made against someone like Dan or John Gingerich.

She made herself small in her corner of the seat. In the light of her own meanness and faults, she wasn't fit to associate with Mark. She bit her lips and answered only a morose yes or no when he tried to carry on the conversation.

He noticed it at once. After she had answered the third statement he made with a dull yes, he, too, subsided into silence on his side of the seat. Andy Gingerich's old buggy was a narrow one and neither could get more than six inches from the other, but suddenly something had spoiled his delightful visit with this girl, and they might as well have had a thousand miles between them. And he had just begun to know her!

For a long mile there was silence between them, accented by the clop-clop of the horse's hooves and the creak of the buggy wheels. Although Mark had fully intended to ask her

250

if he could come in when they got to Dan's place, now he wasn't so sure. Evidently she didn't find him interesting, or she'd keep on talking. He sighed. "She is the most interesting girl I've ever met—and brave!" he thought. "Or she wouldn't work for Dan Gingerich! Ah, well, I'm only a poor missionary-in-the-making, with long hard years of study ahead. Perhaps it is just as well not to get involved with a girl—even a wonderful one like Katie. Oh, but she is pretty! If only I had more to offer," he mused. "My folks are a bit cool toward me since I've decided to go to college and be a missionary; so there will be no help from them, and working your way through college can be a long-drawn-out process. Let her go then," he told himself. "It's not fair to tie her down and make her wait. For all you know, God has other plans for her, anyway."

*   *   *

Two weeks later, Katie was on a bus bound for the Ozarks. Mark was trying humorously to accustom his chosen college to the sight of an Amishman in its classrooms.

GRATEFUL for the darkened windows of the bus that modified the brilliant, early June sun, Katie watched the fertile, black fields of Iowa roll by. After seeing only tree-covered hills of the Ozarks for almost three years, Iowa farms seemed strange. In the Ozarks the grass and gardens had been browning in the heat of summer; here in Iowa everything was the green, green, green of an early Midwestern summer.

Shifting around in the seat, Katie tried to imagine how things would be at home. When she had left, Susan had just made application for membership at Poplar Hill, Andy was ready to leave for his two years of service, and Vernie and Henry were, to all appearances, well satisfied with the church.

Now, Vernie and Henry had both joined Poplar Hill. And not only that, but Andy, back from his service, had found Vernie still unmarried and a member of Poplar Hill. He had swept her off her feet with a whirlwind courtship, disregarding her four year's seniority--and they were to be married in a week. Which was why Katie was going home now and not waiting until September when it would be three years since she'd gone away.

She wondered what Mom was saying about it. Were it as much as she disliked seeing her children leave the church, it was probably a lot! "But at least she had the compensation of having one less old maid around the house," Katie thought. "I expect I'm going to be a sore spot. Twenty-six and not married! Vernie is twenty-eight; Clarie, twenty-four. That would make Henry twenty-three, Mary Ann twenty, and Edna a little over sixteen! How time does fly! Only a few years ago I finished school and Mary Ann and Edna hadn't even started!"

She'd been home only once for fall communion after being gone a year. Dan had been taken into the church without explanation. Apparently his quiet, persistent continuation in church attendance, his faultless obedience to traditions had frustrated the leaders. Why keep someone in the ban who lived a better life than many of his enemies? His conduct was baffling to them, for they expected him to apply for membership at Poplar Hill. But as two years had gone by and he was still faithfully coming to church, there seemed nothing else to do but reinstate him. There were only abstract ideas to hold against him, and, as they were hard to put your fingers on, the church voted him in and chose to ignore any need for explanation. All of this Dan meekly accepted and continued to give out tracts just as before.

None of this had been in any of his occasional letters to Katie. But Susan, whom Katie humorously called her private newspaper, had written long, detailed accounts of news Mom wouldn't write and the *Budget* couldn't. It was Susan who wrote her, that first winter, about Mose Junior and Dan B's Mary being churched because of intimacy before their marriage. And Susan who had written about the fifteen young people who had made confession for bed courtship before communion. Mom might keep a discreet silence about it in her letters, Clarie and Vernie might hint, but it was Susan who wrote the bold facts about Bishop Eli's Edward being drunk at the last horse sale. "If the leaders could do so, they'd church Susan for telling me so much," Katie thought.

Susan also had written about so many people leaving the church and joining Poplar Hill that Poplar Hill had decided to divide. With the new congregation needing ministers three had been ordained out of the lay members, and one of them was, of all people, Mahlon! He had been in the ministry now for a year, and Katie was anxious to hear him preach. She half expected him to preach Vernie's marriage sermon next week, although he wouldn't be able to perform the ceremony; only the bishop would do that.

It was hard to think of Mahlon as a minister and Emma a minister's wife. Still, he had always been able to express his thoughts well and he liked mixing with people, if that helped. But had he really committed himself to Christ or had he gone to Poplar Hill merely to have a car and modern conveniences? Emma definitely had given herself to Christ and had made peace with God, but Katie felt a vague uncertainty about Mahlon. Perhaps, if she could hear him preach, she would know for sure where he stood spiritually.

The bus was slowing. Her thoughts momentarily broken, Katie craned her neck to see which town they were approaching. Someone was supposed to meet her at the county seat, but she did not know who. Henry was gone for his two years of service and was coming home only for the wedding. "Perhaps Mom and Pop will hire someone to bring them to the city to shop and meet me at the bus station," she thought as the bus stopped before a small café to let off passengers and take on new ones.

In a few minutes the bus was on its way again. "Only about eighty more miles and I'll be home," Katie mused, shifting her position and hooking her purse over her other arm. The bus wasn't crowded and for the last fifty miles she had been sitting alone. Whether people shied away from her because of her black bonnet and odd dress, she didn't know, but at least she had a chance for unbroken thought.

"Shall I stay with my church or not?" she wondered, almost aloud. "Is that where you want me, Lord?" she prayed silently, her unseeing eyes gazing across green corn that would be more than knee high by the fourth of July. "Is that what your plans are for me or should I do what Susan and Vernie and Mahlons and so many others have done? Before I left for the Ozarks I didn't know and I still don't. Oh, dear Lord, show me your plan for me!"

It had been easy to put off making the decision while away. At the Fairview Home she had been accepted as she was, enjoying fellowship with persons from other denominations.

What was she going to do at home now? In every letter Susan had asked the same question. "Will I apply for a job in the hospital with Susan or shall I find another job like I had at Dan's before Mandy died or shall I be an ordinary hired girl as I was before coming of age?" Katie questioned herself.

"Just what, besides Vernie's wedding, is bringing me home? Certainly, I could have stayed at Fairview. Am I homesick, perhaps? Do my ears want to hear the clop-clop of horse's hooves and the rasp of buggy wheels on gravel? Have the months in a rocky, hilly land made me long for rolling, green fields and great, spacious barns and clean gardens and white houses?"

Katie couldn't say. "I only know that all spring I've been preparing to go home. When that surprising and almost incoherent letter came from Vernie telling of her approaching wedding, I felt: This is it. You're finished down here and you're to go home to stay. There's work for you there." Thus Katie quietly summarized her feelings.

"Dear Lord," she prayed, closing her eyes and pressing her hands against them. "Dear Lord, if you want me at home with my people, show me what you want me to do next. If you have a job ready for me, lead me to it in your own good time. And, O God, let me make the right decision about the church. If you want me to stay, show me so plainly, dear God. I don't know what's best for me. You show me, please, God."

The bus slowed down again and stopped at another town. How many times had it done that since she'd gotten on last night? There must have been a hundred towns, at least. The next stop would be hers.

*   *   *

"Hey! Yo-hoo, Katie. Over here."

The soft calling, faint above the babble of voices inside the bus depot, Katie knew at once to be Vernie's. She was standing on the edge of the crowd with Andy beside her.

"Hi," Vernie greeted her. "You got here, I see. Did you have a good trip?"

"If you can call driving all night and half a day a good trip, I did," Katie replied, her eyes taking in Vernie's changed mode of dress. "I might have known that if she'd been as fancy as the Amish church allowed, she'd be straining the rules of the new one to the utmost." Katie thought, seeing the trim appearance of Vernie's latest new dress. "I'm glad to be here anyway. Hi, Andy."

"Here, let me have those suitcases," Andy reached over and took them from her. "Is this all you have?"

255

"For now, yes. I had a chance to send a box up with a pickup at the end of the month."

"The car's outside," Vernie told her, leading the way.

Andy opened the trunk and put Katie's bags inside; Vernie settled herself in the middle of the front seat and tugged at Katie's dress. "Get in," she ordered. "My, it's nice to see you. What do you think of the news?"

"You certainly surprised me," Katie exclaimed, knowing Vernie was hoping she'd say that. "Andy, I never knew you had your eyes on Vernie," she told him as he got into the car.

He grinned and looked at Vernie. "I did, though. But I was afraid of her before I left."

"Afraid of me!" Vernie squealed, snuggling close to him. "What on earth was the matter with you?"

"You were so smart. I always felt like a dumbhead around you. Anyway, I didn't think you would care to date a green-horn like me."

"And she wouldn't have," Katie thought. "He wouldn't have got her in those days. I wonder if they act like this in front of Mom. If there is anything Mom hates, it is the sight of lovers acting lovey-dovey in public. 'Do you have everything planned for the wedding?'" Katie asked aloud.

"All but the last-minute things," Vernie reluctantly allowed herself to be drawn away from Andy.

"Who are your witnesses?"

"Didn't I write you? Susan and Henry, because they're both members of Poplar Hill, too," Vernie said.

"Are you having table waiters?"

"Oh, yes, that reminds me," Vernie said. "We're having couples, and we were wondering, Andy and I, if you would care to be Mark Hochstettler's partner?"

"Who!" Katie gave a quick, silent gasp. "Was he still in circulation?"

"Mark Hochstettler. He's related to Andy, you know. I know he is as homely as a scarecrow, but couldn't you stand him for one evening? It would only be a couple of hours."

"He's not homely," Katie thought defensively. "He's just as good-looking as Andy. Besides, he's the nicest boy I ever met. But he's the last person I ever expected to see again!" All this Katie kept carefully out of her voice as she answered. "I thought he was going to college in the East. Did he give that up?"

"No, he's still going," Andy replied. "He's coming out here this summer to work with me on a construction gang."

"Oh, so that's what you're going to do for a living. You didn't tell me yet," she kept her voice carefully casual. She did not want them to know talking about Mark Hochstettler was making her heart race. "Are you going to get a house in town?"

"Oh, we've already got one partly furnished," Vernie assured her. "I can't wait to show it to you."

"Let's see, the wedding is to be a week from--"

"Tomorrow night. We're having an evening wedding. It's supposed to start at five."

"Are you having the reception at home?"

"Of course. But you still haven't said if you'd be Mark's partner for table waiter. Really, I hate to ask you, but could you do it just for my sake? Didn't you have a date with him before you left?"

"It wasn't a date," Katie's voice was even. "He took me to the singing with him one night, that was all."

"I thought Andy said you had a date with him," Vernie replied questioningly.

Katie looked up, saw Andy's eyes on her, bit her lips, and looked quickly away from his quizzical glance.

"Oh, well, if you don't want to, maybe we could shuffle things around," Vernie said resignedly. "Maybe we can get him to be an usher. That way we won't have to find a partner for him."

"I never said I wouldn't be his partner," Katie said too quickly.

"Oh, you mean you would? Oh, you don't know how thankful I am," Vernie said. "I'll be everlastingly glad if you do."

"All right, if you think I'm doing you a favor, I won't tell you otherwise," Katie thought, a small secret smile playing around her lips. "But you can't know how surprised I am to think of seeing him again. Surprised and--and--glad. Maybe this is why I knew it was time to come home." Looking up she caught Andy's quick glance on her. She looked at him levelly. He shook his head ever so slightly as if he couldn't figure her out, a small grin on his lips. Abruptly Katie began to talk of other things.

AS they turned into the lane and drove up to the house, the screen door flew open and Edna came racing down to the gate with Mary Ann close behind her.

"Hi, hi! So you finally got home again. Are you going to stay? My, you look good!" Edna jabbered, her sentences thrown out with no anticipation of an answer.

Katie was out of the car and clasping their hands before she quite realized what she was doing. "Yes, I'm going to stay. Hi, Mary Ann. My, you girls look good, too! Where's Mom? Oh, here she comes."

Katie broke away and ran up the walk to meet her. Mom, a dish towel draped across her shoulder, was slowly coming across the porch and down the steps, partly because she couldn't hurry as the two girls could, and partly because she didn't believe in unseemly display of feelings.

"Hello, Mom."

"Well, here's Katie again."

They clasped each other's hands and searched each other's eyes.

"Her hair gets grayer every year," Katie thought fleetingly. "And I didn't notice those wrinkles on her forehead when I was home last year."

"So, she's still Amish," Mom was thinking, her eyes taking in Katie's black bonnet and plain dress without seeming to. "I wonder how long she'll stay that way, with Emma and Henry and Vernie gone and Edna and Mary Ann fussing to leave for all they're worth, and hard telling what Clarie will do. If some-one would have told me when they were small that all my efforts to keep them with the church would come to this, I wouldn't have been able to keep on living."

"Well, so you're home again," Mom was the first to speak. "Come on in. I don't suppose you've had anything to eat. Did you drive all night?"

"Yes, and no, I haven't eaten. I thought I'd wait until I got home. I'm awfully tired, too," Katie realized as she spoke the words. "Last night I got little catnaps between stops--that's all," she said, following Mom up the steps and into the house, letting the others trail after her with her suitcases.

"Where's Pop?" she asked, standing in the middle of the dining room and taking in the clean disorder of an Amish household getting ready for a wedding. The living room was freshly painted, and it looked as though the girls had persuaded Mom to buy a new living room couch and chair. The dining room table looked small and strange with only one board in it. "I wonder if they don't need it larger to put cookies on to cool," Katie thought, remembering with odd clarity one time when she'd come home late from school and Vernie had chased her from the cookies on the table.

"Pop went to town for some things after dinner. Put your

259

bonnet in the living room, Katie. We'll have something for you to eat right away."

The younger girls wanted Katie to talk all the time, hardly letting her eat. At last Mom chased them out to pick strawberries for supper and told Katie to go upstairs and get some sleep.

Gratefully Katie climbed the stairs to the old room she was still to share with Clarie and Vernie. This, too, had been painted, although the wrought-iron bedsteads decked with new quilt coverlets were the same as long ago when they had been the scene of late evening talks. "I feel like a homing pigeon," Katie thought, dropping off to sleep. "It's right for me to be here again."

*   *   *

Late Sunday afternoon she got to see Susan. They had just come home from church and were sitting in the living room talking (it seemed they never could get caught up) --Pop in a straight chair by the table, Mom in her rocking chair by the window, Katie sitting on the new davenport, with Edna perched on the end beside her. Mary Ann was reading the *Budget* in the new chair. Clarie was upstairs napping.

"Who comes now?" Mom broke off an explanation of why strawberries weren't doing so good.

Edna ran to the door. "It's Susan Gingerich. Oh, she's got her new car."

"Does Susan have a new car?" Katie exclaimed, getting to her feet. "She didn't tell me."

"Yeah," Mom said contemptuously, not getting up. She blamed Susan as much as anyone for enticing Vernie to leave the church. She didn't doubt for a moment that Susan would do her best to get Katie to leave, too. "What good did it do for you to tell your children over and over again when they were small that to be faithful to the traditions of the church was the only way for them to hope to win eternal life? When

260

they were grown, they turned on you and told you the Bible didn't say so, and, feeling justified, left the church, turning all your efforts to nothing," she thought.

Susan was out of the car and coming up the walk. Katie met her on the porch, Edna and Mary Ann behind her.

"Hi, hillbilly," Susan greeted her with a broad smile.

"Susan! How are you?" they grabbed each other's hands, shaking vigorously.

"You look just as good as you always did," Susan told Katie.

"You do, too. **Better I think. Isn't there more of you to look good?**"

"Don't try to compliment me like that!" Susan laughed. "Why don't you come right out and tell me I'm getting fat?"

"You must be living high--a new car--and you putting on weight--"

"Oh, don't get funny ideas. Anyone can pay installments. But really, I'm glad to see you again."

"I know," Katie's face grew serious. "I was looking for you to come over before this."

"I was working all week. And I helped Mom with strawberries when I wasn't working."

"Come on in. Will you stay for supper?" Katie led the way into the house. The girls, after a short greeting to Susan, had gone to look over the new car.

There was only Mom in the living room when they went inside. Pop had taken his magazine and disappeared. It was amazing how quickly he sensed a controversy in the air, Katie thought. Knowing how Mom felt and Susan was, he had fled, rather than stay and take a chance of cool looks turning into hot words. Mom's greeting was courteous but distant, although Susan went ahead and talked as matter-of-factly as always.

"I came over to take you with me for supper," Susan told Katie. "That is, if you haven't planned anything else."

"Katie, aren't you going to the singing?" Mom asked quickly. "You should go to the singing, I think. Don't you want to see the young folks?"

"It doesn't take much to see what she is driving at," Katie thought. "She's afraid I'd rather go to church with Susan." Aloud she answered, "I can, if Susan wants to drop me off there. Are the other girls going?"

"Vernie and Andy will come by and pick us up," explained Edna and Mary Ann who had come back from inspecting the new car.

"How will we all get home?" Katie looked at her doubtfully.

"Oh, we'll bum it. At least half a dozen people go past here. It is always easy to get a ride home," Mary Ann said.

"I can come past there after church and pick you up," Susan assured them.

"Yes, don't worry, Katie. Maybe someone will ask you for a date," Mary Ann said.

"Hum. An old maid like me? I can't imagine that."

"Well, if you're going with me, get your bonnet and we'll go. I'd like to catch up on all the talking we missed while you were gone," Susan urged.

"I'll have to change dresses. Come on up and we'll talk while I dress."

She led the way, followed by Susan, with Mary Ann and Edna bringing up the rear. She found Clarie up and getting dressed, having heard that someone had come.

There was a lively exchange of talk among them all while Katie changed, although Katie noticed that Clarie was rather quiet. She wondered fleetingly what was wrong; Clarie didn't seem to be the same girl. But Mary Ann talked a mile a minute --same as Vernie.

They all trooped down again when Katie pronounced herself ready. As they opened the door, Susan said, "Oh, yes, I almost forgot. There's going to be another wedding."

"Who?" Edna and Mary Ann cried simultaneously.

"Is it anybody we know?" Clarie asked.

"Yes. But you'll never guess; so I'll tell you. Henry Yoder's Anna Mae and Bishop Eli's David."

"Who!" Katie cried.

"I didn't know they went together," Mom said.

"Oh, he's had her two or three times. But Sammy Yoder has, too," Mary Ann said.

"Good night! Is she old enough to get married? She's not even sixteen, is she?"

"She's my age," Edna said. "I'm sixteen."

"But just barely," Mary Ann reminded her. "Your birthday was week before last."

"It is a have-to case," Susan said bluntly.

"Oh, no!" Katie cried. "Not David!"

"Why not?"

"Well, but--but--he always seemed so decent when I worked there."

"Who told you this?" Mom's voice followed her suspiciously.

"The folks did. They were over in that district for church."

Susan walked toward the car without waiting for a reply. Katie followed more slowly. "I can't believe this," Katie said. "It makes me sick--I never dreamed--are you sure it's true?"

"It's awful," Susan agreed. "I didn't tell the half of it either. She doesn't know who the father is."

"No, no, no!"

"It's true, though."

"Yes, but a young girl like that! What started her off wrong?"

"Her mother," Susan said bluntly. "Don't you remember how she used to make fun of the covering bunch? What else can you expect? Ellie belittled and snubbed anyone who wanted to have some standards for courtship. I'd say she's beginning to reap what she sowed."

"Yes, I can see that," Katie agreed slowly. "But I can't help but pity her with all my heart. And David. Oh, it makes me

263

sick, sick, sick."

"David might have amounted to something, if he wouldn't have been Bishop Eli's boy! All his life he heard criticism of young folks who really wanted to live for the Lord alongside of the strictest teaching about rules. You can't blame him if he turned wild."

"I suppose he kept the traditions," Katie said.

"Oh, sure, when it suited him. In church he looked all right. But he had plenty of things behind people's backs that weren't allowed. You remember I wrote you about those young folks who made confession for bed courtship?"

Katie nodded.

"David was one of them I don't know what girls were involved. Anna Mae wasn't running around yet, but I doubt if David ever sat up with a girl if he could go to bed with her."

Katie was too heartsick to speak. "I was impatient with Bishop Eli and Henry Ellie, but I never would have wished this on them," she thought. "I pity Anna Mae and David. If you could have taken those two when they were young and told them not to put their trust in traditions but in the living Christ--if someone would have warned them about the dangers of heavy petting--oh, if, if, if."

Finally she asked, "What's Bishop Eli's Edward doing? He and Fannie Yoder never did make a couple even if--"

"She wanted to," Susan finished for her. "No, Fannie never did get him. Oh, Edward went away after Mose Junior got married. He found more of his kind, I guess. He's been gone for a year or more."

"Are there any young people who have high standards and some spiritual light? So many have left the church and those staying seem to be the wild ones."

"Oh, there are a few. Your younger sisters are some, but--"

"But what?" Katie asked.

"Haven't you noticed that they'd like to leave the old church?"

"They haven't said anything, but I'm not surprised."

264

"Clarie told Edna this spring that Mary Ann says she's leaving as soon as she's of age. Edna wants to go, too, but she's only sixteen, you know. Clarie said Edna joined the church because your mom made her. I guess she's just enduring it until she's her own boss."

Katie nodded. "I've guessed as much. Mom takes care that the conversation is steered away from things like that, and the girls haven't talked about it when we were alone."

"I see that you're still with the old church," Susan said. "Are you going to stay? Your mom would give me fits if she heard me. I know she thinks I'm leading you girls astray."

Katie smiled wanly. "Susan, you don't know how lucky you are to have parents who give you encouragement to live according to the Scriptures. Mom's a good mother, as far as ordinary life is concerned--it's just that she's afraid of breaking tradition--"

"The traditions of the fathers are her god."

"Could anything be blunter than Susan's voice," Katie thought. "Oh, I know it," she said aloud. "But how can you show her otherwise? I thought that maybe--if I stayed and kept the traditions as she wants me to--I could show her that I don't want to be justified by the Scriptures just so I can have more material freedom."

"So you're staying then?"

"Yes. For the present, at least."

"Well, it's your life. I don't see how you'll stand it, though."

* * *

Katie punched her pillow into a different lump, swished the covers, and tried to make herself relax. The events of the last twelve hours kept running through her thoughts like mice, beginning with the moment when Susan dropped her bomb about Anna Mae and David and ending with Edna and Mary Ann knocking loudly on her bedroom door half an hour ago.

There was peace downstairs once more, although a faint

hum of voices from the room beneath her told her that the girls and their dates were still there. Clarie was fast asleep in the bed opposite.

Vernie and Andy came upstairs, said a lingering good-night outside her door, then Andy went to Henry's room and Vernie to the guest room, for, since Katie had come home and none of them liked to sleep double anymore, Vernie slept there. "Vernie is going to have to adjust to sleeping double day after tomorrow," Katie thought, as she tried again to sleep. Once more she changed positions. "If I wouldn't wake Clarie I'd get up and sit by the window. What time is it, anyway?" she thought. "Too bad they didn't have a clock up here." As if in answer to her thought, the clock below gave one single bong. That meant nothing. "It could be all the way from twelve-thirty to one-thirty. But I doubt if it is one-thirty yet. If it were, Mom would beat on the bedroom door to tell the boys it was time to leave," Katie mused. "Tomorrow was a big day--what with the wedding the day after. If the girls didn't go to bed pretty soon, it wouldn't be worthwhile; Mom would get them out again at five.

"Another wedding, Susan had said. Oh, but under such heartbreaking circumstances. What had Anna Mae told her the last time she'd worked at Henry's? 'I'm never going to wear a covering and burn a light when I date.' She certainly hadn't. It wasn't as though a covering and a light had magic powers to keep you from sin--it was only that, if you did wear a covering and burn a light, your standards were high enough to keep you from falling. After all, you weren't going to indulge in heavy petting and bed courtship (even lying on the couch together) if someone could see you. And what girl liked to get a good covering crushed, hard as they were to keep nice?

"It went deeper than that, too. It meant that you realized that you could sin and that you needed Christ to keep you from it. It meant that keeping the outward traditions couldn't

266

save you, but that you needed a power within you.

"But how could you tell people like Mom and Bishop Eli and Henry Ellie that? You couldn't. You had to live among them and show them by your life that you had Christ living in you--something that would be impossible unless God gave you the love and power to do it. I'll do it, Christ," she whispered. "As long as you want me to stay, I'll stay."

*   *   *

Katie stood by the table, rolling pin in hand, pausing a moment to listen to the hubbub around her. Aunt Fannie had come, and her rich chuckle floated in through the opened washhouse door where she was dressing chickens with Elmer's wife and Andy's mother. "Even had I heard that chuckle in the Ozarks, I'd have known that Aunt Fannie was somewhere near," Katie thought. John Sarah's reply was drowned out by the babble from the kitchen.

"Where's the almond flavoring?" Mary Ann asked. "Hey, who took my egg beater?" That was Edna.

"Andy, come help me set up this table," Vernie's voice came from the living room.

"Mom, do you want this ham to be baked or boiled?" That was Emma, who had come to help.

"Their voices are like the rise and fall of a spring wind or a robin's song in the midst of chirping sparrows," Katie mused.

"These are my people. Even if I should ever leave the church, they'll always be mine. You can't cut off the ties of blood and culture. If I live to be a hundred and spend half of my life away from them, they'll always be my people. But I'll stay, Lord," she thought once again. "If that is what I should do, I'll stay."

10

KATIE saw Mark before he saw her. The table waiters had begun to gather soon after three. Katie was in the kitchen getting instructions from Vernie on how to serve. Looking up, she saw Mark on the porch talking with Andy.

"He is just as I remember him, except that he's grown a beard," Katie thought. "So he, too, is still with the church. He must have gotten a new suit--whoever made it is an excellent tailor," Katie mused. "How could Vernie say he was homely?"

"Be sure to remember the cake knife." Vernie's voice thrust through her thought.

"Yes, I know." *Wasn't he thinner?*

"Are you sure you can remember everything I told you? Oh, dear, sometimes I wish we had some precedent to follow instead of having to decide for ourselves which way to do it."

"You should have stayed with the old church, then." Katie grinned. *How did it happen that he had?*

"Uhh!" Vernie gave an impatient snort.

"Oh, don't worry," Katie soothed her. "You're nervous and all upset. Go up and get ready. We'll take care of things and see that you have a pretty wedding." *I wonder if he knows he's to serve with me?*

With a final lingering look at the kitchen, Vernie turned to go upstairs. Mom was out in the washhouse with the younger girls, finishing radish roses. She snorted when the girls cut them to look like roses, but helped just the same. Pop and Henry were putting hay on wagons in the barnyard for those who would come with horses. If the wedding was to begin at five, it was time everybody began to think of getting ready.

After Vernie had gone upstairs, Katie stood for a minute in the kitchen reflecting. "It's funny in a way--Vernie's wishing for precedent to follow--she who had always delighted in leading while she was with the Amish church. But it had been hard to decide on how to conduct the wedding. Every bride at Poplar Hill did things a little differently. It wasn't as though you did as your older sister had done, your mother before that, and your grandmother before that!" With sudden clarity Katie saw that, if you rejected the old culture, you had to set out across the untracked wilderness of a new one. "There's nothing wrong with the old one," she thought. "The wrong comes when you take the old culture and make it your religion. Dear Lord, help me to show my people that."

"Vernie!" Andy called from the porch.

"She went upstairs," Katie answered.

He came into the kitchen with Mark.

"Katie, here's Mark," Andy said. "I suppose you remember each other well enough so I won't have to introduce you."

"Hello, Katie," Mark said, holding out his hand.

"Hello, Mark," she said, giving him her own as Andy disappeared.

"Andy says we're to be partners."

"Yes," Katie answered thinking, "I didn't realize I remembered him so well."

"Dear Lord, is this the girl for me?" he was thinking.

Mom, bringing in the finished radishes, gave a startled look at Mark while she set them down on the table, then looked questioningly at Katie.

"Mom, this is Mark Hochstettler. You know him, don't you? He's related to Andy," Katie explained.

"So? How do you do?" Mom offered her hand to him. "Are you the one that's to be table waiter with Katie?"

"That's what Andy said," he smiled and shook her hand.

"Did you just come?" Mom asked politely.

"Here, yes. But I got back to John's last night."

"Well, Katie will tell you about your work tonight. She knows more what Vernie wants than I do."

More people were coming. The screen doors were banging constantly. Three more table waiter boys were on the porch, partners for Clarie, Mary Ann, and Edna--each boy related to either Andy or Vernie. Susan came with her folks, carrying her dress on a hanger.

Katie gathered the table waiters around the wedding party's table in the living room and went over the instructions from Vernie, the other girls supplying the details she forgot. She and Mark were to wait on the wedding table, Clarie and her partner were to take the rest of the living room, Mary Ann and hers, the bedroom, and Edna and hers, the dining room. They were to sit as partners at the ceremony, with Katie and Mark going first.

The last half hour before they left for Poplar Hill was like a madhouse. The guest room had been taken over by Vernie and Susan; Henry and Andy were getting ready in Henry's room. The two younger girls raced between their room and Katie's and Clarie's, leaving no room vacant for Pop and Mom. It was settled when Mom caught Edna in the hall and sternly told her to stay in one room or the other!

"Strangely, everyone is dressed and ready," Katie remarked to Mom when it was time to leave. "You and Pop and Andy's folks are to ride with Andy's cousin and Mary Ann. The others are to ride with Clarie's partner."

Most of the guests were seated when the wedding party got to church. As Katie followed Elmer, who was head usher, up the aisle to the seats reserved for the table waiters, she tried hard not to be so acutely aware of Mark behind her. They slipped into the pew and stood waiting for the others, then, with a slight rustle, they were seated.

"This is hard on Mom," Katie thought, seeing Mom and Pop and Andy's folks on the bench in front of them. "All her efforts to teach us that the only true way to please God is through the traditions of the fathers have come to nothing. I wonder what Pop thinks about it. I wish I could talk with him. Why couldn't any of us children get close to him? He's always so quiet."

The silence around her deepened, tense with the expectancy of weddings. The big clock above the pulpit showed it to be one minute before five. The door beside the amen corner opened, and the bishop of Poplar Hill came in, followed by Mahlon. They stepped soundlessly across the carpeted aisle and up the pulpit steps, seated themselves, and looked out across the people.

"This is my first chance to hear Mahlon preach," Katie thought. "Susan told me I needn't worry about him, but I am anxious to hear for myself. I thought it was awful when he and Emma left the old church. It took me a long time to get over that. Funny how even after I was saved, I used to think that you had to be Amish to please God."

Beside her Mark shifted his position slightly. Glancing up, she met his eyes and smiled. "Is there a special meaning in our meeting each other once more?" she asked herself. "In the years I worked in the Ozarks, I didn't hear of him once; I'd almost forgotten he existed. Is he still going to be a missionary? Is he planning on changing denominations? Could there be such a thing as an Amish missionary?" The thought made Katie suppress a giggle. "I can imagine how Bishop Eli feels about this. Oh, yes, Bishop Eli's David." The thought of his predicament made her sick at heart. "If ever people needed missionaries, it is my own--and not to send them out either!" she thought bitterly. "They need to be right among us."

The song leader got up. This had been one of those things

Vernie had worried about: Would it be better to have the song leader lead from the front or should he remain seated? They were beginning the second stanza when Katie heard a slight rustle. It was Susan walking up the aisle. Katie caught a glimpse of yellow and looked down at her own light green dress. Vernie's colors were the colors of spring--yellow and green.

Another rustle approached. Vernie came by, looking prettier than ever. "That cream satin is perfect for her," Katie mused. "That was one place where Mom put her foot down that it worked out for Vernie's good. She didn't let Vernie have pure white, but Vernie looks better in this."

Keeping her eyes demurely on the floor, Vernie joined Susan and looked up with a smile to meet Andy approaching her from the other side of the church. "Goodness, I'm going to cry," Katie thought, quick tears welling up. "Why does the sight of Vernie smiling make me cry? Where did I put my hankie?"

The bridal party stood for a moment; then seated themselves in one graceful movement just as the last notes of the song faded away. There was a moment of silence as Mahlon got up to preach.

"I wonder what he can preach that will amount to much in fifteen or twenty minutes. This is a far cry from the hour-long sermons of two preachers that the old church has at weddings," Katie thought. "No wonder some of our people feel that a couple married in a service like this is hardly married! If I can't concentrate better than this, I'll miss out on what Mahlon's saying." With an effort she pulled her thoughts from their ramblings. He was already reading from Ephesians, the fifth chapter. She closed her eyes and let the words penetrate her consciousness.

"Wives, submit yourselves unto your own husbands, as unto the Lord.

"For the husband is the head of the wife, even as Christ is the head of the church: and he is the saviour of the body.

"Therefore as the church is subject unto Christ, so let

the wives be to their own husbands in every thing.

"Husbands, love your wives, even as Christ also loved the church, and gave himself for it;

"That he might sanctify and cleanse it with the washing of water by the word,

"That he might present it to himself a glorious church, not having spot, or wrinkle, or any such thing; but that it should be holy and without blemish.

"So ought men to love their wives as their own bodies. He that loveth his wife loveth himself.

"For no man ever yet hated his own flesh; but nourisheth and cherisheth it, even as the Lord the church:

"For we are members of his body, of his flesh, and of his bones.

"For this cause shall a man leave his father and mother, and shall be joined unto his wife, and they two shall be one flesh.

"This is a great mystery; but I speak concerning Christ and the church.

"Nevertheless let every one of you in particular so love his wife even as himself; and the wife see that she reverence her husband."

"Now what is he going to say?" she questioned herself. She needn't have worried. From beginning to end she listened entranced as he spoke simply of the church, the bride of Christ. Of how Christ had been willing to suffer shame and death because He looked into the future and saw all of those who repented and believed in Him gathered into one as His bride. Of how, down through the years, He had watched and guided that same bride when it seemed as though all signs of her would disappear from the earth. Of how, no matter how he tried, the devil was never able to kill her completely. But most of all, that people of all kindreds and tongues of the earth are the bride. Of how you couldn't put your finger on one denomination and say that was the bride, but that all who called on the name of the Lord in faith and honest repentance of sin were accepted. Of how you couldn't become a member of the bride by doing the works of the forefathers.

He spoke also to the bride and groom on how to have a Christ-exalting marriage, comparing their relationship to that of Christ and the church.

"Oh, that was good!" Katie thought. "Susan was right. I needn't have doubted him. Dear Lord, I'm so glad you're using Mahlon. I was wrong when I wanted him to stay with the old church. He can be used here in a way he never could there."

He had finished, and, stepping back, he was replaced by the bishop who raised his hands. There was a loud rustle as the entire assembly arose in a body for the prayer before the ceremony. Then the bishop began in his deep, rich voice, "Dearly beloved, we are gathered together in the presence of God and these witnesses--"

IN brief snatches Katie and Mark exchanged a few words as they served.

"I heard you just got back from the Ozarks. Did you like it?"

"Oh, I really did. Can you take this tray of sandwiches?"

"How do you find college? Is it hard to get good grades if you didn't take high school?"

"Hard enough. I like it, though. Vernie asked for more coffee."

"Are you going back in the fall?"

"I don't know for sure. Where shall I put these dirty plates?"

While helping Katie dish ice cream, Mark said, "Look here, I'd like to talk to you for more than a few words at a time. Would there be any chance if I stayed tonight?"

Katie's hand posed motionless above the sauce dish, the ice-cream scoop hanging crazily downward. "Yes," she answered and began to dip ice cream again, hoping he couldn't guess how madly her heart was racing.

The evening passed in a fuzzy daze. Katie served and cleared tables automatically. After everyone had been served to drowsy capacity and the gifts were being unwrapped and acknowledged, the tired waiters had supper in the kitchen. Katie only picked at the food. The other girls were just as bad. There had been too much prewedding sampling, too high a pitch of excitement for the last few days; now the girls were jaded and let down.

"I'm so tired I feel silly," Clarie complained after an outburst of giggles about nothing at all.

"We all are," Katie answered.

"I'll be glad when this is over," Mary Ann grumbled. "I hope we don't have to go through this again right away."

"You'd better not talk. I'll bet you're the next one," Edna told her.

"Oh, I'm not! Katie is."

Katie raised her eyebrows in mock inquiry. "Me? Now what makes you think that?"

"Ha, I've got eyes," Mary Ann said knowingly, taking a tiny dip of ice cream out onto a sauce dish.

"It doesn't take very sharp eyes either," Clarie giggled. "Someone's been making sheep's eyes at Katie all day."

"Quiet, please!" Katie whispered fiercely, her eyes on Mark across the room where he was eating and talking with the other boys. What if he heard them? It would be enough to make him leave without talking to her. If he heard, he gave no sign, and Katie showed her relief by making one of her old-time hideous faces at Clarie.

When the last straggling guest had left, Mom and Pop decided that only their own bed was familiar enough to give them rest after the hectic day; consequently the bedroom had to be cleared of chairs and benches, and the bedstead brought in from the washhouse and set up. Mark solicitously helped, and Katie was glad Mom didn't ask why. "After all," Katie thought, "if Mom hates old maids in the family, she'd better not discourage them in what might change their status!"

At long last everyone went to bed. Vernie and Andy had gone to their new house. Katie asked Mom whether Mark could use the guest room. Susan agreed to come by for Mark early the next morning. "I'm glad to do all I can for you and Katie," she told Mark bluntly, "for the last three years have been wasted time between the two of you."

"Come on out to the porch swing," Katie invited Mark. "We won't disturb the folks that way. Mom's terribly tired."

He followed her as she tiptoed softly out to the porch. The moon had come up, and it was almost bright as day. Katie thought, "We'd hardly need that lamp on the worktable inside the window," and laughed quietly at the relativity of rules. She seated herself, and Mark dropped down beside her.

"Are you still going to be a missionary?" she asked.

"Yes, but not in the way I was planning at first."

"How do you mean? Aren't you going out to some mission field?"

"Not in the sense of it being a place in some other country."

"Where are you planning to go then?"

"Katie, have you ever thought what a big field our own people are?"

She gave a sad, short laugh. "Have I? That's all I have been thinking the last few days. Especially since this--" She broke off. Inbred reluctance to speak of such matters with the opposite sex made her stop.

"Since what?" he asked kindly.

"Oh, since this came out about Henry Yoder's Anna Mae and Bishop Eli's David."

"Isn't that a sad story?" he said.

"It makes me feel sick even though I had to admit that it was only what one could expect."

"I know."

"And the worst of it is, things might have turned out differently if their parents wouldn't have been so self-righteous and opposed to any spiritual teachings."

"That's why I say our own people are my mission field."

"But how?" she asked in a puzzled voice. "Do you mean that you're called to be a preacher?"

"I don't know about that. If I am to be a preacher, I'll wait until God ordains me through the lot same as all our preachers are. No, I've decided to be a teacher."

Light broke on her. "Oh, I see. You'll be a teacher and teach in our schools and work among us that way."

"Yes. Could you suggest a better way?"

"No-oo," she said slowly. "But might you be put in the ban?"

"As for being put in the ban, I hope not. I think that if God is leading me in this, He'll see to it that I can work among our people. I thought I'd keep the commandments as well as anyone could just to show our people I'm not trying to justify myself by the Scriptures so I could have more liberty."

"That's one of the first things they say," she agreed. "As soon as you point out that we're put in right standing with God by faith in what Christ does for us--and not by our works--they say, 'Oh, sure, you want more liberty and you pick out Scripture verses just to justify yourself.'"

"How does it happen that you haven't left our people?" he asked.

"I can't explain it," she answered slowly. "Before I left for the Ozarks, I thought I might sometime. I'm not saying I never will, either, but I told God I'd stay."

"A lot are leaving, though."

"I know. It makes it hard to decide to stay when so many

of your family leave and your best friends leave."

"How much longer are you staying?"

"I don't know. Always, if our people accept any spiritual light. But at least until God leads me otherwise."

"That's the way I feel," he said fervently. "I told God I'd stay until they kicked me out!"

"That would be it. If they absolutely refused to listen, you'd have to leave then."

"Listen, Katie. If we both feel this way, and--and--we've met again after we thought we never would--at least, I never thought we would, could you--do you suppose--that is, would you care to go steady with me?"

She sat very still. She couldn't say this was unexpected; she'd been feeling it in her bones ever since she knew she was to see him again.

"Oh, I shouldn't have mentioned it," he said after a moment mistaking her silence. "I can't blame you--if you don't want to. I'm an ugly-looking person and no girl would want--"

"That's not true!" she broke in. "I don't think you're ugly-looking. Any girl would want--"

"Then you would go steady with me?"

"I never said I wouldn't, did I? You didn't give me a chance to answer yet."

A smile broke across his rugged face and spread into his side beard, changing his looks.

"He, ugly-looking?" Katie thought. "How could you think so if you saw that smile?"

*   *   *

The next morning they all wandered around with the letdown feeling that follows on the heels of great excitement. The stack of trays to be washed and the big dishpan of dirty silverware made them, as Mary Ann aptly said, wish they'd made the guests eat with their fingers out of one common dish. Even Mom had less zeal to straighten up than usual. The wedding was a sore spot with her. Had not she seen the raised eyebrows of her own brother's wife at the fancy doings last night? She shuddered to think what her parents would have said about such a worldly wedding were they still living. Even Aunt Fannie, one of whose own children had left the church, had expressed disapproval with a ripple of chuckles that were anything but funny. The worst of it was that at the rate the younger girls were going, there'd be nothing but fancy weddings from now on. If there were any more, that is--which seemed doubtful--the way Katie and Clarie turned down the best boys in the community. Unless this Mark Hochstettler meant anything.

Susan came early for Mark, taking some borrowed dishes with her.

"I'll pick you up for the singing Sunday evening," he murmured by way of good-bye. They were alone in the dining room for a few brief seconds. She nodded wordlessly.

"Mark, I'm ready," Susan's voice came through the screen door. "If you've got anything more to say to Katie, save it for the next time."

"Susan!" Katie protested.

"That's what I'm going to do," Mark said, smiling down at Katie. "Good-bye for now."

Katie went to the kitchen, a glad little song in her heart. She got out a dishpan and began to attack the dirty silverware.

"I'm glad someone feels like working around here," Mary Ann muttered darkly.

"That's what I was thinking," Clarie said, pouring hot water over the silverware. "If the rest of us would have had the tonic she had for breakfast--"

"Oh, fiddle!" Katie told them lightly, squirting some water at them with her fingers.

"I wish two of you would go out and pick strawberries before it gets too hot," Mom cut into their foolery. "We don't need all of you to clean up--you'll just get into each other's way."

"Who's going to do it?" Mary Ann groaned. "I've picked so many my back feels as if it were going to break every time I see that patch."

"Mine, too," Edna eched.

"Clarie, why don't you and I do it?" Katie asked, hands poised above the dishpan. "I haven't picked very often this year, and you haven't either, with your job in town."

"I don't care. Let's hope washing dishes will be easier on this poor girl's back." Clarie grinned, indicating Mary Ann.

Leaving the dishes for the others, they gathered together berry boxes and an empty dishpan, and, tying on sunbonnets and chore aprons, they set out for the patch. The dew was already evaporating off the plants.

"Before we finish, the sun will be hot," Katie said. "That breeze from the south is pleasant now; let's hope it lasts." For a few minutes they picked in silence. Katie was thinking of Mark, a little smile on her face. How good of God to lead them together again! This was different from the way she'd felt about Mose. In a moment of painful clarity she realized that the only attraction she'd felt for Mose was physical. "It was a good thing I wore my covering," she thought soberly. "If I hadn't had a high standard, by the grace of God, I'd have eventually succumbed to his physical attraction the same as Mary did. I'm glad--glad--glad that I quit him before we got into trouble. We never were meant for each other-- the way Mark and I are," she thought, and then put the thought hastily away because after all, he hadn't asked her to marry him yet.

"Katie, how does it happen you haven't left the church?" Clarie's voice shut off her secret thoughts abruptly.

"Why? Did you expect me to?" Katie sat back on her heels and wiped sweat from her nose with the back of her hand.

"Well, yes. I don't think even Mom was expecting you to come home and still be with it."

"I hardly know how to explain it," Katie said slowly, reaching down and picking a berry she'd missed. "When I went to the Ozarks, I didn't know for sure what to do. I wasn't even sure when I came home. Then, when I heard about Bishop Eli's David and Anna Mae Yoder, I don't know--somehow I decided to stay. It seems to me that our church is as big a mission field as you could find anywhere."

Clarie was silent for a minute. "Do you think it's wrong to leave, then?" she asked hesitantly.

"Oh, Clarie, I don't think that way. It's not a case of wrong or right, but where God wants me."

"Well, but do you think we all have to stay?"

"Clarie, would you like to leave?" Katie asked quietly.

"Oh, I don't know what to do. I can't agree with the teachings of the traditions anymore. You don't either--"

"I know."

"But every time I decide to leave, I get to thinking of how we've always been taught that we must deny our own will and--I think maybe it is just my own will that wants to go and--" her voice trailed off with a sad little laugh.

"Are you happy when you decide to stay?"

"No. I'm so miserable about it, it almost makes me crazy. It's just as if something in me were saying, 'go, go, go,' all the time."

Katie absently picked berries, thinking, "What could you tell someone in a situation like this? O God," she prayed, "help me to say the right thing."

"Have you prayed about it?" she asked finally.

"Oh, Katie, I do that all the time. I want God to have His way with me. I tell Him that if He wants me to stay to please make me satisfied with the way things are. I don't know if I don't pray in the right spirit or if my own will gets in the way or what, but--" again her voice trailed off.

"Clarie, maybe God does want you to go," Katie said.

This time Clarie sat back on her heels. She regarded Katie with questioning eyes. "If God wants me to go, why doesn't He want you to do the same thing?"

"Oh, Clarie, we can't know what He's planned for us. Maybe He's planning on sending you someplace to be a witness for Him where you could never go under--under things as they are now. As for me staying, there might be something we--I mean I--can do that you couldn't. Listen, Clarie, when Christ sent out His disciples, did He send them all to the same place or the same people?"

"No-oo," Clarie answered slowly. "They went all over."

"Exactly. And some stayed and worked with the Jews. I think that's about the same way this would apply. For instance, take Mahlon; look how God is using him at Poplar Hill--"

"You didn't like it a bit, when he and Emma left, did you?"

"No, I didn't, but I know now I had no business carrying on like that. Mahlon is being used there in a way that he probably couldn't be in the old church."

"I know. He's on their mission board and one of the main ones for their jail services."

"What would you like to do with your life? Aside from going to Poplar Hill, I mean," Katie asked in a moment of inspiration.

"I'd like to go to college and study to be a teacher," Clarie said simply.

"You! Go to college! I never knew--I never realized--" Katie exclaimed.

"I've just decided this year. Before that I was just going along without much of a goal. I guess I thought I'd work out until I married like everyone else did, and there I was with no boy I cared enough to go steady with!"

"What made you look for something else?" Katie asked, busily picking berries again.

"Your life. I saw that you really wanted to make it count for the Lord, and it made me ashamed of myself."

Katie sat back on her heels, staring at Clarie in astonishment.

"Me! My life! Oh, Clarie, I've never done anything special. Not nearly what I'd like to do."

"I think you have. Just the way you reacted to all those who disagreed with you made me see that you had something worthwhile."

"Clarie, you have committed your life to Christ! When did you?"

"I'm glad you can see it. Or hear it, whichever way you'd say it," Clarie said humbly. "While you were gone, I went to a Bible conference at Poplar Hill with Mahlon and Emma. The speaker pointed out so plainly how each one of us must make a personal commitment to Christ, and I knew I never had. I did then. Everything's different now," she finished simply.

They had stopped picking and were sitting in the half-picked patch, too intent on their conversation to notice the heat of the sun.

"I'm so glad, Clarie. I wanted to ask, but I'm such a coward," Katie said quietly. "I always felt that you girls thought I was religious crazy and a heretic--and all that."

"I never did. I always knew you had something I didn't have. I'm sorry you felt that way, though. I wish I would have told you," Clarie picked a berry absently.

"Vernie told me one time I was crazy," Katie confessed. "I can't say now that I blame her. It was the time when I was still thinking that you had to keep the traditions of the fathers to please God. I guess I was a mournful thing in those days. Anyway, how does Vernie look at spiritual things now? She's left the old church, but does Christ really mean anything to her?"

"I'm afraid He doesn't," Clarie said sadly. "She went just to have more material things."

"I thought it seemed like it. People like that make it hard to convince our people of the liberty we have in Christ."

They began picking again in silence. "How funny things had turned out," Katie thought. "Here I was, too cowardly to talk to Clarie--and all the time I could have. And isn't it funny how I longed to go to high school and never could? Now I don't care anymore. One educated person in the family is enough," her secret thoughts told her. "And Clarie, who had never said anything about high school, wants to go to college. Well, God works in funny ways to get people where He wants them."

"Girls, aren't you about done with those strawberries?" Mom's voice came from the opened dining room window. "I don't see how you can stand the heat anymore."

They looked at each other guiltily. "I didn't notice the heat," Katie said.

"I didn't either."

"What did you say?" Mom asked from the window.

"We'll be done before long," Katie told her. "Don't worry."

They began to pick berries with more fervor than they'd had all morning.

"I hope I helped you," Katie said, after a long moment of steady picking.

"Oh, you have," Clarie assured her. "I know what I'm going to do now."

BY the first of August Mark had asked Katie to marry him and she had accepted. They began to plan their wedding for the middle of September. He decided to transfer to a nearby university to finish his studies. They would rent a house in the community among their own people. He would try to get carpenter work when he wasn't going to school. By another year he would be able to teach in one of the local rural schools. Katie even thought of getting housework in town to help out with expenses so that Mark would have more time for study.

In the weeks before their wedding they were the chief subject of gossip in the community. There were those who predicted they wouldn't stay with the church a minute after they were married, those who openly snubbed Mark because he wasn't content with the same education as his father, and those who staunchly stood by them and wished them God's blessing.

Katie noticed, though, that one tongue was silent, or if she talked, none of her words reached Katie. Evidently the sordid end to Anna Mae's young girlhood had chastened Henry Ellie enough to keep her silent. Even Bishop Eli's pride had been sufficiently humbled to make him give a grudging hand of fellowship to Mark when he asked to transfer his membership from his home congregation.

Old Dan Gingerich was elated over the match. And out of his elation he offered his home to them for the winter, rent-free, while he went to Florida again. The only stipulation he made was that he must, just must, be invited to the wedding. What if he weren't related to them and what if it wasn't customary to invite people you'd worked for unless you'd worked there within the last year? Katie laughed and invited him to the wedding the week before they were published.

"I take all the credit for the match," Susan told them solemnly. "I wrote Mark to come and spend the summer and I urged Andy to offer him a job so he'd be sure to come," she announced.

Katie laughed.

Mark smiled, for they both secretly felt that Susan was only an accessory. Had not God kept them for each other?

*   *   *

285

Holding the lamp erect, **Mom** descended the cellar steps, being careful to close the door so that no one would know where she was. She wanted to check the food for tomorrow undisturbed.

Setting the lamp at the back of a table full of pies, she lifted the cloth covering to survey them. Twelve cherry and twelve raisin pies for dinner tomorrow should be enough for one hundred and fifty guests--what with the cakes and cookies and fruit that were to be served, too. Katie had mildly rebelled at such a large wedding but, after the humiliation of Vernie's fancy wedding, Mom wanted to show her relatives that she could still put on as good an old-fashioned wedding as anyone else.

Over on the shelf a high bulge under another cloth marked the stack of pie shells for supper tomorrow. There were only twenty of those, because only a hundred people were invited to supper. The lemon filling was still to be cooked in the morning, the turkeys to be roasted, and the chicken to be stewed. She had sent the carrot salad home with Emma, Vernie, and Elmer's wife to set in their refrigerators overnight and be brought back in the morning.

Everything seemed ready. Then she remembered the cheeses. Oh, yes, they were still to be sliced, along with the minced ham. There were two crocks of stewed apple slices and two of stewed prunes. Some people no longer served stewed fruit at a wedding, but Mom was going to.

She stood in the middle of the cellar and looked around her. Had she forgotten anything? Ah, yes, the cookies. She turned to check the crock under the table and bumped against a tub of home-grown celery that had been washed after supper. All at once the enormousness of the tasks overwhelmed her. Would she ever get through the next twenty-four hours? Had she the wholehearted support of the family behind her, it wouldn't be so bad. But Vernie made fun of so many of the old customs. Emma raised eyebrows at this or that even though she kept silent, and Mary Ann told her to her face that those things would never be done at her wedding. Clarie and Edna grunted and sniffed at her old-fashioned ideas, and even Pop had asked if she had to make such an expensive wedding.

Come to think of it, Katie had had the least complaints, which was surprising, considering the fact that of all her girls, Katie had always been the most independent and wayward. None of them had been paddled so often, and none of them had been scolded so often, and none of them had broken her heart as Katie had done.

Those years just before Katie had come of age had been the worst. Even now Mom bit her lip as she remembered their sessions over the Scriptures. None of the rest of her children knew so much of them, and not even Emma justified herself with them as often as Katie had. And Pop had not said a word.

How surprising it was to see Katie still faithful to her vows to the church! Mom had expected Katie to change her membership to some higher church. But here she was--Amish--and not only that, she was getting married in the church and, to all intents, was going to stay Amish! Life was full of surprises.

She didn't quite know what to make of Mark. Naturally, she had been suspicious of his faith when he'd come back from South America. She'd openly condemned him when he left for college. But he, too, had remained faithful. You couldn't figure it out.

Oh, well. You bore them and trained them and taught them the best you knew; if they made mistakes after that, at least it wasn't your fault. Picking up the lamp, she slowly climbed the stairs. Tomorrow was a big day and it was already eleven o'clock. Time she joined Dan in bed.

*   *   *

Katie and Mark came out of the counsel room. Downstairs Dan Gingerich was beginning the great hymn during which the wedding party was to make its entrance. Katie paused with her hand on the doorknob, turning to meet Mark's eyes. "This is it," she said to herself. "What if Mark will not be happy with me? What if I disappoint him?" she thought in a moment of unexplained panic. "Make me everything you want me to be, God--for him. If I should fail--I couldn't bear it!"

Mark smiled his slow, beautiful smile. She marveled at that arrangement of facial muscles! One minute his face was bony, with too deep-set eyes; the next moment it was the most compelling face she'd ever seen--the humble goodness of the man shining from within. "With him I can have oneness of soul and spirit," she thought. "I need not fear." Smiling in return, with all her hope and trust in that smile, she turned the knob. She was ready to go down--down to her wedding ceremony and whatever God had in store for them.